MURDER IN REGENT'S PARK

By Christina Koning

THE BLIND DETECTIVE SERIES

The Blind Detective

Murder in Regent's Park

Murder at Hendon Aerodrome

Murder in Berlin

Murder in Cambridge

Murder in Barcelona

Murder in Dublin

MURDER IN REGENT'S PARK

CHRISTINA KONING

Allison & Busby Limited
11 Wardour Mews
London W1F 8AN
allisonandbusby.com

First published as *Game of Chance* in 2015 under the name A. C. Koning
This edition published by Allison & Busby in 2023.

All characters and events in this publication, other than those clearly in the public domain, are fictitious and any resemblance to actual persons, living or dead, is purely coincidental.

A CIP catalogue record for this book is available from the British Library.

10 9 8 7 6 5 4 3 2 1

ISBN 978-0-7490-2968-5

Typeset in 11pt Sabon LT Pro by Typo•glyphix

The paper used for this Allison & Busby publication has been produced from trees that have been legally sourced from well-managed and credibly certified forests.

Printed and bound by
CPI Group (UK) Ltd, Croydon, CR0 4YY

In memory of my mother, Angela Vivienne Koning (1921–1991), who knew the original of the 'Blind Detective' rather better than I did.

Chapter One

A fox had got into the henhouse. There was blood on the snow, the girls said. When he realised what must have happened, he warned them away, not wanting them to see the worst of it. But it was too late, of course. Anne's cries of distress when she saw the carnage – the soft, feathery bodies with heads torn off in what seemed a wanton fury of destruction – told him all he needed to know about how bad it was. 'Go back to the house, both of you,' he said, his anger at the senseless waste of it making him uncharacteristically stern. 'At once, do you hear? Tell your mother on no account to let Joanie out of the house until I've finished clearing up here.' His youngest daughter's fondness for the 'chook-chooks' being uppermost in his mind as he began the melancholy task of disposing of the corpses.

From the silence which reigned over the entire field, he knew there was little chance that any of the flock had survived the onslaught. The irony was that it was in order to make the hens more secure that he'd built the large hut, whose door – he didn't need to check – now hung open, a conduit for slaughter. Which of his two elder children had been careless enough to leave the thing unlatched was something else at which he could make a pretty good guess. Dreamy Anne, always with her head in the clouds, was the most likely culprit. Although, later that day, Margaret would come to him with a confession that it was she who'd left the door open. That was one thing about his children: they stuck up for one another – Anne, on one memorable occasion when they were visiting Edith's brother in Richmond, having jumped fully clothed into the river in order to share the scolding her elder sister was about to receive for having got her feet wet.

Not that it mattered who was guilty – or not guilty – of the oversight, Frederick Rowlands thought grimly as he shovelled bodies into sacks. The sharp tang of blood, mingled with the perennial stink of chicken manure, was mercifully deadened by the extreme cold; even so, it was a disagreeable task. To say nothing of the loss of income it signified. Even if he'd been the sort of father to exact retribution (which he was not), he doubted whether the mild punishment of stopping his middle daughter's pocket-money for a week would quite cover the cost of the disaster.

Nor was it the first setback they'd had in the two years since they'd moved from London to the wilds of Kent. First there'd been Dorothy and Viktor's departure – which had been unavoidable, of course, but had left him running the farm alone; then there'd been that outbreak of Fowl Pest last spring which had decimated the flock, and from which, nine months on, they'd only just started to recover. Well, they could forget about any sort of recovery now. With what had happened that morning, they'd be lucky if they could make it to the end of the month without having to sell up.

No, it wasn't what you'd call the best start to the year, he thought, as he finished tying up the mouths of the sacks with twine. There! That would keep the rats out until he'd time to build a bonfire to dispose of the bodies. It might be possible to salvage some that weren't too badly mauled for eating purposes. He'd see what Edith thought about that; he supposed she'd have heard the news from the girls by now. Walking back towards the house, he braced himself for a tirade of recrimination. But his wife seemed uncharacteristically subdued. Perhaps it was the sight of his face as he walked in the door. 'Is it bad?' she merely asked.

'Very bad,' he replied. Having fallen down in this respect in the past, he now made it a point of principle not to keep things from Edith. 'In fact,' he went on, trying to keep his voice light, 'I'd say it's about as bad as it can be.'

'Are we ruined, then?'

'Oh, not quite that.' He blew on his fingers, feeling the life come back into them. He had a dread of chilblains, his hands being – for him, more than for most others – essential tools of perception. 'There's still the tea shop.' Although this, as they both knew, was a seasonal enterprise only. In the bitter January weather, with snow on the ground a foot deep, they were unlikely to sell many teas, or indeed, fancy cakes – even if they still had the eggs with which to make them.

'Yes.' She didn't waste time, as some women might have, in pointing out this obvious fact. 'Come and sit by the fire,' she said. 'You look half-dead with cold.'

'I could certainly use a cup of tea.'

'I was waiting for you,' she said. 'It's just made. Here you are.' She handed him his tea, then took a thoughtful sip of her own. 'We could always sell something,' she said. 'My pearl necklace, for instance.'

'We're not selling your pearl necklace.'

'I never wear it. And they're quite good pearls, I believe. A cousin of Mother's brought them back from China. We need the money,' she added.

'There are other ways of getting it.' Although he couldn't, at that moment, think of any. 'I'll write to Major Fraser after lunch. Perhaps he can suggest something.' Even as he said it, he knew this was unlikely. The Major had his hands full enough as it was, trying to raise funds for the new rehabilitation centre, without being asked to solve a former inmate's financial troubles. Still, it was worth a try. Because even though more than a decade had passed since Rowlands' days at St Dunstan's Lodge, still the organisation to which he knew he owed everything – his health, his sanity, even his marriage – kept a watchful eye on the vicissitudes of its members' lives.

He was just threading the paper into the typewriter, and thinking of what he was going to say (but how on earth did one *begin* a begging letter?), when there came a ring at the door. 'If it's the Boy Scouts, I've already given,' he sang out. But it couldn't have been the Scouts, after all, because somebody had come in. There were voices in the hall: Edith's, and another, which seemed vaguely familiar. The vicar's, perhaps. There was a new chap at All Saint's, wasn't there? He must be doing his rounds. Funny weather to choose; still, you couldn't fault a man for being keen. He adjusted the paper, then typed the date – Tuesday 1st January 1929 – and the address. 'Dear Major Fraser,' he began. 'I expect you'll be surprised to hear from me, after all this time . . .'

The door of the sitting room opened. Why was the vicar coming in here? He started to get to his feet, forcing a smile, although the last thing he felt like at that moment was engaging in polite chit-chat about the state of the church roof. But as it turned out, he didn't have to. 'Och, don't disturb yourself,' said a voice. It was, after all, one he knew. 'I can see you're busy just now. But if you could spare me a moment or two, I'd be grateful.'

'Inspector.'

'You look surprised to see me.'

'I am, a little. What brings you here? Nothing

untoward, I hope?' As he said it, a dreadful thought occurred to him. He felt the blood drain from his face. 'It isn't . . . anything to do with my sister, is it?'

'Och, no. Rest assured, it's nothing that concerns her. Wherever she might be,' added the policeman drily. 'No, it's you I've come to see. The fact is, I thought you might be able to help me.'

'I can't imagine how.' Rowlands' heart was still beating rather too fast. He took a breath to calm himself. 'Please sit down, Inspector.'

'It's Chief Inspector, now,' said the other, seating himself, with a groaning of springs, in one of their rather less than comfortable armchairs. 'Not that you were to know unless you've been following my career in the newspapers.'

'I can't say I have. Well, congratulations.'

'Thanks. You're looking well, Mr Rowlands. Country life obviously suits you.'

Rowlands couldn't suppress a grimace. 'Well, it *did* suit me, up until now. Quite how much longer my wife and I will be able to keep on living here is anybody's guess.' At once he regretted saying so much; the man had that effect on him, evidently.

'Oh?' said Douglas. 'And why might that be?'

Rowlands explained about the loss of the chickens.

'Unfortunate,' said the policeman, clicking his tongue. 'But it's an ill wind, as they say. Because there's something I'd like you to do for me, Mr Rowlands. And while I can't promise that it will solve your present difficulties altogether, I *can* make it worth your while.' Before he could elaborate, or Rowlands could respond, there was a knock at the door, and Edith came in, carrying a tray. 'I thought you might like some tea,' she said. 'And perhaps a little something after your journey.'

'Scones,' said Chief Inspector Douglas, with relish. 'How very kind of you, Mrs Rowlands. Here, let me . . .' He must have taken the tray from her because there was the sound of its being set down, rather too firmly, on the little bamboo side table. 'Well,' said Edith brightly. 'I'll leave you both to it.'

'Charming lady,' said Douglas as the door closed behind her. 'You're a fortunate man, Rowlands.'

'I know.'

'I'll be Mother, shall I?'

'If you like.'

Their visitor busied himself with pouring out the tea. 'How do you like yours?'

'What? Oh, just as it comes.'

'That's just how I like mine, too. Can't abide stewed tea, mind. It has to be fresh and strong.'

'Yes. Look here, Inspector . . . Chief Inspector, I mean. I'd like to know what this is all about.'

'All in good time,' said the other. 'Why don't you drink your tea, while it's hot? Here you are.' There was the faint percussive sound of a full cup settling into its saucer.

'Just put it down on the table, would you?'

But Douglas appeared not to hear this simple

request. 'Here,' he said again. 'Take it.'

Exasperated at this small failure of communication – did the man understand *nothing*? – Rowlands held out his hand. If half his tea ended up on the carpet, it wouldn't be his fault. But into his outstretched fingers came not the curved edge of one of his wife's best porcelain cups but a straight, sharp edge that might have been that of a knife but was not; it was as thin, certainly, but lighter and less substantial. He knew what it was at once. His fingers went to the raised marks – really no more than pinpricks – in the upper left and lower right-hand corners. 'The ace of hearts,' he said.

'Quite right,' said Douglas, his satisfaction at the success of his 'trick' only too evident from his tone of voice. 'I always said you were a sharp one, Mr Rowlands. Your tea's in front of you, by the way. On the low table.'

'Thank you. Perhaps now you'll explain,' said Rowlands, 'what all this is about?' He held up the playing card, between finger and thumb.

'Willingly,' replied the Chief Inspector. He took a sip of tea. 'Lovely,' he said. 'Hot and strong. You'll have to forgive my little subterfuge, Mr Rowlands. I had to prove something to myself, and you've helped me to do so. As to that particular card – not eighteen hours ago, it was found in the hand of a murdered woman.'

'Christ!' The card fell from Rowlands' hand to the floor.

'You might very well invoke our Saviour's name, Mr Rowlands,' said Douglas, with grim humour. 'Although there's precious little of His goodness and mercy in this sorry business, I'm afraid.'

Rowlands was still trembling with the horror of it. 'You had no right,' he said. 'Supposing one of my girls had come in . . .'

'Ah, I made sure to tell your wife we weren't to be disturbed,' was the reply. 'I'm sorry for giving you such a shock. But it's told me something else I needed to know.'

'I can't imagine what.'

'Can't you?' said Douglas. 'Well, perhaps you will when you know a wee bit more.' He bent down, with a little grunt of effort, and picked up the card. 'This,' he went on, 'is, as you perceived, a playing card. The ace of hearts, as you rightly said. A card of a particular kind, Mr Rowlands.'

'A braille card,' said Rowlands, impatient with what seemed to him an unnecessary spinning-out of the perfectly obvious.

'Indeed. Which is how you came to identify its value and suit so quickly. But it's also, we've discovered, in the nature of a calling card.'

Rowlands was silent.

'Aye,' said the policeman, helping himself to a buttered scone and biting into it with some relish. 'A kind of *message*, if you like.'

'I don't follow.'

'No, I don't suppose you do.' The Chief Inspector sighed, although whether the sigh was on account of human iniquity or because the scone he had just eaten was so delicious, was hard to tell. 'Let me put you in the picture. That card you've just identified was found in the hand of one Winifred Calder – known as Winnie – called herself a dancer, late of Camden Town. About half past twelve last night, the woman with whom she shared rooms – name of Violet Smith, also a dancer – came back to find the place in darkness. Her first thought was that Winnie must've run out of shillings for the meter – but then she switched on the electric light and found the girl lying on the bed. She'd been strangled. Dead no more than an hour, the doctor reckoned.'

'Have you any idea who did it?'

'Not as yet,' replied Douglas. 'Although at first sight, it looked like a routine affair. Woman no better than she should be quarrelling with a boyfriend. The usual thing. But then we found this, your little ace of hearts, and it set us thinking.'

'Yes,' he said. 'I can see that it did.' A thought occurred to him: 'Can you describe the card?' he said. 'I thought we'd been over all that,' replied Douglas. 'It's a braille card. The ace of hearts.'

'I know. I just wondered if there was anything else distinctive about it.'

The Chief Inspector must have taken the card out of his pocket once more, for he said after a moment, 'Nothing particularly distinctive, that I can see. The face is red and white; the reverse side's red and black. That's to say, there's a border of red, surrounding a border of white, patterned with black dots. There's something that looks like a flaming torch in the centre. Why? Is it important?'

'No,' said Rowlands. 'It's not important at all.'

'I suppose you like to get an idea of the look of things, do you?' said the other.

'That's right.'

'I wonder,' went on the Chief Inspector, 'if your wife would mind if I lit my pipe in here?'

'I've a better idea,' said Rowlands. 'If you've finished your tea, why don't we take a walk into the orchard? We can speak more freely there.' Because suddenly the room seemed airless, as if the terrible event which had been alluded to had sucked the atmosphere from it.

'A fine idea,' said the Chief Inspector, getting to his feet. 'You'll need to put a muffler on, though. It's awful cold outside.'

Beneath their trudging feet, the snow had a brittle, icy feel. Rowlands wondered if it would snow again tonight. He sniffed: it was certainly cold enough. Beside him, Chief Inspector Douglas puffed away on his pipe; its pungent smoke hung on the still air. From a mile or so away across the fields, a dog barked. Otherwise it was utterly silent.

'Aye, it's been a bitter winter,' said Douglas. 'And no sign of a thaw yet.' Rowlands made a sound indicative of agreement but said nothing more. 'I take it,' the policeman said at last when they had taken a turn around the orchard, 'that you've worked out why it is I'm here?'

'I imagine that it's to do with that card. You have a notion that the perpetrator of this murder must be a blind man – otherwise why would he leave such a "calling card", as you call it?'

Douglas laughed delightedly. 'There!' he said. 'Didn't I just say you were a sharp chap? Yes, that is what we've surmised although it begs the question, how did he manage it? Not so much the killing itself – there's always the element of surprise in these cases, you know – but getting away unseen. I'm sure I don't have to tell *you* that a man with such an affliction would tend to make himself conspicuous, rather than otherwise.'

'No,' said Rowlands, thinking wryly that being conspicuous was exactly what most blind men spent their lives trying to avoid.

'So if we take it that our man is blind – and of course it might just be a trick of his to make us think so; what you might call a "blind" in itself,' said the policeman, evidently pleased with this turn of phrase, 'then it's a question of checking the movements of each and every blind man who might have been in the vicinity of Camden Town between the hours in question – say ten and midnight. There were a lot of people out last night, of course, seeing the New Year in, and so it makes our job all the harder.'

'I can see that it would. But I still don't understand . . .'

'. . . where *you* come into all this?' The Chief Inspector came to a standstill, and stamped his feet. 'Brr,' he said. 'Chilly. I think we may be in for another fall tonight. It seems to me, Mr Rowlands,' he went on, 'that you're exactly the man to help us. Seeing as how a man in your situation must number amongst his acquaintance a large number of the kind of men we think we might be looking for – blind ex-servicemen, I mean . . .'

'The answer's no,' said Rowlands.

'. . . and seeing,' the policeman continued as if Rowlands had not spoken, 'that you've a particular interest in keeping things dark, as it were, with regard to your sister's whereabouts.'

'You said you didn't know where she was,' protested Rowlands. There was a sick feeling in the pit of his stomach. 'You promised.'

'I promised nothing,' was the sharp rejoinder. 'You know as well as I do that the police don't strike bargains. What I *said*, if I remember rightly, was that we didn't *at present* have the resources to go after her. Given that we're at full stretch, as it is, without diverting valuable time and manpower to chasing off to South America, or wherever it is.' Although he would of course know perfectly well where it was that Dorothy had fled, Rowlands thought bleakly. The dreadful events of two years before were doubtless as fresh in his mind as they were in Rowlands'. It struck him all at once that the place they were standing, beside the stump of the fallen apple tree, was the exact spot where he'd heard Dorothy's confession, all those months ago. A blighted spot, he thought with a shiver.

'Feeling the cold?' enquired Chief Inspector Douglas.

'We can't have you catching a chill. Yes, the unpleasant truth of the matter, Mr Rowlands, is that I only have to say the word for your sister to be taken up. The fact that she hasn't been so far is for the reason I've just given, and – well, because it's suited me to leave her free. But it doesn't mean that I mightn't take a very different view if you can't see your way to helping me.'

'That's blackmail.'

'An ugly word,' said Douglas. 'I prefer to call it persuasion. And I'm not asking you to work for nothing, you know.'

'That makes it worse. You're asking me to . . . to *spy* on people I know. To be a paid informer.'

'I'm asking you to *talk* to a few people, that's all. To keep your ear to the ground, so to speak, and let us know if you hear anything of interest connected with this murder. You do know quite a lot of people in your situation, don't you, Mr Rowlands?'

'If by that you mean blind men, then yes, I do know quite a few. Some of them are my friends. But I suppose that counts for nothing with you.'

'On the contrary,' said Douglas. 'It counts for a great deal. With a man like you, Mr Rowlands, one always knows where one stands. I'd call you a man of principle.'

'A man prepared to compromise his principles, don't you mean?' They had by now arrived back at the house. A smell of roasting chicken, emanating from the vicinity of the kitchen, suggested that Edith was doing what she could to salvage something from that morning's catastrophe. Troubled as he was by the conversation he had just had with Douglas, Rowlands couldn't suppress a smile. That was his wife all over – always looking for ways of turning a bad situation to advantage. And it *did* smell rather good . . . although whether he'd feel the same once they'd been eating chicken for a week, he couldn't say. It crossed his mind to invite Douglas to join them for dinner, but he decided against it in the same moment. After what had passed between them, to have the man sitting at his table, eating his food, and drinking his drink, would be hard to bear. As if he half-guessed this thought, Douglas murmured something about needing to make tracks. 'No rest for the wicked,' he said. 'Nor for those in pursuit of 'em, like myself. Well, good day to you, Mr Rowlands. I'll be in touch.'

'All right.' It seemed churlish not to offer his hand, and so he did so.

It was warmly clasped. 'Good man,' said the Chief Inspector. 'I'm proud to be working with you. Oh, I know you're feeling bad about this now,' he added, resting his free hand for a moment on Rowlands' shoulder. 'But it will seem quite different when you've had a chance to think things over.'

'So what did he want?' asked Edith. It was later that evening; the girls had been put to bed and the news on the wireless listened to. Unemployment was up. Manufacturing down. They weren't the only ones who were having a bad start to the year, Rowlands thought.

Now his wife sat knitting in her chair by the fire, and he sat drumming his fingers and trying to concentrate, without much success, on the book he was reading. Sir Arthur Conan Doyle's *The British Campaign in France*: a heavy book, in every sense. He was still only halfway through the first volume, with another four to go. Braille books took up a great deal more room than the ordinary kind. But even if his reading had been the most frivolous of thrillers, he'd still have found himself distracted. He sighed, and laid the weighty tome aside. Two years ago, he'd have fobbed Edith off with some lame story or other. Now he said: 'He wants me to spy for him.'

'Oh?' She didn't sound as shocked as he'd expected at this bald statement of fact. 'Well, it wouldn't be the first time.'

'No.' He didn't need to point out that, on the occasion referred to, he'd resisted all Douglas's attempts to make him 'peach'. Things were different now. 'You'd better tell me what it's all about,' she said. 'That is, unless he's said not to.'

'He hasn't.' As briefly as he could, he outlined the salient facts. When he'd finished, she was silent for a moment. 'So they think it was a blind man who did it?' she said at last. He shrugged. 'So it would appear. Although it seems rather a long shot to me.'

'Yes. I suppose the card couldn't have got into her possession – the girl's, I mean – by accident?'

'Unlikely. It was in her hand when she was found.

One assumes it must have been put there after death, because . . . Well, let's just say the possibility that she was clutching it all the while that she was being murdered seems rather a slender one.'

'I see that.' Her needles clicked. 'How beastly it all is,' she said.

'Yes. You know, I rather wish you hadn't asked me about it.'

'Oh, I wanted to know,' Edith said. 'I believe one should face these things. I must say,' she went on, in a reflective tone, 'it does seem extraordinary that the police don't have anything else to go on, apart from this . . . playing card. I mean – what about fingerprints?'

'He'd have worn gloves.'

'Surely *somebody* must have heard or seen *something*?' she persisted.

'Well, if anybody did, I'm sure the police will track him down.'

'Or her.'

'What? Oh yes, I see what you mean,' he said. 'Although it might prove a bit tricky, finding this "him" – or "her". Given that it was New Year's Eve. An awful lot of people would have been out and about.'

'All the more chance that one of them saw something,' said his wife.

'Perhaps.' He hesitated a moment, then made a decision. 'There is one other thing,' he said. 'That card. It wasn't just *any* card.'

'It was a braille card, I know.'

'Not only that. The design on the back was a flaming torch.'

'Then that means . . .' She broke off. In her excitement, she let her needles fall. 'Fred, are you *sure*?'

'The Chief Inspector described it to me.'

'Did you tell him what it meant?'

'No. I wanted to think things over first. Because if it's someone at the Lodge . . .'

'You don't really think it could be, do you?'

'I don't know,' he replied.

'I mean, you can buy those St Dunstan's cards everywhere.'

'That's true enough,' he said. 'But you must see how bad it looks. If I'm to take this on – this *sleuthing* business – there's a chance I might find out things I'd rather *not* find out. I suppose,' he added, 'it's a chance I'll have to take.'

Chapter Two

A brief paragraph about the Camden Town murder appeared in the newspaper next day; Edith read it to him at breakfast after the the girls had been sent upstairs to clean their teeth. To the information Rowlands already had, it added not a great deal more. A Miss Winifred Calder, aged twenty-two, had been found dead from strangulation in the early hours of Tuesday morning. The body had been discovered by her friend, Miss Violet Smith (stage name: Violetta L'Amour), who worked as a dancer at the Hippodrome Theatre, and had been returning from an after-show party. '*Winnie was a very quiet sort*,' Miss Smith was quoted as saying. '*Kept herself to herself, really*.' She had known Miss Calder only a few weeks, she said, when the former had answered an advertisement to share furnished rooms. '*It was awful*,' she said. '*Finding her like that. Still warm she was. I don't think I'll ever get over it.*'

Rowlands supposed that the police would already have got whatever there was to be got from the loquacious Miss Smith; still, a visit to Camden Town wouldn't go amiss, if only because it would give him a better idea of the lie of the land. His memory of most parts of London was good – it was, after all, the city in which he'd spent most of his life; even so, it wasn't until he'd walked around a bit and got the smell of the place, so to speak, that he'd know what he was about. A reply to his letter had come by the evening post. The Major would be happy to see him: would midday on Thursday suit him? He replied by return that it would. It would give him time, he thought, to visit the scene of the crime; Camden being conveniently close to Regent's Park.

So it was that he found himself on the half past eight train to Charing Cross, hemmed in by the well wrapped up bodies of a carriage load of City workers. He hadn't been part of such a crowd for a very long time; funny to be back in it now. Very little seemed to have changed in the eighteen months he'd been away: there was still the same dull shop being talked by some; the New Year's Day football results chewed over by others. There was the rattle of newspapers being read and the phlegmy sound of noses being blown. A smell compounded of stale tobacco, body odour and woollen overcoats. He wasn't sorry to be out of it all, and yet in a strange way, he rather missed it.

In Camden High Street, the snow had turned to slush, churned up by the feet of passers-by along the pavement, and in the road itself by the constant traffic of heavy goods vans, trams, buses, taxis and drays, each bringing its own particular brand of noise and stink. But then that was the nature of the district – a rackety place, in Rowlands' opinion. From the boozy gaggle of drinkers awaiting opening time on the pavement outside the Old Mother Red Cap to the market traders bawling their wares in Inverness Street, there was always somebody creating a disturbance. Just now, as he approached the bridge that ran over the canal, an altercation was in progress. A butcher's boy pushing a handcart had chosen to cross the street at the same moment that a lorry full of coal had come thundering out of Hawley Crescent, nearly crushing boy and handcart in so doing. Now both parties voiced their opinion of the other in no uncertain terms.

'You fucking eejit. You could've killed me!' shouted the youth with the handcart as Rowlands drew level with him, so that for an instant he thought it was he who was being thus addressed.

'Shouldn't 'ave been in the fucking way, then, should yer?' was the no less vehement reply.

'I'll get the coppers onto you, I will!' retorted the butcher's boy. 'That's ten shillings' worth of beef you've gone and spoilt. Look at it! All over the street.' This had evidently been the fate of the handcart's load. 'Didjer see what happened?' the lad then demanded of Rowlands.

'I'm afraid not.'

The other made a sound indicative of disgust.

'Dust it down – it'll be as good as new,' jeered the coalman from the safe elevation of his truck. 'Go lovely with a bit o' mustard on Sunday, that will.'

Behind them – to judge from the impatient honking of horns and shouts of 'Get on with it!' – a queue of traffic was building up. Rowlands left them to it and made his way, with a degree more caution than usual, along the icy street. Falling over was bad enough, but to walk slap bang into a coal truck – or have one crash into you – just because you hadn't been paying attention . . . well, you'd have only yourself to blame, that was all. Because paying attention was what you had to do at all times. Stopping and listening at the lights wasn't the half of it. It meant keeping all your wits about you – all your senses, too. Equipped as he was with one fewer than most people had, still he tried to make the most of those that remained. In the dozen years which had passed since a piece of shrapnel had taken away all but a fraction of his sight, he'd had to learn ways of coping. You had to develop a kind of inner eye, he thought; a preternaturally sharp awareness of all that was going on around, that drew on sense impressions – smell, sound, touch, taste – and memories.

Fortunately, he'd always had a good memory: it was what had got him through school, and later through those evening classes at the Working Men's College in St Pancras, which in turn had enabled him to leave the factory for the job at Methuen. It had been Harry who'd encouraged him, of course. 'With brains like yours, you ought to train for a teacher – or a solicitor's clerk,' his brother had said. 'You could do a lot better than *this* job, at any rate.' Although he hadn't minded working at The Lamp, which was the local name for the Swan Edison factory. It was called that, because that was what it made; later, it would turn out shells for the war effort. He'd started on four shillings a week, sweeping up under the trestle tables where the women sat, assembling lamps. Later, he'd moved to the factory floor with the rest of the men.

His task was collecting the waste that fell from from the machines that made the electric bulbs. Little airy things of spun glass they were, with a glowing thread at the heart. When he was sixteen, he was given a machine of his own to operate. It was exacting work, but not as punishing to the nerves and muscles as working in a factory that made heavy machinery. This, though demanding enough, was classified as *light* rather than *heavy* industry. And of course what it produced was light itself. It was something he'd found quite magical. That, thanks to the little bulbs of glass with their tungsten filaments he and his fellow workers turned out by the thousand each day, you could make the sun come out, banishing darkness at the touch of a switch.

Yes, if it hadn't been for Harry he'd never have got the job in the first place. And it was Harry who, when he'd turned eighteen, had persuaded him it was time to move on. And so he, Fred, had started at the College, two nights a week, studying book-keeping and copy-editing. At twenty, he'd got a job checking proofs at Methuen, earning three pounds a week. When the war came, he'd just been promoted to Senior Copy Editor. It had been a good job – one he'd hoped to return to, although of course after what happened, there was no question of that. But it had occurred to him since that the work, exacting as it was, had helped to develop his 'eye' for detail – for the small error that, in a page of otherwise perfect text, threw the whole into disharmony.

Now he stood at the junction of Camden High Street and Kentish Town Road, waiting for the lights to change. He could tell that this was imminent from the sound of idling engines – a Talbot's, he rather thought, and a Vauxhall's, amongst others. A church clock – St Michael's? – struck the half-hour. He'd better get a move on if he were to be at Regent's Park by midday. He drew a breath of the icy air which tasted faintly of coal smoke. Someone in one of the houses nearby was frying bacon. Lovely smell. His mouth watered. The house he was looking for was the one on the corner – one of a terrace, he seemed to recall, at the entrance to Jeffrey's Street. If he hadn't already known it, he'd have guessed this was the place, from the fact of there being a policeman standing outside it. He discovered this when he attempted to approach the front door and found his way barred by a large, serge-clad body.

'Sorry, sir. You can't go in there,' said a voice. A young

man's voice, Rowlands thought: no more than eighteen, at a guess. Rowlands assumed a perplexed expression.

'This *is* Number Three, The Laurels, Kentish Town Road, isn't it?' he asked.

'It's Kentish Town Road, right enough. As to the rest of it, I couldn't say,' replied the other. 'Only you can't go in here, sir – not unless you live at this address, and I reckon you don't, sir. Those are my orders,' he added, with a touch of pride. 'No unauthorised persons is to enter without permission. Didn't you see the notice?'

'No,' said Rowlands. He gave an apologetic shrug. 'I can't, you see. Or not well enough to read notices, anyway.' As the truth of this dawned upon the young policeman, he became all stammering confusion. 'I'm . . . I'm ever so sorry, sir. I never . . .'

'That's quite all right, Constable. It is "Constable", isn't it, not "Sergeant"?'

'Oh yes, sir,' said the other, sounding pleased as Punch at the idea that he might have been taken for his superior officer. 'I only joined up a month ago. Still a probationer, in fact.'

'They give you all the difficult jobs, I shouldn't wonder,' said Rowlands.

'Not half, sir.'

'Standing about in the cold all morning being one of them, I suppose?'

'Yes, sir.'

'Been here long, have you?'

'Since half past six. My relief comes at midday,' said

the constable. 'And won't I be glad,' he added fervently.

'Yes, it's pretty cold still, isn't it?' observed Rowlands, drawing the cigarette pack from his pocket. 'And not even a warm drink or a smoke to keep you going.' He fumbled for his matches and proceeded to light up, turning his back to the wind to do so. 'Beastly windy on this corner! Quite a job to light up. I say,' he went on when the gasper was finally lit, 'you wouldn't care for one, would you?' He held out the pack. The young policeman hesitated a moment.

'Thank you, sir,' he said at last. 'But we're not supposed to smoke on duty.'

'Of course. Rules is rules, eh?' Rowlands exhaled a lungful of aromatic smoke. 'If you like,' he went on casually, feeling a rotter for what he was about to suggest, 'I could keep cave while you go around the corner and have your smoke out of the wind. Anyone comes along, I'll sing out.'

'Well . . .'

'Old trick from my army days,' said Rowlands. 'Two of us out on patrol at a time. Not supposed to smoke either. Danger the enemy'd see the light, you know. A lighted cigarette made a good target. So what we'd do was this: one of us'd light up while the other held his waterproof cape out as a kind of shelter. Cut off the wind, you see, and prevented Fritz from taking a sighting. Then if the one doing the shielding spotted an officer approaching, he'd give his Pal a nudge. Rules,' he added, drawing deeply on his Churchman's, 'are sometimes made to be broken.'

'Perhaps just the one, then, sir,' said the young man, his resolve now utterly broken down by the enticing smell of the tobacco. 'There's only two left in the pack,' said Rowlands, handing it to him with the box of matches. 'Keep the other one for later, why don't you?' Muttering his thanks, the policeman walked off around the corner into Jeffrey's Street. Rowlands waited until the sound of his footsteps had died away before trying the front door. It was unlatched, as he'd hoped – the to-ings and fro-ings of police officers over the past few days having made this a necessity, he guessed. Nothing stirred as he reached the first floor landing, although he supposed from what the policeman had said that there must be other tenants in the place. Perhaps they were all out. Just as he had the thought, a door creaked open.

''Oo's that?' demanded a voice. Elderly. A woman's. He turned his head towards the voice.

'Good day,' he said pleasantly. 'I'm looking for Miss Smith.'

''*Er*!' was the reply. 'You won't find '*er*. She's gorn off. Staying with friends,' the old woman said scornfully. '"Friends"! I know what sort of "friends" they are. If you ask me,' she went on, although he hadn't said a word, 'it should've been '*er* what got it in the neck, and not t'other one. Coming an' going at all hours. It ain't decent,' she shouted after him as, with a murmured apology, he pushed past her. Under other circumstances, he'd have let her ramble on, because there was usually something to be gleaned from even the most inconsequential talk, but just now he hadn't time. Leaving her muttering balefully to herself on the landing below, he climbed the short flight that led to the attic floor. There were two doors; the first was locked. The second opened easily.

If Rowlands had been in any doubt as to whether he'd come to the right place, the first breath he took would have convinced him. It wasn't just the stuffiness of the air, as of a room too long closed up, but something else – something harder to define. Perhaps it was no more than the knowledge of what had taken place in that room, three nights before, that made the hairs on the back of his neck stand up on end – he couldn't say. Only that he felt a powerful sense of unease . . . no, it was more than that. It was fear. From his days as a gunner, he recalled the way that, after the gun was fired, one's ears rang for minutes afterwards with the roar of it. It was like that now; only instead of waves of sound, what reverberated from the walls of this mean little dwelling was the echo of a woman's terror.

He knew – from what particular source he couldn't have said – that strangulation was not a quick death. It could take as long as three minutes while the victim fought, and gasped for air, and lost consciousness momentarily, before waking to fight some more. From the waves of fear and pain he could feel in the room, he conjectured that Winnie Calder had struggled more than most. Bile rose in his throat. He forced himself to take a step into the room, then another, feeling his way cautiously between the various items of furniture with which the flat was cluttered. Here was a deal table, with one, two, three chairs – none of them matching. Had they sat here, Winnie and her killer, on either side of the table, to consume whatever it was the bottle contained, that had been left standing at its centre? He picked up the bottle, unscrewed the cap, and sniffed. Gin. Of the glasses from which the two had drunk – as surely they *had* drunk? – there was no sign; they'd been taken away as evidence, he assumed.

In front of the gas fire was a divan, piled with women's clothes; his exploring fingers found a pair of stays. He dropped them hastily. A smell of stale perfume and sweat rose from the dropped garments. Among the limp heaps of art silk undergarments, and not-quite-fresh blouses, he found a silk stocking, missing its fellow. Had *that* been the instrument of Winnie Calder's destruction? His skin crawling, he moved towards where he guessed the bedroom must be. He knew from what the Chief Inspector had said that it was there that the body had been found. But even if he had not been told, he would have known it. Because here, the feeling of terror was at its most intense. You could almost taste it, he thought, with a shiver of disgust. Had she led him inside, poor unsuspecting Winnie, only to find there was no way out, and that this was to be her tomb?

His fingers fumbled behind him at the door. The key, as he had guessed, was on the inside of it. And so the murderer had gone about his business, safe in the knowledge that he would not be disturbed. Were someone to return unexpectedly, all he had to do was to wait until the coast was clear before letting himself out. Winnie Calder and Violet Smith must have had some sort of arrangement as to which had the use of the bedroom, Rowlands thought. Whoever had 'company' would lock the door – just as the killer had done – leaving the other to make her bed on the divan. Which was no doubt what Violet – or Violetta L'Amour, as she'd called herself – would have done if the bedroom door had not stood open. He pictured the scene: Violet stumbling tipsily up the attic stairs at midnight, and finding the flat in darkness. Grumbling to herself as she fumbled for the light switch, 'Might've left a lamp on for us', then seeing the door of the bedroom ajar: 'Win! You awake? I've had such a night, you wouldn't believe.' Opening the door. 'Winnie! Wake up! I want to talk. Don't be a spoilsport, Win . . .' Reaching to switch on the bedside lamp. Then the sight that met her eyes . . .

He'd reached the foot of the bed: an iron bedstead it was, with a cheap horsehair mattress. It had been stripped, of course. Fighting back the waves of nausea which threatened to overwhelm him, Rowlands forced himself to stand there, in that place of horror, and bring his thoughts to bear on what had happened there. The desperate, near-silent struggle which had taken place on this bed between a woman about whom he already knew too much and a man of whom he knew nothing. Or almost nothing. He knew that the man had climbed the stairs, as he himself had done, a few minutes earlier; that he'd sat at the rickety table and drunk gin from a greasy bottle, and then – having taken a silk stocking from the slatternly heap on the divan – had followed the girl into the bedroom and locked the door behind him. That he'd moved swiftly and surely across the room, to where the girl was undressing, or perhaps already lying on the bed. That, without giving her time to react, he'd slipped the stocking around her throat. Had twisted it until it tightened, into a ligature.

Rowlands found he was trembling with the sheer effort of making himself stay in the room. He could feel sweat on his upper lip. He gripped the rail of the bedstead so tightly he felt his knuckles crack. *The place was in darkness when she got back* . . . It was Violet Smith he meant. Yes, the flat had been in darkness; he remembered that Douglas had said so. Didn't that suggest that the man who'd done this dreadful thing had been accustomed to moving about in the dark? That he was in fact a blind man? He did not want to believe it – and yet the implication was all too obvious.

A floorboard creaked. He felt his blood turn to ice. There was someone in the flat – he was sure of it. Hardly daring to breathe, he stood frozen to the spot, straining his ears to catch the faint sounds from the next room. The sounds of someone breathing. Of someone moving quietly around. The wild thought that it must be the murderer, returned (as murderers were said to do), possessed him. He drew a deep breath. Murderer or not, he'd meet the fellow face-to-face. Suiting the action to the thought, he turned to face the door, which he'd pulled shut behind him, and which was now slowly opening. There was a moment's startled silence. Then: 'What the devil are you doing here?' said a voice.

Rowlands breathed again. 'Hello, Chief Inspector,' he said innocently. 'I was just taking a look around.'

'So I see,' said the other drily. 'I suppose you know that members of the public are strictly forbidden to enter a building where a crime has taken place until the police have finished with it?'

'Yes, I realise it's a bit irregular.'

'"Irregular" isn't all it is. There's the small matter of corrupting an officer of the law to take into account.'

'I hope you won't be too hard on him,' said Rowlands. 'Coming up here was entirely my own idea. He'd not the faintest notion of what I was up to.'

'I don't doubt it,' replied the policeman. 'He needs to be a bit sharper, in my view. Silly young fool. I've already torn him off a strip for deserting his post.'

'Oh come now,' said Rowlands. 'It was only for a moment.'

'It need only take a moment for a crime to be committed,' said Chief Inspector Douglas grimly. 'I must say, Mr Rowlands, this wasn't what I was expecting from you. I rather hoped by now you'd have got on with that bit of investigation we talked about.'

'As a matter of fact, I was just on my way to Regent's Park Lodge,' said Rowlands.

'Good.' replied the Inspector. 'I can give you a lift, as it happens. I've a car waiting.' Ushering Rowlands ahead of him out of the door, he closed it behind him. They descended the stairs to the cramped hall, which had the smell of dust, boiled cabbage and bad drains, that houses of this kind often had. The Inspector opened the front door, and the noises of the street rushed in – a dog barking, a child crying, a dray rumbling past – sounds that seemed to Rowlands, after the oppressive quiet of the flat, to speak of life, and warmth, and welcome normality. Two steps led to the little railed off area fronting the street. 'That'll do, Jones. You may stand at ease.' This, from the Chief Inspector's sharper tone, was to the young policeman Rowlands had bamboozled, whose feelings towards his deceiver he – Rowlands – could very well imagine. 'I shall want a detailed report,' Douglas went on, still to his subordinate, 'of everyone who passes this spot – man, woman or child – between now and twelve hundred hours – is that clear?'

'Sir,' replied the young man, in a voice that conveyed a good deal of the emotion he was feeling. 'Good. Carry on, then.' Just then, a car pulled up alongside, and the driver got out. 'You took your time, Andrews,' said the Inspector as the former went around to open the door. 'Yes, sir. Beg pardon, sir.'

'This is Mr Rowlands. You're to to drop me off at the station first, and then you're to take him to Regent's Park Lodge.'

'Sir.'

'And on the way,' Douglas said to Rowlands as both got into the back of the big Wolseley, 'you can tell me what conclusions you've come to about our murderer.'

'Oh, I think it's a bit early for that, don't you?' said Rowlands. 'I mean, the only couple of bits of evidence we've got are pretty insubstantial, to say the least.'

'And what pieces of evidence are those?' asked the policeman slyly.

'I . . . well . . . the playing card, obviously,' replied Rowlands, cursing himself for his blunder.

'You said *two* pieces of evidence,' persisted Douglas.

'Yes. You said the flat was in darkness when Miss Smith returned to it. She herself said that the body was still warm. It occurred to me,' said Rowlands reluctantly as the car sped along Arlington Road and turned into Delancey Street, 'that he – the perpetrator – might still have been on the premises when she – Miss Smith, that is – entered the building. It would have been easy enough for him to let himself out and slip past her on the stairs.'

'But what makes you think . . .' began Douglas. Then he gave a satisfied chuckle. 'I see what you're driving at. You mean the flat was in darkness because he didn't need to see what he was doing. He could manage perfectly well without the light.'

'Yes,' said Rowlands. 'That is what I meant. It doesn't prove anything, but . . .'

'It's certainly food for thought,' said the Chief Inspector.

Chapter Three

'So,' said Ian Fraser when the usual pleasantries had been exchanged, and they were comfortably ensconced in the room he called his study, which had once been the drawing room when the house was in private hands. 'What can I do for you?' They were sitting on either side of a good fire that was presently singing away to itself and throwing out plenty of heat so that Rowlands – still shaken by his visit to the drab furnished rooms where Winnie Calder had met her death – felt himself relax for the first time that day. The warmth of the fire, combined with that of the tea he'd just drunk, and the slices of hot buttered toast he'd just consumed, produced a pleasant drowsiness, against which he knew he'd have to guard.

Because, notwithstanding the simple animal pleasures of being warm and well-fed – to say nothing of the pleasure he felt in being back here again, at the Lodge – the fact remained that this visit was nothing but a sell: a fraud he was about to perpetrate on a man he liked and respected; a man to whom he owed a debt of gratitude. Hadn't the Major (as he always thought of him) been the man who'd rescued him from the slough of misery into which he'd fallen after being discharged from hospital, in the autumn of '17? *Then* he'd been fit for nothing; a useless wreck. The Major had given him his life back. By taking him on at the Lodge, he'd offered Rowlands not only the chance to learn new skills, which in turn had enabled him to earn a living, but had given him back his self-respect. And this was how he was going to repay him: with lies and evasions.

He took a deep breath. 'Well . . .' he began; then stopped. He couldn't bring himself to do it: to pull the wool over the Major's eyes. Spinning some yarn to cover up his true intentions. It went against everything he thought was right.

'I rather gathered, from your letter,' said the Major, perhaps attributing a different cause to Rowlands' silence, 'that things hadn't been going as well as might have been expected – with the farm, I mean.'

'No. The fact is . . .'

'These are difficult times,' said the older man. 'A lot of people are struggling. This hard winter we've been having hasn't made things any easier.'

'That's true,' said Rowlands. He was feeling more and more awkward. *Damn* Douglas. He'd half a mind to tell him to take a running jump. Let him get his information another way. But then he remembered Dorothy. The way she'd clung to him, tears streaming down her face, that last time on the quayside at Southampton Docks. Could he really take the risk that the Chief Inspector wouldn't carry out his threat of having her arrested if Rowlands refused to co-operate? And so he made himself go on: 'We've had some setbacks, I have to admit. In fact, the farm's not really what you'd call a "going concern". But it wasn't about that I wanted to see you.'

'Oh?'

'The fact is,' said Rowlands, hating himself for the ease with which the lie emerged, 'I've been wanting to organise a reunion.'

'I see,' said Major Fraser, although he clearly didn't.

'A get-together, d'you see?' Rowlands plunged on. 'Of all the London Pals – I mean, of course, anyone who's living in the London area as well as those who served in London regiments. One loses touch so easily.'

'Indeed,' said the Major. 'And what form would this . . . ah, *reunion* be likely to take?'

'I suppose that depends on the number of men who want to take part,' replied Rowlands smoothly. 'Of course,' he added, with a laugh he hoped didn't sound as false to the Major as it did to him, 'there's a chance we might end up with no more than a few chaps in a pub somewhere . . . that is, if not very many decide to come.'

The Major considered this. 'It might be rather jolly, all the same. And if you get a bigger turnout?'

'Well,' said Rowlands. 'That's where I was hoping you'd come in. Could we hold our get-together here, do you think?'

'I don't see why not,' replied the other. 'In fact, I think it's a splendid idea. You can use the Rec room, if you like. I suppose you'll be wanting a bar?'

'It might help to attract a few more people,' said Rowlands.

'Splendid,' said the Major. 'Consider it done. I suppose we'll have to wait and see what kind of numbers we get before deciding.'

'Rather,' said Rowlands. 'As you say, we ought to see what kind of response we get when we contact people. With regard to that,' he went on, keeping his tone casual, 'I'll need names and addresses. Telephone numbers, too. I don't suppose . . .'

'Oh, we can supply all of that,' said the Major. 'Names by the score. You'd better check with me before you start getting in touch, though. Just in case. Some of them have died, you know,' he added gently, in case his meaning had not been made sufficiently clear. 'We try to make a note of it when it happens, but we're not always as up to date as we'd like. I'm sure you wouldn't want to be the unwitting cause of distress to anyone.'

'No,' said Rowlands.

A silence ensued which neither seemed in a hurry to break. Rowlands took a sip of his tea, recalling other times he'd sat there, in just that spot in front of the fire, talking things over with this man whose opinion he valued above all others. There'd been one time in particular, two years ago, after Gerald Willoughby died . . . He flinched at the memory. 'So,' said the Major, breaking into these thoughts, 'if that's all you need from me, I don't see any difficulty in achieving it. Would you like to borrow Doris for a day or two?' This was his secretary, Rowlands surmised. 'I'll have to check that she's all right about it, of course, because it'll mean some extra work, what with all the telephoning, but I feel sure . . .'

'Oh, I wouldn't expect her to do that,' said Rowlands quickly. He smiled. 'As you may recall, using the telephone's rather in my line.'

'Yes, I know,' said Major Fraser. 'And I'd be the last man to want to do you out of a job! The only difficulty is that not all our records are in the shape we'd want them to be. I mean, some of them are, of course, but we're talking about hundreds of names and addresses. When it's the wives who supply these – which it often is, you know, writing being less of a chore for them, on the whole – then it's a matter of getting the information transcribed into braille. All rather time-consuming, I'm afraid. Not to say expensive,' he added ruefully. 'So you see, you'll need a sighted helper if you're to get through the list in reasonable time.'

'If it's all the same to you, I was thinking of asking Edith – my wife – to help me,' said Rowlands, to whom the idea had only just occurred.

'Oh. Well, that makes things a lot simpler,' said the Major. 'If you like,' he went on, warming to the theme, 'you can use one of the offices as HQ – that is, if your wife doesn't mind traipsing up to Regent's Park from . . . where is it you're living now?'

'Kent,' replied Rowlands. 'No, she won't mind.' He fervently hoped that this would prove to be the case.

'Good. Let me know when you'd like to make a start, and I'll tell the girls to get the room ready for you. We might even be able to run to a fire,' the Major laughed. 'Can't have your good lady freezing to death, now can we?'

'No,' said Rowlands. 'As a matter of fact,' he went on, with a mounting horror at his own deviousness, 'I was rather hoping to make a start right away. That is, if any of the chaps are about.'

'Right-ho.' The Major got up, rubbing his hands together briskly in what Rowlands recognised as a characteristic gesture. 'I can see that you're a man for striking while the iron's hot.' He wandered across the room – to the window, evidently, for his voice came from that direction. 'I think you'll find some of our long-term residents about the place somewhere. There's a football practice just finishing, I believe.' And indeed, from outside could be heard the sound of voices, raised in jocular dispute: 'I tell you, it was offside . . .' 'The workshops are closed today, of course. Much too cold. You'll probably find some people in the Smoking Room.

Would you like me to come with you, to make some preliminary introductions?'

Rowlands hesitated. Without wanting to give the impression that he was up to something, he very much wanted the Major not to be a witness to his enquiries. 'Oh, I think I can manage, thanks,' he replied, with an airiness he did not feel. 'I still remember my way about.'

'I don't doubt it,' was the reply. 'You always had an excellent memory, as I recall.'

It was true what he'd said to the Major: he remembered the place like the back of his hand. Even though a decade had passed since he'd left, its layout was still imprinted on his mind. There was the old Lodge itself whose spacious, high-ceilinged rooms – always a little chilly, even in summer – had a special echo that, even now, he could have distinguished from that of any other place. There was the cluster of workshops surrounding the main building, in one of which he had been set to work in his first week, learning how to use a hammer and nails without hitting his thumb – at least, no more than the usual number of times for a beginner. These wooden purpose-built huts echoed to their own variety of sounds: from the sawing of wood to the tapping of tacks into leather soles (boot-making being one of the more popular trades the men here were taught). The singing and whistling which accompanied these activities was something he'd always associate with this place – a snatch of one such tune found its way, irresistibly, into his head:

Oh! You beautiful doll,
You great big beautiful doll,
Let me put my arms about you,
I could never live without you . . .

Exiting from the Major's study, he turned right after five paces, into the first of the network of corridors that connected one side of the building with the other. These corridors – each with its guide-rail and strip of linoleum along the left-hand side to remind one which way one was going – had offered him his first chance of independent movement. After years of managing the trick without benefit of rails or strips, he found he no longer needed them. Still, it was pleasant, for a moment, to let his hand remember the way it had been when he'd had to rely on such mechanisms to find his way through the dark.

He began with the library – always his favourite room, which smelt all year round of books and the leather upholstery of its worn but comfortable chairs. Just now, it smelt also of woodsmoke, from the fire that was burning merrily away in the grate. He went towards it. 'Chilly today,' he said, by way of greeting to the men who were seated on either side of it. He thought he detected a third man, over by the bookshelves, but he wasn't sure. He listened, heard a floorboard creak. Yes, there was someone there.

A grunt of agreement came from the man seated nearest to him. 'I'll say.'

'More snow's forecast, according to the wireless,' said Rowlands. You could rely on the weather to get most people talking.

'I thought that was Scotland,' objected another voice – that of the man on the other side of the fire.

'Perhaps it was,' replied Rowlands, drawing nearer to the fire and rubbing his hands appreciatively as he felt its warmth. He smiled. 'You can be pretty sure of snow in Scotland, at this time of year.' He turned his face towards the first man. 'Name's Rowlands, by the way.'

'Carstairs.' The voice had an elderly, querulous sound. The more recent intake were mainly older men, the Major had said – 'not striplings, like your lot,' he'd added, smiling. The effects of phosgene and mustard gas had been slower in some cases, leaving the men afflicted with enough sight to get by until the effects caught up with them. 'We've had quite a few men your age and older who've only just gone blind,' he'd said, the smile having vanished from his voice. 'For some, it's been a process of gradual deterioration; for others, it's come upon them suddenly after years of being able to see. They don't, as a rule, adjust as well to blindness as younger men do,' the Major had added, with what Rowlands thought must be a degree of understatement. Carstairs, he guessed, must be one of these: a man embittered by what had happened to him, perhaps all the more so because he'd thought himself one of the lucky ones.

'I've just popped in for a chat with the Major,' Rowlands went on easily. 'Former inmate, you know.' He laughed. 'Still miss the old place, rather.'

'Do you? I find that extraordinary.'

'Well I know *I'll* pine for this place when and if they ever kick me out of here,' said a voice with an agreeable north country accent, from over by the bookshelves.

'Is that you, Mortimer?' said Rowlands, wondering if his ears deceived him.

'The very same. How are you, old man?' They shook hands. Mortimer's handshake, it seemed to Rowlands, was less vigorous than he remembered, that is, if his memory was to be relied upon. Surely old Mortimer had always been the sporty type? One of their best rowers – and a champion sprinter. The kind who'd clap you on the back and almost knock you off your feet. He'd been a superb horseman, too, Rowlands seemed to recall – a skill acquired during his days in the army, no doubt. *This* man seemed a shadow of his former self . . . 'What are you up to these days?' the one-time champion now asked. 'Still enjoying country life?'

It seemed easier to say yes.

'Glad to hear it,' said Mortimer, drawing nearer the fire. 'I tried that once, but I didn't get on with it,' he added vaguely. 'No sticking power, you know. This is Phillips, by the way,' he added, touching Rowlands' arm, to indicate the man who'd said that snow was forecast for Scotland.

'How d'you do?' muttered Phillips.

'Phillips and Carstairs are two of our new boys,' said Mortimer. 'Joined us just before Christmas. In time for the New Year's Eve Ball, wasn't it?'

Rowlands pricked up his ears. 'Oh yes. I went to a few of those myself, in the early years. Was it a good turnout?'

'Over a hundred,' replied Mortimer. 'Not as good as in some years, but then most chaps have got families.'

It occurred to Rowlands that a list of all those who'd attended the event might prove useful, if only as a way of excluding names from his list of potential suspects. After all, if you were dancing the quickstep in Regent's Park, he argued with himself, you couldn't be murdering a girl in the Kentish Town Road . . . But he dismissed the argument as specious. In any case, it wasn't his job to provide alibis. 'How's that wife of yours?' said Mortimer, breaking into these thoughts. 'Still as good a dancer as ever?'

'Oh yes.' Although in point of fact, he couldn't remember the last time he and Edith had been to a dance. There didn't seem to be the time for such activities these days. 'But what about you?' Rowlands went on. 'Are you still with the firm in . . . Carshalton, wasn't it?' Import-export, he rather thought.

Mortimer gave an uneasy laugh. 'Oh, that came to an end a long time ago,' he said. 'The firm was cutting back on staff. You know how it is.'

Rowlands didn't, but he could guess. 'Hard luck,' he said.

'It could have been worse,' was the reply. 'At least I had a job to go to. That is, if you can *call* it a job, putting books back on shelves all day long.'

'Doesn't sound too bad.'

'It isn't. It's just that . . .' He let the sentence tail off. 'Don't think I'm not grateful to the Major for taking me on,' he said after a moment.

'Of course not.'

'I was just getting on with it when you arrived,' Mortimer went on, starting to move in the direction of the library shelves on the far side of the room. 'Don't mind if I carry on, do you?'

'Not a bit,' said Rowlands, turning to follow him.

'Watch out for the trolley,' said Mortimer. There came the sound of heavy volumes (and braille books *were* heavier than most) being lifted onto shelves.

'I'd lend a hand if I knew where things went,' said Rowlands. It occurred to him as he spoke that he ought to be pumping Mortimer for information. The thought made him feel rather sick.

'Oh, that's all right,' said Mortimer. 'It would take too long to explain it. I've got a system, you know. Bit of an improvement on the last one, in my opinion.'

'Yes, what happened to old Ackroyd?' asked Rowlands, fingering the spine of the topmost book on a pile still waiting to be shelved. *The Woman in White*. Edith had read that to him, a year or so ago. She had a liking for Victorian shockers; his own tastes ran more to history – and poetry when he could get hold of it. But it wasn't fair to expect his wife to sacrifice so many of her leisure hours reading things she found tedious, or – as was the case with some of Mr Eliot's recent offerings – utterly incomprehensible.

'He retired,' was the reply. 'Didn't you get the letter, asking for a subscription?'

'Oh yes, of course. A clock, wasn't it?'

'And a set of cufflinks. He was a decent sort, was old Ackroyd. One of the old school.' Both men were silent a moment, as if in acknowledgement of this irrefutable fact. Then Mortimer said in a low tone, so as not to be overheard by the men sitting over by the fire: 'The fact is, there've been a lot of changes since you were here . . . since we were both here,' he corrected himself. 'It isn't the place it used to be. There isn't the camaraderie, for a start. It's a different crowd altogether from the chaps we knew. Some very queer fish among them, I can tell you . . .' He broke off as the door to the library opened, and someone put his head in.

'I was looking for Vance,' said this interloper.

'Well, he isn't here,' said the man who'd been introduced as Phillips.

'Any idea where I might find him? Only he owes me five shillings.'

'Try the Rec room,' said Mortimer. 'There was a group of them in there playing cards when I last looked.'

'Thanks awfully.' He let the door bang shut behind him.

'Not quite the calibre of men we were used to,' said Mortimer softly, adding in a louder voice: 'There! That's done. I don't suppose,' he said to Rowlands, 'you've time for a beer?' Rowlands felt for his watch. It was a quarter to one. He'd promised Edith he wouldn't be too late back. But then the thought of what Mortimer had said – *some very queer fish* – seemed too good a lead to ignore.

'I hadn't realised the premises were licensed these days,' he said lightly. 'There *have* been some changes if so.'

'Oh, it's still the same as far as all that's concerned,' laughed Mortimer. 'You know how hot the Major is about the men drinking. No, my watering hole is the Albany, just across the park. They do quite a nice pint of Ordinary there.'

'Sounds good to me,' said Rowlands, resolving to limit himself to a half. Edith hated it when he came home stinking of beer, and in any case, he needed to keep his wits about him.

They were passing the Rec room when there came a great shout: 'Coo! What a carve-up!' A burst of laughter followed. 'I say,' said Rowlands. 'Isn't that old Agnew? Don't tell me he's still knocking around?'

'He is, indeed. Been back a good while now. Why? Do you want to speak to him?' But Rowlands was already through the door and halfway across the room where a group of perhaps a dozen men were *in situ* – some lounging, he surmised, in the circle of armchairs nearest the fire, from which direction came the sound of the wireless, and of football results being discussed. The card tables – of which at present only one was occupied – were over by the window, as of old. Of the four players, Agnew was the only one known to him. It occurred to him he'd need to get to know the others. This was as good a way as any.

'Agnew!' he accordingly cried, advancing towards the table.

'Rowlands, old man – is that you?' A small commotion as of a chair being scraped back followed.

'Large as life and twice as ugly,' said Rowlands with a smile. The two men shook hands, Rowlands reminded as he did so of the difference in their respective heights: Agnew couldn't have been more than five foot six. He wondered how tall the murdered girl had been; he must remember to ask Douglas. It was difficult – although by no means impossible if the victim were lying down – to strangle someone much taller than oneself. 'I thought you'd gone up north.'

'I did, but I came back,' said Agnew. 'Couldn't keep me away from the old place.'

'No more than you could keep Mortimer here away,' replied Rowlands. 'But I mustn't keep you from your game,' he added, conscious of a certain restiveness on the part of those still seated around the table. 'What are you playing?'

'Solo,' said Agnew.

'Ah, my old favourite! When I think of the halfpence I've won and lost around this very table . . .'

'Oh, we play for a lot more than halfpennies these days, don't we, chaps?' said a voice Rowlands didn't recognise.

'Shut up, Vance,' said another voice. There was an awkward silence.

'So where'd you got to when I interrupted?' asked Rowlands, to cover this.

'South had just propped and West copped,' replied Agnew. 'I'm North, you know, so it's me to go next.'

'Yes, we're still waiting for you, old boy,' said Vance rudely. 'Hearts are trumps, remember?'

'Gosh, it takes me back, all this,' said Rowlands, cheerfully ignoring this hint. 'Hours and hours I must have spent playing Solo and all its variations. Name's Rowlands, by the way,' he added, addressing the dealer.

'Vance,' said this individual, with ill-concealed impatience. 'Now, about this call of yours—'

'Awfully sorry, old man – should've introduced you,' said Agnew, cutting across him. 'Reggie Vance is South, as you've probably gathered. West is Broomfield, here . . .' A grunt from Broomfield. 'And East is Williamson.'

'How d'you do,' said the last mentioned, with scarcely more warmth than the others. Mortimer was right, thought Rowlands. Things *had* changed – and not for the better. Well, it made his job easier, if anything. He needn't care so much about putting people's noses out of joint.

'Williamson,' he said in a reflective tone. 'I knew a Williamson, once. In the army it was. Charlie Williamson. Nice lad. Field gunner. Don't suppose he could be any relation, could he?'

'Not that I know of,' was the reply.

'Pity, that. He was from Camden Town, I seem to recall. Ran a fruit and veg stall off the High Street. He was engaged to be married, too. Showed me a photograph of the young lady once. Pretty girl. What was her name again? Cissie? No – Winnie. That was it. Winnie Calder.' But if he hoped to elicit a response by this less-than-subtle mention of the dead girl's name, he was disappointed. All he got was a bemused silence, broken by a yawn from Vance.

'Much as I'd like to hear more about your no doubt varied acquaintance, old man,' said the dealer in a bored tone, 'we do have a game to finish.'

'Yes, of course,' said Rowlands. 'Good New Year, was it?'

'Come again?'

'The New Year's Eve Ball. Mortimer was just telling me about it. Sounds like a jolly affair. I take it you all went?'

'I was there,' said Agnew. 'Wouldn't have missed it for the world. Plenty of free beer – I must say, the Major never stints one in that regard! Good little dance band, too – wasn't it, Broomfield?'

'Yes, they weren't half bad,' said Broomfield grudgingly. There was a sound, indicative of agreement, from Williamson. Only Vance said nothing.

'Well, that's good to hear,' said Rowlands. 'Next year I'll be sure to come and bring the missus. I say!' he added, checking his watch, 'Is that the time? We'd better get a move on, Mortimer old chap, if we're to have that drink. Enjoy your game,' he said to the rest of them. 'Nice to see you again, Agnew.'

'Yes. Don't make it so long next time, will you?' said Agnew.

'I won't,' said Rowlands.

As he reached the door, he heard Vance say, in a voice he hadn't bothered to lower: 'Who *was* that chap? I thought he'd never go.'

'You see what I mean?' said Mortimer in a low voice as they walked along the corridor that led to the exit. 'They're not a friendly crowd, that new lot. Not the way we were, with everyone mucking in together.'

'Yes,' said Rowlands. 'I do see that. Agnew's just the same good sort, though.'

'Oh, *Agnew's* all right.' They reached the entrance hall where both put on coats and mufflers, Rowlands pulling the thick woollen scarf up around his face to make up for not having a hat. In this weather, he'd almost been tempted to break his rule, but the resulting loss of light, especially on such a dark day, wasn't worth it; he'd rather put up with the cold. Fortunately, his hair was still thick, even though he'd be thirty-nine next birthday. 'It's that Vance I don't care for,' continued Mortimer as they stepped out into the freezing air. 'Chap's a bounder, if you ask me.'

'Yes. *He* wasn't at the New Year's Ball, was he?'

'Not that I recall. Other fish to fry, no doubt. Why do you want to know?'

'Just interested,' said Rowlands. They'd reached the Broadwalk, he guessed; their footsteps crunched on the gravel – the only sound in that still, cold air. 'How many of the actual residents were there that night, do you think?'

'Hard to say,' was the reply. 'Around twenty, I'd say – at least when I was there. I didn't stay for very long.' He gave a laugh, without any mirth in it. 'My rotten lungs playing me up, you know.'

'Bad luck,' murmured Rowlands. 'So how many are currently in residence?' he asked, keeping his tone casual.

'We've twenty-eight at the moment. No – thirty. I was forgetting Carstairs and Phillips. Not like the numbers we had in the old days.'

'No,' said Rowlands. He was grateful for this since it made his task a good deal easier. If twenty of the men had attended the New Year's Eve party, then that just left ten whose movements he'd need to track. Of course, that wouldn't rule out anyone who wasn't a resident of the Lodge but lived in the London area, he reminded himself. As Edith had pointed out, playing cards with the torch design could be bought in any tobacconist's. The fact that the murdered girl had been holding one such card proved nothing, he told himself.

He was first to the bar at the Albany and, ignoring Mortimer's protests, ordered a pint of Ordinary and a half for himself. It was the least he could do, he thought, after interrogating his friend as he had, even though the latter seemed blissfully unaware of having been interrogated. Mortimer, in fact, was only too happy to talk – their mutual reminiscences of the old days when they'd both been young and newly blinded, being enough to keep the conversation going. 'I must say, it's good to get out of that place for a while,' said Mortimer. 'One gets awfully fed up talking to the same lot of fellows. Nice to see an old Pal. You'll drop in again before too long, won't you?'

'As a matter of fact, it'll be sooner than you think,' replied Rowlands. He explained about his plans for the reunion.

'So *that's* why you were so interested in the New Year hop!' said Mortimer, with the air of one for whom the penny had finally dropped.

'Yes, I was trying to get an idea of the kind of numbers we might attract,' agreed Rowlands, feeling like the lowest kind of scoundrel. Lying to one's superior officer was bad enough, but lying to one's friends . . . It was unforgivable.

'Jolly good idea, if you ask me,' Mortimer was saying. 'Getting some of the old gang together. It'll be quite like old times.'

'Yes,' said Rowlands. After this, a silence fell. Both sipped their beers, content to let the buzz of conversation going on around wash over them: 'Think they'll cancel the fixtures this Saturday? If the snow holds off, I was going to take my boy to the match . . .' 'Seen that Watson of theirs? He's scored more goals this season than the rest of 'em put together. If they keep this up, West Ham'll be top of the League, you mark my words . . .' Nice chap, old Mortimer, thought Rowlands. Not that they'd ever been especially close, even in the old days, but there was a feeling of camaraderie you had with those you'd known when you were young which was like nothing else. 'Well,' he said, finishing his drink. 'Best be getting along, Mortimer, old man.'

'Sure you won't have another one?'

'No, thanks all the same.'

'Another time, then?'

'That'd be grand.'

The two men shook hands, and Rowlands left him sitting there in the pleasant fug of tobacco smoke and beer. One thing he missed about his old life was the London pubs, he thought. The one in the village was nice enough, and served a very decent pint of ale. But even after two years, he couldn't walk into the place without feeling himself a stranger.

'How did it go today?' said Edith when they were drinking their tea in front of the fire, the girls having been sent to bed long ago. Blowing the steam from the surface of the scalding liquid, Rowlands considered what to tell her. After the day he'd had, he didn't feel much like talking. He'd been chilled to the bone when he got in, and had barely been able to manage more than a bite of dinner (it was chicken again: rissoles this time). But he owed it to Edith to put her in the picture, he thought. And so, as succinctly as he could, he told her all he'd been up to since catching the half past eight that morning, leaving out only what struck him as irrelevant, or – in the case of his odd moment of communion with Winnie Calder – as too horrible to mention. Mercifully, Edith, perhaps sensing his reluctance to be drawn on certain matters, kept her questions to a minimum. When he got to the part of his tale that concerned the Lodge, and his spur-of-the-moment idea about arranging a reunion, she said only, 'That would be one way, of course.'

'One way of what?' he said.

'Why, of finding out what they were all up to that night,' she replied.

'Yes,' he said. 'The thing is, Edie, I'm going to need some help.'

'Oh, I'll help you,' she said. 'You couldn't manage on your own.'

'No. But the girls . . .'

'It's high time Mother came for a visit,' she said. 'The girls'll be perfectly fine with her for a few days. We'll need to stay in London, of course.'

'Yes. I must say, Edie, this is awfully good of you.'

'I want to be of use,' she said, with a fierceness that was all the more startling because it was so quietly expressed. It struck him that Edith had her own ideas about all this. 'If I telephone first thing, Mother can be here by tomorrow evening. Then we can make a start on Saturday – if that's soon enough for your friend the Inspector.'

'It'll have to be,' he said, and kissed her.

Chapter Four

A game was in progress: he could see the cards flash down. Ace, king, queen, knave. And hearts were trumps. He couldn't see their faces. The faces of the players, around the table, that is. But he was used to that. The cards, though, were quite distinct. He could feel their smooth surfaces under his fingers – the little pattern of raised dots that designated their value. Ten, nine, eight, seven . . . It was time to call, surely? He was North, and West had propped, so it was up to him to cop: 'I'll take you,' he ought to have said. Yet the words wouldn't form themselves. He could only watch helplessly as the cards came down. 'Any interest?' said the man on his left in a sneering tone (he thought it must be Vance, from the voice). 'Any interest?' And all he could do was to sit dumbly by and watch the cards fall down. Six, five, four . . . If he could only see their *faces*, he thought, then everything would become clear.

But now a bell was ringing, sharp and insistent, on and on it rang. He couldn't keep his mind on the game because of it. Damn it. What *was* that sound? 'Fred – wake up!' It was Edith's voice. 'Wake up!' she said again. 'You're wanted on the telephone. It's the Chief Inspector calling.' This brought him wide awake. He flung himself out of bed, and grabbed his dressing gown. Almost broke his neck falling downstairs, in so much of a hurry to reach the instrument was he. They'd had it installed the previous year, because Edith said that if she was going to have to live in the middle of nowhere, she should at least be able to get in touch with the outside world without having to walk a mile to the nearest telephone box. Now the thing sat like a squat bomb, waiting to explode with its load of bad news. He knew before the other spoke what the news would be.

'There's been another one,' said Chief Inspector Douglas, flatly. 'Shoreditch. Thought you might like to take a look.'

'Yes, Chief Inspector.' He was conscious of how fast his heart was beating. 'Shoreditch, you say?' If he hurried, he could make the seven-thirty. The District Line would take him to Whitechapel. He could walk from there. 'If you'll just tell me the address.'

'I'm sending a car,' said the Chief Inspector. 'It should be there within the hour.' He hung up before Rowlands could say anything more. Not that there was anything he wanted to say.

The car arrived as he was finishing his breakfast. He'd just time to grab his coat and scarf, and the overnight bag Edith had packed for him while he was dressing, before the sound of the Crossley's engine in the lane outside was followed by the scrunch of heavy boots on the path. In a little over an hour, their speed seldom dropping below 50mph – or so Rowlands was informed by the young sergeant sent to collect him – they were in Shoreditch High Street. 'It was the least I could do,' said the Chief Inspector in a tone of great affability. 'Since you're so interested in visiting the *scene of the crime*,' he added with scarcely veiled irony. The scene in question was very different from the shabby diggings where Winnie Calder had met her untimely end. That had been bad enough, but this was worse: a narrow alley running between a public house on one side and a warehouse on the other. Rowlands sniffed, and then wished he hadn't. The smell was of urine, tomcats and overflowing dustbins. 'We haven't got a name, at present,' said the Chief Inspector. 'But she was young, like the other one. About twenty-five, I'd say. Pretty, too – or she was before our man got hold of her.'

'You're sure it was the same man?'

'Oh yes. Same method. And *this* was found stuffed down the front of her dress. No fingerprints, of course, so he must have worn gloves.'

Rowlands removed his, before taking the card that

Douglas was holding out. 'The king of hearts,' he said after a moment.

'Spot on,' said Douglas. 'I must say, you're awfully good—'

'Was this where she was killed?' asked Rowlands, cutting across him. They had gone a little way into the alley – five paces, no more.

'We think so. O'course, we won't know the full story until the surgeon opens her up.'

'What time would this have been?' asked Rowlands, choosing not to respond to the casual brutality of the policeman's remark.

'Sometime between eight and ten o'clock last night, the doctor reckoned,' Douglas replied. 'They never *will* be drawn to say exactly when.'

Rowlands thought, *I left Regent's Park at three. Plenty of time for any one of them to have got from there to here*, and then reproached himself for the thought. There was nothing to tie either of the killings to the Lodge . . . or only one thing. And even that might have been no more than a coincidence. On an impulse, he stretched out his arms; he could just touch the walls on either side. The bricks felt cold and slimy. It was a dreadful place for a life to end – among the smells of stale beer emanating from the pub, and the stench of piss. 'Where does this lead?' he said, gesturing to show it was the alley he meant.

'It's a dead end. There's a gate, but it's kept locked. He must have lured her in here . . . not that she'd have resisted at first.' Rowlands must have looked blank, for the Inspector said: 'She was doing business, I'd guess. A cold night for it, though.' Rowlands was silent. There was *something* . . . He couldn't pin it down. He was still clutching the playing card. It struck him that the murderer had held it, too, only a few hours before. Perhaps he, too, had run his thumb over its surface, just as Rowlands himself was doing, to feel the pattern of raised dots that, to one such as himself, indicated its value.

'Is it from the same pack?' he asked, holding it up.

'It would seem so,' replied the Chief Inspector. 'Which means there's a strong possibility that it came from Regent's Park Lodge. Oh, I know all about that,' he added drily. 'After you were so interested in the pattern on the back, I had my sergeant look into it. Those cards are produced to St Dunstan's own design.'

'You can buy them anywhere,' said Rowlands.

'No doubt,' was the reply. 'Still, I'd have preferred to hear it from you, Mr Rowlands. I hope there's nothing else you've been keeping from me?'

'No.'

'Glad to hear it.'

'Who found her?' said Rowlands.

'The pot boy at the Fox when he was putting out the empties this morning, at seven o'clock. We're questioning him now.'

'And nobody heard anything? Last night, I mean.'

'No one's come forward – yet. Although if you ask me, even if anybody *had* heard something, they'd have carried on minding their own business, if you get me.'

Rowlands thought about it. The sounds of a struggle – of a woman's cries, swiftly stifled – might well have passed unnoticed or, if they were noticed, have been attributed to another cause. He wondered at what point she had known what was happening to her, the as yet unnamed victim: when what she had taken for one kind of tryst had turned into a more brutal encounter entirely. How narrow it was between these clammy walls! There was scarcely room for two people to stand side by side. A dead end. It had certainly proved to be that for *her*.

He realised his teeth were chattering.

'Had enough?' said the Chief Inspector. 'Then let's get ourselves in the warm, shall we? They'll do us a cup of tea at the station. We'll need it, before our next port of call . . .'

'How tall was she?' interrupted Rowlands. They had by now emerged onto Paul Street whose unexceptional sounds of motor vehicles passing, and someone shouting a greeting to someone else across the way, were a welcome contrast to the cold silence of the alley.

'That I can't say for certain,' replied Douglas, 'only having seen the young woman lying down, you understand. And not lying straight, neither, but sort of crumpled.'

'Yes.'

'You'll have a chance to find out, though,' went on the policeman, in the tone of one about to offer a delightful treat. 'It isn't what you'd call regular procedure, as you're not a relation of the deceased, but since you're helping us with our enquiries, as it were, I don't think it'll do any harm for you to come along. We'll just have our tea, because it's always so perishing cold, even on the hottest day.'

'Where are we going?' said Rowlands.

'Oh, didn't I say? To the mortuary,' was the reply.

'So,' said Chief Inspector Douglas as they sat drinking their tea in front of a newly stoked up coal fire, in an office hastily prepared for the purpose by the presiding officer at Shoreditch Police Station. The tea, Rowlands was pleased to discover, was strong, freshly made and piping hot. 'How did you get on yesterday, at the Institute?'

'We prefer to call it the Lodge,' said Rowlands. 'Or St Dunstan's. Either will do. And I got on quite well.' Briefly, he outlined his plan for getting in touch with former inmates.

'Yes, I wondered how you'd tackle it,' said Douglas blandly. 'Quick thinking on your part, coming up with that reunion story.'

'I can't say I liked doing it,' said Rowlands.

'No. But it had to be done. You do see that now, don't you?'

'Yes.'

'Good. So do you think this fellow Vance might know something?'

'I didn't say that,' said Rowlands.

'No, but it sounds as if he's the only one without an alibi for New Year's Eve. And the Kentish Town Road is only a stone's throw from the Lodge, as you call it. All we have to do is find someone who remembers seeing him in Shoreditch last night, and we've got our man. Well, if you've finished your tea,' he said, pushing back his chair, 'we'll go and take a look at the lady in question. Speaking of ladies,' said the Chief Inspector as they walked briskly along the corridor that led to the exit onto Shepherdess Walk, 'I take it your wife's aware of the, ah, *confidential* nature of what we're doing? Since she'll be assisting you,' he added.

'Of course.'

'That's good. Thank you, Sergeant,' he said to the officer who had risen from his desk at their approach. 'We can see ourselves out. Inspector Dawes is already at the hospital, I take it?'

'Yes, sir.'

'Good. Well, carry on.'

A car was waiting for them outside. 'Royal London Hospital,' said Douglas to the driver as they got into it. 'And be quick about it. While we're on the subject of what we do – and don't – want people to know,' he said in an undertone to Rowlands, 'I think it's high time we took the public into our confidence, so to speak. The Press boys are clamouring for details, of course, and they'll be all over the case now that there've been two murders. Aye,' he concluded with an air of grim satisfaction, '"Playing Card Murders – Another Victim?"

or some such nonsense'll make a fine headline in the evening papers, don't you think?'

'It's what he wants,' said Rowlands, not knowing how it was he knew it to be so, but knowing it was true, all the same.

'All part of the game he's playing, you think?'

'I would imagine so.'

'Well, it's time we took him on at his precious game if that's what he's in it for,' said Douglas. 'We need to find out what he's up to. See if anyone else – one of your St Dunstan's chappies, for instance – can cast some light. Playing games!' he added in a disgusted tone. 'Time was when villains committed murder for a good solid reason. Money, generally. A woman, sometimes. But this! It makes no sense at all.'

'Oh, I think it does,' said Rowlands. 'At least to our murderer. I should imagine it makes perfect sense to him.'

At the hospital, they were admitted, through heavy rubber doors, to a large cold room. The echo it gave off was enough to give Rowlands an idea of its size; as for what it contained, he was never more grateful for his blindness than at that moment. At least he didn't have to *see* what lay upon that table, nor on the tables around it, each of which, he supposed, must have borne a similar cargo. The smell was enough, though. Part medicinal, part cloacal, it took him back a dozen years to the hospital where, with other comrades wounded as he had been – and some whose injuries were far worse than his own – he'd spent the first week of his recovery. There'd been a heavy bombardment for days, and the hospital couldn't keep up with the numbers; some men had lain on pallets on the floor. The air had been thick with their groans and with the stench of death. It was this he could smell now. He felt his gorge rise at it.

'So what can you tell us about her?' he heard the Chief Inspector say, and was dragged back to the present and the unspeakable thing they now confronted. The doctor who'd performed the post-mortem allowed a moment's pause before replying.

'I take it you're referring to the woman who was brought in this morning?'

'Aye,' said Douglas, with scarcely concealed impatience. 'That's the one.'

'I've already said all this to the other chap.'

'Inspector Dawes, I suppose you mean?' said Douglas coldly. 'Well, you can say it again to me.'

'All right, all right. Let me see,' said the doctor, evidently consulting his notes. There was the sound of a page being flipped over. 'Ah, here we are. Female: name and circumstances unknown. Age: about twenty-five. Height: five foot five.'

'There you are,' said Douglas to Rowlands.

'Had given birth, but not recently.'

'How did she die?'

'I was coming to that. Strangulation,' said the doctor.

He had what Rowlands thought of as a fruity voice. It lent an air of theatricality to the horror of which he spoke. 'Although there was bruising on the scalp which suggested that she'd received a blow to the head immediately before death.'

'Time of death?' Douglas might have been asking the time of the next train.

'Between eight and ten o'clock, I'd say. Contents of the stomach indicate she'd eaten a fish supper and consumed at least a pint of porter not long before her death. Let's say time of death was ten o'clock, to be on the safe side.'

'Any signs of sexual congress having taken place?'

'None.'

'Strange,' murmured the Chief Inspector. 'Well, I think that's all.'

'What colour are her eyes?' said Rowlands, surprising himself. There was a startled silence before the doctor spoke.

'Blue, I think. I'll just take a look. Yes, they're blue. Greyish-blue. Though of course rather reddened now. The blood vessels do tend to burst in these cases, you know.'

'Hair colour?' Rowlands wasn't sure why he wanted to know, but it seemed important.

'Fair. Here, see for yourself,' said the doctor. He must have thrown back the sheet at that moment, because a stronger smell than the one that had been disagreeably filling Rowlands' nostrils now arose.

Blood, and – not quite masked by its metallic tang – another, fouler stink.

'I can't.' Rowlands turned his face away from the awful intimacy of that smell. The body in its final nakedness. Stepping back, to place some distance between himself and the poor abandoned thing that lay upon the table, he collided with a trolley loaded with instruments; a few of them fell to the floor, with a skittering crash. 'I'm sorry,' he said, although whether it was his clumsiness he was apologising for or his failure to confront the worst, he could not have said.

'It takes some people like that,' said the doctor cheerily. 'We get used to it, of course, in our respective lines of work, don't we, Inspector?'

'Chief Inspector,' said Douglas. 'Yes, I suppose we do. Thank you, Doctor. That'll be all. Come along, Mr Rowlands. You look as if you could do with a drink – and something a wee bit stronger than a cup of tea, too.' He must have consulted his watch then, for he added, 'What d'you know? We're in luck. They'll be opening in fifteen minutes. I believe we've time for a swift half.'

At a table next to one of the windows in the public bar of the Blind Beggar, Rowlands waited while Douglas fetched the drinks. The pub was still quiet, with – he judged from the subdued hum of conversation – no more than a dozen regulars present. The clacking of 'bones' and occasional hoarse cries of 'Out!' and 'I win!' from an adjacent table told him that a game of dominoes was in progress. He'd never taken to the game, but it had been popular at the Lodge for a season. A wintry sunshine fell through the glass; he could feel its faint warmth on his upturned face. It had been thoughtful of the Chief Inspector to choose this particular table, knowing as he did his companion's preference for the lightest part of any room. Or perhaps his choice had been dictated by discretion rather than out of any consideration for Rowlands – it being the one furthest from the other tables. 'Didn't I tell you it'd be cold in there?' said Douglas, setting down the brimming glasses.

'Yes.' Rowlands took an appreciative draught of his Burton's. 'It certainly was that. Your health, Chief Inspector.'

'You needn't call me that here,' said Douglas in a low voice.

'No, of course not.' So he'd been right about the table. He hoped that the rattle of the dominoes had been loud enough to cover his slip. 'I wanted to ask you—' he began, but the policeman cut across him.

'Yes, I think the Gunners'll do well this season,' he said in a voice loud enough to carry. They talked football for a few minutes, and then Douglas said in an undertone, 'So what do you want to know? Keep it general, if you would. No names.'

'All right. I was wondering if there was a pattern to be discerned in all of this.'

'Lockdown!' came the shout from the next table, and then a burst of laughter.

'A pattern?' echoed the policeman.

'Well, *similarities* between the . . . ah . . . incidents,' said Rowlands. 'Apart from the obvious,' he added.

'Our game of chance,' you mean, the Chief Inspector said. 'You could say it imposes a pattern of its own.'

'Smack down the bone, Charlie, we haven't got all day.'

'Yes. But aside from that, are there any resemblances between the young women in question? Hair colour, build – that sort of thing.'

'Oh, we thought of that. But apart from the fact that they were both young, fair-haired, and what you might call reasonably good-looking . . .'

'Take a bone from the boneyard, Alfie, if you ain't got a match,' said a voice from the dominoes table.

'. . . I'm afraid there isn't very much to go on at all. Just these blessed playing cards.' He took a last draught, and set down his empty glass with a resonant clink. 'Who put them there? That's what we've got to find out – and soon, before there's another one . . .'

'Double six!' came the cry from the players' table.

Outside the pub they parted – the Chief Inspector to talk to the Press; Rowlands to make his way, via the Metropolitan Line, to the small hotel in the Marylebone Road where he was to spend the night, and where Edith was to join him the following day. He knew he could have asked to stay at the Lodge, in the married men's quarters, but somehow the idea hadn't appealed to him. To be billeted under the same roof as the men whose movements he was spying on (there was no other word for what he was doing) would have been more than he could stomach. Even so, he was starting to regret the decision a little as he rang the bell, and was admitted, after a brief hiatus, to the cramped hallway of the Belmont Hotel (prop. Mrs A. Philpotts). Here, in an atmosphere redolent of floor wax and furniture polish, he signed the register and was handed a key by the said proprietress – a fat woman, he guessed, from her stertorous breathing. 'Breakfast's at seven,' she said, adding with a martyred air, 'I can do you a boiled egg, or there's porridge.'

He could imagine what the porridge would be like. 'A boiled egg will do very well,' he said.

'No baths after ten o'clock,' went on the lugubrious Mrs Philpotts. 'It's a double room,' she said doubtfully, as if noticing for the first time that there was only a single occupant.

'Yes, that's all right. My wife'll be joining me tomorrow.'

'Only we don't get many married people. Mainly commercial gentlemen,' explained his hostess. There was really no answer to this, and so he merely smiled.

'If you could just direct me towards the lift.'

'There's no lift.'

'The stairs, then. And no, I don't need any help,' he added, in response to a grudging enquiry as to whether he'd want the 'boy' to bring up his bag. 'Room Ten, you said, I think?'

'End of the corridor,' called Mrs Philpotts after him. 'You can't miss it.'

Once inside the room, he felt exhaustion overwhelm him. The combination of an early start and the unpleasant experiences of the past few hours had had a debilitating effect. He felt ready to drop, even though his watch told him it had only just gone one o'clock. He realised in the same moment that he was ravenously hungry, having eaten nothing since a hastily consumed breakfast at seven that morning. He wondered if the permanently affronted Mrs Philpotts would consider doing him a ham sandwich, or some such. What he really wanted, more than this, was a bath. After a few hours in the sooty London air, he felt covered in grime from head to foot. The smell of the morgue was in his nostrils still. Perhaps a good long soak in hot water would wash it all away. But the effort involved in undressing and unpacking his dressing gown and spongebag, and then walking back along the corridor to the carbolic-smelling communal bathroom, was suddenly too much. Instead, he lay down fully dressed on the bed's slippery sateen eiderdown, and fell into a heavy, dreamless sleep.

He awoke with a start, and the consciousness that something was wrong, somewhere. Someone was banging on the door. It was the landlady, he realised.

'Just a minute.' Groggily, he got to his feet. His head was splitting; two hours' unrestful sleep in a stuffy room had left him feeling worse than before. He opened the door a crack. 'Yes?'

'Telephone call for you. A woman,' said the proprietress suspiciously. She emitted a juicy sniff. 'Says she's your wife.' Not waiting to hear any more, Rowlands dashed out into the corridor and ran towards the stairs, which he descended at a gallop. He found the telephone, which was on the front desk, almost at once and seized the receiver with alacrity.

'Edith, is that you?' His heart was pounding, and not because he'd run downstairs. His experiences of the past few days had made it all too easy to imagine catastrophe.

'Who else were you expecting?' she laughed, and at the sound of her laughter he felt himself relax.

'I don't know. You took me by surprise, that's all. Is everything all right?'

'This isn't a public tellyphone, you know,' said Mrs Philpotts disdainfully as she regained her seat behind the counter.

'I heard that!' said Edith. 'Don't worry, I'll keep it brief. I just wanted to let you know that I'll be with you tomorrow about four. Mother's catching an early train. The girls send their love.'

'Send them mine,' he said. 'And to you, of course.' It wasn't possible to say more, with that dragon sitting there. But as he replaced the heavy receiver in its cradle, he thought: There's nothing that matters more. The girls and Edith, and keeping them from harm. Yes, that was all that mattered.

After a rudimentary wash – the geyser wouldn't be lit for two hours yet, Mrs Philpotts had told him with undisguised satisfaction when he'd enquired about a bath – he'd set off for Regent's Park. A year living in rural Kent had made him less confident in traffic; it took him all of five minutes to get across the Marylebone Road, along which what seemed an unbroken stream of omnibuses, taxis and motorcars roared, belching out noxious fumes. Only the dread of having some well-meaning passer-by take him by the arm to help him across, forced him to chance it at last. With the heavier vehicles, one was on safer ground, of course, because they made such a fearsome racket; even so, it was with a pounding heart that he made it to the opposite pavement, and stood getting his bearings. Here was Gloucester Place, with beyond it, Dorset Square; then Glentworth Street, at the end of which was St Cyprian's church. You could get into the Outer Circle that way. In the two years he'd spent at the Lodge, he'd got to know these main thoroughfares and the side streets that ran off them as if he'd been born in this part of the world – which in a sense, he had been. If you counted the life he'd had after 1917 as a new life (it had certainly been different from the old), then this network of streets with the park at its centre had been the first he'd known, in the way he was, thereafter, to know the world.

Outside Baker Street Underground Station, a news vendor was bawling 'Playing Card Killer Strikes Again!' Douglas had got what he wanted then. He bought a paper, on the off-chance that there'd be someone at the Lodge who'd be able to read it. Otherwise he'd keep it for Edith to see. Entering the park by the York Gate, he quickened his pace – always a relief, once you were out of the crowds – and struck out towards the right. If he timed it correctly, he'd just be in time for tea. Reaching, after a few minutes' brisk walk, the middle of the great open space, he drew a deep breath of the icy, faintly pine-scented, air. Being here, at this season, and at this time of day, brought back memories of earlier days when, returning from a row on the lake or from a game of football, he'd felt the same keen glow of anticipation at the prospect of hot tea, a warm fire and the company of his peers. Around him, the wide lawns, now covered with a fresh layer of snow, resounded to the barking of dogs and the shouts of those engaged in walking them. It was funny – he'd never taken to the idea of a dog; he believed some of the men now had them, as an aid to getting about. But when he'd first come here, in '17, the very thought had been anathema. Almost as bad as having to carry a white stick: a sign that you were *different*.

Chapter Five

Tea was being served in the library: the appetising smell of hot buttered toast wafted towards him as he opened the door, and pleasant sounds of cups being raised and replaced in saucers, and of teaspoons clinking against the rims of cups, overlaid the murmur of conversation. He caught fragments of the same as he moved towards the fire, around which the familiar half-circle of armchairs had been drawn up.

'. . . if you want my opinion, it's all rot.'

'Thing is, the game's about *strategy*.'

'That's all my eye, and you know it. It's about luck, pure and simple.'

'Any ideas on Five Across? "Murder most foul and unnatural" . . . Eight letters.'

Rowlands found a seat and sat himself down in it. 'Is there a cup of tea in the pot?' he enquired, of no one in particular.

'Might be,' came the reply, from one of those already ensconced there. Phillips, he rather thought. 'Who wants to know?'

'Fred Rowlands. We met yesterday.'

'Did we? I'll take your word for it. Frightfully confusing, keeping track of all the people one meets when one can't see their faces.'

'I suppose it is,' said Rowlands, for whom it was not. He supposed it must be more difficult for those who hadn't had to get used to remembering voices and tricks of speech from the beginning, the way he and the rest of his generation of St Dunstaners had.

'Tea trolley's over by the door,' said Phillips, perhaps to make up for his earlier gruffness.

'Thanks.' Rowlands got up again, and retraced his steps towards the trolley and its freight of urns and cups. But as he was reaching for a clean cup from the pile, another voice – Mortimer's – said, 'I shouldn't bother with that. It'll be stewed by now. I must say,' he went on, 'you don't believe in letting the grass grow under your feet, do you? I mean, here you are, back again.'

'Oh, I thought I should make a start,' replied Rowlands mildly. He poured himself a cup of tea and took a sip. It *was* stewed. Still, beggars couldn't be choosers. 'I don't suppose there's a slice of toast left, is there?' he said. 'Only I forgot to have any lunch.'

'I think we can do better than that,' said Mortimer. 'Plum cake.' He cut what turned out to be a generous slice, put it on a plate and handed the plate to Rowlands. 'One of the wives brought it.'

'Mine, as a matter of fact,' said a voice from the fireside. Not one Rowlands recognised. 'Well, it's jolly good cake,' he said, through a mouthful of moist crumbs. 'You must thank your wife from me, Mr . . .'

'Bingham's the name.' A pleasant, light tenor voice. 'Don't believe I've had the pleasure.'

Rowlands introduced himself.

'Rowlands. I know that name. Weren't you a rower?'

'Well, it *was* a long time ago. But yes, I used to row a bit. I was never as good as Mortimer, though.'

'Oh, as to that . . .' Mortimer started to say when the door opened and someone else – a woman, evidently – came in, wafting carnation scent, and talking with what seemed to Rowlands excessive animation.

'Now, you'll just have to wait until I've had my tea, Mr Carstairs. I've been gasping for a cup all afternoon.'

'I'm afraid you won't think much of this, Miss Clavering,' said Mortimer. 'Poor Rowlands here has been making the best of it, but it's really not fit to drink.'

'Like that, is it?' said the girl. 'Well, I'll just have to ring for a fresh pot.'

'And some more toast, please, Doris,' said another voice, with a lazy drawl that made Rowlands' hackles rise. Vance. Might have known *he'd* be hogging the fire.

'All right, all right! Don't all shout at once,' said the young woman thus addressed, seeming not at all put out by such familiarity. She must have pressed a bell, for a moment later the housekeeper appeared. 'Ah, hello, Mrs Britcher. Do you think we could have some more tea, please? And another plate of toast.'

'I'll see what I can do,' said the housekeeper, with a sniff.

'Thanks ever so. You *are* a dear,' said Doris Clavering sweetly. 'Old cat,' she muttered, just loud enough to be heard by those nearest to her as the door closed behind Mrs Britcher. 'Now then, Mr Carstairs – what was it you wanted me to read to you? Something to do with stocks and shares, wasn't it?'

'My share holdings, yes,' replied Carstairs, with an edge of impatience. 'Anaconda Copper Mines and Anglo-Java Rubber. Oh, and you might let me have the figures for British Imperial Tobacco while you're about it.'

'And then you can read me the racing results,' said Vance. 'Had a little flutter in the two-thirty, don't you know?'

'Right you are,' said the girl. 'Now, where did I put that paper?'

'Will this do?' said Rowlands, taking the folded-up *Evening News* from his coat pocket.

'Thanks,' said Miss Clavering, taking it from him. 'I don't think we've met, have we?'

Rowlands introduced himself.

'Oh, I know who you are now!' said the girl. 'You're

the one that's organising the reunion.'

'That's right.'

'Ever such a good idea, I think. Getting the boys together. I was only saying to Major Fraser this morning—' She broke off abruptly. 'Oh, Lord! Not another one! What *is* the world coming to, I wonder?'

'What's that, Doris?' called Vance, from his place by the fire.

'There's only been another poor girl murdered,' replied Miss Clavering, with a relish she was unable entirely to conceal. 'Looks like the same chap that did the last one in – that girl in Camden Town.'

'Well, don't keep us all in suspense,' said Vance. 'Read it, why don't you? Nothing like a jolly good murder, I always say.'

'But Miss Clavering—' came a pained voice.

'Yes, Mr Carstairs, I haven't forgotten about your shares. Now, let's see . . . Ah, here we are! "*Playing Card Killer Shows His Hand*" – rather good, that, don't you think?' Miss Clavering's voice took on the 'stagey' quality some people adopted when reading aloud. '"*Police hunting the killer of Winifred Calder, a dancer, found strangled on New Year's Day in Camden Town, have issued a warning to the public to be extra vigilant, after the body of a second woman was discovered in a Shoreditch alley early this morning* . . ." How horrid!' she exclaimed delightedly.

'But what's it got to do with playing cards?' interjected Phillips.

'I was coming to that,' said the girl. 'If you'll just have patience, Mr Phillips. "*Police were alerted to a possible link between the two deaths by the discovery of a playing card in the possession of the deceased – also a feature of the earlier case* . . ." Gruesome, isn't it? "*Asked to comment, Chief Inspector Alasdair Douglas of the Metropolitan Police, who is in charge of investigating the murders, said: 'What we appear to have here is a series killer – that is to say, an individual for whom one murder is not enough. The placing of the playing cards at the scene of each crime suggests that he believes himself to be playing a* game *with the police. I should like to take this opportunity of reassuring the public that the police have matters very much in hand – and that, if any such* game *is being played, there can only be one possible* winner: *the force of Law and Order*'" . . . Well!' said Doris Clavering, 'If that isn't a challenge, I don't know what is. I just hope . . .' She gave a theatrical little shiver, 'that our murderer, whoever he is, doesn't decide to take it up.'

'Oh, I shouldn't worry,' said Vance. 'I have it on good authority that he only goes for blondes.'

'How can you be sure I'm not?' she replied sweetly. Vance laughed immoderately at that. 'Oh, I say! Jolly good! But I've always had you down as a redhead.'

'Auburn,' she said. 'And not out of a bottle, neither.'

'Miss Clavering . . .' Carstairs renewed his appeal.

'Yes, Mr Carstairs. Be right with you. What I want to

know is: will he strike again?' said the girl in a thrilled undertone. 'I mean, they don't often stop at two, these types, do they?'

'You seem to know an awful lot about it, Doris,' said Vance slyly. 'Know many of these *types*, do you?'

'The cheek of it!' cried Miss Clavering, going off into a peal of giggles. 'Why, I take an interest, that's all.'

'Idiotic girl,' muttered a voice in Rowlands' ear. Mortimer again. 'What Major Fraser can have been thinking when he took her on, I really can't imagine.'

Rowlands was saved from having to reply by the arrival of another latecomer, who turned out to be the Major himself. 'I say, it sounds awfully jolly in here! What's all the excitement? I could hear your voice from along the corridor, Doris.'

'Ooh, hello, Major. Yes, we were just talking about this latest murder.'

'And what murder's that?' enquired the Major gravely.

'Well, I couldn't really say. That is, they don't say very much about it in the paper,' replied the girl. 'All they've said is it's the same chap that did the other one – that girl in Camden Town.'

'Oh yes,' murmured Major Fraser. 'Shocking case.' There was a moment's silence. 'So who's in this evening?' he went on, making it clear that this marked an end to the previous subject. 'I thought I heard your voice, Vance.'

'Guilty as charged,' drawled Reggie Vance, from his place by the fire.

'Phillips? Carstairs? I know I can rely on both of *you* to swell the merry throng.'

'Afternoon, Major,' sang out both these gentlemen. Murmured greetings from others came from different quarters of the room.

'Hello, Major,' said Rowlands. 'I thought I'd look in, too,'

'Ah, Rowlands. Jolly glad you did,' came the reply. 'I hope you'll stay to dinner?'

'That's awfully good of you,' said Rowlands, feeling the invidiousness of his position all the more at this fresh evidence of the warmth of the Major's regard. 'But you see, I don't have my dress clothes with me. That is, they're back at the hotel,' he added lamely.

'Oh, we're very informal here. Quite a few of the men don't bother with dressing, you know,' said the Major, who always did.

'Well, in that case . . .'

'Splendid. Dinner's at seven. We dine rather early here, as I expect you remember,' added the Major apologetically. 'It leaves the rest of the evening free for cards, and all that sort of thing. Are you a Bridge player, Rowlands?'

'I play a bit.'

'Then we'll have to see if we can get up a table or two later this evening.'

'Oh, there'll be a game going on, Major – you can be sure of that!' said Vance, who had evidently been listening to this exchange.

'Yes, you like your game of an evening, don't you, Vance?' said Major Fraser, with a certain edge. 'Doris, I've signed those letters, so you can get them off to the post.'

'Yes, Major,' said Miss Clavering meekly. 'Only I was just waiting for Mrs B to bring some fresh tea and toast.'

'Have your tea by all means,' said her employer, in a warmer tone than he had used in addressing Vance. 'But do make sure you don't miss the last post. I want that letter to Sir Neville Pearson to be on his desk tomorrow morning. Fundraising, you know,' he said to Rowlands in an undertone. 'It's a large part of my job these days, I'm afraid. If you're at a loose end in about half an hour,' he went on, still addressing Rowlands, 'why don't you drop by my office? There are a couple of things on which I'd like your opinion.'

'With pleasure,' said Rowlands. Half an hour should give him ample time to get to know every man in the room he'd yet to speak to, and to improve his acquaintance with those – like the amiable Bingham – he'd only just met. It wouldn't have been his preferred way of going about it – having to *force* a process which under normal circumstances could take weeks, if not months. He recalled his early days at the Lodge, soon after he'd been invalided out of the army in 1917. *Then*, the camaraderie felt by all the men – a sense of shared experience, not only of being blind, but of the war that had made one so – had helped to carry them over the awkwardness of first meetings. Now . . . well, he gathered it was different, that was all. Their blindness aside, these men, he guessed, had very little in common.

'Sherry?' said the Major, opening the drinks cabinet he kept for such eventualities in his office. 'Or would you prefer whisky? We've time before dinner.'

'Whisky, please.'

'Good man.' The Major poured out a couple of generous glasses and handed one to Rowlands. 'Well,' he said. 'Here's luck. So tell me,' he went on when both had drunk to this, 'how are you getting on? With your plans for getting the men together, I mean.'

'Oh, not so bad.' Rowlands hoped his embarrassment wasn't as obvious to the other man as it felt to him. 'Quite a few of the chaps I spoke to are fairly keen.' And quite a few were anything *but* keen, he amended silently. Carstairs, for one. 'What! Catch me turning up at a reunion after I leave this place?' he'd exclaimed. 'I've had quite enough of it already to want to do *that*.' Major Fraser seemed satisfied with this reply, however.

'Splendid,' he said. 'And your wife joins you tomorrow, what?'

'That's right, sir.'

'Jolly good. It'll be like old times for her, too, I imagine?'

'Yes.' Edith had been a VAD. The months she'd spent at the Lodge, teaching men newly returned from the Front how to quickstep, or acting as coxswain while a man getting used to the art of sculling rowed her around the lake, had been some of the best fun she'd ever had, she liked to say. 'A different chap every day. Some of them *very* attractive. And then *you* came along,' she'd add wryly. 'And put an end to all that.'

'I wonder,' said the Major, with the air of slight abstraction which had characterised his utterances since Rowlands first came in, 'whether *she'll* see a change?'

'Well . . .'

'Oh, I don't mean just that the men here are all a good deal older,' said the Major. 'Although there *is* that, you know. They're not as lively as your lot were – always larking around, like a pack of schoolboys. Remember those entertainments we used to put on? *Babes in the Wood* was one, I seem to recall. Strapping six-foot chaps got up as village maidens. Bawling out the songs in ridiculous falsetto. Brought the house down when they did their closing number.'

'"If You Were the Only Girl in the World",' put in Rowlands.

'That's the one. Those were good times,' said the Major. There was a brief pause while he lit a cigarette. 'Now?' he went on. 'Well, I'm not so sure.' Rowlands, who had formed his own opinion of the present state of things at the Lodge, judged it best to say nothing. 'Yes,' said the Major. 'It's a different generation now, with different preoccupations. Not the same spirit as in the old days, of all mucking in together. Only to be expected, I suppose . . .' He broke off. 'I say – I *am* sorry. You must think me awfully rude. Here I am, smoking away, and never so much as offered you a light.'

'That's quite all right,' said Rowlands. 'I've got my own.'

'No, I insist. Do help yourself. There's a box on the table in front on you. That's what comes,' said the Major, 'of getting caught up in something. One forgets one's manners. Now. Where were we?'

'You were saying that things hadn't been the same lately,' said Rowlands, holding the cigarette he had taken from the heavy silver box alongside the match as he struck it: an old trick, from the early days of his blindness. It meant that at the moment of ignition, the end of the cigarette was level with the flame. Useful in all weathers, he'd found.

'So I was.' The Major exhaled a lungful of smoke before continuing. 'The fact is, I've a feeling there's something not quite right going on . . .' His voice tailed off. 'Hard to put it into words, really. I mean, take this business of the card-playing . . .'

Rowlands was silent.

'Oh, don't get me wrong,' said the Major. 'I like a good game of Bridge as well as the next man. It's awfully good as a way of training the memory, if nothing else, and people do seem to get a lot of fun out of it. Rather more than that, sometimes.'

'I know some people take it very seriously.'

'*Too* seriously, if you want my opinion,' replied the Major. 'A game's a game when all's said and done. I don't hold with all this competitiveness. To say nothing of the financial aspect. Oh, I know what goes on.' He took a sip of whisky before continuing. 'And of course the game wouldn't be the same unless there was money involved. A few shillings lost and won makes it all the more exciting. It's when it gets *beyond* that, that the whole thing starts getting out of hand. I mean, strictly speaking, we don't allow gambling here.'

'No,' said Rowlands.

'Of course one doesn't want to seem like a killjoy by absolutely *forbidding* the men to play for money. But it can't be allowed to take over, if you know what I mean?'

'Oh, yes,' said Rowlands. 'I know exactly what you mean.' Thinking, as he spoke, of men he'd known in the army, for whom every occurrence, from the most trivial to the deadly serious, was a betting opportunity. How many shells would go over before there was a direct hit. Who'd be the first to go home with a Blighty one, and who wouldn't be going home at all . . . He thought, too, of the queue in front of the betting shop when he was a lad. Men spending half their wages in the pub, and the rest on a two-way bet in the three-thirty.

'Sometimes I think it's become a national obsession,' said the Major. 'I mean, take the City. All that buying cheap and selling dear. Men making fortunes one day, and losing 'em the next. What's that if it's not gambling?'

'I'm sure you're right,' said Rowlands, who knew very little of what went on in the City – if by that one meant the banks. For him, the word 'City' had a geographical connotation, merely. It was where he'd worked for seven years, that was all. He knew its streets and alleys as if they were the lines of his hand; and yet he couldn't say he had more than a cursory understanding of what went on behind the fortress-like walls of its banks and counting houses, although in his successive journeys to and from Saville & Willoughby's offices in Gracechurch Street he must have rubbed shoulders with scores of people who worked in those very institutions. He thought of TS Eliot's lines in *The Waste Land* about the crowd flowing over London Bridge. He'd been part of that crowd once. When he'd read the lines – or rather when Edith had read them to him – it had brought it all back: the inexorable movement of the crowd and the sound of its hurrying feet, and all the other, no less familiar, sounds which together made up the texture of the experience. The low rumble of taxicabs and buses. The hollow booming of ships' sirens in the distance. The chiming of the clock on Southwark Cathedral. Sounds which would forever echo in his dreams.

He became aware that the Major was speaking: '. . . rather afraid that it's been getting out of control lately. Naming no names, but one or two of our more recent arrivals have been upping the stakes a good deal, if you take my meaning. Causing no end of bother. Why, one man came to me only the other day in a terrible state—' He broke off abruptly, as if conscious he might be revealing too much. 'Time it was nipped in the bud – the gambling, I mean. Trouble is,' the Major said, with an awkward little laugh, 'the men tend to clam up when

I'm around. Nobody wants to be the first to point the finger. So I'd consider it a favour if you'd keep your ear to the ground, as it were, and let me know if you hear of anything untoward.'

'Well . . .'

'Oh, I wouldn't want you to do anything you don't feel comfortable doing,' said the other hastily. 'It's just that . . . if you did hear of anything . . . *unusual* . . . well, you might just let me know, that's all.'

'I'll do what I can, sir,' said Rowlands, grimly reflecting that this was the second time in as many days that he'd been asked to become a spy.

Dinner was an unexpectedly pleasant occasion, Mrs B having excelled herself, the Major said. Mulligatawny soup, followed by veal cutlets, duchess potatoes and creamed spinach, with treacle tart to follow – the whole of it washed down with what seemed to Rowlands, admittedly no connoisseur, to be a very decent claret. Aided by this, conversation flowed, and the mood, which had seemed crabbed and awkward at tea, was genial. The Major was to his right, Bingham to his left; Agnew and Mortimer sitting opposite. For the first time since his return here, Rowlands felt that he was surrounded by friends. It occurred to him through the agreeable haze brought on by a little too much food and alcohol, that perhaps after all the Chief Inspector had got it wrong, and that there was no connection between the murders of those two girls and anyone at the Lodge. The playing cards might be nothing but a blind, as Douglas himself had said. Although it *was* odd, he thought, the way Vance had known those girls were blondes. Had there been anything in the paper about that? He'd have to find out.

The talk moved from politics (the recent troubles in Afghanistan) to sport (England's hopes in the Ashes), and from sport to theatre. Bingham had been to see *Plunder*, the new farce at the Aldwych. 'I must say it was jolly good,' he said. 'Lot of nonsense, really, but he writes a corking line, does Travers. Have you seen it yet, Rowlands?'

Rowlands said that he had not.

'Oh, but you must! Take the wife, next time you're up West.' Bingham chuckled, as if at a reminiscence too amusing not to share. 'Silly stuff, you know. But the scene with the jewel thieves being hauled over the coals at Scotland Yard had me howling with laughter, I can tell you.'

'I'll keep it in mind,' said Rowlands, thinking he'd had quite enough of Scotland Yard these past few days.

'Good concert last night at the Wigmore Hall,' put in the Major diffidently. 'I heard it on the wireless. Bartok, you know. A bit on the modern side for me. What do you make of his stuff, Rowlands? Not really *music*, is it, when all's said and done?'

'Well,' said Rowlands, who'd developed quite a liking for the avant-garde in recent years. 'I suppose it's all a matter of taste.'

'I can't be doing with all that foreign stuff,' put in Agnew, from across the table. 'I like a nice tune, myself. Something with a bit of heart to it. *Irene*. Now *that* had some lovely tunes.'

'If it's all the same to you, I suggest we continue this artistic discussion in the Rec room,' said the Major. 'Mrs B will be wanting to clear away. And then we'll see about setting up a game of cards for Rowlands here.'

'Oh yes,' said Rowlands, whose taste for games of chance had considerably diminished during the past week. Now, what had been a lighthearted pastime seemed charged with significance. Every time he made a bid, it would be as if an invisible policeman stood at his elbow, watching his every move.

As before, the game was Solo Whist, although Phillips put in a half-hearted plea for Bridge. 'So much jollier, playing with a partner, I always feel.'

'You can do that with Prop & Cop,' said Vance. 'Although personally I like to play Solo. I like to win my own tricks.' Remembering his 'commission' from the Major, Rowlands wondered whether he ought not to manoeuvre himself onto Vance's table. He couldn't imagine it'd be much fun playing opposite the man – a player only out for what he could get, and not too particular about how he got it. But in the end he found himself on the second of the two tables that were set up on the far side of the room. The Major, having been invited to join them, politely declined.

'D'you know, I think I'll sit this one out. Never much of a hand at cards. Chess is much more my line. Are you a chess man, Winterbourne?' This was to one of the group of men who'd taken possession of the chairs around the fire.

''Fraid not,' came the reply. 'Too brainy for me, I'm afraid. Draughts is more my game.'

And so it was Rowlands, Mortimer, Agnew and Bingham at one table; Phillips, Broomfield, Williamson and Vance at the other. On Rowlands' table, Agnew was dealing. Hearts were trumps. 'I'll bid Prop,' said Bingham to Rowlands on his left, but Rowlands had already ascertained that his own cards were poor. 'I'll play *Misère Ouverte*,' he said.

'We'll see about that,' said Mortimer. 'Pass.'

'Pass,' said Agnew.

'Two of hearts,' said Rowlands, putting it down.

'Bad. Very bad,' said Mortimer. 'Five of hearts.'

'Four of hearts,' said Agnew.

'Seven,' said Bingham. 'Looks as if I've taken this trick, curse you. Three of spades,' he continued, opening the next round of bidding.

'Five,' said Rowlands, discarding this.

'King,' said Mortimer, with a groan.

'Jack, said Agnew. 'Your trick, Mortimer.'

'Don't I know it?' said Mortimer. 'But the game's not over yet.'

At the next table, they were playing Abundance. Vance was winning; his self-satisfied crowing could be heard above the rest. 'I tell you, if we were playing for more than halfpence, I'd be doing all right for myself tonight.' There was a dry cough from over by the fireplace where the Major was sitting. A moment later, he got up.

'Think I'll leave you chaps to it,' he said. 'There's a play on the wireless I want to catch. Good night, all.'

A chorus of 'good-nights' followed as he made his way to the door.

'Anyone want to raise the stakes?' said Vance as the door closed behind Major Fraser. 'What about you, Broomfield old man? You've had some good cards tonight.'

'I'll pass, old chap, if you don't mind. Bit of a difficult month, you know, what with my buttery bill to pay, and all that.'

'Suit yourself,' said Vance. 'You, Phillips?'

'Well . . .'

'Ace of diamonds,' said Mortimer, making further eavesdropping impossible.

'Queen.'

'King.'

'Three,' said Rowlands. 'Your trick again, Mortimer.'

'It's a funny old game, this,' said Mortimer, with the wheezing laugh that had become habitual with him. Lungs, poor devil, thought Rowlands. 'A funny old game. You lose to win, and you throw away your best cards in order to get the other man out. But it doesn't always work out. Six of clubs.'

'Four,' said Agnew.

'Two,' said Bingham, snapping it down briskly.

'Oh dear,' said Rowlands. 'I suppose that means I'll have to play my king.'

'And you came so close to losing everything,' said Mortimer, pushing the cards towards him. Rowlands shrugged.

'You know what they say,' he said lightly. 'Lucky at cards . . .' Mortimer laughed. The laugh ended in a coughing fit.

'Yes, they do say that, don't they?' he said, when he could speak.

Another few games followed. Agnew and Bingham teamed up for Prop & Cop, and won their required eight tricks. Mortimer played an unsuccessful Solo hand. He had better luck with a round of *Misère Ouverte*, as did Rowlands, who, with good cards this time, won the next round of Abundance.

At the next table, Vance had hit a losing streak. 'Just as well we didn't agree to play for shillings, or you'd have been cleaned out by now,' Phillips took pleasure in pointing out.

'Ah, but I'd have won it all back next time,' retorted Vance.

'Well, *I've* had rotten cards all night,' said Williamson morosely. 'So I can't say I'm sorry we were only playing for halfpence.'

'The trouble with you, young Williamson, is that you've no competitive spirit,' said Vance, in the jeering tone which seemed habitual with him. 'It's what you need to be a really good player.'

'Not to mention luck,' put in Broomfield cheerfully. 'Ace of spades. My trick, I think.'

Walking back that night across the deserted park, Rowlands reflected on the evening's events, which had left him with a distinctly uncomfortable feeling. Something wasn't right, the Major had said, and Rowlands could only concur. Although what exactly the source of the wrongness was, he couldn't have said. Vance's influence, though doubtless unsavoury, couldn't by itself account for the pervasive mood. Yes, there was something rotten somewhere, Rowlands thought. The trick would be to find out what it was – and who was responsible. Arriving back at the Belmont Hotel, he was relieved to find the lobby deserted. He didn't think he could have faced another inquisition from the formidable Mrs Philpotts. He climbed the stairs and let himself into the room, which smelt faintly of mice and of infrequently turned mattresses. Edith would have something to say about this, no doubt. But he was too tired now to care about the room's deficiencies. All he wanted was to get his head down; let everything else go hang.

But the blissful unconsciousness he'd been anticipating proved harder to achieve than he'd hoped. As he felt himself drifting off to sleep, the horror he'd been keeping at bay for the past few hours returned with a vengeance. That ghastly feeling of being *closed-in* he'd had that morning, in the grim little alley behind the pub. He could smell its fetid smell now, feel the sensation he'd had, standing there, between those sweating walls. A feeling of faintness, of choking, suffocating . . . One could have put it down to an excess of imagination, he supposed.

Then there were those awful few moments at the hospital. The terrible sense of *absence* he'd felt, standing beside the mortuary slab. A young life cut off before its time – and with such brutality. Not that he hadn't seen death before – it had been all too regular a part of his existence once. But at least those deaths had been for a cause – albeit what had come to seem a dubious one. This was worse, somehow, because of the calculation which had gone into bringing it about. You couldn't even call it a crime of passion – nor the death which had preceded it. If they told you nothing more, the playing cards told you that much. These were cold-blooded killings of innocent victims: the worst kind of murder, he thought.

Chapter Six

Edith's train was five minutes late. 'They were still clearing the line in Kent,' she said, reaching up to kiss him; there'd been another fall of snow in the night. 'We sat in a field outside Yalding for ages.'

'Not literally, I hope.' Rowlands took the suitcase from her, and linked his free arm through hers. He was surprised at how much of a difference it made to have her there. 'No. Although it couldn't have been much colder if we *had* been out of doors,' she replied. Around them, crowds of people were moving, with varying degrees of purposefulness: those who'd just disembarked from trains heading towards the Strand and the buses which would take them to the shops of Regent Street; those responding to announcements about outbound trains changing in a moment from stationary bodies, patiently studying train times, to briskly energetic beings. 'Excuse me! May I get past? Thanks awfully'.

The extraordinary volume of sound which filled the air around, echoing and re-echoing in that enormous vault, never failed to amaze him: the murmur of conversation overlaid by the shouts of porters and the shrieking of whistles – above all, by the tremendous noise made by the trains themselves as they let out great bursts of steam. What a very *loud* world we seem to have made, he thought. And the smells! Oil, smoke, soot and grease; the smell of people's clothes, and that of their luggage – leather suitcases, tin trunks, packing cases filled with straw – as well as their newspapers: cheap paper and the pungent smell of ink. 'How are the girls?' he asked as they made their way across the forecourt towards the exit.

'Oh, just the same,' replied his wife. 'It *has* only been a day since you saw them.'

'I know. It seems longer, somehow.'

'Joan was a bit clingy when I left,' Edith went on. 'Mother had to distract her with a biscuit.'

'That would do the trick, of course.'

'Anne seemed happy enough to see me go. But then she does adore her grandmother. I sometimes think,' she added in the bright tone she used when she was upset, 'that she'd rather have Mother than me.'

'I'm sure that's not true,' he said, thinking it probably was. Anne and her mother had never really got on.

'Margaret sent you her love,' Edith concluded, as if she had not heard his last remark. 'She promised to look after Granny and the little ones while I was away.'

Rowlands laughed. 'An old head on young shoulders, our Meg.' They'd reached the steps leading down into the Underground. 'I say – would you like a cup of tea? Something to eat?'

'That'd be lovely,' said Edith. 'You know, it's rather fun to be back here again,' she added as they emerged from the great arched entrance onto the wide, roaring thoroughfare that lay in front of it. 'Ages since I was out and about on my own – I mean, without the children.' Her words were drowned in the cacophony of growls, shrieks, coughs and groans emitted by the stream of motor buses, taxis, heavy goods vehicles and motorcars that thundered past, each adding its own peculiar note to the din. Some were so deep that they gave one an uncomfortable feeling in the viscera, others so shrill they made one's ears vibrate. After the complex smell of the railway terminus, came that of the street. This, too, combined the pleasant and unpleasant: the stink of burnt oil and petrol mingling with the aroma of frying onions, from the numerous cheap restaurants along the Strand, and with the sweeter smell of oranges and apples from the hawkers' barrows near the station's mouth.

'Is the ABC all right?' asked Rowlands as they waited their turn to cross at the traffic lights. 'We could go somewhere smarter if you like.'

'Where do you suggest? The Ritz?' Edith seemed in high spirits.

'I don't see why not. It isn't everyday I have my wife to myself.'

'Oh, the ABC will do very well for me,' she said. 'So how's the detecting going?' his wife went on when, having secured a table in that popular establishment, they faced one another over tea and cakes. From around them, came the subdued clatter of cake forks against plates, interspersed with the murmur of conversation.

'All right. Although I wouldn't call it *detecting*.'

'Wouldn't you?' Edith took an experimental mouthful of cake. 'Bit dry, this. Probably made with margarine. I should have thought,' she went on, in the same light, conversational tone, 'that that was exactly what you'd call it. You're trying to find things out, aren't you?'

'Yes. But I hardly think this is the place.'

'Fred, dear,' she said. 'There couldn't *be* a better place. At the table next to ours on the right, a mother and daughter are discussing the latter's wedding plans. They can't agree on the bouquet. Mother thinks roses would be suitable for June, but daughter is of the opinion that lilies-of-the-valley would be more artistic. On our left, an elderly lady is telling another elderly lady about her visit to her nephew's house in Scotland. The other lady has just been showing her photographs of a new grandson, so I imagine this to be a kind of revenge. Over by the window . . .'

'All right,' said Rowlands. 'You've convinced me.'

'Good,' said Edith sweetly. She reached across and patted his hand. 'After all, what possible interest could anybody have in what a dull old married couple like ourselves has to say?' Then she was silent, sipping her tea as he outlined, as succinctly as he could, the events of the past thirty-six hours, glossing over those – such as his visit to the mortuary – which seemed unfit for her ears, and touching briefly on what the Major had said to him the previous evening.

'Do you think there *is* something going on at the Lodge?' she said, when he had finished.

'Yes. That is . . . it's hard to say. There's an atmosphere, certainly.'

'But one, you think, that could be attributed to a cause other than that of murder?'

It seemed to Rowlands that this last word fell into one of those silences that occur for no particular reason in a crowded place. He was doubtless imagining (since he had no way of confirming) the sidelong glance from the mother and daughter at the next table, their attention distracted at last from the niceties of place settings, and the elderly spinster raising a shocked lorgnette at the mention of a subject more compelling than the beauties of Inverness-shire. 'If you've finished your tea, we ought to be going,' he said, raising a hand to signal to the Nippy to bring the bill.

* * *

After a brief visit to the hotel to drop off Edith's suitcase, during which his wife succeeded in impressing on an uncharacteristically subdued Mrs Philpotts the necessity of a thorough airing of the room before they returned to occupy it, they made their way across the park towards the Lodge. Rowlands had been all for getting a taxi, but Edith wouldn't hear of it. 'What! Spending all that money to go the long way round when we can be there in ten minutes if we take the short cut? I'm not *that* infirm yet, you know.'

'I never said you were,' he protested. 'It's cold, that's all.'

'I think I can stand a bit of cold,' she said. 'Besides, I've been looking forward to seeing the lights.' Because of course it was already dark, although it was not yet five. The lights she was presently looking at, although not a patch on the West End's, he supposed, seemed to satisfy this desire. She walked along happily, her arm tucked into the crook of his, commenting upon things that struck her fancy, just as she'd used to in the days of their courtship when – it occurred to him with a sudden access of sentimental feeling – they'd walked these very streets together, arm in arm as they were now. He'd been newly blinded then, and the world was one that had to be learnt afresh, with none of the familiar signposts to guide him. That's where Edith had come in, of course – her guidance as much to do with letting him discover things for himself as with keeping him out of scrapes, although she did that, too.

'Do you remember . . . ?' he started to say, as having crossed Marylebone Road by Marylebone Town Hall, they strolled slowly along in the direction of Madame Tussaud's.

'Yes,' she said, before he'd finished asking the question. 'I remember. It seems like only yesterday.'

The spring of 1918. He'd been blind for just over seven months – the first four of them lost to the painful process of recovery, and the still sharper pangs of despair. Edith had got him out of all that, as surely as if she'd reached out a hand and pulled him up out of a deep pit. It was she, in a very real sense, who'd taught him to 'see' the world again; had shown him that there was a world worth caring about. Now, as they entered the park they'd spent so many weeks exploring – from Rose Garden to boating lake, and from there to the chained up and silent zoo – he squeezed her hand. 'Are you sure you feel like going through with this?' he asked.

'Oh yes.' She returned the slight pressure. 'It'll be all right, you'll see. Why, this takes me back!' she cried, as a few moments later the Lodge came into view. 'The dear old place. Just as it was.' Because by now their footsteps were crunching on the gravel path that led to the front door, and the smell of leaves in the shrubbery – *laurels? Rhododendrons?* – now penetrated the icy air. They rang the bell. 'Quite as if we were visitors instead of old inmates,' said Edith – and were then admitted, his wife having to submit to

Ellen's exclamations of surprise and delight: 'Miss Edith! Can it really be you? Well, I must say, you don't look a day older,' before they could go a step further. The Major, as was his style, was more reticent, confining himself to a murmured, 'Well, well! Miss Edwards . . . Mrs Rowlands, I should say. How very nice to see you.' All of which Edith endured with a good grace, seeming, in fact, rather to enjoy the attention. Poor girl, she had little enough of it, Rowlands thought, recalling how very much his wife had always liked company.

'Now, we've time for a sherry before dinner,' the Major was saying as he ushered the Rowlands into his private sitting room. 'And then you must tell me all about life in Staplehurst.' When Rowlands protested that really, they'd only looked in for a minute, Major Fraser had squashed him at once. 'Nonsense! You've kept your wife to yourself all this time, Rowlands. You must allow me the pleasure of her company this once. Although,' he went on, addressing Edith this time, 'I'm afraid you'll find us very dull these days, Mrs Rowlands. We're not the cheerful crowd we used to be.'

'Well, *you* haven't changed a bit,' said Edith warmly. The conversation shifted to other things. Only when they were alone for a few minutes before dinner – the Major having gone ahead to organise Mrs B, as he put it – did she express her true opinion. 'Something's worrying him,' she said. 'You can see it in his face. He looks ten years older.'

'Well, he *is* ten years older,' Rowlands pointed out. 'We all are, if it comes to that.'

'That's not what I meant,' she said.

After dinner, the company repaired as usual to the Rec room. Card tables were set up as before; but for Rowlands the prospect held little enjoyment. 'Do you fancy a game?' he started to say to Edith but the Major would have none of it.

'Oh, but Miss Edwards . . . that is to say, Mrs Rowlands – I can't seem to get out of the habit of it, you know – *do* say you'll play the piano to us! You used to play very well in the old days, as I recall.' It was in vain that Edith protested that she was out of practice, that she'd forgotten all the tunes she knew, and that she was sure they'd all much rather not be distracted from their game by her caterwauling. 'Anyone who wants his game of cards is welcome to it,' said the Major firmly. 'Speaking for myself and, I imagine, for a good number of others, I'd prefer the rare treat of hearing some good music. I think you'll find the piano's in tune. We had Mr Briggs to see to it only last month, in time for the Christmas concert, you know.'

Edith's playing, although a little hesitant at first, gained in confidence as she went on and her fingers familiarised themselves with the keyboard. A short piece of Bach – 'the easy one that all the children learn' – was followed by a Chopin *Nocturne*. It seemed to Rowlands, struck by the sensitivity of her playing, that there were sides to his wife's character with which he was still unfamiliar. The warmth of the applause from the semicircle of men around the piano showed that others had been as moved as he was. 'Quite beautiful,' said the Major. 'And now, Miss Edw . . . Mrs Rowlands, perhaps you'll play us some of the old songs? You'll find the music somewhere in that pile on top of the piano.'

But Edith was already picking out the notes of a tune that was familiar to them all. A love song: one that spoke of heartache and the pain of loss. It could not but bring back memories of that time, so vivid still in mind when they had all been young, and life had been both terrible and beautiful. It was a song which would forever be associated with the war, although it wasn't one of the marching songs which had been designed to keep their spirits up. This was decidedly melancholy, and yet its sadness made it more bearable, somehow, than any amount of cheery uplifting stuff. As Edith began singing, the room fell silent: the clicking of chess pieces ceased; even the card players stopped bidding. It was as if for those few moments, time was suspended. They might all have been a dozen years younger, and back in uniform.

Roses are shining in Picardy,
In the hush of the silver dew,
Roses are flow'ring in Picardy
But there's never a rose like you!

And the roses will die with the summertime,
And our roads may be far apart,
But there's one rose that dies not in Picardy,
'Tis the rose that I keep in my heart . . .

As the last notes died away, the hush that had accompanied Edith's playing was prolonged for a moment longer. Then someone – it was Bingham – broke the silence. 'Thank you, Mrs Rowlands,' he said, his voice husky. 'I think I speak for all of us when I say that that's just about the loveliest thing I've ever heard.'

'Well,' said Rowlands as, later that night, they walked back across the frozen park. 'You certainly seem to to have made a conquest of Bingham.'

'Go along with you,' said Edith, not sounding entirely displeased at the remark, however. 'He's a married man.'

'It doesn't stop some men.'

'I wouldn't know about that,' his wife said demurely. 'Although,' she went on, with a note of mischief in her voice, 'he *is* rather nice-looking.'

'I'd better watch out,' said Rowlands.

'You had indeed.' She tucked her arm more securely into the crook of his. 'I hope she's got a good fire going in that room,' she said, meaning the proprietress of their hotel. 'I can hardly feel my fingers and toes.'

'Then we'd better get you back in the warm as soon as possible,' he said. 'So aren't you going to describe my rival to me?' he went on as both quickened their pace. 'Surely you owe me *that* much?'

'You first,' said Edith. This was their old game.

'Oh, all right. I'd say he was just under six foot – an inch shorter than me. Athletic, but not burly.' He'd become adept, over the years, at judging a man's height and build from his handshake; also from the height at which his voice emerged. A simple trick, really, but it often foxed people who weren't themselves blind, and hadn't had to make the mental efforts required at a first encounter.

'Good so far,' said Edith. 'Colouring?'

'Oh, as to that . . . sandy?'

'I'd say fair.'

'Fair, then. Blue eyes?'

'Green.'

'Oh well, you can't win 'em all,' said Rowlands cheerfully. 'A nice chap, Bingham – even if he does fancy my wife. What did you make of the others?' They'd reached the park gates, which were locked at this time of night. Rowlands presented his pass. 'Sorry to trouble you so late,' he said to the gatekeeper, who – with a great jangling of keys and wheezing of breath – was opening the wicket for them.

'Right you are, sir . . . Mum,' said the man; then: 'Why, thank you, sir,' as Rowlands slipped a coin into his hand.

'You were saying,' he said to Edith as they found themselves once more in the Marylebone Road. 'About the others . . .'

'I don't think I'd quite got around to saying,' she

replied. 'But if you want my opinion, there's something not quite right about the place. The Major knows it – he was looking quite drawn and grey. Still the same dear old duck, of course, but his heart's not in it. I thought Mr Mortimer was looking ill, too. He hardly said a word all evening.'

'Yes,' said Rowlands. 'Trouble with his lungs, I suppose.'

'He was gassed, wasn't he? Such a terrible thing. He used to be such a sporty type, too. Or am I confusing him with someone else?'

'No,' he said. 'That's Mortimer, all right. What did you make of Vance?' He tried to keep his voice neutral, but Edith knew him too well to be fooled by that.

'You don't think much of him, do you?' she said. 'Not quite officer material, is he?'

'I don't believe he was ever an officer.'

'Perhaps not. A slippery customer, is our Mr Vance, I'd say. That toothbrush moustache doesn't help. And I can't abide a man who uses so much brilliantine.'

'Build?' asked Rowlands, who realised that he'd yet to shake Vance's hand.

'Average, I'd say,' she replied. 'Five foot eight, or nine. Does it matter?'

'Only that the women – or at least one of them – were tall.'

'Oh. I see.' She thought about it. 'You mean the man would have had to have been taller – to get his hands in the right position to . . .'

'Yes,' said Rowlands as they reached the steps of the Belmont. 'That is what I mean. And there's another thing . . .' He told her what Vance had said about the murderer's supposed taste for blondes.

'That does seem suspicious,' said Edith. 'Although I suppose it's just possible that it might have been mentioned in one of the papers . . . that they were both fair, I mean.'

'Or it could just have been a lucky guess,' said Rowlands. Conversation was suspended as they entered the lobby, out of consideration for the other guests – of whom, it occurred to Rowlands, he had seen neither hide nor hair. Perhaps it being the off-season, he and Edith were the only ones. 'The stairs are this way,' he whispered, taking her by the hand. Now it was his turn to guide her; there would be no need to switch on the electric light. But a moment later, as if in answer to this thought, there came a click. A yellow glare flooded the room. A voice cried: 'So! You're back then, are you?'

There was a startled pause. It was Edith who spoke first – although, as she said afterwards to Rowlands, seeing Mrs P in her flannel wrapper and curl papers was enough to deprive anyone of the power of speech. 'Yes, thank you, Mrs Philpotts. We were just going up. I trust,' Edith added, 'that the room's been thoroughly aired?'

'Aired!' came the reply, delivered in a tone of heavy sarcasm. 'I don't know about aired. What I *do* know is that there's been a tellyphone call. From the police.'

'Ah, that'll be Chief Inspector Douglas,' said Rowlands, silently cursing the man. What did he mean by putting the wind up the old biddy? 'Did he leave a message?' he added smoothly.

'Did he leave a . . .' Mrs Philpotts seemed momentarily to have run out of breath.

'. . . message,' Rowlands finished for her. 'No? Never mind. I wonder,' he went on, in a speculative tone, 'whether it's too late to telephone Scotland Yard?'

That did it as far as Mrs Philpotts was concerned. 'I'll have you know,' she said, drawing herself up, Edith said later, 'with awful majesty' – 'that this is a *respectable* hotel.'

'Perhaps, after all, it is a bit late,' said Rowlands, cutting across this tirade. He had taken a step towards the stairs, drawing Edith with him when the telephone rang: shockingly loud in that confined space. Almost without thinking, Rowlands retraced his steps and picked up the receiver. 'Hello?'

'Ah, Rowlands – that you? Good,' said Chief Inspector Douglas. 'I've been trying to get hold of you all evening.'

'So I gathered.'

'Yes, I'm sorry about that. But I wanted to let you know . . . the fact is, there's been a development.'

'Not another . . . ?'

'No, not that. A piece of information, merely. If it means what I think it means it could change the course of the enquiry altogether.'

'I see,' said Rowlands, trying to make sense of this.

'But I mustn't keep you,' said the Chief Inspector. 'Won't make you very popular with the old dragon, will it?' He chuckled drily at his own joke. 'Why don't I send a car for you in the morning? Nine o'clock suit you?'

'Fine,' said Rowlands. 'But what about my wife?'

'Och, yes, she's there with you – I'd forgotten that,' said Douglas. 'Perhaps,' he added casually, 'she could go shopping. Buy herself a hat.' But Edith, when this was put to her a few minutes later in the privacy of their bedroom, was not amused. 'What! Having got me all the way up here to help with the investigation (this was overstating the case somewhat, but Rowlands knew better than to point this out), he wants me to go and look at *hats*? The man must be mad. What are we to say to the Major?'

'I'm sure we'll think of something.'

'The whole thing's preposterous,' said Edith, pausing midway through the lengthy process of brushing out and re-plaiting her hair: her nightly ritual. 'I must say, if this is the way the police go about conducting a murder enquiry, it's no wonder so many of them go unsolved.'

'I think you're being a little hard on the Chief Inspector,' said Rowlands mildly. 'We haven't yet heard what it is he has to say.'

Edith gave a sniff. 'All I can say is,' she said, 'is that it had better be good.'

* * *

True to the Chief Inspector's word, there was a car waiting outside the hotel at nine the next morning; what was surprising was that Douglas himself was not in it.

'The Chief said as I was to take you and the wife to St John's Lodge,' said the sergeant who had been delegated to drive them. 'Said he'd a mind to join you there later.'

'All this chopping and changing!' Edith muttered darkly as the car pulled out into the Marylebone Road. 'One would have thought a man in his position ought to be more decisive.' Rowlands gave a non-committal grunt. There were times when it was easier not to disagree with Edith. He let his thoughts drift as, moving slowly on account of the traffic, the car turned down Albany Street. At this rate, they'd have been quicker walking. He wondered what Douglas's piece of information would turn out to be, and why it had made such a difference to the investigation. Well, he'd know soon enough, he supposed, when Douglas turned up at the Lodge. He hoped the Chief Inspector wouldn't give away their connection. He felt bad enough about the double role he was playing – part confidante, part spy – without being revealed as such. 'Oh!' exclaimed Edith suddenly. He felt her lean forward abruptly as if something outside the car had caught her attention.

'What is it?' he asked.

'Nothing.' She sat back in her seat again. 'I just thought I saw someone who looked familiar. But I must have been mistaken. You know,' she said in a louder tone, to the police sergeant. 'You should have gone down past Park Square Gardens. This is the long way round.'

'Yes, Mum,' said the young policeman.

'Quite dreadful, the traffic in London these days,' remarked Edith to her husband. 'Every road jam-packed with vehicles – motor buses, lorries, trams. It quite ruins the look of the streets. You're lucky you can't see it.'

'I can hear it,' said Rowlands. 'Not to mention smelling it. I suppose that's one advantage the country has over the town: you can breathe without getting a lungful of petrol fumes.' They'd entered the Outer Circle by this time, and were about to turn down Chester Road, which led to the Inner Circle and the gates of the Lodge. It occurred to Rowlands that he should warn his wife not to let on that she knew the Chief Inspector. For the same reason, it wouldn't do to be seen arriving in a police vehicle. He tapped on the glass. 'You can let us out here,' he said to the sergeant. 'We can walk the rest of the way. You don't mind, do you?' he added, sotto voce, to Edith. 'Only I don't think it would be quite the thing for us to arrive in style.'

'No, I suppose not.' They got out of the car. 'There's still quite a lot of snow about,' she said. 'Lovely and white, too – not like the horrible slush you get in the busier streets. The girls were building a snowman when I left,' she added, sounding suddenly forlorn.

'Look, it's only for a few days,' he said.

'I know.'

Arm in arm, they began to walk across the lawn towards the Lodge, their feet softly crunching on the crystalline stuff with which it was covered. Mysterious, magical stuff, thought Rowlands, transforming the drab, dirty world to a thing of wonder. No wonder children loved it so.

'Do you think we might telephone,' said his wife, 'just to see how Mother's coping?'

'We'll do it the minute we get there,' he said, patting her hand in its slightly worn and inexpertly mended kidskin glove.

Chapter Seven

But, as it turned out, it was some time before that or any other call could be made. Because, just as they'd taken off their overcoats and hung them up, and were stamping their feet on the mat to rid their shoes of traces of snow, the Major came out into the hall. 'Ah, Rowlands . . . Mrs Rowlands . . . Is that you?'

'Present and correct, Major,' said Rowlands.

'Good, good. You'll find the office is set up, telephone and all. There should be a decent fire too. I asked Mrs B to see to it especially.'

'Thank you,' said Rowlands.

'I must say, I appreciate your taking the time to do this,' the Major went on. 'You especially, Mrs Rowlands.'

'Glad to be of help,' said Edith.

'Only before you get started on your telephoning, I wonder if you'd mind stepping into my office for a moment?' Major Fraser lowered his voice, although as far as Rowlands could tell there was no one else about. 'Something rather *untoward* has come up.' Half-prepared for what this 'something' might be, Rowlands was able to behave with equanimity when, having ushered them in and closed the door of the office behind them, the Major said: 'Mr and Mrs Rowlands, do let me introduce our visitor. This is Chief Inspector Douglas of Scotland Yard.'

'Chief Inspector.' Rowlands held out his hand, and felt it warmly grasped. 'Mr Rowlands,' said Douglas.

'Fred Rowlands is one of our former residents. A veteran of Passchendaele, you know. He and his good lady are helping to organise a reunion for the men.'

'That sounds like a very good idea,' said the policeman.

'I thought so, too, when Rowlands proposed it,' said the Major. 'Do sit down, Mrs Rowlands. There's a chair next to the fire. Rowlands, you take the one opposite. Warm you both up after your walk.' He cleared his throat; a nervous habit. 'Chief Inspector Douglas was just explaining that we – that is, we residents of the Lodge – might be able to help him with his enquiries . . . Is that the right phrase?'

'Quite right,' said the Chief Inspector.

'It's this dreadful murder case, you know,' the Major went on. 'That poor young woman in Camden Town. I suppose it's near enough – although we're hardly what you'd call on the doorstep,' he added mildly. 'As for the other gel, she was found in Shoreditch, wasn't she?'

'We have to eliminate all possible suspects,' said Douglas – rather woodenly, Rowlands thought.

'Suspects?' said the Major. 'I'm afraid I don't quite follow.' Douglas allowed a pause to elapse. Perhaps he was studying the other's face – looking for a guilty twitch, or a furtive expression. Well, he would look in vain, thought Rowlands. You wouldn't meet a straighter man than the Major.

'You'll have seen what it said in the papers about the playing cards left at the scene?' said Douglas, suddenly abandoning his stolid manner for an altogether more businesslike mien. 'That is, you'll have *heard* . . .'

'Yes, yes,' replied the Major, with the slight edge of impatience he sometimes betrayed at the clumsy literal-mindedness of the sighted.

'Well, it transpires that the playing cards in question were braille cards,' said the policeman.

'I see.'

'I suppose that does narrow the field,' put in Rowlands, judging that some response from him might be called for.

'Indeed it does, Mr Rowlands,' said Douglas. 'But then again, the field, as you put it – are you a racing man, by the by? – seems to have widened somewhat in the past twenty-four hours since we found the second body. We found *this* – cut out of the *Evening News* two days ago – amongst the effects of the girl in Shoreditch. Name of

Mary O'Reilly,' he added casually – Rowlands guessed for his benefit. 'Perhaps you'd be kind enough to read it aloud, Mrs Rowlands?'

Edith must have taken the clipping from him, for a moment later she cleared her throat and read: '*Artist's Model sought. No experience necessary. Tall, grey-eyed blonde preferred. Good terms. Apply Box 1042.*' Rowlands was silent, remembering that conversation in the hospital mortuary: '*What colour are her eyes?*' '*Greyish-blue. Though of course rather reddened now . . .*'

'So you think you might be looking for an artist?' said Major Fraser.

'Or someone pretending to be an artist,' said Douglas.

'That doesn't fit terribly well with the braille cards idea,' observed the Major in a speculative tone. 'If you see what I mean.'

'A blind artist,' said Edith, catching on at once. 'It does seem rather improbable.'

'Not if you've seen some of the pictures these chaps produce,' said the Major wryly. 'Frightful daubs, some of 'em, as I recall. Noses where ears should be and eyes all skew-whiff. You'd think the feller would've had to have been blind in order to paint 'em.'

'Be that as it may,' said the Chief Inspector, 'it does, as you say, beg the question. If our man's a painter, then why the braille cards? Unless it's all part of his game – to muddy the waters, that is.'

'I don't think it's that,' said Rowlands, from his seat next to the fire. 'I think it's all as plain as daylight. To him, that is. The playing cards mean something, all right – otherwise why would he have taken such care to leave them? As for the advertisement, surely that was just a way of attracting the attention of his victims? I imagine most women might like to think themselves worth being painted.'

'Not this one,' said Edith. The laughter this sally provoked brought about a necessary relaxation of tension.

'Oh, come now, Miss Edwards!' cried the Major gallantly. 'I'm sure you do yourself an injustice.' The Chief Inspector seemed to concur.

'Well, I'm not much of a one for paying compliments,' he began. 'But it seems to me . . .' He broke off. 'Did you say "Miss Edwards"?' he said to the Major.

'I'm afraid I did. Mrs Rowlands was one of our VADs, during the war. She was Miss Edwards then. I can't seem to break the habit of calling her by that name.'

'Yes, it makes our work doubly difficult – women changing their names,' said Douglas. 'The reason it took us so long to discover the identity of the Shoreditch victim was that she'd registered herself at her lodgings under her maiden name. Her married name was Lintott. Husband a farrier. A bit too fond of drink, according to the neighbours. Took off some time ago, leaving her in the lurch, so to speak. We haven't been able to trace *him*, either.'

'I can't help feeling,' said the Major, 'that a man like that – I mean with a definite relationship to the deceased – would be a far more likely suspect than one with no such connection.'

'Like I said,' the Chief Inspector replied – reverting to his wooden manner, Rowlands observed – 'we have to eliminate *all* possible suspects, not just the obvious ones. Ah, Sergeant . . .' This was to one of his subordinates, who had just come in. 'I take it you're ready for me?'

'Yes, sir,' said the young policeman smartly. 'Company assembled in the Recreation room, sir. Twenty-eight in all. Two absent. One in the sick bay, the other visiting his mother.'

'I can vouch for both,' said the Major.

'Good.' Douglas was suddenly all briskness. 'If you'll excuse me, Major . . . Rowlands . . . Mrs Rowlands. I'll just have a word. Need to establish each individual's movements on the days in question. Routine, you know.'

'I suggest you use the library as your HQ,' said the Major. 'It's usually empty at this time of day, except for Mortimer . . . Our librarian, you know. But I expect you'll need to talk to him, too.'

'Oh, we'll be talking to everyone,' said Chief Inspector Douglas. Then he was gone, closing the door behind him.

'Well,' said Edith when they were alone once more – having found their way to the office set aside for their use. 'This *does* put a different complexion on things.'

'Does it?' said her husband. 'I'm not sure that it does.'

'A blind artist? Oh, come on . . .'

'He might not always have been blind,' he said.

'No. I suppose not.' She was silent a moment. 'So you still think it might have been one of the people at the Lodge?'

'Shh.' His sharper hearing had detected a footstep in the corridor. A moment later, Doris Clavering put her head around the door.

'Settling in all right?' she said brightly. 'The Major said I was to see to it that you have everything you need.'

'Thank you, Miss Clavering,' said Rowlands; then: 'I don't believe you've met my wife.'

'Charmed, I'm sure. Well,' said the girl after a brief pause, 'I'll leave you to it. Funny,' she added, as if the thought had just occurred to her. 'We were only talking about it the other day – that girl's murder, I mean – and now we've got the police giving everyone the third degree.'

'Hardly,' said Rowlands, with a laugh. 'I'm sure it's just routine. The police,' he went on, conscious that he was parroting the Chief Inspector's line, have to eliminate all possible suspects.'

'So you think they *do* suspect someone at the Lodge?' said Miss Clavering. It was so much an echo of what Edith had said, that he guessed she had indeed been eavesdropping.

'I don't think anything of the sort,' he said, with a smile. 'And now, if you don't mind, I really would like to get on with these telephone calls.'

'Right you are,' she sang cheerily, and then, to Edith:

'*Ever* so nice to meet you.' Edith said nothing until the tip-tap of the secretary's heels along the corridor could no longer be heard. Then she said: 'Rather full of herself, that young woman. I wonder what the Major was thinking.'

'Mortimer said much the same thing,' said Rowlands, now seated at the desk. He reached for the telephone and drew it nearer to him. 'Let's get started, shall we?' Edith reminded him that they had not yet made the call to Staplehurst. 'And Mother'll be expecting it,' she said. 'As will the girls.'

'All right, all right,' he said good-humouredly. 'But don't let your mother keep you talking. We've a lot to do.' While he waited for Edith to make her call, he let his thoughts drift. It was strange being back at the Lodge; unsettling, too. As if by some slippage of time he'd been transported back ten years, to this place – at once so familiar and unfamiliar – where he'd once been young and newly cast into a darkened world. Now, as then, he had to find his way through the labyrinth. There were clues to follow, as there had been in that first and most perfect of Daedalus's creations. The question was, were they the right ones, or would they lead to his becoming ever more hopelessly lost?

He became aware that Edith was speaking. 'Mother sends her love.'

'That's nice. Everybody well?'

'Anne had a tummy-ache last night, but she's fine today,' said his wife briskly. 'So do we have a date for this event? The reunion, I mean.' He shrugged.

'I hadn't thought about it. Sometime after Easter?' She must have consulted the calendar, for she said, 'How about the first of June? It's a Saturday.'

'Saturday 1st June it is,' he said. 'Who's my first call to?'

'*Abel, J*. It's a suburban number. *B, Y, W . . .*'

'Bywood. That's the code for Purley and Kenley,' he said promptly. He dialled the numbers as she read them. He didn't have to ask her to repeat them even though she rattled them off quite fast. Seven years as a telephonist for a firm of City solicitors had left him with a good memory for figures. Abel, J. was out; it was his wife who answered. Yes, she thought John would like to come to a reunion on the first of June very much indeed. Would it be families as well? Rowlands said that was still to be decided. 'Families!' he said with a groan, replacing the receiver. 'I hadn't thought of that. I suppose the fact is that most of them – that is, most of *us* – have children.'

'We'll hold it outside in the grounds,' said Edith crisply. 'In a marquee if it rains. Next: *Adcock, R*. No, that one's "d" for deceased. *Andrews, P*. It's a London number, I think. *G, E, O . . .*'

'Georgian. That's Ealing,' said Rowlands. He dialled the number. After it had rung a few times, a man answered, sounding irritable.

'Yes?'

Rowlands explained about the planned reunion. This

time, the response was less than encouraging. 'A reunion? Why would I want to come to that?'

'Well,' said Rowlands. 'It would be a chance to see people.'

'"See" them? But that's just my point. I can't *see* anybody.'

'No more can I,' said Rowlands evenly. 'So you'd be in good company.'

'I don't think so, if it's all the same to you,' said P. Andrews in a withering tone. 'What! Trek all the way to Regent's Park to talk to a lot of men I haven't seen – as you put it – in more than ten years? No thanks!' And he put the phone down.

'Cheerful chap,' said Rowlands. 'If we get many more like him, we won't need that marquee, after all.'

But Archibald, M. and Armitage, K. proved more enthusiastic. 'I say – what a ripping idea!' exclaimed the former, while the latter offered to get in touch with his own group of St Dunstaners: 'We meet once a month, you know, at the Crown & Anchor,' said Keith Armitage eagerly. 'Guy Bishop, Ralph McArthur, Jimmy Gilby and myself. We were were part of the first intake in '15, you know. It'll be good to see the dear old place again.' It was the Lodge he meant. 'Quite like old times.'

'Yes,' said Rowlands, knowing those times were gone.

It was a long-distance call, and so it would be ten minutes or more before the various connections necessary to open a line between London and Cornwall could be made. He only hoped the old boy would be in. But after three or four rings, the receiver was lifted. 'Hello? St Ives four-nine-one,' said a voice. A woman's voice. Rowlands was momentarily taken aback. But then he remembered.

'Mrs Nicholls?' he said. 'It's Frederick Rowlands – I don't suppose you remember me?'

'Oh yes,' said Cecily Nicholls. 'You're John's friend. I'll just see if he's about. He was feeding the goats, last time I looked.' She must have laid the receiver on its side, for what Rowlands heard next was muted, but still audible: 'Jack! Telephone call for you.' A moment later, there came a voice Rowlands never heard without a lifting of the heart:

'I say, you old devil – is it really you?'

'You'd be in trouble if it wasn't,' he said drily.

'Oh, I knew from what Ciss said that it had to be you,' said Ashenhurst with a laugh. '"John's friend". There aren't so many of *those* left, I can tell you.'

'Pull the other one.' Even though it had been two years – more – since they'd last met, at the funeral of a fellow St Dunstaner, they fell at once into the old easy way of things. 'I can't believe there aren't some decent folk in St Ives.'

'Oh, we've made a few friends, Ciss and I. But it isn't the same as when you've both been through a bloody war together.' The lightness of Ashenhurst's tone might have led one to believe he was joking. Rowlands knew he was not. 'So,' Ashenhurst went on, 'to what do I owe the pleasure of this call? It must be something important if you're ringing all the way from London. Not another comrade called home, I hope? I'm getting rather fed up with funerals.'

'No, it's not that.' Suddenly, Rowlands knew he couldn't lie to Ashenhurst. 'The fact is, it's about a murder case.' Ashenhurst gave a soft whistle.

'Another one? You *do* get yourself into some scrapes, don't you, old man?' This was an allusion to something which had happened two years before. The West case. It had been in all the papers for a season. Of his own part in discovering the perpetrator of the crime, Rowlands had been obliged to be circumspect, even with his oldest friend. But he'd conveyed enough for Ashenhurst to get the idea that he'd been more than just a bystander. A great deal more, in fact . . .

'Yes,' he said. 'I suppose I do.' Briefly, because this call would be costing quite a bit, he outlined for Ashenhurst the facts of what the Press had so memorably dubbed the 'Playing Card Killings'.

Ashenhurst got it at once, of course. 'Well,' he said, when Rowlands had finished, 'I don't see that I can help you very much. The cost of train fares from Cornwall being what it is . . . to say nothing of the beastly weather we've been having . . . pretty much rules me out as a suspect, I'd say. Not that there aren't a number of women I'd like to seize by the throat . . . Ciss is clicking her tongue at me for that! But I imagine you and your Detective Chief Inspector will be concentrating your efforts in the London area, won't you?'

'Yes,' said Rowlands. 'It's just if you think of anything . . .'

'Oh, I'll be straight on the blower – you can count on me for that!'

'Thanks.' It occurred to Rowlands that he hadn't asked how things were going with the hotel. Business had fallen off quite a bit lately, Ashenhurst had intimated in his last letter. But before he could frame the question, his friend said:

'Well, it's been good to chat, old man, but this call must be costing you a fortune.'

'There is one other thing,' said Rowlands, remembering the ostensible purpose of his call. 'I don't suppose you'd be interested in coming to a reunion this summer?'

'Just try and keep me away,' said Ashenhurst.

'That was seven and a half minutes,' said Edith when he'd put the phone down.

'I know. I'll pay for it,' he said. 'No reason why St Dunstan's should bear the cost of a personal call.'

'It isn't that so much,' his wife said. 'Although I think we ought to pay for it – and the one to Mother, too. It's just that we've several hundred calls to make, and we're still only on the "A's". How *was* he, by the way?'

'The same dear old fellow. Always so cheery.'

'You know,' said Edith, 'when all this is over, you really ought to go and see him. Cornwall's not so far away – and the sea air will do you good. You've been looking a bit peaky, lately.' He got up and went over to where she was sitting, at the desk across from his. Surprised, she turned her face up to his as he bent to kiss her. 'What was that for?'

'Nothing,' he said, 'I just felt like it, that's all.'

At five, they packed up for the day, although Edith said she'd have been happy to carry on, 'Because we're still only a third of the way through the alphabet, and I'm not in the least bit tired.' So far they'd had eighty-six firm acceptances, twenty-one possibles, eight refusals and eleven not-at-homes. 'At this rate, we ought to manage it in three days quite comfortably.'

But Rowlands had other plans. 'I don't know about you, but I've had enough of telephones for one day. We'll go back to the hotel and get changed, and then head down to the West End for a bite of supper before the show.' It had been Bingham who'd put the idea into his head at dinner the night before last, with his talk about going to see *Plunder*. Rowlands didn't care for farce, but a good thriller was a different matter. It was a choice between *Blackmail* at the Globe, *Jealousy* at the Fortune and *The Last Hour* at the Comedy. *Blackmail* won.

'It's a good thing I thought to pack an evening dress,' said Edith as, an hour later, they sat in the taxi threading its way through the early evening traffic in Regent Street. They'd a table booked at Kettner's, which was only a step from Shaftesbury Avenue. 'I'd hate to have let the side down.'

'You couldn't do that if you tried,' he said. By mutual agreement, they'd set aside all talk of the murders and of their part in pursuing the suspects. If indeed that was what they were doing, Rowlands thought. He'd had cause to wonder, during the past few days, if the whole thing wasn't just an elaborate game that Douglas was playing. A blind artist with a penchant for games of chance. It was too fantastic – like something out of a melodrama.

They had seats in Row F of the stalls; he liked to be near enough to hear every word, and Edith always enjoyed seeing who was in the front five rows. Once she'd spotted Douglas Fairbanks, with a *very* smart lady – not Miss Pickford – on his arm; on another occasion, they'd been two rows behind the Prince of Wales. Of course, this wasn't a First Night, so they were unlikely to see any *stars*, but the play had had very good notices – the delectable Miss Bankhead no doubt being the reason for most of these. Waiting for the house lights to go down, Rowlands let the familiar – and to him eternally fascinating – sounds of the theatre wash over him. The buzz of conversation as the seats around them filled up: 'I saw her in *Conchita* – the one where she comes on carrying a monkey. *Too* killing . . .' The atmosphere of excited anticipation. From beside him, came the rustle of chocolate papers as his wife selected her favourites from the box he had bought her, and her whispered comments on their immediate neighbours. 'People seem to be wearing a lot of black this season. And diamanté. It looks quite elegant, I think.'

This didn't require a reply, and so he said nothing,

content to take in what was his to take in: the smells as well as the sounds. Cigar smoke wafting from the doorway to his right where someone was evidently enjoying a last-minute smoke in the corridor. Quite a decent Havana, Rowlands thought. *La Corona*, or *Flor de Fonseca*, perhaps. He didn't smoke the things, and so he'd never developed a nose. A whiff of brandy on the breath of the man to his left. A woman's perfume . . . My God, he thought, it *can't* be. 'What a beautiful gown that woman's wearing,' said Edith suddenly. 'Molyneux, I shouldn't wonder . . . Oh!'

'What is it?'

'Nothing. Isn't it time they started?' she said impatiently. 'It's half past.'

'I'm sure they will before long.' *That perfume. He'd have known it anywhere.*

'I do wish people would sit down instead of standing about talking.'

'I didn't realise you were so keen to see the play.'

'I'm not. It's just . . .' But then the bell rang, and the latecomers took their seats with a great rustling of skirts and murmuring of apologies, 'Frightfully sorry to disturb you, but may we get past?', and the play began.

Within minutes, Rowlands wondered if he'd made the right choice. Not that Edith wasn't broadminded about such things, but it was evident that the story that was unfolding in front of them was of a decidedly risqué kind. Or perhaps it was simply the presence of the leading lady which made it seem so. 'Sex Appeal', 'It' – whatever you called it, she had it in spades. From the very first moment that she walked on stage, the atmosphere in the theatre felt electric. It was something to do with her voice, he thought, although she doubtless had other qualities not apparent to him. Its husky, smoky timbre was that of a woman who had crammed a lot of living into a few short years, if one believed what the papers said about her.

He concentrated his attention on the unfolding drama. Even without being able to see what was happening, he could get most of what was going on, although long pauses of the significant kind were often hard to interpret. Fortunately this play didn't have too many of those. In the first scene, a young woman, played by Miss Bankhead, quarrelled with her lover, a Scotland Yard detective (was there no escaping from Scotland Yard? Rowlands wondered). By scene two, she – Miss Bankhead – had taken up with another man, an artist of dubious reputation, and had agreed to accompany him to his studio. By scene three, what had started as mild flirtation on the girl's part – a chance to make her boyfriend jealous – had deteriorated into something uglier. 'You knew what you were coming to when you came in here tonight,' sneered the artist as he locked the door, while the girl's reply, shrill with panic – 'What do you mean? Give me that key!' – conveyed that things were rapidly getting out of control.

Rowlands was conscious of Edith sitting, stiff with disapproval, beside him. Perhaps, after all, it had been the wrong choice. A struggle ensued, with the girl (he presumed) getting the worst of it. There was the sound of a dress being ripped. A cry from the girl – 'Let me go!' Further sounds of a struggle. Sounds of a woman choking . . . 'I don't think I can bear this,' murmured Edith in his ear. 'He's got his hands around her throat . . . Oh!'

Her exclamation was drowned in a collective gasp from the rest of the audience. 'What's happened?' he whispered.

'She's killed him,' his wife whispered back. 'Stabbed him with the bread knife. Right through the heart.'

Chapter Eight

'I must say,' said a voice. 'I thought Cyril was awfully good – didn't you?' The question wasn't addressed to him, and yet at the sound of that voice he felt himself blush to the roots of his hair. He prayed that Edith wouldn't notice – or, if she did, that she'd remain unaware of the reason for his confusion. Of course that was impossible. She'd known (he realised now) before the curtain went up. The woman in the Molyneux gown wasn't just any woman. The perfume she was wearing, of which he'd caught such a tantalising whiff, should have told him that much. 'Hel-lo!' It was the voice again, this time, closer to. 'Well, isn't this too marvellous for words?'

He stumbled to his feet, forcing a smile. 'Lady Celia.'

'I *thought* I saw you, just before the lights went down,' she said. 'But I wasn't sure till now. How very nice to see you. And Mrs Rowlands, too.'

'Yes,' he said. 'We were just . . .'

'*Lovely* to see you again, Mrs Rowlands. Are you enjoying the play?'

'I . . .'

'Frightfully exciting, isn't it?' Celia West went on. 'Natalia almost shrieked aloud in the murder scene, didn't you, darling? Oh, forgive me. I haven't introduced you. This is a friend of mine. The Countess Rostropovna.'

'How do you do?' said a queenly voice, with an unmistakably foreign accent. 'Celia, we really should be going. We said we'd meet Dickie in the Champagne Bar.'

'Oh, let him wait. Unless . . . I don't suppose you and your wife would care to join us, Mr Rowlands? We've time for a glass of champagne before Act II. A friend of ours is in it, you know. He's the detective. *Do* say you'll come! I want to know whether you think she'll get away with it – the murderess, I mean.'

The bar, like others to be found in theatres of its era, was circular, and built around a central atrium, up which the noise of a great many people talking at once rose, as if through a funnel. Here, they found Dickie – otherwise known as the Honourable Richard Fairfax – with a friend, introduced as Bunny, whose real name Rowlands never did find out. If Dickie seemed a little nonplussed to discover that their party was to be augmented by two more, he soon rose to the occasion: 'Waiter! Another bottle of the Perrier-Jouët,' he cried, ignoring Rowlands' protests that he and Edith hadn't meant to barge in, and that in any case, with a mere fifteen minutes to go before the start of the second act, there'd hardly be time for them to drink a whole bottle. 'Nonsense! There's oodles of time,' said the redoubtable Dickie. He was seconded by his friend:

'Always time for a glass, you know.' This was said in confidential tones to Rowlands' neighbour on his right, the Countess Rostropovna, who emitted a tinkling laugh.

'But of course! You can never have too much champagne. Or so my dear father believed. "*Cherie*," he used to say, "For a woman to drink anything else is vulgar. But with champagne, one need never be vulgar." Dear Papa! I have always remembered his words,' she added, heaving a deep sigh. From her accent, Rowlands supposed she must be Russian: one of that nomadic tribe of the dispossessed which had pitched its tents in all the capitals of Europe since the Revolution, and whose members, to a man – or a woman – were always found to have 'lost everything' in that imbroglio.

His interest in the lady was no more than cursory, however. With Celia West sitting across the table from him – Dickie having commandeered another four of the flimsy little gilt chairs with which the bar was furnished – and with Edith on his other side, it was as much as he could do to keep a sense of equilibrium. But then she'd always had that effect on him – Lady Celia. From the moment, two years before, when he'd first heard her voice, she'd ensnared him, body and soul. It was no good pretending that it wasn't so; all he could hope for was to conceal the extent of his feelings for Celia West from his wife. Although that, he guessed, was something of a lost cause. Edith knew perfectly well how things stood. After all the lies he'd told on Lady Celia's behalf two years ago his wife was hardly likely to believe him now when he said the other woman meant nothing to him.

She was saying something at that moment, in her beautiful voice, whose tones, between warm and cool, he'd tried to describe to himself on so many occasions. 'Honeyed' was the best he'd come up with, although that didn't convey the slight catch in the voice, like a crack in a crystal bowl, which made the sound so beguiling. 'So tell me *everything*. I want to hear *all* about it.' This was directed at him – the note of intimacy was one she had used with him before. It was quite different from the brittle raillery with which she addressed her friends. 'All that you've been up to since we last met.'

'There isn't a lot to tell.' He was damned if he was going to discuss his recent troubles with the chicken farm, in front of these supercilious *society* types. He could just imagine the remarks, afterwards: 'What extraordinary people Celia knows! Quite sons-of-the-soil, don't you know?' She seemed to pick up something of his reluctance to be more explicit, because her next remark was of a vaguer sort. 'I do so envy you, living in the country,' she said. 'Delightful, isn't it?'

'In the summer, perhaps,' said Rowlands. He sipped his champagne. The dry, faintly acidic taste of it on his tongue, combined with the heady effect it was having on his brain, was inseparable from the way she made him feel: exhilarated, and a little off-kilter.

'Oh yes,' agreed Celia West. 'In the summer, it must be too divine. And the children,' she went on, directing this enquiry towards Edith, Rowlands supposed, from the slight alteration of her tone. 'How are the children? Such ducks, I thought them.'

'They're very well,' replied Edith calmly. It was evident to Rowlands that his wife was determined not to be dazzled by Lady Celia or her friends. 'Getting quite big now, of course.'

'Of course,' said Celia West, with a sigh, in which – to Rowlands, at least – a great deal was conveyed. Her own childlessness. The disastrous marriage – brutally cut short by murder – and its consequences, which had fatally undermined her future security. He wondered what her life was now, in the aftermath of that catastrophe. If present company was anything to go by, it hadn't changed for the better.

'Drink up,' said Dickie Fairfax as the first bell interrupted these reflections. Around them, people started moving towards the doors. 'We've time for another.'

'I couldn't possibly,' said Edith. 'Or I'll never be able to follow the rest of the play.'

'I shouldn't worry about *that*,' said their host cheerfully. 'Play's a lot of rot, anyway. *She's* a corker, though, isn't she? You can see why a man would be prepared to risk his neck for *her*.'

As the actors made their bows, and the leading lady took her curtain calls, Rowlands sensed a restiveness on his wife's part. 'We really ought to go,' she murmured, 'if we're to get to the Underground in time.' There was plenty of time before the last train and they both knew it; what was really bothering her, he guessed, was that she might again be forced to endure another meeting with Celia West.

'All right,' he said, getting to his feet – but just then the woman who had been uppermost in both their thoughts, he supposed, swept past them along the aisle.

'Oh, Mr Rowlands,' she called back over her shoulder. 'We're going for a bite of supper at the Café de Paris. Do join us if you like.'

'Thanks, but we've already dined,' he said, ushering Edith ahead of him towards the exit.

'Just as you like,' Lady Celia said carelessly. They were separated at this point by the press of people coming out into the aisle from the seats on either side, so it wasn't until they were descending the stairs, a few steps behind Celia West and her companion, that she turned towards him once more. 'I'm having a party next Saturday,' she said. 'I do hope you'll both be able to come?'

'Well . . .' They'd reached the foyer by this time

where the crowd was at its most dense, with those queuing for coats pushing in one direction, and those who'd already retrieved them moving as determinedly in the other, and so he was prevented from replying at once – which was perhaps just as well, he thought. In the queue in front of him was the jovial Bunny, who had evidently been given the task of collecting the ladies' cloaks. He hailed them loudly.

'Jolly good play, I thought,' he said. 'Though I did think the little woman got off rather lightly, what? After all, she *did* stick a knife in the chap.'

Rowlands, just then occupied with handing his cloakroom ticket to the attendant, made a vague sound signifying agreement. In truth, distracted as he was by the sudden reappearance in his life of the woman about whom he'd almost made a fool of himself, he'd barely followed the rest of the play. There'd been something about a pair of gloves that had been lost. The blackmailer had got hold of one of these, of course. Then it had been up to the murderess's boyfriend, the Scotland Yard detective (so admirably played by Lady Celia's friend) to rescue his beloved from the gallows. Quite how he'd done it wasn't clear to Rowlands, but the whole thing had ended satisfactorily enough, with the blackmailer being framed for the killing (surely a rather unorthodox procedure on the part of a Scotland Yard detective?) and conveniently bumped off before the truth could be revealed. He helped his wife into her coat, then put on his own. During the past two days, there'd been no more snow, but the air was still bitterly cold. Ahead of them, Lady Celia and her entourage began to descend the short flight of steps that led from the theatre's double doors into the street. He could hear her, still talking about the play, and laughing at its absurdities: '. . . too preposterous when he pulled out the gun.'

It was then that it happened. Without warning, a flash of white-hot light erupted in their faces. Annihilating. Blinding. 'What the . . . ?' He almost lost his balance and fell headlong. Only Edith's catching hold of his arm just in time prevented this ignominy. The flash was accompanied by a devil's chorus of voices: 'Lady Celia! Over here, Lady Celia!'

'Oh, how *tiresome*,' he heard her say.

His heart was still hammering from the shock of the flash going off in his face. It was all too reminiscent of another occasion – only then the blindness brought about by the sudden explosion of light hadn't been temporary, as it would be on this occasion, for those who'd been caught in its glare. He found he was trembling. 'It's all right,' Edith told him. 'Just a flashbulb.' Around them, the hubbub was still going on:

'Lady Celia! A minute of your time, if you would . . .' There seemed no end to it. Fortunately, at that moment, Dickie Fairfax took charge:

'Taxi!' he cried, stepping forward. 'I say – taxi!'

'Really, Celia,' said Natalia Rostropovna, sounding far from amused. 'I wish you had warned me that there would be photographers. I hate all this kind of thing, as you know.'

'I don't much love it myself,' was the reply. 'Oh, *do* hurry up with that taxi, Dickie!'

'Lady Celia!' One of the reporters had, it seemed, broken through. 'Is it true that Lord Edgecombe has popped the question? Will it be a spring wedding?'

'I wish you'd leave me alone,' she said.

'But our readers want to know.'

'Lady Celia has already asked you to leave her alone,' said Rowlands, with quiet fury. 'I suggest you do so.'

'And just who do you think you are?' jeered the journalist. 'Sir-bloody-Galahad?' Rowlands was saved from having to reply – and perhaps from a more physical response to the taunt – by the arrival of the taxicab.

'At last,' said Celia West. 'Get in, Natalia.' She touched Rowlands' sleeve. 'Can we drop you somewhere?'

'No, that's quite all right.'

'Well, if you're sure . . .' She got into the cab. 'You will come to my party, won't you?' she called from inside it. 'Eight o'clock. Cadogan Square.'

'That's kind of you, but . . .'

'I'll expect you,' she said.

Edith waited until the cab had pulled away from the kerb before she spoke. Around them, the crowd of theatregoers and passers-by who'd stopped to see what the fuss was all about was starting to disperse. 'I was thinking of going home on Tuesday,' she said. 'Wednesday at the latest. I can't really ask Mother to cope with the girls on her own for much longer.'

'No, of course not.'

'*You* ought to go to the party, though,' she went on brightly. 'Since she seemed so very keen for you to be there.' They both knew it was not her mother to whom she was referring.

'Oh, I don't suppose she meant it for a moment,' he said.

Sunday was a quiet day. They got up at what was, for them, an unusually late hour, bathed, breakfasted – Mrs Philpotts having excelled herself by producing a lavish repast of eggs and bacon, grilled tomatoes, mushrooms and devilled kidneys – and then turned to the papers. The Belmont took the *Sunday People* and the *News of the World*, and so Rowlands, sitting over his second cup of coffee, had the pleasure of listening to his wife read selected passages aloud. This had been their habit since they'd first started walking out together: she'd skim through the paper first, to get the gist of the news, then give him the salient points before going on to read out particular items that struck her fancy. She began with the *People* – which wasn't his favourite paper, being too much given to stories about the smart set and other nonsense, in his opinion, but beggars couldn't be choosers and it *was* a Sunday. After the grim events of the past few days, it was a relief to find that the rest of the world was preoccupied with matters no more unsettling than the Queen's gift of a set of blue-enamelled teaspoons and tea-knives to Miss Barbara Grosvenor, on the occasion of her wedding to Lieutenant Viscount Dromwich RA, at St Martin-in-the-Fields, and the safe arrival in Paris of Lady Bailey, in her De Havilland Moth, piloted all the way from Cape Town. Ever since Miss Johnson had shown the way – and that American woman before her – you couldn't open a newspaper without reading about one of these stunts. Crazy, it seemed to him, to be risking one's neck just for the hell of it. He remembered the Flying Corps boys, during the war, swaggering around in their leather jackets as if what they were doing was the most fun in the world instead of being what it was – a deadly business. Most of them lasted about three weeks. He'd a vivid memory of watching one of these dogfights in the cloudless summer skies over Ballieul, from the relative safety of his gun emplacement. A Fokker Eindecker versus a BE2. These last were deathtraps, he'd been told, which stood no chance against the superior German model. He remembered the way the flimsy-looking craft had banked and turned, in intricate figures of eight, leaving white smoke trails that seemed, at that distance, like chalk lines scrawled across the blue. He and, he supposed, all the others watching this deadly aerial ballet, had held their breaths, as if the very act of doing so could keep *their* champion airborne.

Even though there'd been those amongst his company who'd envied the RFC crews for being, quite literally, above it all – the stink and the mud and the clamour of shellfire – he hadn't been one of them. In a world of terrible deaths, it was one of the most terrible, he knew – to fall from the sky in a cloud of burning gas. Like Icarus, he thought – another beautiful, foolhardy youth in search of glory. Now, it seemed, the women were following suit. '"*And so*"' Edith read, '"*an hour after landing at Villecoublay, the dauntless aviatrix, still in her flying coat and boots, was getting out of a taxicab at the Ritz Hotel in Paris . . .*" I must say,' his wife went on, 'I call that remarkable, don't you?'

'Certainly,' he said. 'Just promise me you won't be asking for flying lessons next week.'

'As if I would!' There was an edge of impatience in her voice. 'Seriously, Fred, you have to admire what she's done. To fly all the way from Africa, single-handed. For a woman, too.'

'I've agreed it's a wonderful achievement. But is there any other news?'

'Oh, you!' She flicked through the next few pages. 'I suppose you'll be wanting the sport?'

'If you wouldn't mind,' he said meekly. 'Just the Test Match report will do.'

Edith gave a gusty sigh. 'Cricket. Always cricket. All right, here we are: "*Melbourne. Saturday evening. England was in a strong position at close of play, after superb batting from Hobbs and Sutcliffe . . .*"'

'Thank you,' he said, when she'd got to the end. 'Now read me something that interests *you*.'

'You might regret those words,' said Edith. 'All right, then. "*In its eagerly awaited January Sale, Dickens &*

*Jones is offering elegantly styled musquash coats, reduced to 29 guineas, knitted jumper-suits in a range of attractive and serviceable colours for 18*s. 9d., *and dainty sealskin shoes at 29*s. 6d. *the pair . . .*"'

'All right, all right. What does the *News of the World* have to say?' It must have been underneath the *People*, for she folded this up before unfolding the other. Almost at once she gave a gasp. 'What is it?' Rowlands said. 'Don't tell me you've seen something you fancy in the Harrods sale?'

'It's *us*,' she said, cutting across him. 'We're on the front page. With *her*.'

'Who?'

'Lady Celia. And that friend of hers, that Countess. There's a photograph. Large as life.'

'I say! Do you mean to say we're headline news? How exciting!'

'You could call it that,' said Edith.

'Well, aren't you going to read me what it says?' he asked. 'You forget I won't be able to appreciate the full effect of this unprecedented eventuality unless you do.'

'There isn't much,' she said flatly. 'Just a caption to the photograph: "*Lady Celia West, enjoying an evening out at the Globe Theatre last night. She was accompanied by the Countess Rostropovna, who is presently staying with Her Ladyship in Cadogan Square.*" That's all.'

'You mean they haven't printed *our* names?' he said. 'That was very remiss of them.'

'You can joke about it, Fred, but it's really rather

embarrassing,' said Edith, casting the *News* aside. 'Having one's face plastered all over the papers like this. What Mother will say I can't imagine.' Rowlands could imagine it quite well – his mother-in-law's horror of vulgarity of any kind being all too familiar to him. But he kept this thought to himself.

'Is it a good photograph? Of us, I mean.'

'Not particularly.' Edith gave a disgruntled sniff. 'I'm standing behind you, so you can only see part of my face and a little bit of my dress. *Your* face is completely visible, however – just behind Lady Celia. You look stunned. As if you've been shot.'

'That's rather how I felt,' he said drily.

'And that Countess Whatyoumaycallit – if she *is* a countess, which I rather doubt. There are so many of them, these days, that one does begin to wonder. Anyway, she's looking even more terrified than you are. As if someone were about to pull out a gun and shoot her.'

'Maybe she had a narrow escape during the Revolution,' Rowlands said. 'I say, do you suppose there's any more coffee?'

'I'll ring,' said Edith. 'At 7*s.* 6*d.* a night, I think they might run to a fresh pot.'

Then for the next few days, everything went quiet. They got on quite fast with the telephoning – the two of them forming rather an efficient team, Rowlands said to Edith, combining as they did her quickness at reading out names and telephone numbers from a sometimes hard to decipher list, with the manual dexterity he'd acquired from seven years of working at a switchboard. By Tuesday afternoon, they'd almost finished; there were just the 'Ws' and 'Ys' to do. 'It looks as if it'll be a fair turnout, after all,' he said, setting the heavy receiver back into its cradle, at the end of a string of calls. 'If even half the people who've expressed an interest turn up, we should have well over three hundred.'

'And that's not counting the families,' Edith reminded him. 'I do think it would be nice to include the families,' she said. 'The girls would so enjoy a treat.'

'We'll have to see what the Major says,' replied Rowlands, knowing that Major Fraser, soft-hearted where women and children were concerned, would almost certainly allow himself to be persuaded. With the last of the calls made, and the list of prospective guests typed up by the obliging Miss Clavering, he and Edith could call it a day. They'd travel back together by the early train, first thing on Wednesday morning. But, as with so much in life (he was later to reflect), it didn't turn out like that. Wednesday morning duly arrived, and they'd breakfasted, then packed their bags. This hadn't taken long, since neither Rowlands nor his wife had brought more than a bare minimum of clothes with them. Edith, with dresses to see to, had taken somewhat longer than the five minutes Rowlands had needed. And so it was that, as he stood settling their bill at the front desk, he was the one to take the call. With the proprietress sitting there, her breathing more stertorous than ever as she calculated the extent of what she was owed in shillings and pence, Rowlands ought by rights to have let her answer it. But as the phone began to ring, he didn't think twice before picking up the receiver. 'Hello?' he said. And then when the other had spoken: 'Yes, it's me. What can I do for you, Chief Inspector?'

Douglas didn't waste time on preliminaries. 'We're getting closer,' he said. 'Told you we'd flush him out eventually, didn't I?'

'Why – what's happened?' asked Rowlands, feeling, in spite of himself, his pulse begin to quicken. 'There hasn't been another one?'

'Not that,' replied the Chief Inspector. 'But he's shown his hand, all right.' Rowlands said nothing, and after a moment, Douglas went on, 'It's those damned playing cards. He's only gone and sent one through the post to a young woman in Cadogan Square.'

Chapter Nine

'Well,' said Celia West. I must say this *is* a surprise. I'd hoped I might be seeing you soon, of course, but I hadn't realised it would be *quite* so soon.'

'No,' said Rowlands. 'I suppose it is rather unexpected.' His choice of words appeared to give her pause.

'Yes,' she said after a moment. 'It's certainly that. But do sit down, won't you? It feels so odd, with you both *looming* over me like this.'

'Thank you,' said Rowlands. But before he could find his way to a chair, the Chief Inspector replied for them both.

'I'm afraid this isn't a social call. We're here on police business. At least,' he corrected himself, '*I* am. Mr

Rowlands is merely assisting me with my enquiries.'

'Then perhaps,' Lady Celia said brightly, '*he* could sit down?'

'I'll stand if you don't mind,' said Rowlands quickly. A brief, uncomfortable pause ensued. He took advantage of the moment to take stock of his surroundings: something at which he'd become adept, over the years. The room in which he and Douglas were now standing was a large one, he deduced, from the way their voices got lost in the space around and above them. The floor was some highly polished surface – parquet, he rather thought – with a carpet of peculiar thickness and softness in the centre of it. There was a fire burning in the fireplace – which was marble, he guessed; its warmth could be felt several paces away. A clock ticked quietly on the mantelpiece. On the far side of the room were two tall windows, from which a cold, bright illumination fell. Here, on a sofa surrounded by an archipelago of little chairs – over which one had to take care not to trip – Lady Celia had disposed herself, 'like the Queen of Sheba', Douglas said afterwards, disapproval all too evident in his voice.

'I suppose,' said the object of Rowlands' thoughts after a moment, 'you'll be wanting to talk to Natalia?'

'If that's the Countess Rostro . . .' The Chief Inspector must have consulted his notes. 'Rostropopova,' he managed eventually.

'Rostropovna.'

'Yes, well, whatever she calls herself,' said Douglas. 'I do indeed want to talk to her. As soon as possible if that doesn't *inconvenience* you too much.' It was said with heavy irony. Celia West chose to take the words at face value, however.

'Oh, it's no trouble at all. I'll ring, shall I, and ask if she's ready to see you?' While the Chief Inspector was digesting this remark, she must have touched a bell, because a moment later the maid appeared in the doorway. 'See if the Countess is dressed yet, will you?' said Lady Celia carelessly. 'Tell her there are two gentlemen waiting to interview her – is that the right word?' she added sweetly. The Chief Inspector gave an embarrassed cough.

'Quite right,' he said.

'Not that I've ever had the experience,' she went on when the door had closed behind the servant. 'Of being interviewed by the police, I mean. For which I'm heartily grateful,' she added, as if to herself. Another awkward silence fell. It struck Rowlands that she knew exactly what she was doing. It was a game she had played before – a kind of teasing, in which it was always a man who was the victim of the tease. A dangerous game, which had once almost led to her ending up on the gallows. Of the two men now in front of her, one had done his best to put her there, the other had tried his utmost to save her. It wasn't a state of affairs she seemed in any hurry to forget.

The door opened; the maid reappeared. 'Countess says as she'll be with you directly,' she said.

'Thank you, Truscott,' said her mistress. 'And bring some tea. I for one could do with a cup,' Lady Celia went on, still in the same abstracted tone as if she were talking to herself. A few more minutes ticked away. 'I suppose it would be out of the question to ask what your role in all this is, Mr Rowlands?' she said at last. 'I mean – assisting the police. You seem to be making rather a habit of it, if you don't mind my saying so.'

'Of course not.' He hesitated. 'The fact is . . .' Again, Douglas took it upon himself to intervene.

'The fact is that it's confidential business. A murder enquiry,' he added, with rather more emphasis than seemed warranted. 'But I suppose there's no harm in telling you. It's to do with these playing cards.'

'I rather thought it might be,' she replied.

'Yes, well, if you've guessed that, then you know why we're here – and why Mr Rowlands has been so invaluable. It's something we've kept out of the papers, you see, but it may provide the key to the whole puzzle. Because there's something about these particular cards that's special, as I imagine we'll find when we come to examine the one your friend has received . . . where *is* your friend, by the way? She seems to be taking rather a time getting ready.'

'She'll be having her bath, I expect,' said Celia West calmly. 'Do go on about the playing cards. It all sounds fascinating.'

But the Chief Inspector seemed suddenly to remember to whom he was talking. 'I'd like you to answer a few questions first, if you'd be so kind,' he said stiffly. 'How long has this Countess of yours been staying with you?

I take it she *is* staying here, and that this isn't her permanent address?'

'Oh no, she's only been here a week or so,' said Lady Celia vaguely. 'Perhaps three weeks. Yes, that's right. She came to me just before Christmas. She hadn't anywhere else to go, poor thing. All her family are dead, you know. Killed in the Revolution. She doesn't have a permanent address, as you call it. Although, now I come to think of it, there does seem to be some dreadful old aunt, or cousin, or something, in Paris. Always threatening to cut her off without a shilling if she doesn't do as she's told . . .' The door opened. 'But here she is,' said Lady Celia. 'You can ask her yourself.'

It wasn't the Countess Rostropovna, however, but only the servant with the tea tray. 'Put it down over there,' said Her Ladyship. 'I'll pour it myself. And then tell the Countess she needn't hurry herself unduly, but that we'd all be terribly glad if she could appear before too long. She's too poor to afford a maid of her own, you know,' she added when the girl had gone. 'So I let her borrow mine. She's quite helpless without someone to look after her. Brought up in palaces and so on before the Bolsheviks took over.' The Chief Inspector made a sound indicative of mingled incredulity and disgust at this further evidence of the decadence of the ruling classes.

'You seem to have been a good friend to the Countess,' said Rowlands, to avert what he sensed might be an explosion to that effect from his colleague. 'Given that she has, as you say, nowhere else to go.'

Intent on pouring tea, Lady Celia did not reply for a moment. 'Oh, as to that . . .' she started to say, when the door opened.

A breath of some exotic perfume – tuberose, jasmine – wafted towards them. Then a voice said, with the slightly theatrical overemphasis Rowlands recalled from his first encounter with the lady a few nights before. 'I have kept you waiting. For this I am sorry. But you see, I have had many things on my mind.'

The brief pause which followed this somewhat overdramatic entrance was broken by Lady Celia: 'Will you have a cup of tea, Natalia?'

'Thank you. I will.'

'You prefer it black, don't you?'

'With lemon. Yes.' The Countess gave a little laugh in which there was the tiniest element of self-deprecation. 'The Russian way.'

'Countess Rostropovna,' said Douglas, evidently making a supreme effort to control his temper, 'you received, did you not, a communication in this morning's post?' Another pause ensued while the Countess sipped her tea, then set down her cup in its saucer.

'Yes,' she said in a low voice. It occurred to Rowlands, for the first time, that she was very frightened.

'May I see it?' said the Chief Inspector, in a tone of infinite patience.

'It is in my room,' was the reply. 'On my dressing

table.' She made a move to get up. 'I will get it.'

'Truscott can go,' intervened Lady Celia, and the maid having appeared almost on the instant – perhaps, Rowlands thought, she had been listening at the door – she commanded: 'Bring the letter from the Countess's dressing table, will you?'

'I'd rather my sergeant fetched it *if* you don't mind,' said Douglas. 'I don't suppose,' he added with a resigned air, 'that it'll make any difference at this stage, but you never know, do you?' He went to the door and spoke in a rapid undertone to the man that stood outside it. 'And mind,' he was heard to say in conclusion, 'you take care how you handle it.'

'I suppose you must be thinking of fingerprints,' said Lady Celia brightly.

'I was. Although I doubt there'll be much that'll be of much use to to us.'

'Well, for what it's worth, I should think there'll be at least three sets,' Lady Celia replied. 'The butler's, although he'd have been wearing gloves, of course, and the maid's – that's my maid, Agnes, not the parlourmaid – and Natalia's. And mine. I think,' she added in a thoughtful tone, 'we were fairly careful about handling the thing, once we realised what it was, weren't we, Natalia dear?' Before she could reply (or perhaps, Rowlands thought, the Countess had merely nodded her head), the door opened to admit the Detective Sergeant.

'Sir,' he said, handing what Rowlands supposed to

be the envelope containing the playing card to his superior officer.

'That'll do, Withers. You can wait outside,' said Douglas. 'Ordinary sort of envelope,' he remarked, considering it. Nothing special about it. Posted yesterday at 5.30 p.m., in Westminster. Name and address typed. We might be able to do something with that . . . Here's the card. Ah! There's a letter with it.'

'Yes.' The Countess seemed to hesitate. 'It was that which made me realise that it was not . . . how do you say? *Une blague*.'

'A joke,' supplied Lady Celia.

'Oh, it's no joke,' said the Chief Inspector grimly. He read the note aloud, for Rowlands' benefit: '"*You're next*," it says. Charming and to the point – I don't think! Then there's this . . . If you'll hold it by the upper right-hand corner, I'd appreciate it,' he said to Rowlands, putting the card into his hand. 'There's not much chance of any fingerprints, but . . .'

'The queen of hearts,' said Rowlands. There was a little gasp from Lady Celia; then she said, 'Of course. How stupid of me. *That's* what's special about your playing cards. Do you see, Natalia? They're cards meant for the blind . . . Oh, don't upset yourself!' For the Countess had burst into tears.

'He is going to kill me,' she wailed. 'He says it there – "*You're next.*" Oh what will I do? What will I do?'

'Now, there's no need to take on,' said Douglas. 'Nothing's going to happen to you if I and my men have anything to do with it. But I'll need a bit of help from you first. What I need to know is exactly when you came to receive this letter and its interesting little enclosure – thank you, Mr Rowlands, I'll have that back now – and if there was anything particular which led up to your receiving it. Anything at all which, when you look back on it, strikes you as suspicious.'

'Well, we knew there was something funny about the whole thing from the word go, because of the playing card,' said Celia West. 'We'd read about the murders in the paper of course, and so . . .'

'I'd like the Countess to answer for herself *if* you don't mind,' said the Chief Inspector. 'Now, Countess, at what time did you receive this letter?'

'I . . . I don't know exactly,' came the subdued reply. All trace of the theatrical had gone from the Countess Rostropovna's manner. 'About eight, I think. The maid came in with my tea and . . . and told me there was a letter for me.'

'This was the lady's maid, I take it?'

'Yes. Celia's maid. Agnes.'

'We'll be talking to her later,' said Douglas. 'So you received this letter at around eight. It's eleven o'clock now. What made you wait so long before calling the police?'

'I . . .' Again, the Russian seemed lost for words. 'I didn't think,' she said at last, 'that it was important.'

'Not important? When someone who'd already murdered two people had threatened to kill you?'

The gentleness with which Douglas had addressed the Countess up to now had been replaced by a harsher manner. 'I should have thought it was *very* important!'

'I told you,' said the young woman, in an exhausted tone. 'I thought it was a joke . . . that a friend, perhaps, had sent it.'

'Funny sort of a friend,' said the Chief Inspector. 'So then you decided it was in earnest, I take it?'

'Yes. I . . . That is, Celia thought . . .'

'It didn't seems like a joke to me,' said Celia West. 'I thought it was pretty foul, if you want to know.'

'Indeed,' said Douglas. 'So then you called the police?'

'Celia called them. I . . . I was too upset.'

'Quite natural, under the circumstances,' said Douglas. 'Wouldn't you say so, Mr Rowlands?'

'Yes. Would it be all right, Chief Inspector, for me to ask the Countess a question?'

'Ask away.'

'It's just this: I was wondering if the Countess could cast any light on an aspect of the case which has been puzzling me . . . The fact of the playing card's being a braille card. That is – as Lady Celia has said – a card meant for the use of blind people. Does that mean anything to you, Countess?' There was a moment's silence. Then Lady Celia said, 'Natalia's shaking her head, Mr Rowlands. Natalia, darling, you'll have to speak out if Mr Rowlands is to understand you.'

'It means nothing,' said the Countess Rostropovna, in a voice from which all expression seemed to have been expunged. 'Nothing at all.'

'She was lying, of course,' said Douglas as the car which was taking them back to Scotland Yard moved out into the stream of traffic along Birdcage Walk.

'Yes, I rather think she was,' agreed Rowlands. 'She was frightened, too, I thought.'

'Hardly surprising, given that our man seems to have decided to switch his attention from artists' models to titled ladies . . . even if this one *is* of the foreign variety. Well, there's not much we can do if she won't come across. I've left a man on duty. He's to report directly to me if he notices any suspicious goings-on in the neighbourhood of Cadogan Square.'

'I did wonder,' said Rowlands guardedly, 'whether Lady Celia mightn't be the one to ask about . . . well, anything which might have struck her as unusual. After all, she was the one to call the police.'

'Yes, she's a sharp one, all right,' admitted the Chief Inspector. 'I suppose,' he added, with a grudging air, 'we owe her a vote of thanks – this being the only real lead we've had in over a week. One thing I did wonder,' he went on, 'was how our man came to pick on her – the Countess, I mean. Knightsbridge being a goodish way from Shoreditch, if you get my meaning.'

'I believe I can help you there,' said Rowlands. He described his encounter with Lady Celia and the

Countess at the theatre a few nights before, not forgetting to mention the photograph that had appeared in Sunday's papers. When he'd finished speaking, the Chief Inspector let out a whistle. 'So that's how he cottoned onto her! Saw her picture in his paper on Sunday morning and thought he'd play for higher stakes, so to speak.'

'Perhaps,' said Rowlands. 'Only . . .' He broke off, frowning. 'If it *is* the same man – and the braille card indicates that it must be – then he's overlooked the rules of the game, or is playing a new one.'

'I don't follow.'

'Up till now,' said Rowlands, 'he's been playing Solo. A form of Whist, you know, played with four or more players. You begin with hearts as trumps, which is what he led with, if you recall: the ace, and then the king. And he's been going from north to east, which means south should have been next, you know, if one were going clockwise, which is what the game requires.' Beside him, the policeman made an impatient movement, as if he wanted to say something. But Rowlands was not quite finished. 'I suppose,' he said doubtfully, 'Knightsbridge does count as south? Although I'd have tended to call it west, wouldn't you?'

Travelling back on the train to Staplehurst, it occurred to Rowlands that the key to the whole thing must lie with the murdered girls. There had to be some reason why they had been chosen for the – admittedly dubious – distinction of being the 'Playing Card Killer's' first victims. It struck him that he knew very little about either of them other than their ages, their heights (both tall), the fact that they were fair-haired – attributes they shared with the Countess, apparently. 'I'd say she was a looker, if you like those kind of looks,' the Chief Inspector had admitted when pressed for a description. 'A good figure on her – statuesque, you might say – and yellow hair coiled into a bun, you know, not shingled, the way most women nowadays have it. I do like a woman with a decent head of hair,' the Chief Inspector had confided. 'My late wife, now . . .' he'd started to say, then recollected himself. 'Yes, I'd say she was a handsome piece,' he'd concluded.

Well, that was no surprise, thought Rowlands, alone in the swaying carriage of the moving train. Both the dead girls had been pretty blondes, too. As for their circumstances – both seemed to have been remarkably alone in the world. Winnie Calder had had an aunt, Rowlands recalled; as to whether there were any other family members extant who might have mourned her passing, he was still in the dark. Then there was the errant husband of Mary O'Reilly – Lintott, the farrier. He wondered about Lintott. Hadn't there been a child, too? He resolved to ask Douglas about that.

Still, aunt or no aunt, child or no child, the fact remained that both women had been solitary creatures – part of that great diaspora of the orphaned and dispossessed which had spread across the globe since the war. Here were fatherless children in abundance; widows in their hundreds of thousands. An army of mourning wives and mothers – enough to fill all the graveyards of Europe if those had not been full already. By a cruel irony, many of those bereft of their loved ones had themselves been lost to the terrible plague which had decimated the world's population in the immediate aftermath of the war, killing more people than the war itself. Yes, it wasn't surprising, he thought, that the dead women had been so alone.

He thought of the Countess. How frightened she had been! Pretending to make light of the whole business – the letter and its sinister enclosure – when all the while she had been shaking in her shoes. He'd heard it in her voice even though she'd tried to conceal it. Yes, she'd been afraid for her life all right . . . It occurred to him that she, too, was alone – her family the victims of another kind of fever, which was that of revolution. Although Celia West had mentioned an aunt. There was always an aunt, he thought. It was another effect of the war. The countless unmarried women – maiden aunts and bachelor girls, who together formed a sorority of sorts. Women who looked out for one another, who provided money and shelter in extremity, as well as the comfort of friendship. Sharing confidences (he supposed) over the teacups. Offering small kindnesses: the loan of a pair of silk stockings, or a lady's maid.

The train, which seemed to have been going slower and slower since it had passed Yalding, now gathered speed. Another ten minutes and he'd be home. He started to gather his traps together. Violet Smith, he thought suddenly – that was the name of Winnie's friend, wasn't it? The dancer. Another bachelor girl, he guessed. It struck him that a visit to Miss Smith might prove illuminating. Because surely she – or someone – must have seen *something*? He thought, it's time I started playing a more competitive game.

Edith made no reference to his meeting with Celia West and the Countess, and so he felt it incumbent upon him to describe it in detail – all too mindful of the time, two years before, when he had been wont to keep such things to himself. She listened without interruption until he had reached the end of his narrative; then she said: 'You think, then, that her life really is in danger, this Countess of yours?'

'She isn't *my* Countess. And yes, I do think so.'

'It couldn't just be . . . well, a hoax, or something?'

'I very much doubt it. I can't imagine,' he said, 'why anyone would want to lie about something like that.'

'Can't you?' Edith was silent a moment. 'Some people will do anything to get attention.' He knew it wasn't the Countess she meant.

'I don't think that's the case here,' he said carefully. 'She seemed genuinely taken aback when she learnt it was a braille card, for instance.'

'Ah.' They were sitting over their coffee after dinner,

for which the girls had been allowed to stay up, in celebration of their father's return – 'as it's been a week since you went away,' Edith said. The presence of the children and Edith's mother had made conversation at the meal necessarily general. The planned reunion of St Dunstan's old boys had been the topic of conversation, Helen Edwards remarking that she hoped they were suitably grateful for all the trouble which had been gone to on their behalf. 'Such a lovely idea – a summer party,' she had added vaguely. 'It quite makes me long for those parties we used to give in Alverton Avenue – do you remember, Edith? With the men in white flannels and blazers, and the girls in *such* pretty dresses, all frills and lace. You never see such dresses nowadays. Lovely times,' she added dreamily. 'All gone now, of course.'

When they'd had their dinner – a boiled ham, the last of that winter's salting, with roast potatoes and mashed swede, and an apple pie to follow – there was the washing-up, which Mrs Edwards insisted on doing, 'Because the girls and I have had such *fun* together this week doing the chores, haven't we, girls? And I wash all my china by hand at home.' This was a slight distortion of the truth since the china referred to was only the best tea service, not to be trusted to Mrs Edwards' tweeny, who came in to do the rough. But with the steeliness of which this almost excessively gentle little woman was capable, she had her way, and the kitchen soon resounded to the banging of pots,

'*Careful*, Anne, darling!', and the clatter of plates into racks. Exhausted by these labours, Edith's mother then took herself off to bed, having refused coffee – 'it keeps me awake, you know' – and sacrificed what was left of her evening to reading stories to the girls: 'Such fun! It quite takes me back to when you and dear Ralph were small.'

So it was that the events uppermost in Rowlands' mind – and, he suspected, in Edith's – had had to wait until the two of them were alone. Now he said: 'It must have been the photograph that put him onto her. The one you came across in the paper. The fact is,' he added, in case she'd missed the point. 'if it hadn't been for you I'd never have known about it.'

'I suppose not. Which suggests,' she said, 'that your Chief Inspector's been barking up the wrong tree.' He waited for her to say it, although he'd already worked it out for himself. 'Because if it was the photograph,' said Edith, 'then it suggests he isn't blind at all.'

'No,' he agreed. He reached across and took her hand. 'Do you know,' he said. 'Between us, I think we make quite a good detective.'

'Hmff,' said Edith, not sounding too displeased by what he'd said, however. 'I suppose,' she went on after a moment, 'you'll be going to that party of hers on Saturday?' He didn't pretend not to know whose party it was she meant.

'I don't know,' he replied. 'That rather depends . . .'

On you, he was going to say, but thought better of it. 'I don't *have* to go,' he said.

'I think you ought to.' She leant across and gave the fire a vigorous poke, so that a shower of sparks flew up. '*She'll* be there, won't she? The Countess, I mean. Perhaps,' she added, settling back into her chair, '*he'll* be there, too. Our murderer.'

Chapter Ten

Someone was screaming. '*No! No! No!*' A high wailing that seemed to go on and on. It was a sound he'd heard before, more times than he cared to remember, during the war. Men in pain often wept like children. But this time it really was a child, he realised, waking, groggy with sleep, to find himself in his bed at home.

'Edith?' he said.

'It's all right,' said his wife. 'I'll deal with her.' Now the screams had turned to sobs.

'Mummy, Mummy, Mummy . . .' It was Anne, of course. She'd always been prone to nightmares.

'Shh, shh,' he heard Edith say, from the room the girls shared, next to theirs. 'You've had a bad dream, that's all.' Then came Margaret's voice – his sensible eldest child: 'She said there was a fox. But there isn't a fox, is there, Mummy? It was just part of the dream, wasn't it?'

'Yes,' said Edith. 'Now go back to sleep, both of you. Hush, Anne. There's nothing to be afraid of.'

Violet Smith was staying with a girlfriend – a fellow dancer – in Kentish Town, sleeping on the put-you-up in the sitting room until she got herself settled somewhere else. 'I'm not going back *there* again,' she told Rowlands with a little shudder. 'Not after what happened. Seeing her like that, poor kid, and *him* not gone so very long before, by all accounts. It makes me come over all cold, it really does.' Rowlands said that he quite understood. 'You're nice,' said Miss Smith warmly. 'Not like that other one. Grumpy old stick *he* was. "If y'ull just tull me yurr moovements on the nicht in question, Miss L'Amour . . ."' she said, in cruel but accurate mimicry of the Chief Inspector's tones, '"we'll mebbe get somewhurr." But you're different. More refined, I'd say. All the same,' she added, 'you're not what I expected. I mean – don't get me wrong,' she said, 'but it does seem a bit funny. A blind copper.'

'I'm not a policeman,' said Rowlands.

'So what's your interest, then? Don't tell me you're a friend of the family?'

'No.'

'Good. Because if you'd said you were, I'd have sent you away with a flea in your ear. She didn't *have* any family to speak of, didn't Win. Only her auntie, out

Sidcup way. And you won't,' said Violet Smith, 'get much change out of *her*. Deaf as a post, she is. But here I am,' she cried suddenly, 'forgetting my manners! Won't you have a cigarette? They're Turkish.'

Rowlands had already gathered as much from the smell of the room – the sweetish aroma of Miss Smith's preferred smokes, mingling with that of the scent she wore (something musky and rather overpowering), overlaid with the smell of dust; he supposed that the demands of a dancer's life didn't leave much time or inclination for housework. He declined the cigarette.

'I'll smoke my own, if you don't mind.'

'Be my guest,' said the girl. Both lit up; then she said: 'So what is it you want to know? I've told it all to the other one, already – my movements on the night in question. Quite lively ones they were, as a matter of fact!' She gave a little shriek of laughter. 'Seeing as I was onstage that night,' she added, in case he'd missed the point. Rowlands smiled.

'At the Hippodrome, wasn't it?'

'That's right. I've got a six-month engagement in the new Jack Buchanan show – *That's a Good Girl*,' she added helpfully. 'It's a corker. I can get you tickets, if you like.' She hummed a little snatch of tune under her breath.

'Thanks,' said Rowlands. 'And you were home just after midnight . . .'

'Yes.' She made an impatient movement, which set her bracelets jangling. 'I *said* all this to the other man.'

'Yes, of course,' said Rowlands hastily. 'And I'm sure

there's no need to go over it all again. What I really wanted to know was if you'd noticed anything, well, *odd* about Miss Calder's behaviour in the days leading up to her murder.'

'Odd?' echoed the dancer.

'Well – different.'

Violet Smith took a long drag on her cigarette, then exhaled the smoke slowly as if giving herself time to reflect. 'D'you know, I believe she was a bit different, now I come to think of it,' she said. 'Sort of . . . excited, I suppose you'd say.' Rowlands held his breath. 'It was getting the job, I imagine.'

'And what job was that? A dancing engagement?'

'Bless you, no.' Violet Smith's laugh ended in a coughing fit. 'Sorry,' she said when she could speak once more. 'It's just that Win didn't have what it took to be a dancer. Not a grain of talent in her body. Couldn't sing a note, either. As for her acting . . .' Miss Smith blew a cloud of scented smoke in his direction. 'Let's just say she only got call-backs because of her looks. 'Course,' she added scornfully, 'there's always *some* producers who'll go for a pretty face and figure. But if a girl's got two left feet, then that lets her out as far as getting the plum parts. Dancing's hard work,' she concluded, 'although you mightn't think it.'

'I appreciate that,' said Rowlands. 'But you said . . .'

'About the job? I was coming to that. It was something she'd seen in the paper the week before. Artists' models wanted, that sort of thing.'

'Go on,' said Rowlands.

'There's not a lot more to tell. She'd written to the Box Number it gave and got a reply. Chap said she sounded just what he was looking for.' She emitted another shriek of laughter. 'Sort of thing they *do* say, isn't it? But she was very pleased with herself about *that*. Thought she was on the up at last, poor kid. *Men!*' said Violet Smith, putting all the cynicism of her twenty-seven years into the monosyllable.

'I don't suppose' said Rowlands, keeping his voice casual, 'that you got to see this man?'

'No, I didn't. Here!' said Miss Smith. 'You don't think he might have been the one who . . .'

'I don't think anything just at present,' he said. 'But it does seem a coincidence, to say the least, that Miss Calder had been in touch with this person so soon before she died. Did she mention a name, by any chance?'

'No. All she said was he was ever so nicely spoken. He'd asked her to sit for him, she said. Offered her five shillings an hour—'

'You're saying she'd actually *met* this man?' he said, cutting across her, with a feeling of rising excitement. At last he was getting somewhere. But his hopes were dashed a moment later.

'I don't know about that,' said Violet Smith. 'All I do know is that she spoke to him on the phone. There's a box at the end of our street. All excited, she was when she came in from making the call. "Five shillings an hour!" she kept saying, as if it was five hundred pounds. "That's two pounds a day. Just think what I'll be able to buy with that!" Only wish I'd been paying more attention at the time,' said Violet Smith, her voice not quite steady. 'I'd have told the silly kid to throw his five shillings an hour back in his face, the swine.'

As he crossed Pont Street and entered the Square at the north end, the collar of his best overcoat turned up against the driving sleet, and the hat Edith had persuaded him to wear pulled down at an angle over his face, he thought how very much a stranger he was in this world. Celia West's world was what he meant. He'd known it the first time he'd heard her voice on the telephone, two years before; all that had happened thereafter had only served to confirm it. Still, he could console himself with the knowledge that – on this occasion, at least – he was acting in a professional capacity. When, in the car driving back to Scotland Yard the other day, he'd let slip that he'd been invited to Lady Celia's soirée, Douglas could not have been more delighted than if he'd thought up the stunt himself. 'But of course you must go, man!' he'd cried. 'Don't you see? This is a great chance for us. You'll be there as a guest. Who'll know you have any other reason for being there?'

'And will I have any other reason?' said Rowlands. The policeman laughed. 'Of course. You'll be there to keep your ear to the ground, as it were. To let me know at once if anyone resembling our man shows his face.' His wife and the Chief Inspector, Rowlands reflected wryly, evidently thought along similar lines.

Now, as he reached the far side of the Square, he could

hear the low rumble of taxicabs drawing up in front of the mansion block where Celia West's flat was to be found. Here, a servant waited with an umbrella, to offer shelter as far as the front door. Disdaining this, Rowlands climbed the short flight of steps and rang the bell; the door immediately opened and a voice said, 'Good evening, sir.' The butler, Rowlands guessed, or a footman, hired for the evening, perhaps. Cadogan Square, though undoubtedly one of the better parts of SW1, was still, he supposed, a step down from Mayfair. He handed his coat and hat to the man, and crossed the hall to the drawing room. This, too, was flung open as if by invisible hands, just like in the fairytale the girls had loved so when they were little. He gave his name to the man who'd opened the door, and heard it announced, although it struck him that there was little chance of its being heard over the infernal racket that greeted him. Music – jazz, of the hot variety – issued from a gramophone nearby, but even this, played at top volume as it seemed to him, was almost drowned out by a cacophony of voices, all shouting to be heard about the din.

'Beastly weather . . .'

'Yes. We wondered if we'd ever get here from St John's Wood.'

'I don't suppose you've seen Bunny, have you?'

'What?'

'I *said* – I don't suppose you've seen Bunny?'

'I say – can't a chap get a drink around here?'

The room was full of people – he guessed around fifty

or sixty in all: the deeper chest notes of the men's voices, overlaid by the lighter tones of the women's. 'Oh my *dear*, you never *saw* such a sight . . .' There was a smell of cigar smoke, fresh flowers and expensive scent. It was very hot. 'So I was saying to Nina Killen . . . do you know Nina? Yes. The sister. *That* one . . .' Surrounded by so many competing sources of sound, it was an effort to get his bearings. Now. Fireplace to the right, connecting doors to the left. Windows straight ahead. In front of the windows a sofa where she had sat to receive them. Except that now all the furniture would have been removed, or pushed back against the walls, he thought. 'No, no! I meant his *second* wife, not the first . . .' Standing there, ill-at-ease in evening dress, he felt himself an imposter – as if he'd blundered into the wrong room by mistake and would soon be found out, and evicted. 'Cocktail, sir?' said a voice at Rowlands' elbow. He'd have preferred a beer. 'Do you have any whisky?' he said.

'I'll see what I can do, sir. Will that be with soda, or without?'

'Just as it comes, thanks . . . On second thoughts, you'd better put some water with it.' It wouldn't do to get tight, given that he was supposed to be here in an official capacity. Spying, in a word, he thought disgustedly. He seemed to be doing rather a lot of that, these days.

'Mr Rowlands!' came a voice he knew. At once he felt his heart lift.

'Lady Celia,' he said.

'How very good to see you. But isn't your wife with you?' she asked.

'She had to stay with the children,' he said. 'She . . . she sends her apologies.'

'Of course,' she murmured. 'The children.' As if in her world, having children could ever have made a difference to whether one might attend a party, or not. 'But I hope you're being looked after?' she said, suddenly recalled to her role as hostess. 'You haven't got a drink. You ought to have a drink.'

'Thanks. I've everything I want,' he said, and indeed at that moment, his whisky arrived. Invisible hands, he thought.

'What's funny?' she said. He'd forgotten how well she was able to read him.

'Nothing. It seems like a good party,' he said.

'I'm *so* glad you could come.' She put her hand on his arm for a moment, reinforcing their moment of intimacy. Or perhaps she did it with everyone, he'd no way of knowing. She lowered her voice. 'Especially after this business with poor Natalia.'

'How *is* the Countess?' Although in truth he was rather more interested in the Countess's friend.

'Oh, bearing up, you know,' she said. 'It's all been rather unpleasant for her.'

'Yes,' he said. He hesitated a moment. 'Lady Celia . . . I was wondering . . .' But before he could form the question, there came another voice: a man's light baritone. '*There* you are, Celia! I've been looking for you everywhere.'

'Hello, Johnny.'

'Comes to something,' went on this voice, with just a shade of petulance, 'when a chap's fiancée goes off and leaves him in the lurch so that he's forced to talk to perfect strangers.'

'What rot. You've known half of them since you were born.'

'It's the other half I seem to have got stuck with. She really does know some extraordinary types.' The young man Lady Celia had introduced as Johnny now addressed Rowlands in a confidential tone. 'Artists, and Russians, and I don't know what else . . .' He sounded more than a little tight, Rowlands thought. 'We haven't met, have we?' he went on. 'Name's Edgecombe. Everybody calls me Johnny.'

'Frederick Rowlands.'

'I say – *you're* not an artist, are you?'

'No.'

'Mr Rowlands is a friend of mine,' said Lady Celia. 'And I'll thank you to be civil to my friends.'

'No offence,' said Johnny Edgecombe.

'None taken,' replied Rowlands. An awkward silence ensued, broken after a moment, by Edgecombe.

'See you've got yourself a whisky,' he said. 'Call that a proper drink. Not like this muck . . . *Cocktails!*' he said in a disgusted tone. 'Can't understand what people see in 'em, frankly.'

'Which I suppose is why you've had three already,' said Lady Celia sweetly. 'Come on, Mr Rowlands.' She took his arm. 'I'll introduce you to some people.' They began to make their way across the room.

'That's right,' came Edgecombe's voice after them. 'Leave me to fend for myself!'

'I must apologise for Lord Edgecombe,' murmured Celia West in Rowlands' ear as they manoeuvred themselves between a laughing group, at the centre of which was Dickie Fairfax, and another, composed solely of men talking politics. 'He's just had a bit of bad news. Although I don't suppose,' she added, as if to herself, 'it'd have made the slightest difference to his behaviour whether the news were bad or good.'

'Why, it's the lovely Celia!' called out Fairfax, breaking off from telling what sounded like a slightly off-colour story. 'Celia, the belle of every ball.'

'Don't be an ass, Dickie.'

'But it's true!' He, too, appeared to have consumed more than his fair share of cocktails, thought Rowlands, congratulating himself on having avoided the same. 'B-beautiful Celia. Wouldn't *be* a party without her.'

'Think the market'll hold?' said a voice behind Rowlands. 'You never know, the way things are going in Shanghai. Glad I've got my shares tied up in gilts . . .'

'You and I must have a talk,' said Celia West in an undertone. 'I want to know all about these murders.'

'I'm afraid there's not a lot I can tell you.'

'Oh, I know it's all supposed to be hush-hush,' she said. 'Isn't that what they say in detective stories? But I thought, as I'm rather involved . . . Oh, Natalia! *There* you are! You know Mr Rowlands, don't you?'

'We have met.' The Countess's tones could not have been more glacial.

'And this is Percy Loveless. Mr Loveless is an artist,' said Lady Celia. 'He had a marvellous exhibition in Cork Street only last year. Loveless, I want you to meet Frederick Rowlands. He was in the war, too, you know.'

'Which regiment?' demanded the artist.

'Royal Artillery.'

'I was with the Artists' Rifles. Bloody awful show. Most of 'em bloody amateurs.'

'Most of us were,' said Rowlands.

'Yes, but not like this lot,' said the other, with what seemed a characteristic vehemence. 'Never done a day's work that didn't involve paint and charcoal. Six weeks' training, and that was it. Launched upon a career in soldiering. You never saw such a bloody shambles.' It seemed all too apposite a word, and so Rowlands, conscious that there were women present, changed the subject.

'What do you paint, Mr Loveless?'

'Bodies,' was the curt reply. 'Heads. Speaking of which, you've got rather a good head yourself. Decent angles. Not like some of these overfed piglets.' He gave a contemptuous guffaw. 'Might as well paint cushions. *You've* got bone structure.'

'Be careful, Mr Rowlands,' laughed Celia West. 'Or you'll find yourself sitting for him. Not the most enjoyable experience, I have to say.'

'Only because you wouldn't keep still,' said Loveless. 'Women do fidget so. Wriggle, wriggle, wriggle. Sex-starvation, no doubt. Although,' he went on, raising his voice so that no one in the vicinity could avoid hearing what he had to say, 'I can't be expected to satisfy all the women in London.' The brief, startled pause which followed this announcement was broken by Natalia Rostropovna. 'Celia,' she said, in a pained voice, 'I wish you would let me have a pin. My dress seems to have a tear.'

'Oh, Meadows'll see to it,' was the reply. 'You'll find her in my bedroom.'

'Thank you,' said the Countess, her icy disapproval of the present company apparent, even to Rowlands. Without another word, she stalked away.

'Now *there's* a young woman who could do with my services,' said Loveless, not lowering his voice an iota, although she could hardly have been out of earshot, Rowlands thought. 'Wouldn't mind painting her, either – even if she *is* a bitch. Bitches make the best subjects, though.'

'Thanks,' said Celia West, with a laugh. 'You're too kind.'

'Oh, *you're* just a delicious piece,' said the artist lazily. 'No man in his right senses could resist the chance to get *you* down on canvas. No, the Rostropovna's handsome enough for my purpose. But I don't like her. There's something not quite right about that woman.'

'Don't be horrid about poor Natalia,' said Celia West. 'You mustn't listen to him, Mr Rowlands. Loveless is appallingly rude about everyone.'

'I see it as my role,' came the unabashed reply. 'Like the satirists of old. England's rotten to the core – and London's the worst of it. Full of the dregs of a ruined civilisation. Pansies, prostitutes and pimps. The idle rich and the downtrodden poor. I make it my business to 'hold the mirror up to nature', as it were.'

'It sounds rather a bleak view of things,' said Rowlands. 'I'm not surprised that people find it an uncomfortable experience, being painted by you.'

'Oh, they love it when I insult them,' said Loveless. 'Think it's all part of the act. Of course I mean every word – but most of 'em are too stupid to see that. As a matter of fact,' he added casually, 'some of my finest pictures have been of people I loathe. It seems to bring out the best in me.'

'Well, I'm sorry not to have seen your work,' said Rowlands. 'As you've probably noticed, that isn't an omission I can put right, either.'

'Yes, I saw you were blind straight away. Doesn't matter at all, for my purposes. I seldom bother with painting eyes – and when I do, they're usually blank, like the eyes in Greek statues.'

'Or Modigliani,' put in someone.

'Bugger Modigliani. No, you'll do very nicely, I think.' Rowlands must have looked his surprise, for the artist added, with some acerbity, 'I want you to sit for me. I shan't want you long. A couple of sessions should do it. It's for a big piece I'm working on: *The Descent of Christ from the Cross* . . . Don't look so shocked, man. I wouldn't expect you to do it for nothing. Although I can't offer much. I'm still waiting,' he added bitterly, 'for some of my wealthy *patrons* to pay me.'

'It isn't that,' said Rowlands, feeling his face flame. Did the man have no sense of decorum? 'It's just . . .' But then it struck him: if it was an artist – blind or otherwise – that they were looking for, then the cantankerous Mr Loveless might offer an introduction to the world in which such a man might move. 'I'd consider it a privilege,' he said.

'Good man. Shall we say first thing, Monday morning? There's the address.' The artist scribbled something on a piece of pasteboard, and slipped it into the breast pocket of Rowlands' dinner jacket. 'No need to wear the boiled shirt, either. Just your ordinary clothes will do.'

'All right,' said Rowlands. He finished his whisky.

'You need another of those,' said Loveless. 'Only way to get through a thing like this. Waiter! bring us two more whiskies.'

'At once, sir.'

'I must say,' said Celia West, 'for a man who hates parties, you spend rather a lot of time going to them. Didn't I see you at Pamela Farnham's the other day?'

'Touting for business,' was the reply. 'And I don't *hate* parties – I simply see them for what they are. Manifestations of the zeitgeist. Puppet shows. A *danse macabre*, whose participants are the living dead of Europe, and its upstart scion, America. The decadent, the dull, and the diseased.'

'Can't we have a more cheerful subject?' said the

man who had mentioned Modigliani. 'I didn't come here for one of your lectures, Loveless. I get enough of those as it is.'

'Did I mention the dimwitted, in my catalogue of Dunces?' said the artist, but his venom seemed to have subsided for the moment, for which Rowlands was glad if only because it made it easer to pay attention to some of the others. The man who had spoken out introduced himself as Edgar Pickford. 'Oh, I write a bit,' he said, when asked what it was he did. 'But you won't have heard of me.'

'Mr Pickford is a poet,' said Celia West. 'A rather good one, though he's too modest to say so. And this is Iris Barnes. Iris is a writer, too.'

'Of sorts,' said Miss Barnes, with a laugh. Rowlands felt his hand firmly grasped and shaken. No shrinking violet, this, but a healthy, Modern Girl. 'I write about films, for the newspapers. Filthy job, but someone's got to do it.'

'It sounds interesting,' said Rowlands politely. Although what interested him more was that Celia West had chosen to surround herself with such people – artists, poets, journalists – rather than those of her own set. Although this was in evidence, too. Across the room, came the braying tones of Dickie Fairfax's voice, 'put a tenner on Lucky Boy each way, at a hundred to one, and he came in second. Good little morning's work, I call it . . .'

'Sometimes I feel that there's nothing I'd like more than to see the tumbrils rolling along Piccadilly,' muttered Percy Loveless in Rowlands' ear. 'With Madame la

Guillotine set up in St James's Park. Think of it! All the useless parasites dealt with at one fell swoop. I'm thinking of doing a picture on the subject, as a matter of fact. '*À la Lanterne*' might be a good title.'

Supper was announced. 'I say, Loveless,' said Pickford. 'Are you going to stand here gassing all night, or are we going to get something to eat? I haven't had a thing all day.'

'That's hardly my fault,' said Loveless. 'If you will starve yourself in a bloody garret . . . I suppose you think it's good for your art, or something . . .'

'Oh, stow it,' was the cheerful reply. 'I'm going to get some supper. Coming, Iris?'

'Rath*er*. Listening to Loveless sounding off about Art and Civilisation always gives me an appetite.'

'Silly bitch,' said the artist affectionately. 'Now *she* does know how to sit still. Sat for me a year ago, for a picture I submitted to the RA last summer. Lovely thing. And *she* isn't so bad, either.' With Celia West on his arm, and Loveless on his other side, still talking, Rowlands joined the general movement towards the supper room. 'Profile like a knife blade, and that black hair. I do love the Mediterranean type. Not like these insipid, English blondes.'

'Careful!' laughed Lady Celia. 'Or you'll be going without your supper. Don't believe a word of what he says,' she added, to Rowlands. 'He's only rude about people he likes. The women, anyway.'

'There are no women I like,' interrupted Loveless. 'A man in my position can't afford to *like* women. One either makes love to them, or paints them. Sometimes both. As for liking them . . .' But his remarks were drowned out in the blast of sound which greeted them as they entered the adjacent room. The gramophone had now been replaced by a live band, playing hot jazz and popular tunes from the latest shows. As they took their places in the queue for the supper table, Rowlands recognised one such number, now being energetically performed by the trio of double bass, piano and saxophone. It was the song Violet Smith had been humming the day he'd met her – something from that show she was performing in, he supposed. Let Yourself Go, was the refrain.

'Awful tripe,' muttered Loveless gloomily. 'Although I suppose it does have a certain crude vitality.' He must have helped himself to the comestibles on offer, for a moment or two later he went on, through a mouthful of food, 'I quite like the saxophone player, I must say. Fine Negro head, of the classical type. I wonder if he'd agree to sit for me? He'd do for my second Roman soldier . . . I can recommend the salmon mousse, by the way.'

'Thanks,' said Rowlands, starting to fill his plate. He wasn't particularly hungry, but he thought it might be advisable to eat something. Two whiskies on an empty stomach wasn't exactly an aid to concentration. Now, taking advantage of the momentary lull in the flow of Loveless's talk, he moved away from him, and – avoiding the busier centre of the room where he was more likely to be jostled – found a perch on a sofa in front of one of the big windows where he could eat his supper in peace. Here, he could let the syncopated stridencies of the jazz band wash over him, as well as the sounds of talking and eating – of forks being scraped against plates and of glasses being drained and refilled – made by the thirty or so people who now occupied the supper room. Snatches of talk caught, momentarily, at his attention: '. . . of course, reducing the rate from seven per cent to six and a half will help to stabilise things, I fancy . . .'

'. . . if this snow keeps up, I can kiss goodbye to my day out with the Beaufort . . .'

'. . . the *second* wife, not the first . . .'

None of it meant anything, he thought. The frivolous chit-chat of a lot of self-absorbed people. He resolved to make his excuses and leave as soon as it was decently possible. There was nothing for him here. But then a voice he knew – and to which he could have listened to all night, given the chance – said, in an undertone, 'You're being absurd.'

'Am I?' This was Johnny Edgecombe, in a voice thickened by anger, and drink. 'Then explain to me why you've hired a detective to watch me.'

'I tell you, it's nothing to do with you! He's a friend, that's all.'

'He was here, with that policeman, two days ago,' said another voice: Natalia Rostropovna's.

'What if he was?' came the reply. 'He's here tonight as

a friend. And I've no control over what my friends do – as you of all people should know, Johnny.'

'What's that supposed to mean?' His voice was sullen – that of a small child reproached for some misdemeanour. Celia West's reply, when it came, was cool: 'You can hardly expect me to jump for joy when the man I'm engaged to marry gets himself mixed up with a lot of Fascists.'

'I do wish you'd keep your voice down.'

'Why? Are you ashamed of the connection?' said his fiancée. 'I should've thought you'd have wanted to advertise it! In fact, I'm surprised you're not wearing a black shirt this very minute.'

'Celia, if you're determined to quarrel . . .' began Edgecombe angrily; then he broke off. 'But here *is* your friend,' he said coldly. For Rowlands, feeling the invidiousness of his position, now rose from his seat, drawing attention to his presence with a discreet cough. 'I've come to say goodbye,' he said. 'I've had a most pleasant evening.'

'Oh, you can't go yet,' said Lady Celia, putting a hand on his arm to detain him. 'It's not even ten o'clock. There's still the dancing to come. I'm sure you're a good dancer. You seem to be good at most things.' There was a disgusted snort from Edgecombe at this; a moment later, he walked away, with the Countess at his side, evidently. Because suddenly Rowlands found himself alone with his hostess.

'I'm sorry,' he said. 'I seem to have upset your fiancé.'

He hesitated a moment. 'I couldn't help overhearing what he said.'

'He was being ridiculous,' replied Celia West, in a bored tone. 'Seemed to think it was some kind of reflection on his honour that you were here. As if he might be a suspect for these murders. Which perhaps he is,' she added slyly. 'Let's sit down, shall we?' she went on. 'I feel as if I've been on my feet all night.'

Chapter Eleven

They withdrew to the sofa where Rowlands had been sitting some minutes before. This was set within an embrasure, out of which a set of French windows opened onto a terrace. Full-length brocade curtains hung down on either side of it, which partly screened the occupants of the sofa from the rest of the company. The volume of noise emanating from the far side of the room where the musicians now began a spirited rendition of 'Lady, Be Good', only added to the perverse sense he had of being, somehow, alone with her in the midst of the crowd. A waiter passed at that moment with a tray of champagne. Lady Celia relieved him of two glasses. 'There you are,' she said, putting one of them into Rowlands' hand. 'Well, here's luck.'

‘Here’s luck,’ he said, taking a sip. It struck him that he’d had more champagne this past week than in the previous twelve months. That was to do with her, of course. The very taste of the stuff – faintly acidic, sparkling – was one he would always associate with her. That, and the headiness that came after . . .

‘You were going to ask me something,’ she said.

‘Yes. I wondered if there was anything else you wanted to tell me.’

She seemed to hesitate. ‘Do you mean about Natalia?’

‘Yes.’ Sensing that she had more to say, he waited. In spite of the noise that was coming from the room beyond, where they were seemed preternaturally quiet. He could hear the champagne fizzing in the shallow glasses. ‘It’s just that she’s a friend,’ she said.

‘I’m not asking you to betray a confidence,’ he replied, although that in fact was exactly what he was asking. ‘But two women are dead . . .’

‘I know.’ She gave a little shiver. ‘How perfectly foul it all is!’ Again, he was silent. ‘I heard her crying,’ she said, so softly that he almost missed it. Unconsciously, he leant towards her. He could smell the champagne on her breath, the perfume in her hair. ‘It was later that night – the day the letter came. Around one in the morning, I think. We hadn’t long gone to bed when I heard her. It woke me up, as a matter of fact. I got up, and went to see if she was all right. It was then that I heard her say something. Something rather odd,’ she said. Rowlands held his breath. ‘She’d been weeping, you see, but then she broke off as if she were trying to pull herself together. Then she said, "My God. What have I done?"'

'What happened then?'

'Nothing. I knocked, and said, "Are you all right?" and she said, "Perfectly, thanks." And then I asked her if she wanted anything, and she said no, and I went back to my room and got into bed and fell asleep.'

'You didn't ask her what she'd meant by what she'd said?'

'No. I wasn't sure it had meant very much at all. What do you think?'

'Oh, I think it meant *something*, without a doubt,' said Rowlands. 'Although at present I'm not sure exactly what.'

Later, as Lady Celia had promised, there was dancing. He must stay at least for the first few numbers, she said. It was a good little band, didn't he think? They'd played at the Kit-Kat Club only last week. Nor would she accept his excuses that he was too out of practice to join in, and that, in any case, he had two left feet. 'It isn't like you to lie, Mr Rowlands,' she said, when they were moving around the floor to the strains of 'Let's Misbehave' – a little more uptempo than he was used to, but he was managing so far. 'I must say, I'm disappointed in you.' The lightness of her tone belied the severity of her words, and so he smiled. 'I'm afraid I don't know what you mean.'

His dance companion gave a soft laugh – a sound which, by itself, was enough to bewitch him. Having her in his arms like this – feeling her slender body in its diaphanous silk chiffon gown pressed against his – as together they moved around the floor, was intoxicating. The delicious *scent* of her was almost more than his ravished senses could bear. 'Another lie!' she laughed, tapping his cheek in mock reproof. 'I shall start to think the worst of you if this goes on.'

'Is this about my dancing? Because I can assure you, I'm usually much worse than this.'

'No it's not your dancing – or rather, saying that you couldn't – although *that* was another shocking fib! It's that you pretended not to understand me a moment ago when I asked you if you suspected anyone here of being involved in the murders.'

'I wasn't lying. I've no idea who the murderer might be. He could be here – or anywhere.'

'So you admit he could be one of my guests?' she persisted.

'There's a possibility,' Rowlands replied. 'But that wasn't,' he added, 'the reason why I came. To . . . to spy on your guests. That would have been despicable.'

'Would it? I think it would have been eminently sensible. Perhaps,' she went on, as the song to which they had been dancing came to an end, and another began. 'I could be of some help. Let's sit this one out, shall we?' She took his hand and drew him towards a convenient alcove. 'The fact is,' she said when they were seated, 'it seems to me that you're at something of a disadvantage.' He made a wry face at this. But she went on, 'Oh, it's not because you can't *see* these people, but because you don't *know* them. Not that you're missing a great deal,' she added, sotto voce. 'So my idea is this: why don't I describe them for you? Or at least as many of them as possible. Then at least you can say to that Inspector of yours that you've done your job.'

'Lady Celia, I'm not sure . . .'

'Oh, *come* on. It'll be fun,' she said. 'I've always wanted to be a detective. Now, first and foremost, you'd better tell me what kind of man we're looking for. I take it we *are* looking for a man?'

'Yes.'

'Thought so. Strangling's a man's crime, isn't it? And what sort of a man is he? Tall? Short? Fat? Thin? Red-haired, with a pronounced limp? No, I thought that would be too easy,' she said, when he had shaken his head in answer to all these questions.

'The truth is, we don't have any idea what he looks like,' said Rowlands. 'Only that he may be blind.'

'Well, that lets out everyone here – except you,' she said.

'Or at least that he may have some connection with the blind.'

'Ah, now that makes it more difficult.'

'It's also possible . . .' Rowlands hesitated, then decided he had nothing to lose. 'That he may be an artist, or in some way involved in the art world.'

At this, Celia West gave a crow of laughter. 'Now *there* I can help you! I know lots of artists. Several of them are here tonight. Loveless you've met, of course. I should think *he'd* be perfectly capable of strangling a woman. Do you need a description?'

'Well . . .'

'He's tall – about six foot one, I'd say. Burly, but not fat. Beautiful hands. Age: early forties. Quite handsome, in a rather dissolute way. Dark hair – what there is left of it. Eyes: brown, I should say. I haven't been to bed with him,' she added casually. 'In spite of the impression he might have given you that I had.'

'I didn't think for a minute . . .'

'No. I just wanted you to know, that's all. Oh, and he wears glasses when he's painting, which give him rather an owlish look. He's much too vain to wear them in public, of course. Thinks they'll spoil his manly beauty,' she laughed.

'What about his friend, Mr Pickford?' asked Rowlands, thinking that he'd heard enough both from and about Loveless for one evening.

'Oh, Edgar's a pet,' she said. 'I doubt he'd have the strength to strangle anybody. He's rather delicate – his chest kept him out of the war, you know. I'd put his age at thirty-six or -seven. He's short – around five foot four, at a guess, and slight. Sandy hair, freckles, glasses. He's a marvellous poet.'

'Perhaps,' said Rowlands, thinking that at this rate, they'd be here all night – not that the prospect displeased him in the slightest – 'you could give me a brief tour of the room, mentioning anyone who might be of interest . . . the men, that is,' he added reluctantly, for it was tempting to ask her to describe the whole scene: the room, with its white-and-gold panelled walls and ornate ceiling, its mirrors, its candelabra . . . That, at least, was how he envisaged it – it might have been painted bright scarlet, for all he knew. He'd have liked to ask her to describe the women's dresses, too, so that he could have told Edith about them afterwards. But then they really would have been there all night.

'All right,' she said. 'Starting at the door, and moving in a clockwise direction, we've got Lady Brampton, in a rather risqué frock for a woman who'll never see fifty again, dancing with her son-in-law, Giles Newby. He's a stockbroker, I believe. Thirty, or thereabouts. A face rather like a frog and pale blond hair. Protuberant eyes, also pale. What Lavinia sees in him, apart from his money, it's hard to tell. Next to them, are the Risleys. Married a year ago, and still very much in love.' There was the faintest edge in Lady Celia's voice. '*Look* at the way he's gazing at her, the silly young fool, as if he wanted to eat her up. She's very pretty, is Clarice Risley, but rather stupid,' she said with a yawn. 'He's good-looking too, in a rather dull, shopwindow dummy sort of way. Age: about twenty-five. Patent-leather hair, and wears his evening dress awfully *well*. I'm sure they'll have beautiful children,' she added, without enthusiasm. 'Next to them . . .'

But his ear had caught a familiar voice. 'I *say*, you chaps . . .'

'Isn't that Mr Fairfax?'

'Yes, that's Dickie. Rather pie-eyed, I'm afraid. But Dickie's a dear. I've known him all my life. He couldn't kill anyone unless it was by *boring* them to death with his awful jokes.'

'Even so . . .'

'Thirty-eight, five foot nine, reddish hair, receding chin. Does Something in the City,' she said. 'Between you and me – and much as I adore him – he's not *clever* enough to be a killer,' she laughed. 'Just at present, he's talking to Maurice Le Fevre. Now he *is* rather sinister,' she said. 'Terribly rich, you know. Runs a sort of dining club for gentlemen, in his spare time. They meet once a month, to smoke cigars and talk politics. It's he who's got Johnny involved in all that nonsense.' The laughter had gone from her voice. Rowlands said nothing, sensing she wasn't quite finished. 'Yes, it's rather queered the pitch where Johnny and I are concerned,' she went on, 'as I expect you'll have gathered earlier. The fact is, I don't approve of some of Johnny's friends – at least, not Le Fevre's crowd. I wouldn't have asked him tonight, only Johnny insisted.'

Le Fevre. The name was familiar, although just at that moment, Rowlands couldn't think why. He made a mental note to ask Douglas what he knew about the man. 'Could you describe him?' he prompted since she seemed, suddenly, abstracted.

'Who, Le Fevre? Nothing easier. I'd put his age at around sixty. He's of medium height. Perhaps five foot eight, or nine – although he seems taller. I expect it's the way he holds himself,' she said. 'Rather grandly, you know, as if he expected to be looked at. He's not fat, exactly. Corpulent. Is that the word? His hair's grey, worn rather long. An aquiline nose. Thin lips. A cold blue eye. Which is actually quite an accurate description, because the other one's glass. He wears a monocle, to disguise it, but it's a false one – no doubt about that.'

'Really?' Rowlands felt, for the first time that evening, a prickle of unease. 'Then he's . . .'

'Half-blind,' said Lady Celia. 'Which should make him at least half a suspect, in my view.'

'What else do you know about him?'

'Not a great deal. Pots of money, as I've said, although where it came from, I've not the least idea. Hello!' she said. 'That's rather queer . . .'

'What is it?'

'Oh, just that he and Natalia seem to have got talking. I wonder what exactly *they're* finding to say to one another? Natalia can't bear anything to do with politics. And he's hardly what you'd call a ladies' man.'

Further discussion was curtailed by the reappearance of Lord Edgecombe, in conciliatory mood. 'I say, Celia, are you going to sit talking half the night, or do I get my dance?'

'All right. Don't run away,' murmured Celia West in Rowlands' ear as she rose in answer to her lover's summons. 'We've still half the men in the room unaccounted for.'

'What's that?' said Johnny Edgecombe suspiciously.

'Nothing that need concern you, my angel,' replied his fiancée, with acid sweetness. 'Thirty-one, six foot two, former Guards officer, blue eyes, black hair, devastatingly handsome,' she said, over her shoulder, to Rowlands. 'He makes up for in looks what he rather lacks in brains, poor darling.'

Left to his own devices, Rowlands found his thoughts returning to what Celia West had overheard, the night she'd woken to the sound of weeping. Natalia Rostropovna's anguished cry: *My God, what have I done?* The words – like so much in this case – were ambiguous. *What have I done to deserve this?* might have been one interpretation; he rather thought there was more to it than that. Looked at in another light, the words implied culpability. If the Countess were guilty of something, he had to find out what. 'You're looking very thoughtful,' said a voice. It was the cheerful Miss Barnes, Edgar Pickford's friend. She sat down beside him on the sofa with a little groan. 'Gosh, that's a relief!' she said. 'I feel as if I've been dancing on red-hot coals for the past hour – like the wicked queen in the fairytale. I say, I hope you don't mind my crashing in on you like this?'

'Not a bit,' he said, making room for her.

'Only I was *desperate* to sit down. I hate this kind of party,' she said, with sudden vehemence. 'There's never any *real* conversation. Just a lot of aimless people wandering aimlessly about, saying fatuous things.' It was rather what he thought himself, but he felt it incumbent on him to protest if only for Celia West's sake.

'It isn't as bad as all that, surely? I've met some quite interesting people.'

'If by that you mean Celia's arty friends – amongst which I have the honour to count myself – then I suppose that's why we're invited,' Iris Barnes said. 'To add spice to an otherwise undistinguished crowd.'

'Well, speaking as someone who's not in the least distinguished . . .' he began, but she cut across him. 'Oh *you*! You're not like all the rest. I could tell that the minute I saw you.'

'Is it as obvious as all that?' he said wryly. She really was a forthright young woman. Nor did she seem embarrassed by her gaffe. 'What? Oh, that. No, it's not obvious at all.' She must have studied him for a moment, for she added: 'Your eyes look quite normal, in fact. What was it – mustard gas?'

'Shrapnel,' he said. 'Damaged the optic nerve, apparently.'

'Bad luck. I don't remember much about the war,' she said. 'I was still at school. Lots of the girls were in mourning, for brothers, or fathers, you know. They used to read out the names in Assembly. *Pro patria mori*, and all that . . . On Armistice Day, they gave us a half-holiday.'

'That was decent of them.'

'You really aren't a bit like Celia's other friends,' said Iris Barnes. 'Men friends, I mean. I suppose you're in love with her,' she added in an offhanded tone. 'Oh, don't look like that! Most men of my acquaintance are. I can't see it myself. Not that she isn't attractive, of course, but there are lots of attractive women. Celia has men blowing their brains out for her . . . I say, have I said something wrong?'

She couldn't have known, Rowlands thought. It would just have been a half-remembered story she'd read in the papers. He forced a smile. 'I'd rather talk about something else, if you don't mind. Tell me about being a film critic. It sounds like an interesting job.'

'It has its moments.' The music, which had come to an end, now started up again. 'I say, would you care to dance? I rather like this one.'

'I'd be delighted.' And so, to the jaunty rhythms of 'Don't Keep Me in the Dark', Rowlands heard all about Miss Barnes's admirably independent life, sharing a bachelor flat in Maida Vale with a fellow journalist – 'Leonora Prynne. She writes a column for the *Mail*. Household Hints, you know . . .' and reviewing for *The Spectator* three times a week. This week's offerings were mixed: Pola Negri in *Loves of an Actress* – 'which really tells you all you need to know,' said Miss Barnes witheringly. Patsy Ruth Miller in *Hot Heels* – 'sometimes I despair of the film industry. I mean, do we really need *another* film about dancers in a vaudeville show?' Emil Jannings in *The Patriot* elicited her approval, however. 'He's a marvellous actor. The way he conveys emotion through look and gesture alone is quite sublime. I don't suppose you've seen the film, have you?'

'No.'

'Of course not. Stupid of me.'

'My wife likes a good musical,' he said quickly. 'We saw *The Singing Fool* a few weeks ago.' But he never got to tell her about *The Singing Fool*, because at that moment there came a commotion from the next room. A woman's voice, screaming.

With a murmured apology to his dancing partner, Rowlands moved swiftly towards the sound, pushing his way through the crowd of revellers – some of whom were still dancing while others were arrested in the act of dancing. In his haste, he was less careful than usual about avoiding collisions, finding himself more than once in unwelcome contact with some portly, dinner-jacketed male, or with the naked, perfumed back of a female in a satin evening gown. Once he trod, heavily, on someone's foot. 'Watch where you're going, can't you?' said the owner of the foot, indignantly. At last he reached the double doors connecting the room where the dancing was going on with the other one. Here, a row was in full swing. 'You swine! I suppose you think that's funny!' screamed the Countess, for it was she. 'Laughing at me! I'll teach you to laugh at me!'

'But dash it all,' said another voice – Dickie Fairfax's. 'All I *said* was hearts were trumps. It's up to me to choose, you know, because we're playing Abundance.' But this only made things worse.

'There you go again!' shrieked Natalia Rostropovna.

'Taunting me, with your talk of hearts and trumps.' So that was it, thought Rowlands. For those who didn't like dancing, card tables had been set up. Here, Bridge – or in this instance, Solo Whist – was being played. 'I think there's been a misunderstanding,' he said. 'I'm sure Mr Fairfax didn't mean any harm by what he said.'

Natalia Rostropovna drew a long, shuddering breath. '*You*,' she said. 'I might have known *you* would be at the bottom of this.'

'I'm afraid you've got the wrong idea.'

'*Spying* on me,' she said, with peculiar venom. 'Trying to catch me out. Oh, don't think I don't know *your* game!'

'Countess, I assure you . . .' he began, when there was another intervention.

'Natalia, darling, *do* be quiet, there's a dear,' said Celia West, appearing, to Rowlands' immense relief, from the next room. 'You're upsetting my guests.'

'Celia, this man has threatened me.'

'Oh, I *say*!' This was Dickie Fairfax. 'I mean, far be it from me to question a lady's word, but . . .'

'Be quiet, Dickie.'

'If you say so, old thing,' he said humbly.

'Now then – what's it all about?' said Lady Celia to her friend. 'You said he threatened you. That's a pretty strong word.'

'I was passing by this table,' replied Natalia Rostropovna, in tones of offended dignity, 'on my way to fetch my shawl. I was feeling the cold a little, you understand. Your English houses,' she observed tartly, 'are not warm. Suddenly this . . . this *wretch* calls out, "Hearts are trumps. Consider yourself dead. You don't stand a chance."'

'I was talking to Bunny,' put in Fairfax.

'He was, too,' said that gentleman. 'I'd taken so much money off him in the last game, that he wanted his revenge, that's all.'

'I do hope,' said Lady Celia, distinctly, 'that you're not using my house as a gaming parlour.'

'Oh, not a bit of it, old thing. We were only playing for ha'pence, you know – weren't we, chaps?' There was a general murmur of agreement from those around the table.

'Good,' said Celia West. 'Because Mr Rowlands here is very good friends with Chief Inspector Douglas, of Scotland Yard.'

'*Spying* on me,' muttered the Countess, bitterly.

'Natalia, why don't you go and lie down for a little while?' said her friend, in a tone in which solicitude and firmness were equally mixed. 'You're overwrought. Please say to the Chief Inspector,' she went on, now addressing Rowlands, 'that I appreciate his keeping an eye on the premises.' Rowlands must have looked perplexed, for she said: 'Oh, yes. There's been a man watching the house all evening. Wearing plain clothes, but I suppose that helps him to blend in better. He's out there this very minute – or he was when I last looked. He was here yesterday, too. I do think these poor policemen earn their money, don't you?' she said.

Douglas, when this remark was relayed to him, seemed puzzled. 'But there *wasn't* a man there tonight – I told him he could go early since you'd be on the premises. And in any case, our man's a uniformed officer.'

'Odd,' said Rowlands.

'Very. Although we *have* had a man keeping an eye these past forty-eight hours, as she says. Wouldn't do to find ourselves with another corpse, on top of the others,' he added. 'Especially not one of the aristocratic Russian variety.'

'I see that,' said Rowlands. He was sitting in the Chief Inspector's office, at Scotland Yard. It was after one; he'd heard Big Ben strike the hour as the taxi taking him to Charing Cross sped along Whitehall. He'd missed the last train, of course; there was nothing for it but to find a convenient bench, on which to wait for the milk train. Passing Horse Guards Parade, he came to a decision. 'You can let me out here,' he said to the driver. Too late, it occurred to him, as he stated his name and purpose to the officer at the desk, that he might, after all, be disappointed. It *was* late; surely even Douglas had a home to go to? But the Chief Inspector, it turned out, kept hours every bit as unsociable as his own. Not that Rowlands was in the habit of wandering about late at night when he was at home. There, the fatigue resulting from the hard, physical labour of running a smallholding was usually enough to overcome his chronic insomnia. It was a common complaint amongst the blind, he knew. With darkness one's waking condition, it was sometimes hard to change from that state to one of unconsciousness, especially when – as now – one's mind was racing with all that had happened in the past few hours. Douglas, in any case, seemed unsurprised to see him. 'Ah, Mr Rowlands! I was hoping you might drop by,' was all he said. 'Care for a cup of tea?'

'That'd be grand.'

'Better than champagne, eh?' said the policeman when the tea had been brought.

'Much better,' said Rowlands.

'So tell me,' said Douglas, blowing on the surface of his tea to cool it, 'what it is you have to tell. I gather you *do* have something to tell?'

'Yes.'

'Well, let's hear it, man,' said the Chief Inspector. Then he said nothing more until Rowlands had finished speaking. Even though his account of the evening's events was as concise as he could make it, it still took him upwards of ten minutes. At the end of this, there came a long pause. 'So what do you make of it?' Douglas said at last. 'That thing she said.' Rowlands knew it was the Countess he meant.

'It rather sounds,' he replied, 'as if she knows something.'

'Doesn't it just, by God?' Having finished his tea, the

Chief Inspector now lit his pipe. 'Time I had her in for questioning.'

'You can't do that,' said Rowlands, perhaps rashly.

'And why not?' Douglas sounded genuinely puzzled.

'Because the information was given in confidence,' said Rowlands. 'I hardly think we can use it.'

'Don't you, now?' This time, there was an edge of sarcasm in the other man's voice. 'It seems to me, Mr Rowlands, that you're rather quick to tell the police their business.' Rowlands did not attempt to deny this. 'Well,' said Douglas after a moment, 'I'll leave things as they are for now. The fact is, we've more than enough to be getting on with as it is. We've managed to track down Lintott.'

'Oh! The husband.'

'As you say, the husband. Not that he's been a bit of use to us. Living in Leeds for the past three months, the blighter. Says he hasn't seen his wife since last October. We're checking his story, of course, but it looks as if he's out of the picture.'

'Wasn't there a child?'

'What?' The Chief Inspector rustled his notes. 'I believe you're right. Yes, here we are. A son. Aged six. Lives with his grandmother.' Six. The same age as Anne, thought Rowlands. 'Poor little mite,' he said.

'Then there's the matter of Miss Violet Smith,' said the policeman.

'I went to see her.'

'So I gather,' said Douglas, with heavy irony. 'I assume

you were getting around to telling me of that visit?'

'Of course.'

'That's good,' said the Chief Inspector. 'Although, as it turns out, you needn't bother. She's been to see me herself.'

'Oh?'

'Aye. Apparently, she'd remembered that Winnie Calder had a meeting with a man who wanted her to model for him, two days before she was killed. Said she hadn't realised it might be important until she'd talked to you.'

'Ah,' said Rowlands.

'Ah, indeed,' said the Chief Inspector. 'It seems to me you've rather a way with women, Mr Rowlands. First Miss Smith, and then Lady Celia West – pouring out their hearts to you. Perhaps,' said Douglas, 'I should get *you* to talk to the Countess.'

'She doesn't like me.'

'Yes, so you've said. Strange, that,' said Douglas. 'Still, it sounds as if you'll have your work cut out for you next week.' Rowlands' expression must have been perplexed, for the other laughed. 'Why, man, having your portrait painted's what I mean. Not to mention keeping an eye – if that's the right expression – on Mr Percy Loveless, RA. Funny, that,' he went on, evidently warming to his theme: 'To think that *you'll* be studying *him*, at exactly the same time that *he'll* be studying you.'

'Yes, I suppose it does have its funny side.'

A hush had descended on the building, which in

daylight hours reverberated to the sound of typewriters and the brisk to-ing and fro-ing of people; their voices, too. Now, it was silent. A great echoing box, Rowlands thought. Sitting there, on his hard chair, in a room that smelt of pipe smoke and dust-covered files, he felt as if the two of them – he and Douglas – must be the only ones awake. He knew it wasn't the case, of course – there'd always be someone on duty, no matter how late it was. Criminals, like insomniacs, tending to keep odd hours. And yet it was hard to shake off the feeling of emptiness, engendered by the profound silence. It was as if the room, and everything around it, had disappeared. He himself had disappeared. *He* was an absence, merely – a thing of 'darkness, death; things which are not . . .'

'Come again?' He must have spoken aloud.

'Nothing,' he said. The Chief Inspector got to his feet, yawning hugely, and scraping his chair on the floorboards. At once the room, and its inhabitants, came back into focus. 'I reckon we've done all we can do tonight,' he said. 'What do you say to a bite of breakfast? I know a little place not five minutes from here.'

'Sounds good to me.'

'That is,' said the other drily, 'if a *gentleman* attired as you are' – he meant the evening dress, Rowlands supposed – 'isn't too grand for the Cosy Corner café.'

Chapter Twelve

Over eggs and bacon, washed down with a cup of bitter black coffee, Rowlands felt his spirits revive. His companion, too, seemed similarly restored. As much as the food, it was the cheerful atmosphere of the place which had brought this about, Rowlands thought. It was hard to remain blue when you were surrounded by people eating and talking. Most of these were taxi drivers, to judge from their conversation: 'So I says to him, I says, "*You* might think it's quicker to go down Regent Street, but I'm here to tell you Shaftesbury Avenue's the quicker way . . ."' There was a strong aroma of cigarette smoke, coffee and frying bacon. After a few minutes, Douglas pushed his plate away with a contented sigh, and reached for his pipe. 'Don't mind, do you?' he said. Rowlands shook his head. 'My Lizzie always used to complain that it spoilt the taste of the food,' said the policeman. 'Used to make me go outside, to smoke on the front step.'

'My wife doesn't like me smoking in the house, either.'

'It's ten years to the day that I lost her,' said Douglas.

'I'm sorry.'

'Our boy, too,' the other man said. He finished filling the pipe, then lit it. 'It was the influenza. She nursed our Davy when he went down with it; then it took her, a week after it took him.' Rowlands was silent. There was nothing to be said. After a moment, Douglas said, in a different tone, 'I'm interested in what you've told me about Maurice Le Fevre. I've heard of the man, of course – who hasn't? But as far as I know, we've nothing on record against him. Which isn't to say,' he added, 'that there's nothing against him.'

'No,' said Rowlands. 'But I'm only repeating what Lady Celia told me of his . . . activities. She . . .' He hesitated. 'She doesn't like the man.'

'Hardly surprising, if he's the one responsible for getting young Johnny Edgecombe into bad company,' said Douglas, his pipe now drawing nicely. 'Not that he needs much encouragement in that respect! Edgecombe Hall's already mortgaged up to the hilt. From what I hear, it won't be long before he'll have to sell it if he keeps on the way he is.'

'Oh?' said Rowlands.

'Gambling,' was the reply. 'Oh, yes. I think you'll find our handsome Lord Edgecombe is rather addicted to games of chance.'

The train was twenty minutes late, because of the snow, but he was still home by half past six. Edith was already up, seeing to Joan. 'Good morning,' she said. 'Or is it still night with you? You look as if you could do with a few hours' sleep.'

'You're not far wrong,' he said, with a groan, stripping off his jacket and the shirt he'd put on clean twelve hours before, and which now reeked of sweat and cigarettes. But he didn't feel like sleep – the walk home from the station had done more than a little to revive him. Tramping across the snowy fields, he'd drawn great breaths of the icy air, which had tasted clean – not like the petroleum-scented air of the city. It felt good to be back in his own home, amongst those he loved. A world away from the overheated drawing rooms of the smart set.

When he'd washed and shaved and put on clean clothes, he joined his wife downstairs in the kitchen where she was giving the baby her breakfast. 'Do you want anything?' said Edith.

'Thing!' shouted Joan. She had taken to repeating words that took her fancy.

'A cup of tea would be nice,' he said.

'Tea! Tea!'

'It's already made,' said his wife. She poured it, then

set the cup in front of him. 'I put two sugars in. You look as if you need it.' Having settled Joan down in her highchair with a piece of toast, Edith sat down at the table, opposite him. 'Well,' she said. 'Am I going to hear about this wonderful party?'

'Party!'

'It wasn't all that wonderful.'

'Was the murderer there?' This wasn't a word with which Joan was familiar, but she did her best. 'Murda, murda, murda,' she muttered darkly.

'I can't really say.' He sipped his tea. 'There were certainly a number of possible candidates there. Loveless, for one.'

'Loveless?'

'He's an artist.'

'Ah,' she said. 'Go on.'

She listened without further interruption until he got to the part about the quarrel, and Natalia Rostropovna's uncalled for attack on Dickie Fairfax after he'd said that hearts were trumps. 'Just a minute,' she said. 'That reminds me of something. Let me see . . . Now, where did I put it?' She rummaged around in the pile of newspapers they kept by the back door in readiness for lighting the stove. 'Ah! Here we are! I knew I had it somewhere. Now, what do you make of this?' She unfolded the paper with a little shake, and read aloud: '"*N. – Hearts are Trumps in 1929. The Queen must die. The winner, Jack, remains to play the game.*" It was in the Personal column two days ago. It caught my eye, because of the playing cards business, and so I . . . Oh!' she cried as Rowlands, jumping up out of his chair, caught her in his arms and kissed her. 'You darling,' he said.

'What have I done to deserve this?'

'Don't you see?' he said. 'You've only managed to establish a definite link between the Countess and the murderer.'

'Murda, murda, murda,' chanted Joan.

'No wonder she was so frightened when Fairfax made his – presumably quite innocent – remark about hearts being trumps. She'd already seen something very like it in the paper. She must have jumped out of her skin. Oh, you're so *clever*,' he cried, kissing her again. The door opened and his two elder daughters came rushing in – Anne in the lead as usual. 'Daddy! Daddy! Why were you laughing, Daddy?' she demanded. He scooped her up, and planted a kiss on her curly head. 'I was just telling your mother that she's a fine detective.'

'I'd like to be a detective, when I grow up,' said Margaret. His serious child. 'Do they let girls be policemen, Daddy?'

'They do. Very useful they are, too. I see no reason,' he said, reaching out to include her in his embrace, 'why you shouldn't end up as Chief Constable, one of these days.'

'Kiss for Joan,' said his youngest child, never one to be left out.

'And here it is,' he said, suiting the action to the word. 'Now,' he went on, when this affectionate interlude was at an end. 'Who wants to build a snowman?'

At nine o'clock on Monday morning, he presented himself at the address Loveless had given him, in Ossington Street. It was hardly the most fashionable part of London, he thought – didn't most artists live in Chelsea? This was practically Notting Hill. Still, it wasn't far to walk from the Underground station, for which he was glad if only because of the filthy condition of the streets, in which last night's snow, trampled into slush by thousands of passing feet, didn't hold out much hope for the preservation of his best suit. There'd been an argument with Edith about this. He'd wanted to wear his everyday suit, because hadn't Loveless as good as told him not to be too dressy? But she wouldn't hear of it. 'What! The very first time you go to have your portrait painted' – she spoke as if there would be others – 'you turn up looking like a tramp.'

'I don't look like a tramp. This was a perfectly good suit when it was new.'

'Well, it isn't new now. What's wrong with your blue suit?'

'Edith, the man particularly said I wasn't to be too smart.'

'He said not to wear evening dress. That doesn't mean looking shabby.' And so it went round and round, as their quarrels always did. In the end, he wore the blue suit to please her, and because he suspected, from the little he knew of the ways of artists, that it wouldn't matter a hoot.

Now he stood at the top of a flight of six steps leading up to the front door of Number 33. He rang the bell and waited, shivering a little in the icy wind that funnelled down the street between the ranks of tall, white houses on the one side, and two-storey brick cottages on the other – a memory of visiting a cousin of his mother's years ago, in Moscow Road, supplied these details. A few minutes passed. Surely it was Monday morning Loveless had said? This was the right house – the address was on the card Loveless had given him. So where on earth *was* he? He pressed the bell again; the sound could be heard echoing hollowly inside the house, but no sound of approaching footsteps followed. Suddenly, from somewhere below the level of the pavement, came a loud hissing: '*Shh*! No need to disturb the whole house!' said a voice he recognised as the artist's. 'It's this way. Take care. The steps are a bit slippery.'

Steadying himself on the railings – for it was indeed slippery – Rowlands descended again to street level, and from thence, via another flight of steps, to a basement area where Loveless awaited him. 'I must say, you're nice and early,' remarked the artist, with grudging approval. 'Come in. The studio's at the back. I live in this bit,' he added superfluously as a smell of stale food, dust and infrequently washed sheets announced a domestic area. 'You can leave your coat in here. Lavatory's through there, if you want to . . .'

'No, that's all right.' Having divested himself of his overcoat, as Loveless had suggested, Rowlands now wished he'd kept it on. It was far from warm.

'And this is where I work,' said Loveless – again, unnecessarily as far as Rowlands was concerned, for the smell of linseed oil, turpentine and oil paint was overpowering. 'Sit down, sit down,' said the artist. 'No – not there! That picture's still wet,' he explained, too late since a smear of paint now adhered to the sleeve of Rowlands' jacket. 'Over there. Mind the table!' Again, a warning issued a fraction later than it should have been. The table in question, Rowlands found, in his brief skirmish with it, was laden with tubes of paint, tins of raw pigment, jars of thinner, brushes and other paraphernalia of the artist's trade. 'You almost had that over,' said Loveless. 'Good thing you didn't. It would have made a hell of a mess. You'll find a chair by the window. Yes, there. In the light. There isn't much of it today, but we'll manage, I think. I suppose,' he added, 'you'd like some tea?'

'If it's not too much trouble.'

'No trouble at all. I've a gas ring in here. Quite convenient, you see . . .' Throwing out the odd remark – 'Trains all right, I take it?'– Loveless fiddled about for a few minutes boiling water (in a pan; the kettle had a hole in it, he said) and making what turned out to be a pot of very weak tea. Hot water with a few leaves in it, thought Rowlands, gingerly sipping his from a chipped cup. It struck him, as he listened to the man rambling nervously on, that this was a very different Loveless from the blustering showman of Lady Celia's party. He'd suspected even then that the artist's manner had been all an act – hadn't he himself admitted as much? Only when the undrinkable tea had been drunk, and they got down to business, as Loveless put it, was there a return to his old, confident self. 'We'll start with a couple of quick studies,' he said. 'No, just as you are is fine. I don't believe in too much posing. I won't, in any case, know how I'm going to *use* you until I've drawn you, if you follow me?'

'I think so.'

'Good,' said Loveless, from the far side of the room. There followed sounds of an easel being adjusted, and of paper being torn to size. 'As I believe I said to you when we met, you've a fine head of the Aryan type, if that means anything to you. Good sharp planes. A good large nose, too, of the aquiline sort. I like a good nose – it gives me a point of reference, you understand.'

Rowlands nodded, although in truth it was all so much artists' shop to him. He knew the planes of his face well enough – he had to shave them every morning. As for his nose. . . 'Hold still!' shouted Loveless. 'That's it. Keep looking towards the left. I'll tell you when you can move.' There came the scratching sound of charcoal moving energetically across a sheet of paper. After this, there was no more conversation. Rowlands took advantage of the silence – made more intense, somehow, by the minute sounds which interrupted it – charcoal scratching; a tap dripping – to take stock of his surroundings. The room, he guessed, was not a large one. It would have been made smaller still by the amount of stuff with which it was cluttered. In addition to the canvases stacked along the wall, there was the table containing materials into which he'd blundered, a folding screen which stood beside it, and which he'd also almost succeeded in knocking over, several chairs, and – doubtless – other items he couldn't see. Quite a ramshackle affair, and not at all the popular conception of an artist's atelier. It was queer, he thought, the places you ended up.

'Don't smile!'

Rowlands adjusted his expression accordingly. The scratching continued. He let his thoughts drift. Where was it all going? he wondered. A blind artist. A playing card. A woman weeping. *My God, what have I done?* It had to mean something, and yet he could make no sense of it. *The Queen must die. The winner, Jack, remains to play the game . . .* 'Don't frown,' said Loveless. 'Sorry.' It occurred to Rowlands that he wasn't getting very far with what he'd come here to do – which was to pry into Loveless's affairs. Specifically, those to do with the Countess Rostropovna. Was it more than a coincidence that they'd been at the same party? 'Find out as much as you can about him,' Douglas had said as they'd parted in the early hours of Sunday morning. 'Who his friends are. Where he goes. You might even,' he'd added casually, 'ascertain where he was on the nights of the 31st of last month and January 3rd.' Fat chance of *that*, thought Rowlands, if they were to sit in silence for the whole session. But just then Loveless called out, 'That's it for now. You can relax. Care for a cigarette?'

'Thanks,' said Rowlands, flexing neck and shoulder muscles stiff from prolonged immobility. Although it *had* only been a fifteen-minute pose, Loveless pointed out. 'You wait till you've been sitting for me for two hours,' he guffawed. 'You'll feel it then!' He returned to his easel a moment, evidently to consider what he'd done so far, for he gave a satisfied grunt. 'Not bad, not bad at all,' he said. 'I think I've begun to *get* you.'

'I wish I could see it.'

'Yes, it's a pity you can't,' replied the other. 'You're not familiar with my work, I think you said?'

'Unfortunately not.'

'A great pity. I had quite a big show in the autumn of 1914, as a matter of fact – just before I joined up. At the Doré galleries. I don't suppose you saw it?'

'No.' He'd have been at Aldershot, waiting to be sent to France. Although he'd been once or twice to the National Gallery while he was on leave. He'd liked the Turners. And Constable. He couldn't remember having seen any paintings by modern artists, though.

'Of course, my work's moved on a bit since then,' Loveless was saying. '*Then* it was all to do with Vorticism, and Futurism, and all the other *isms* that were knocking about at the time. A necessary breaking with the moribund traditions of the past. Pater, and Whistler, and all the rest of that sickly *fin-de-siècle* stuff. *Now*, I'm more interested in trying to capture the essential *form*. The carapace, if you like. Art should be about *surface*. The dead shell, not the living, pulsating flesh. Putrefying flesh, too. I saw enough of that on the Western Front – as I expect you did, too. No. Art should transcend the merely human. It should be hard, cold, *dead*. Yes! The best art has always been about death.' It wasn't easy, Rowlands found, to interrupt Loveless in full flow. But he made an effort: 'I imagine,' he said, 'that you've painted a good many people?'

'A few. I've had no choice,' replied Loveless. 'It was either that or starve. Unlike some of my fellow *artists*' – he pronounced the word as if it had a foul taste – 'I don't enjoy the benefit of a private income.'

'You did a portrait of Lady Celia, recently, I gather?' Rowlands persisted.

'Yes. Not a bad effort,' was the reply. 'She paid over the odds for it, of course – or rather, that boyfriend of hers did. He can afford it,' said Loveless bitterly.

'And the Countess Rostropovna?' said Rowlands. 'Have you painted her, too?'

'She doesn't have any money,' said the artist. 'So it'd hardly be worth my while. Although she *is* a lovely piece. A true Slavic blonde. Cheekbones you could cut yourself on, and those cold grey-blue Russian eyes. Why do you ask, anyway?' he added suspiciously. 'Do you fancy her yourself?'

'I'm a married man.'

'So am I,' said the other. 'I don't see what difference it

makes. Women!' he exclaimed, with some heat. '*They're* the enemies of Art, if you want my opinion. Always wanting one to settle down with them. Having babies when one least expects it. It's *death* to the creative spirit.'

'I can see that it might be,' said Rowlands. 'Is the Countess married, do you know?'

'All these questions about the Countess!' said Loveless. 'I shall begin to think you're in love with her.' He yawned. 'Either that, or you're in the pay of the People's Commissariat. Sent to check up on renegade White Russians.' Rowlands' heart gave a jump. He forced a smile. 'I don't think I'd make a very good spy,' he said.

'Why not? You've got ears, haven't you? Right,' said Loveless, suddenly brisk. 'If you've finished your gasper, we'll get back to work.'

At around four o'clock, Loveless put down his brushes, yawned, stretched, and said: 'I think we're about done for the day.' This was welcome news to Rowlands, who, for the past hour, had been wondering if the sensation of red-hot pins and needles he was feeling in his left shoulder blade was merely a consequence of his having been frozen in the same attitude for the past three hours, or if it meant something more sinister. Now he let himself relax, with a grunt of relief. 'Extraordinary, how tiring sitting still can be,' he said.

'Yes,' said the artist indifferently. He'd lit a cigarette, and was now, Rowlands guessed, from his silence, engaged in studying the painting on which he had been working.

'It'll do,' he said after a moment, confirming this suspicion. 'Not a bad start, although it'll take a bit more work before it's right. I take it you can come next week?'

'Of course.' Although privately Rowlands wondered just how much more of his time he could commit to what seemed, to say the least, a rather desultory form of investigation. Not that he hadn't found out quite a lot, in the course of the past five hours. He now knew a great deal more than he had before about Modern Art – or Loveless's opinion of it. He knew which painters Loveless liked – Goya, Cézanne, 'bits of Picasso' – and which he disliked: Burne-Jones, for his 'neurasthenic sex-dolls'; Whistler for his 'pastel-coloured fogs'; Duncan Grant for just about everything: 'Gaudier-Brzeska had more talent in his little finger than Grant and all his tribe of Bloomsbury dilettantes can muster in their entire bodies,' he said, during one such outburst. 'And *he* was blown to bits at Neuville while *they* sat out the war in comfort.'

In addition to this useful augmentation of his artistic knowledge, Rowlands learnt a few other things. That Loveless, although given to bombast and fond of provocation, was actually quite reserved and shy. That his numerous affairs with women were a way of evading deeper commitment. He was, Rowlands guessed, rather lonely. As to his movements on the night of the 31st December, he'd been only too happy to tell Rowlands about *those*. 'New Year's Eve? I was at a party at the Chelsea Arts Club,' he said. 'Went home with the most marvellous girl. Jessie Dismorr. I don't suppose you've met her? Artist's model. Married, unfortunately. A lovely piece.'

January 3rd's movements had been harder to pin down if only because there was no way of framing the question that would not arouse suspicion, Rowlands thought. 'Where were you on the night of last Thursday fortnight?' was all too reminiscent of the Police Court. Rowlands had tried a more subtle approach. 'Have you always had a studio here?' he began. They'd broken for lunch, at this point. Bread and cheese, washed down with a bottle of beer.

'What? Oh no – I've only had this place for eighteen months. Had to do a moonlight flit from the last one. Adam and Eve Mews. It's off Kensington High Street. I owed the landlord rather a lot of rent, so that was that.' Loveless took a meditative bite of his sandwich. 'Before that I was in Fitzroy Street . . . No, that was after. It must have been Earl's Court. Horrible place. It stank of boiled cabbage.'

'But you've always been in this part of London?' Rowlands persisted. 'Never lived in the East End? Whitechapel, or . . . or Shoreditch?'

'Shoreditch? No,' was the reply, through another mouthful of sandwich. 'Can't imagine why I'd want to go there.'

'I suppose it might be cheaper,' ventured Rowlands.

'Yes, but you'd be cut off from everything. The West End galleries. The clients. I don't imagine,' added

Loveless slyly, 'that the Countess Rostropovna would be very pleased at having to trek all the way to the East End to have her portrait painted.' With which Rowlands had to be content. Damn it all, he thought angrily as – their meagre luncheon having been consumed – he took his place on the model's throne once more. If Douglas wants to know where the man was on the night of the 3rd, he can ruddy well ask him himself.

'You're scowling,' said the voice from behind the easel. 'Do try not to pull faces while I'm painting you – there's a good chap.'

After that, both were silent for a while – the one absorbed in his thoughts, though trying his best not to scowl, the other in his work. Now Loveless stood cleaning his brushes at the sink as Rowlands prepared to take his leave. 'Twenty-five shillings all right?' said the artist, in an embarrassed tone.

'Oh. Rather. Thanks,' replied Rowlands, putting on his coat. He took the money – two ten shilling notes and two half-crowns – and put it in his pocket, recalling what Violet Smith had said about her flatmate's excitement at the prospect of just such wages. 'Five shillings an hour!' He gave an involuntary shiver. 'Hope you've not caught cold,' said Loveless. 'I try to keep the place as warm as possible, but coals eat money.'

'I'm fine,' said Rowlands. 'Well, good night.'

'Yes, it *is* like night out there, although it's not half past four,' Loveless said, opening the door. 'See you next week. Same time if you can make it.'

'I'll be there.' The two men shook hands. Loveless's clasp was firm and dry; his hands smelt of the turpentine with which he had cleaned them. 'Beautiful hands', Celia West had said. Was it possible that these same hands could have grasped a woman around the throat and squeezed the life out of her? Rowlands very much hoped not. To his surprise, he found that he was beginning to like Loveless.

Chapter Thirteen

As he ascended once more to street level, an icy blast caught him full in the face. His eyes began to stream. Strange that they could still weep, though near useless to him in other respects, he thought. He fumbled in the pocket of his overcoat for a handkerchief. At that moment, a car drew up alongside him. A window was rolled down. A voice said, 'Get in.' Accustomed as he now was to such unscheduled appearances by the Chief Inspector, he made no reply, but did as he was ordered. 'You were a long time,' said Douglas when he had given an instruction to the driver, as a result of which the vehicle made a U-turn, and headed back towards the Bayswater Road. 'Another five minutes, and I'd have come in to haul you out.'

'Which would rather have defeated the object of the exercise,' said Rowlands.

'What? Oh, I see what you mean,' grunted the policeman. It seemed to Rowlands that the Chief Inspector had something on his mind; well, he would learn what it was soon enough, he thought. Although it wasn't until some minutes later, with the car now moving at quite a pace along the broad highway that ran beside Hyde Park, that Douglas broke the silence. 'You were right,' he said. 'He *was* playing by the rules – it's just that we didn't know it.'

'Oh?'

'His next murder was "South", after all,' said Douglas. 'We've just been informed by the local police.'

'When did you hear?'

'The call from the Lewisham station came through an hour ago. A group of lads had stumbled across a body, in Telegraph Hill Park. That's New Cross.'

'I know.'

'They thought it was a snowman, at first. Covered, you see,' said the Chief Inspector, in a voice that sounded strangely unlike him. 'It seems,' he went on, in the same choked voice, 'as if it had been there for several days. What with the snow, you see . . .' The Chief Inspector broke off.

After a moment, he said: 'Same method as before. Strangulation.'

'And the playing card?' asked Rowlands. 'In her handbag,' said Douglas. 'No, don't go down Oxford

Street. It'll be murder at this time of day,' he added in a louder voice to the driver. 'Cut along Park Lane, then Grosvenor Place, and Vauxhall Bridge Road.'

'Sir.'

'I've told the Inspector who's dealing with the case – Graves; a good man – to leave the body where it was found,' said Douglas. 'I just hope his chaps haven't destroyed too much of the evidence, trampling over the scene,' he added glumly. 'Of course, it'll be dark by the time we get there. Not that it'll make much difference to you, I fancy?'

'None at all,' said Rowlands.

'So tell me,' went on his companion idly as they rounded Hyde Park Corner and entered the stream of traffic that flowed past Marble Arch. 'How did you get on with our friend, Mr Loveless, today?' He listened in silence as Rowlands gave him the upshot of his meeting with the artist. 'But I don't think,' he said, concluding this account, 'that he's our man. He's got an alibi for New Year's Eve, for a start . . .'

'We'll need to check that.'

'. . . and, in any case, Chief Inspector, he doesn't strike me as the type to go in for this sort of thing.'

'What? Murder, you mean?' Douglas laughed. 'Believe me, when you've met as many murderers as I have, you come to realise that there's no such thing as the murdering *type*. Any man's capable of murder, given the right circumstances.'

'I think Mr Loveless is more interested in painting women than killing them,' said Rowlands.

'And not just *painting* them, either, from what I've heard,' was the rejoinder. 'The fact remains, we're looking for an artist – or someone with a grudge against artist's models, at the very least. Someone who might have sent that letter to the Countess.'

'Yes, I know. But just because a man talks about art and death a lot doesn't mean . . .'

'Oh, he talks about death, too, does he?' said the policeman. 'What exactly does he say?'

'Nothing with any bearing on the case,' replied Rowlands hastily. 'Just a lot of theoretical stuff. I'm afraid it was all rather above my head.'

In front of Victoria Station the traffic was at a standstill. 'Tram's broken down up ahead,' reported the driver, with what seemed a degree of satisfaction.

'Well, cut through Pimlico. Good God, man, do I have to drive the car myself? At this rate,' Douglas muttered, 'the Police Surgeon will have packed up and gone home, and who could blame him?' Traffic accidents notwithstanding, they were at the scene by a quarter past five. They parked in a side street off Pepys Road. 'It's a bit of a climb,' said Douglas as they crossed the wide street towards the park. 'Icy underfoot, too. Do you want to take my arm?'

'Thanks. I'll manage.' Rowlands was in any case familiar with the lie of the land. When they'd lived in Honor Oak Park, he and Edith had sometimes brought the children here. They'd catch the tram to New Cross Gate, then walk up the hill to the park. There was a band that played on Sunday afternoons. He'd sit on a bench near the bandstand and listen for half an hour or so while Edith took the girls to buy ices. Classical pieces of the lighter variety were what the audience liked, and popular tunes, of the more sentimental kind. 'I'm Looking Over a Four Leaf Clover' and 'Bye Bye Blackbird' being particular favourites, he recalled. For him, these melodies would always evoke the smells of new-mown grass, and of tarmac, melting in the sun; the shouts of children playing Hide-and-Seek and King of the Castle, and the murmured endearments of young men to their Best Girls, from neighbouring benches.

Now, in the dead of winter, the park presented a very different aspect. There was no smell but the smell of cold; no sound but the crunch of snow under their feet, and the rattling cough of the young police constable sent to meet them. 'This way, sir,' he said. ''Spector Graves said as I was to show you. It's ub at the tob there, by the badstad,' he'd gone on to say, between coughs.

'If we'd known that, we could have parked a bit closer,' grumbled the Chief Inspector. Having been cooped up indoors all day, Rowlands was glad of the walk, however. Even with all this snow, it'd only take them five minutes, he thought. He checked his watch, feeling the small raised dots on the face that denoted the hours. Twenty past five. He wondered how long it was all going to take, he averted his mind from the thought of what *it* meant, and if he ought to telephone Edith to say he'd be late.

'Over here, sir.' The path up which they'd been

climbing, now levelled out. It was here, Rowlands remembered, that the bandstand stood, with a semicircle of benches across from it. On summer evenings when the band was playing, there'd be quite a crowd. Just now, it seemed no less crowded, but with policemen, he guessed, instead of music lovers.

'Herd of elephants couldn't have made more of a mess,' observed his companion wearily. 'Just look at it! If there ever *were* any decent footprints, they've been trampled into slush by these clodhopping oafs . . . Ah, Graves,' he went on, in what Rowlands recognised as his official voice. 'Good to see you. Filthy night for it, eh? Now, what have you got for me?' The two men went a little way off from where Rowlands was standing, and conferred in low voices. Towards the end of this exchange, Rowlands heard his own name mentioned. A moment later, he felt a touch on his arm. 'Mr Rowlands, come over this way, if you please. This is Inspector Graves.'

'Mr Rowlands.' The two men shook hands. 'Chief Inspector Douglas tells me you've been doing a bit of investigating for us?'

'Well . . .'

'I don't, as a rule, approve of members of the public interfering in police business,' said Graves. A South Londoner, Rowlands thought. He'd resent anyone outside his manor getting involved in what he'd consider to be an entirely local affair. That would include the Chief Inspector, who, being from Scotland, could hardly be expected to understand the ways of English criminals. 'However,' went on Graves, with evident reluctance, 'I gather you've got some special knowledge of the case.'

'Not really,' replied Rowlands. 'Unless you count a familiarity with braille playing cards as special.'

'Och, it's rather more than that!' interrupted Douglas impatiently. 'Through his contacts in what you might call the "blind world", Mr Rowlands has helped us to open up several very promising lines of enquiry.'

'Impressive,' was Inspector Graves' reply. 'Be that as it may, we still don't have a perpetrator. Just another body. Speaking of which, would you care to take a look, sir? The mortuary van's arrived, but they'll wait until I tell them.'

'Good man' said Douglas. 'Yes, I might as well take a look at her. Over here, Rowlands. She's on the bench, just under the tree.' Which cleared up a matter that had been puzzling Rowlands. She was seated, then. That explained why the boys who'd found her had mistaken her snow-covered form for a snowman. Once again, it was a relief not to be able to see what was there; although he could not stop his imagination supplying details not made explicit by the others' remarks.

'Hmm. Not a pretty sight,' said the Chief Inspector. 'Was she like this when she was found?'

'More or less,' replied Graves. 'Doctor had to clear some of the snow off her to examine her. But we left her in position, as you ordered.'

'Quite right. Not that it'll help us much. How long do

you reckon she'd been lying – or rather, *sitting* – here, when she was found?'

'Doctor reckons two to three days. That's why she's that funny colour. O'course, the cold doesn't help. Shame, really. Nice-looking girl like that.'

'Do we have a name yet?'

'Elsie Alsop. Works – or rather, *worked* – as a barmaid at the White Hart Hotel. One of my chaps is down there now, talking to the landlord.'

'Good. Any boyfriends?'

'We don't know any more just yet.'

All the while that the policemen were talking, Rowlands had been conscious of a mounting horror. It was the same feeling he'd had in Winnie Calder's rooms in Camden, and in the filthy little alley where Mary O'Reilly had met her end. A feeling that was more than just the natural outrage any decent man might feel at a young life's being wasted. This was visceral. A sick sensation he knew all too well from his army days. The creeping fear you felt as you heard the shells going over. The dread that, this time, it'd be your turn. The relief when it turned out not to be your turn, after all. Yes, that was it. It was a feeling of fear. It had been in that dreadful little room, and in the alley where the girl had died. It was here, now, in this frozen park. He could almost taste it. 'Cause of death?' said a voice. It was the Chief Inspector. 'Broken neck,' said another voice – the doctor's, Rowlands surmised. 'Done from behind, at a guess. Easy, when the victim's sitting down. Ah, good evening, Chief Inspector. I thought it was you.'

'Mr Williams. Sorry to drag you out on a night like this.'

'All in the line of duty, you know.' A Welshman, Rowlands thought. 'Nasty business. Then there's the matter of this playing card, you know . . .'

'Yes,' said Douglas. 'You've got it there, have you?'

'Yes.'

'Mr Rowlands, would you mind?'

Rowlands took the card from the doctor's outstretched hand. 'Jack of hearts,' he said, and handed it back. It all seemed a rather unnecessary piece of theatre. Couldn't they *see* for themselves what it was? Then it struck him that this was Douglas's way of establishing his bona fides with Inspector Graves. 'I think,' he ventured to say, 'that this means that the letter the Countess received two days ago was no idle threat.'

'My feeling exactly,' said the Chief Inspector. 'All right, Mr Williams, you can take her away now. Mr Rowlands has a theory that our man has been playing a little game with us,' he said to Graves as the three of them walked back toward the gate. 'That is to say, a game of cards. Solo, I think you said?' he added, addressing Rowlands.

'Yes.'

'You don't say?' said Inspector Graves.

'You sound a bit dubious, Charlie, said his colleague, 'but I can tell you, it's the best lead we've got. Three bodies in three different districts of London. North, East,

South. A fourth woman – in West London – receiving a death threat . . .'

'So what's it supposed to mean?' said Graves, with the air of someone humouring a lunatic.

'You're obviously not a card player,' replied Rowlands, 'or you'd see the significance of the pattern the Chief Inspector's just described. North, East, South, and West is the direction of the play, in a game of Whist. It's as if our murderer has turned London into a giant card table,' he added. 'So far he's been winning every trick. But with a little patience, we can still beat him, I feel.'

The car dropped him off at New Cross Gate Station; he'd get the train from there to London Bridge, then change for Charing Cross and his train back to Kent. 'Well, good night,' said the Chief Inspector. During the brief drive down the hill, there'd been no suggestion that Rowlands should accompany him to the White Hart Hotel where he and Inspector Graves were headed; nor had he – Rowlands – felt inclined to invite himself along. That was police work – the identifying, and interviewing, of suspects. He wasn't a policeman, as Graves had made a point of reminding him. What exactly he was, he wasn't entirely sure: an auxiliary, perhaps – although there were uglier words for it. One thing he *was* certain about, was that he was dead tired. A day spent sitting for Loveless, followed by that dreadful hour at the murder scene, had just about done him in. No, let Douglas and his cohorts do what they were paid to do, which was, slowly and painstakingly, to sift through the evidence that would eventually lead to the arrest and conviction of a killer. Perhaps, this time, he thought, there would be more to go on: *someone* who'd seen *something*. He supposed the Chief Inspector would let him know.

Huddled in a corner seat of an empty compartment, in a train that seemed to be jogging on forever, he thought over the events of the past few hours. The car appearing as if out of nowhere. *Get in*. The silent trudge through the snowbound park. He felt chilled to the bone. It was if the cold he'd experienced in those moments had penetrated to his very marrow. It seemed fanciful to suppose that it was the chill of death he felt: the utter stillness – the terrible *absence* – of the thing that had sat upon the bench. You couldn't call it a woman. It bore as much relation to the living being – the young woman that was Elsie Alsop – as the park in winter bore to its summer incarnation. One spoke of life, the other of all that was life's opposite. 'Absence, darkness, death, things which are not,' he muttered, shivering in his corner as the train ground slowly on.

Next morning, he woke with a scratchy throat and the feverish sensation that presaged a cold. He was *damned* if he'd be ill, he thought stubbornly. It was probably just the effect of a bad night. 'Just tea for me,' he said as Edith got up from the table where she'd been giving Joan her breakfast, to make him his usual eggs and bacon. 'I knew it!' she said severely. 'You shouldn't have stayed out so long last night. Now you've caught a chill. Let's hope it doesn't go to your chest.'

'All right, all right,' he said, holding up his hands in mock surrender; although he knew she had a point. His lungs had never been the same since that ghastly affair at Loos in '15 when gas from the canisters they'd launched against the Germans had blown back across the British lines. A case of being 'hoist by your own petard' if ever there was one, he supposed. Just then the tuneless whistling of the boy on his bicycle, followed by the flapping of the letterbox, told him that the paper had come. 'I'll get it,' he said. Returning with the folded slab of newsprint, he placed it in front of Edith. 'Eat your nice egg, Joanie,' she said, before responding to his mute request. Moving swiftly past the Births, Deaths and Marriages, and the columns of advertisements requiring the services of Cook-Generals, House Parlour Maids and Lady Typists, she found what she was looking for at last. 'Here we are. "*Woman Found Dead in Park.*" Do you want me to read it?'

'Please.'

'Only Mother and the girls'll be down in a minute.' And indeed, the children's voices could be heard at the top of the stairs. 'The blue one's mine!' – 'No, it isn't. Yours is the green one . . .'

'Just the salient points.'

'There's not much,' she said, summarising rapidly: '*Body of young woman found in Telegraph Hill Park, New Cross, on Monday night. Dead woman identified as Elsie Mabel Alsop, twenty, a barmaid, of 5, Kitto Road, SE14 . . .*'

'Any mention of the playing card aspect?'

'Let me see. Yes, here we are: "*Police suspect Miss Alsop may have been another victim of the so-called 'Playing Card Killer', but this is 'only one of a number of possibilities' said Inspector Charles Graves . . .*"' She broke off suddenly, as their two elder daughters, still arguing about hair ribbons, came clattering in, followed, at a more measured pace, by their grandmother. So, Graves had a better theory, did he? thought Rowlands. *That*, at any rate, was no surprise.

'Are you quite sure you're well enough to go out?' Edith said as, a few minutes later, he stood pulling on his gumboots by the kitchen door.

'There's a lot that needs doing,' he replied. 'I've still to clean out the sheds. They'll need to be properly sterilised if we're to restock in the spring.' She sighed. '*Are* we going to restock, do you think?' When he said nothing, she went on: 'I mean, it'll cost money to buy new stock – you know that as well as I do – and the only money you've earned this month is what you've got from the Chief Inspector.' He couldn't suppress a feeling of irritation. The last thing he felt like, with all that was going around in his head, was to have to face an inquisition on their future. And so he spoke more sharply than he meant to. 'What are you saying, Edith? Do you want us to give this up – is that it?'

'With things as they are . . .' – she meant money, or

their lack of it – 'I don't see what else we can do.'

'I thought you liked it here,' he said.

'I do. And it's wonderful for the children. But . . .'

'Let's talk about this later,' he said. He opened the door, letting in a cold blast of air. But his wife wasn't quite finished. 'I think you ought to go back to London,' she said. 'You know it's the only chance of your ever finding work.'

He spent the next couple of hours scrubbing out the large shed with Lysol, to rid it of the lingering stench of fox. It was hot, dirty work, and his shirt was soon sticking to his back with sweat. He worked on, nonetheless, determined to finish the job. It had to be done – and not just for the reason that he had given Edith. Because even if they decided not to carry on, the farm and its outbuildings would still have to be in a fit state to be put on the market. And so he toiled grimly on, sweeping up the damp and dirty straw from the floor of the hut, and washing down its walls and the perches where the hens had sat – all too exposed, as it turned out, to the marauding predator . . . *Such* a waste, he thought, reminded once more of that catastrophe. Even as he swept and scoured, he knew that, for him, the rural life had only ever been a stopgap. Edith was right: his future, such as it was, lay in London. 'I must need my head examining,' he murmured. To want to exchange all this – space, quiet, and clean air – for the crowded streets, the noise and stink of the city, seemed like utter perversity. And yet, during these past few weeks of his conscription as Douglas's aide-de-camp (if that was what he was), he'd never felt so alive – so *engaged* with what he was doing. 'Daddy?' came a small voice from outside the shed. He stuck his head out. 'What is it, Meg?'

'Granny says would you like a cup of tea?'

'That'd be nice. I say – don't come any closer, will you? This disinfectant's rather nasty stuff.'

'I won't,' said Margaret. 'May I stay and watch?'

'If you like. Although I've nearly finished.' He emptied the pail of its dirty water, and wiped his hands on a piece of rag. 'There! That'll do for now. Aren't you supposed to be at school?' he asked as they began to walk back towards the house. 'School's closed. It's because of the snow,' replied his daughter.

'That's rather jolly, isn't it?'

'Yes,' said Margaret. 'Although I like school, too,' she added, with her customary scrupulousness. 'Miss Church is teaching us French.'

'*Très bien*,' he said. '*Comment t'appelles-tu?*'

She thought about it for a moment. '*Je m'appelle Marguerite*,' she replied carefully. 'We've French names, you see.'

'Oh ho, so you're really a little French girl, are you?' he said.

'Only sometimes,' said Margaret.

It wasn't until that evening that he heard from the Chief Inspector. The girls had been put to bed. Mrs Edwards had not delayed long before following them, 'I find this country air makes me so sleepy . . .' Now Edith was reading to him, as was her nightly custom. They'd begin with the papers; then, if both felt up to it, carry on with a chapter of whatever book it was they were currently tackling. Just now, it was *Great Expectations*. So, after a brief skim of the rest of the day's news – the King was making 'slow and steady progress', his doctors said; Exmoor was snowbound; Chelsea had beat Everton by two goals to one at Stamford Bridge – they turned again to the tale of lies and half-truths and unrequited love in which they were now caught up. '"*He calls the knaves, Jacks, this boy! said Estella with disdain* . . ." She really is the most awful little cat,' remarked Edith. '"*And what coarse hands he has! And what thick boots!*"'

But they weren't to get much further that night with poor Pip's humiliation at the hands of his femme fatale, because just then the telephone rang. 'I'll go,' said Rowlands. As before, Douglas didn't bother to announce himself. 'I thought you'd like to know how things stand,' he said, without preamble. 'The fact is, we've made an arrest.'

'Oh!' Familiar as he now was with the Chief Inspector's predilection for springing surprises, Rowlands still found himself taken aback. 'That's very gratifying.' Douglas emitted a sound not unlike the sound of steam escaping from a kettle. 'Gratifying! Aye, it's gratifying all right. That Charlie Graves is a fool,' he said. Rowlands thought it best to make no comment. 'He's got it into his head that it's the boyfriend,' the Chief Inspector went on, 'Just because it usually is, in these cases.' His accent was becoming more decidedly Scottish the more indignant he grew. 'What he can't seem to get into that thick skull of his is that this *isn't* like all the other cases . . .'

'No,' said Rowlands. 'What evidence is there against this man – the boyfriend?' he asked. 'Not a lot,' was the reply. 'Although they'd had a quarrel, it appears – he and the dead girl. Something to do with her seeing another man. It was that which got Graves excited.'

'Does he have an alibi for the other murders? This man you mention.'

'His name's Bert Mullins. Works in the Dockyards in Deptford. As for his alibi, or lack of it, that's what Graves is presently engaged in finding out. I'm letting him have his way,' added Douglas, with a grim little laugh. 'At least for the moment.'

'I see,' said Rowlands, wondering why all this couldn't have waited until the morning. But then Douglas said: 'Even if he's wasting his time, I see no reason why you should waste yours. I'd like you to go down there – discreetly mind! – and talk to a few people. Just in the way you have up to now, you know. Quite casual. Nothing too official.'

'Chief Inspector, I don't quite see . . .'

'No, I know you don't,' said the other. 'But trust me. It's the little, inconsequential things that can make all the difference. Sometimes people don't know what it is they *do* know, if you get me,' he said. 'And you're just the man to get it out of them.'

Chapter Fourteen

They were just pulling the shutters up in the public bar of the White Hart when Rowlands walked in. It was some time before the landlord, whistling softly under his breath as he polished glasses, or rubbed up taps, or engaged in some other no less essential task, appeared to notice him. 'What'll it be?' asked this individual at last, with no very great warmth of expression. 'Pint of Charrington's.' Rowlands wasn't, as a rule, much given to drinking at this time of day, but this was work, not pleasure. He judged from the quiet that he must be the only customer; but then a phlegmy cough from across the room told him that there must be at least one other here: an old man, from the sound of him. The phrase 'spit and sawdust' sprang, irresistibly, to mind. 'Nippy, out,' he said while the landlord was drawing his pint. The only response was a grunt. He tried again: 'Think we'll be in for some more snow tonight?'

'I couldn't say.' This was barely civil; perhaps it was on account of the fact that he, Rowlands, was a stranger? And yet the pub was hardly what you'd call out of the way, situated as it was on the main Lewisham road. 'That'll be *5d*.,' this distinctly unwelcoming host added, in the same surly tone. Making a mental note to cross this particular hostelry off his list, Rowlands drew a handful of change from his pocket and, with a dexterity born of long habit, rapidly sifted the coins he found there in one hand while raising the glass to his lips with the other. 'There you are.'

'Thanks,' was the gruff reply, a shade warmer than before. 'Here,' the landlord went on, 'I haven't seen you in here before, have I?' Rowlands agreed that he had not. 'Thought you was somebody else,' said the man, with a more conciliatory note in his voice. 'One of them reporter chaps. We've had a few of 'em hanging about the place this past couple o' days. Asking questions.'

'Oh?' said Rowlands, with what he hoped seemed no more than polite interest. 'Why's that?' But just then the arrival of two more customers demanded the other's attention.

'Morning Ron. Morning, Stan,' he said. Two pints of the 'usual' were pulled, without further ado. Only when these had been set on the counter in front of the thirsty pair, did the White Hart's landlord return to the subject he had been about to broach to Rowlands. 'I was just saying,' he said – addressing these regulars – 'as how we've had quite a lot of attention from the Gentlemen of the Press.' He gave the words a heavily ironic intonation.

'Nosy buggers,' opined the man called Stan, taking a noisy draught of his beer. 'If you'll pardon my French.'

'Well, it's their job, ain't it?' said the man addressed as Ron, evidently at pains to be scrupulously fair. 'You could say,' he added defensively, since he was evidently in the minority with regard to this opinion.

'Poking their noses in,' said Stan. 'Where they're not wanted. If you ask me,' he added, 'it only encourages it. Printing all that stuff about, you know . . .' He lowered his voice. '*Sex crimes*. Gives people ideas. Stands to reason.'

'What's *that* supposed to mean?' came another voice – a woman's – from the doorway. 'You know as well as I do, Stanley Robinson, that Bert Mullins is a decent sort. You ought to be ashamed of yourself, casting aspersions . . .'

'I never . . .' he protested weakly, but the woman – whoever she was – was now in full flow: 'You've a dirty mind, you have, and I don't care who hears me say so.'

'Now then, Ruby,' said the landlord in a wheedling tone. 'I'm sure Stan didn't mean nothing by it.'

'Then he oughtn't to have *said* nothing,' was the tart reply. 'I just hope,' she added darkly, 'that Bert doesn't get to hear of it. Wring your neck for you, he will. 'Scuse *me*.' the young woman said to Rowlands. 'Only I need to get by. *Some* of us have work to do.' He realised that he must have been blocking her way to the bar. He apologised, and stood up to let her pass. 'Thanks,' she said grudgingly. A section of the counter was lifted up, and then let fall with a bang. 'I'll be in the Snug,' she added, 'if anybody wants me. The brass in there is a disgrace.' Nobody spoke until the door into the Snug had shut behind her. Then the landlord said, 'She's a fierce one, is our Ruby.'

'Sharp-tongued,' agreed Stan, who'd had the worst of it. 'But then it stands to reason she'd be upset,' was the reply. 'Seeing as how she and Elsie worked together.' There was a murmur of agreement; then silence as the men sipped their pints.

'I'm afraid you'll think me awfully dense,' said Rowlands, into this conversational lull, 'but are we talking about that poor girl who was found in the park a couple of nights ago?'

'We are,' said the landlord. 'She worked here, as a matter of fact. Good little worker, too.' Rowlands nodded and took a sip of his beer, trying to make it last without it seeming that he was doing so. It wouldn't do to get too fuddled, this early in the day. 'Yes, it were a terrible shock when it happened,' the landlord was saying. 'She was behind the bar night before last, you know. I still can't quite believe it.' His voice took on the slightly sing-song cadence of someone reciting a well-rehearsed tale: 'We closed up at nine-thirty, as usual, then Elsie mopped the floor – I always like it clean and ready for next day,' he added, as if he might have been thought reprehensible in expecting this. 'Then I stood them all a drink – Elsie, Ruby and Joey – that's the lad who collects the glasses. I always say,' he went on, in sentimental vein, 'that if you treat your workers fair, you'll get a better day's work out of 'em.'

'Stands to reason,' muttered Ron, with the air of one who had heard all this before. 'But it was only one drink she had – a sweet sherry; I poured it myself. Police was trying to say she were the worse for drink, but it weren't so.' Just then the door opened to admit a cold blast of air and with it some more customers. 'Shut that door, for Gawd's sake, Alf Briggs, it's perishing out there.'

'You can say that again, an' all,' was the reply as accompanied by the curious sound – part shudder, part whistle of appreciation – the English make on coming in from the cold, the newcomers (four in all, Rowlands guessed) approached the bar. 'Pint o' Plain, Jack, if you'd be so kind,' went on the man who'd spoken first.

'Right you are, Sid. Same for you, Walter?'

'Make mine a pint o' Mild.'

'Pint o' Mild coming up. Alf? Yours is a pint o' London, if I'm not mistaken . . .'

'You ain't.'

'Pint o' London it is.'

'An' I'll have another,' said the fourth voice. '*Need* it, after the morning I've 'ad . . .'

'Like that, is it?'

The other grunted in affirmation. Then the only sound was the agreeable one of beer being dispensed into glasses, and glasses being set on the brass drip-tray on top of the counter. 'We was just talking,' the landlord said slyly, completing these operations, 'about Elsie. What happened. All that.'

'Shocking, that was,' remarked the pint of London, smacking his lips as the first draught went down. 'What sort o' man chokes the life out of a sweet little thing like that?'

'Queer sort o' bloke,' replied the pint of Mild. 'Want my opinion, there's a lot better things to be done with a girl like that. *One* thing in pertickerlar . . .' He sniggered.

'Now then, Walter Smedley, there's no need for such talk,' said the landlord severely. 'Never meant nothing by it. All I said was she was a cracker – which she was,' the offender muttered.

'The paper said there'd been an arrest,' said Rowlands, interrupting this contretemps.

'That's right,' said the landlord. 'Local lad. Name of Mullins.'

'I gather he was walking out with her – with Elsie, that is?'

'He was,' replied the other. 'But that don't mean he killed her.'

'No.'

'Seems to me,' said Ron, 'the police is very quick to pick on New Cross lads. Stands to reason whoever done this was an outsider.' There was a murmur of agreement, followed by a general supping of pints. Rowlands thought he had heard enough. He finished his beer and, with a nod to the assembled company, made for the door. As it swung to behind him, he heard the landlord say: 'Stone blind, poor beggar. You wouldn't have thought it, would you, to look at 'im?'

Out in the street, Rowlands hesitated a moment, then made a decision. The saloon bar, as was the case in most public houses of the Victorian age, had a separate entrance off the street. With an air of confidence he did not feel, he pushed open the weighty door, whose etched glass panel doubtless portrayed some device – a hart at bay, perhaps – related to the name of the establishment. The bar, as far as he could tell, was empty – no one at that time of day being willing to pay the penny extra per pint that would ensure more salubrious surroundings and a better class of clientele. The Snug lay between the saloon and public bars. As, cautiously, he opened the door, he could hear sobbing. 'We're closed,' said a voice that was barely recognisable as that of the young woman who had been so bold in defence of Bert Mullins. Then: 'Oh. It's you. You was in there earlier. With *them*.' She blew her nose sharply. 'What can I do for you?' she said coldly.

'I gather you knew Elsie Alsop?' he said gently.

'What if I did?'

'I'm . . . I'm making enquiries about her death on behalf of the family,' he said. 'I thought you might be able to help.'

'I can't see how. I've told the police all I know. Which

wasn't much,' she added. A suspicious note entered her voice. 'What family are you talking about, anyway? Elsie didn't have a family, that I know of. Leastways, she didn't have no mum and dad – they died when she was a kid. Both in the same week, she said, of the influenzer.'

'Did she ever mention a brother?' he said, playing for time.

'No. She never.'

'She was engaged to Bert Mullins, wasn't she?'

'Was she? You'll have to ask him. Who *are* you anyway? Some kind of copper? Asking questions . . .' She sounded on the verge of tears again.

'I'm trying to find out who killed Elsie, that's all,' he said. 'And to do that I need to know as much about her movements in the days and hours before she died as I can. Who she saw, where she went, what she said – anything at all, in fact, however trivial, which might cast light on what happened to her. But if you don't think you can help . . .'

'I never said that,' she replied. She hesitated, and he held his breath, waiting for what she would say. But before she could speak, there came a shout from next door: 'Ruby! Ain't you finished them taps yet?' A moment later, the connecting door opened and the landlord thrust his head round. 'There's customers to serve,' he said; then, catching sight of Rowlands, 'You still 'ere? I'll tell you straight, 'ooever you are – this is a respectable house. My girls ain't allowed followers.'

'I was just leaving,' said Rowlands. 'If you think of

anything,' he added addressing Ruby, 'you can drop me a note.' He took out the propelling pencil and notebook he carried in his pocket for just such eventualities, tore out a page from the pad and carefully printed his address. It was a long shot, but it had sounded just now as if she'd had something to tell him.

After leaving the pub, Rowlands caught the bus up to Regent's Park. It was a long, slow journey, but he didn't mind that: it gave him a chance to put his thoughts in order. For the life of him, he couldn't see where this case was going. It was all very frustrating, he thought. So far they had nothing – or nothing much – to go on. Three dead women, all blondes. An advertisement, that two of the three had answered, for an artist's model. Four playing cards: ace, king, queen, jack. A fourth woman, who evidently knew more than she said about the significance of the card she'd been sent. She's the key – the Countess, he thought. But how, he wondered, was he to get her to talk? I must see her, he decided, knowing, as he made that resolution, that this would necessarily involve him in seeing another woman as well. He brushed the thought away; after all, he would only be doing what Douglas had ordered him to do. Talking to people. Listening to what they had to say. Being alert for that one, apparently inconsequential, fact which might prove significant.

''Scuse me, love . . .' The fat woman who had been sitting beside him now made a move to get up, wheezing heavily as she did so. He rose to let her past, and got a whiff of Yardley's Lavender soap – not quite obscuring the muskier smell of sweat. The bus lumbered on along the Old Kent Road, becoming increasingly full as it journeyed westward. Despite the freezing weather, the atmosphere inside the vehicle was hot and stuffy – a consequence of there being too many bodies jammed closely together, in too small a space. The talk, which was sporadic, was of the weather: 'Horrible, ain't it?'; the King: 'Very poorly he is, poor soul . . .' and the price of coal: 'Shocking.' A good many people seemed to have colds. At the Bricklayer's Arms, Rowlands got up to to let a young woman with a grizzling baby sit down. 'Thanks, ever so.'

'Don't mention it.' He thought longingly of the cup of tea he hoped he'd be offered when he reached his destination. It was the only thing he *was* looking forward to; the prospect of the meeting itself made him feel distinctly uncomfortable. But after all the shenanigans – police investigations and the like, to say nothing of his own little piece of skulduggery – he felt the Major was owed some sort of explanation. At the Elephant, the bus disgorged its load of passengers – all South Londoners, Rowlands surmised, for whom a journey North of the River was a rare, if not unheard-of, event – these respective areas of London being as widely separated as to customs and habits as France and Germany. Not that Rowlands had ever set foot in Germany – nor would he, for a thousand pounds. Although he'd known some decent enough Germans in his time – his brother-in-law,

Viktor Lehmann, being one of them. He wondered what old Vic was up to now.

This train of thought could not but lead to speculations as to the whereabouts of his wayward sister. He hoped, wherever she was, that she was well and happy. Nor could this wish be separated from feelings of guilt, which had to do with the part he'd played in bringing about her current exile. He shook his head from side to side, to dispel these unhappy thoughts. 'It's too bad,' he murmured under his breath. '*I* call it a disgrace' said a woman next to him. 'Seven minutes late we are already, and I've an appointment at the hospital to keep.'

He was at Regent's Park Lodge by half past two; it occurred to him as he rang the bell that they might all still be at lunch. But he found the Major in his study. 'Come in, Rowlands, old chap, come in. Disturbing me?' he replied, in answer to his visitor's polite enquiry. 'No, you're not disturbing me in the slightest. As for luncheon . . .' – this had been Rowlands' next question – 'I don't usually bother with much, these days. Can't seem to fancy it, you know.'

'You ought to keep your strength up,' said Rowlands, in a jocular tone at odds with his present state of mind. 'We can't have the CO falling ill.'

'I suppose not.' The Major pressed the electric bell on his desk. It rang sharply in the next room. 'But you don't sound awfully well yourself, if I might say so.'

'It's just a cold, sir.'

'So what can I do for you?' asked the Major. Rowlands

hesitated, wondering how candid he could allow himself to be. 'There are a few things I wanted to talk to you about . . .' he began. But just then the door opened and Doris Clavering bounced in. 'Yes, Major? What is it? Ooh, fancy seeing *you* here, Mr Rowlands! You've become quite a stranger.'

'Some tea, Doris,' said the Major, cutting across this effusion. 'And bring a cup for Mr Rowlands, will you?'

'Right you are,' said Miss Clavering sweetly. The Major remained silent until the brisk click-clack of high-heeled shoes had faded away along the corridor. 'I know she can seem rather bumptious at times,' he said. 'But she doesn't mean it, really. And it's nice having a young person about the place. Wakes us all up.'

'Yes,' said Rowlands.

'But you were about to ask me something? It's about this reunion, I take it?'

'Well, yes . . .' Although it hadn't been the reunion that was uppermost in his mind at all. He knew he should be honest with the Major about his involvement with Chief Inspector Douglas. But he didn't know how to begin. How *did* one tell a man one liked and trusted that one had been lying to him?

'It sounds, from what Doris has been telling me, that you and your wife have made excellent progress,' said the Major. 'She was only typing up the list of names the other day. Over three hundred acceptances, she said.'

'Then there are the families,' said Rowlands miserably. He couldn't do it, he thought. To confess that he'd been *spying* on people here – his own former comrades amongst them.

'Oh, we must certainly have *them*! Wives, you know. Terribly important in what we're trying to do. Kiddies, too, of course. Invite 'em all, I say.'

'I think we'll probably need to hire a marquee. In case of rain,' mumbled Rowlands, feeling perfectly wretched. His head was aching, and not just because of his cold. Guilt took its toll on the body.

'Excellent idea! We must have a dance band, too,' said the Major. 'You might try the one we had for the New Year's Eve Ball. Ernest Melvin and His Tennessee Toe-Tappers, I think they were called. Doris'll know.'

'Did I hear my name taken in vain?' said Miss Clavering archly, entering at that moment with the tea tray.

'We were just discussing the plans for our summer reunion,' said the Major.

'The Fête, you mean? *Such* a good idea,' opined his secretary.

'We were wondering about a band.'

'Ooh, yes. You'll have to have music. And games. A Tug of War. Test Your Strength. A coconut shy. Oh, it's going to be *ever* such fun!' she cried. 'Milk and sugar, Mr Rowlands?' After a few more minutes of this bright banter, Miss Clavering left them, and the conversation turned to other things. The plans for the new Centre at Ovingdean was one that currently absorbed the Major's attention. 'It'll be marvellous when it's done,' he said.

'Quite the latest design, you know. I was given a tour by the architect, only the other day.'

'But surely it isn't built yet?'

'No, of course not,' the Major laughed. 'We'll need to find the money, first! I only meant a tour of the model, you know. But one can get quite a good idea of how it will look from that. It rather resembles an aeroplane in shape, with a glass cockpit – which is the central staircase – and wings on either side. There'll be a great wide sun lounge, looking out across the sea. Wonderful for sunbaths for the men, you know. Then there's the dining hall. Much bigger than the one we've got here, with lots of small round tables instead of the refectory type. Much friendlier, you know.'

'Good for card games, too,' quipped Rowlands, and then wished he'd kept the remark to himself. The Major's mood, hitherto buoyant, now grew sombre. 'Ye-es,' he said doubtfully. 'Although I rather think we'll try and keep those to a separate room.'

'Good idea,' said Rowlands; then, despising himself, he added casually: 'I hope our Mr Vance has been behaving himself lately?'

'As far as I know,' replied the Major. He was silent a moment as if considering whether or not to go on with what he had to say. 'Although I had a rather *odd* encounter with him a day or so ago.'

'Did you?'

'Yes. It was in the corridor, outside the library. He seemed in a tearing hurry. Almost ran me down, you know. When he realised who it was, he said he had to talk to me.' Rowlands felt a prickle of excitement. 'What about?' he asked, keeping his voice level. 'He didn't go into details,' replied the Major. 'All he said was that "something very peculiar" was going on, and that he'd like to tell me about it.'

'And has he?'

'Not yet,' said the Major. 'But you know, the men do get bees in their bonnets about all sorts of things. Vance has probably got himself worked up about nothing . . . Hello!' As, having tapped perfunctorily upon the door, someone came in. 'Who's that?'

'It's Mortimer, sir. Just wanted a word about . . . I say – have you got company?'

'It's only me, Mortimer old man,' said Rowlands, getting up to shake the other's hand.

'Rowlands? Good to see you,' came the reply. 'I can come back another time,' said the librarian to Major Fraser. 'No need,' was the reply. 'Rowlands and I were just having a jaw . . . '

'Well, if you're really sure I'm not intruding . . . It's about these new talking books. Should we invest in the scheme, do you think? Only the discs are rather expensive.'

'Yes, but it's such a marvellous thing,' said the Major. 'Have you heard about this, Rowlands? They've got actors reading one's favourite novels, and recording it onto a disc. Then you play it back – as you would a recording of a concert, you know – and it's exactly like being read aloud to.'

'It sounds a splendid idea,' said Rowlands. 'But I've got my own talking book at home. She's called Mrs Rowlands.'

'Well, for those of us who aren't lucky enough to have a woman at home, these discs are the next best thing – eh, Mortimer?'

'Oh yes,' said the other. 'Why – are you going already?' he said as Rowlands made a move towards the door. 'I'd hoped we might have time for another drink.'

'Sorry,' said Rowlands. 'But the woman in question'll be awfully cross if I miss my train home. Some other time, perhaps?'

'I'll hold you to that,' said Mortimer.

Chapter Fifteen

Then, for the next few days, nothing out of the ordinary happened. Rowlands' cold was worse, and Edith insisted he should stay inside in the warm as much as possible, even though he'd protested feebly that he'd far too much to do around the farm to waste time loafing about. But she was adamant. 'You were fortunate enough to return from the war in one piece,' she said. 'Or just about. You'd look rather silly succumbing to pneumonia after all that, wouldn't you?' With which he could only concur. And so he sat by the fire, and tried to get on with his reading – painfully slow at the best of times – of Sir Arthur's monumental tome. But it was heavy work in every sense, and it was a relief to put it aside to play with the children or chat to his mother-in-law about this and that, her return to Dorset having been delayed on account of the weather. When she could spare the time from her domestic chores, Edith read to him. Thanks to his present state of inactivity, they were getting on quite fast with *Great Expectations*. Pip had by now embarked on the next stage of his adventures, having arrived at Lincoln's Inn where the lawyer's clerk Wemmick was setting him straight about the realities of London life:

> *'Is it a very wicked place?' I asked, more for the sake of saying something that for information.*
>
> *'You may be cheated, robbed, and murdered in London. But there are plenty of people anywhere who'll do that for you.'*
>
> *'If there is bad blood between you and them,' said I, to soften it a little.*
>
> *'Oh! I don't know about bad blood,' returned Mr Wemmick; 'there's not much bad blood about. They'd do it, if there's anything to be got by it . . .'*

Not a great deal had changed since those words were written, Rowlands thought. For the most part murder – as Wemmick had pointed out – was an opportunistic crime. And yet . . . 'bad blood'. He wondered how much *that* was a factor in the playing card affair.

On Sunday, he was well enough to accompany Mrs Edwards and the girls to church while Edith got on with the cooking. They went round by the lane as the snow was still too thick across the fields for an elderly lady and three small children to manage without getting themselves soaked through – although if he'd been on his own, he'd have gone that way. There was nothing he liked better than a good long walk, to blow the cobwebs away. You could go as fast as you liked across the meadows, too, without the risk of bumping into things or people which was so much a feature of city life, whether you were blind or not. Yes, I must need my head examining, he thought, to think of leaving all this.

The sound of the bells, with their tumbling cadences, came clear and loud through the crystalline air. As they reached the church, the wavering strains of the organ could be heard. 'Jesu, Joy of Man's Desiring'. That would be Miss Pargetter; it was one of her set pieces. They stamped the snow off their boots in the porch and went in. The smell of candle wax, incense and damp which greeted him as he pushed open the heavy oak door, was one he had known all his life. He shepherded his mother-in-law and the girls to the pew where the family usually sat, and – with Margaret's whispered assistance – found the right page in the hymn book for Anne. Then, as he had done many times before, he let himself slip into the familiar ritual, allowing its comforting rhythms to wash over him, letting his thoughts drift. These revolved around a single image: a game of chance, in which the cards were not pasteboard oblongs, but human beings. A doubling, lying game, played against an as yet invisible opponent. He thought, Vance knows something. The

Countess, too . . . then came to, with a guilty start, as everyone stood for the next hymn.

Owing to the inclement weather, the congregation was smaller than usual, and there was a raggedness to the singing and to the intoning of psalms. As the vicar rose to give the text for the sermon that was to follow, a chorus of coughs and sniffs reverberated around the church. Joan, who was sitting on her father's lap, took the opportunity to ask for a drink in a loud, clear voice. 'Shh, Joanie,' he told her. 'Later.'

'Be sober, be vigilant,' said the Reverend Rickards, in his pleasant Oxford drawl, 'because your adversary the dev-il, as a roaring li-on, walketh about seeking whom he may devour . . .'

Well, he could certainly vouch for that, Rowlands thought. The devil, in whatever guise he had chosen to adopt these past few weeks, had certainly been walking about. The question was, whom would he devour next? When the service was over, and he'd shaken the vicar's hand – 'Oh, dear,' lamented the latter. 'Not a very good turnout this week, I'm afraid' – and Mrs Edwards had exchanged greetings with some of the local ladies, they made their way home. Rowlands, carrying Joan on his shoulders, suited himself to his mother-in-law's slower pace while the other two ran on ahead. The words of the text returned to him. 'Seeking whom he may devour,' he murmured under his breath. Yes, that was what evil was like: an all-consuming rage. A passion, that was as strong as love. 'I don't much like the look of that sky,' murmured Helen Edwards, at his elbow.

'More snow, do you think?'

'I'm afraid so.'

Just then, the girls ran up, laughing. 'Daddy, you held your hymn book upside down!' cried Anne. 'It was ever so funny.'

'Maybe I can read upside down,' he said. 'Had you thought of *that*?'

'Daddy's so clever he doesn't need to read the words,' said loyal Margaret. 'He's got them all in his head, haven't you, Daddy?'

Loveless was waiting for him when he arrived at nine sharp; the door opened at Rowlands' first knock. 'Well, don't just stand there,' said the artist. 'You're letting all the heat out.' It was certainly a little warmer in the studio than it was outside, although not by a very great margin. 'I've just lit the fire,' said Loveless, preceding Rowlands into that apartment. 'It should be piping hot in here soon. I thought we'd start with a few standing poses,' he went on as his sitter divested himself of his coat. 'Just to warm up.' This was more than fine with Rowlands, and so, following the other's brusque commands – 'Over there. Yes. Now face me. That's it. Stand just as you are. Quite natural. Yes. Like that' – he took up his position. The sound, familiar from the last session, of charcoal moving in great sweeps across coarse-grained paper, began. Being drawn wasn't as tiring as on the first occasion, he found, partly because he now knew what to expect, but mainly because the poses were shorter: three or four minutes instead of fifteen or twenty. Even so, he was just starting to feel the tension in his calf muscles from standing too long in the same position, when Loveless called out: 'All right, you can relax for a minute.' Rowlands did so. 'Now I'd like you to take up another pose. Still standing, as before, but with your arms raised above your head. Like Christ on the cross. Oh, don't worry,' Loveless added, perhaps seeing the fleeting look of consternation that passed across his subject's face. 'I'm not planning to use you for the main figure. I've already got a model for *that*. Chap who makes my suits, as a matter of fact. German Jew. He'll do very well for my Christ.'

Rowlands took up the position, which proved much harder than the one before. At least the fire was starting to take hold; he could feel its welcome heat upon his back. The furious scratching of charcoal began again. After two minutes, Rowlands had pins and needles. He wriggled his fingers to relieve the strain. 'Hold still!' barked the voice from the easel. Two minutes more passed, and he felt as if the blood had drained from his arms entirely. 'All right,' said Loveless, just as Rowlands was wondering how much more he could take. He'd never realised how hard being an artist's model could be. It made him see the women who did this for a living in a different light. 'No, I was thinking of using you for another figure in my central group,' the artist went on, as if there had been no break in the conversation. 'St Peter, as a matter of fact.'

'I'm glad it's not Judas,' laughed Rowlands, chafing the life back into his arms.

'The archetypal spy? Your face isn't villainous enough,' replied Loveless. 'I've got someone else in mind for *him*. You'll do very well for St Peter.'

'He betrayed Christ, too,' said Rowlands.

'Yes, but it wasn't for money. He was afraid, that's all. A lot of us were afraid,' said Loveless softly.

They worked for another hour, then stopped for tea and cigarettes. The tea, Rowlands was relieved to find, was drinkable this time. Perhaps one of Loveless's wealthy clients had paid up, at last. 'I don't think you've ever told me what it is you do,' said the artist. 'From the look of your hands, I'd say you worked out of doors. But you don't seem the type for manual work.'

Rowlands explained.

'And how, if you don't mind my asking, do you come to know Celia West? I know she's famous for not minding about such things – she asks *me* to her parties, after all! – but even so, I wouldn't have thought your respective social circles would tend to overlap much.'

'It's a long story,' said Rowlands.

'Which is a polite way of telling me to mind my own business,' said the artist, sounding not at all put out by the rebuff. 'I begin to like you more and more, Mr Rowlands. And I'm a man, as you will have gathered, who doesn't like many of his fellow men. Shall we carry on?'

In accordance with Loveless's instructions, Rowlands took up the seated pose from the week before. This required less of him than the standing poses, and as the powerful smell of oil paint and thinner once more filled the room he let his thoughts drift, familiar enough now with Loveless's working practices to know that conversation from now on would be one-sided: brief commands – 'Keep your head up' – interspersed with desultory comments on the state of the art scene. 'Saw a show at the Mayor a couple of days ago. Some awful muck, of course, but a rather good thing by Wadsworth . . .'

There was something odd about the whole affair, Rowlands thought. It had struck him just now, when Loveless had made his sly remark about social circles. That was it, he realised – the thing which had been troubling him. Because what, after all, was the *connection* between the world of the Countess Rostropovna and that of the three dead women? There was none. All the dead were from what you'd call humble backgrounds. All three might have been said to have belonged to what the French politely called the demi-monde . . . A dancer. A prostitute. A barmaid. Their circles could never have been those of the Countess. So why had she, of all the other Society ladies in London, been singled out? There has to be a reason, he thought. Could it have to do with the fact that she was a Russian? An exotic bloom, amongst the home-grown flowers . . . Perhaps that was what Lady Celia saw in her – her *difference* from conventional society? And Celia West, as he had every reason to know, had a taste for the unconventional. Still, it was a puzzle. What could possibly link her to those others, he wondered, apart from the colour of her hair?

'You can rest now,' said Loveless after another three-quarters of an hour. Rowlands had hardly noticed its passing, so caught up had he been in these tortuous reflections. Grateful for the respite, he yawned and stretched. 'I thought we might go to the pub for lunch,' said Loveless. 'They do quite a decent pint of Charrington's at the Prince Albert.' Fifteen minutes later, they were comfortably settled in that establishment, each with his beer and a hot meat pie in front of him. There was a fire here, too – a rather more efficient one than the one in Loveless's studio; seated as near to it as he could be, without catching fire himself, Rowlands felt its warmth through every fibre of his body. Edith used to laugh at him for his fire-worship, as she called it, but once you'd been as cold as he had – and how cold they'd been, and wet through, those terrible months in '17 – you learnt to value every scrap of heat. 'Nice pint,' he said, savouring the rich, hoppy taste of it as it went down.

'Not bad, is it?' In those few minutes, Loveless had seemed to unbend. The brusque and rather arrogant manner had been replaced by something altogether more genial. 'I prefer this place to some of the others,' he now confided, 'because you can be pretty sure that you won't meet any artists. Not like some of the pubs further west,' he added. 'Kensington Church Street is becoming impossible. As for *Chelsea* . . .' Rowlands sipped his pint. It didn't seem to him that a response was required. After a few moment's contemplative silence, broken only by the shouts of the darts players in the adjacent bar, Loveless went on: 'It may strike you as strange that I'm not fonder of my fellow practitioners, given that we're all engaged in much the same effort.' He took a long draught of his beer. 'Keeping the flag flying for Art, you might say . . . ('Ohh! Triple! Nice one!') . . . But you see, over the years, I've come to regard many of these people not as comrades-in-arms, but as the enemy. I don't know if that makes sense?'

'Perfectly.'

'Good,' said Loveless. He took another draught of beer. Then, as if the thought had just occurred to him, he said: 'I heard an interesting piece of news about your Countess the other day.'

'Did you?'

'Yes. She's done a bunk.'

'*What?*'

'Oh, I'm sorry – has it come as a shock? Yes. Pickford told me. He happened to call round at Cadogan Square. The place was in uproar, he said. Apparently, they'd just searched her room, and found she'd taken everything. Clothes. Jewellery. The lot. Celia was most upset.'

'When *was* this?'

'I don't know exactly. Two or three days ago, I suppose. Why? Is it important?'

'Very.' Rowlands got to his feet. What a fool I was, not to have anticipated this, he thought. 'I'm afraid I'll have to cut our session short,' he said.

'But you haven't even finished your drink.'

'I'm sorry. I really have to go.'

'All right.' Loveless sighed. 'I suppose you won't tell me what this is all about?'

'I'm afraid I can't.'

'How very mysterious! I think that's probably what made me think you'd make a good subject,' said the artist drily. 'Your air of mystery. Well, goodbye, Mr Rowlands. I do hope you'll be back to sit for me soon. That portrait's shaping up very nicely.'

He was glad, now, that Edith had made such a fuss about his wearing his best suit. Not that he bothered much about his appearance as a rule; as long as he was presentable – which meant not standing out – that was enough for him. But on this occasion, it was good to know that he didn't look a complete scarecrow. It had now been ten minutes since the maid had showed him into Lady Celia's drawing room. The last time he'd been here, it had been full of people; noise; smoke; music and laughter. Now a profound quiet reigned, broken only by the soft ticking of the mantelpiece clock. As he sat, perched on the edge of a chair whose slippery damask upholstery did nothing to improve its comfort, he found his anger in no way decreased by the enforced delay. So she'd keep him waiting, would she? It was a tactic with which he had become familiar, during his years working in an office. A way of establishing who was in charge. Well, they'd see about *that*! But when at last Lady Celia appeared, murmuring apologies, Rowlands found himself disarmed at once. 'You see, I didn't know how I was going to *face* you,' she said. 'I suppose you know she's gone?'

'Yes.'

She didn't ask how it was he knew. In her world, it seemed, secrets could not be kept for very long. 'The past few days have been like a nightmare. Oh, it's been wretched! I can't tell you,' she said, flinging herself down with a great sigh upon the sofa, 'how very glad I am to see you.'

'Have you told the police about the Countess's disappearance?'

'How could I? They'll probably think I *planned* it with her. But I didn't,' she said, sounding close to tears. 'You have to believe me. I didn't.'

'Of course I believe you.'

'Thank God. I'm so glad it's you who've come, and not that Chief Inspector. *He'd* want to arrest me.'

'I doubt that very much.'

'You know,' she said, 'it is a comfort having you here. I've been at my wits' end.'

'Perhaps,' said Rowlands, 'you'd better tell me about it.'

'All right. It was last Thursday, I think – no Friday . . . Oh, forgive me. Would you like a drink? A whisky, or something?'

'No thanks.'

'Well, I'm going to have a gin. I feel I need it.' She got

up and went over to where he guessed the drinks cabinet must be. There was the sound of liquid being poured into a glass. 'Damn,' she muttered. 'There's no ice.' She must have rung a bell, for a moment later, the maid appeared. 'Bring some ice, will you?' she said. 'Yes, m'lady.' A few minutes elapsed while they waited for the girl to return. Lady Celia resumed her seat on the sofa. 'Won't you have a more comfortable chair?' she said after a moment.

'This is fine, thanks.'

'Just as you like.' The silence which followed this brief exchange seemed to Rowlands to be charged with meaning. It occurred to him that this was the first time he'd been alone with her since that time – still vivid in memory – at her house in Hill Street, two years before. Even then, they hadn't *really* been alone, he thought. At the memory of that febrile hour, and all that it had entailed, he felt a painful blush begin to rise. It seemed as if she must have been struck by a similar thought, for she said softly, 'How strange it is, your turning up like this, just when I needed you! It reminds me . . .' But at that moment, the maid came in with the ice, and whatever it was of which Celia West had been reminded, he was not to hear it. 'Now where was I?' she merely resumed when, with a tiny hissing sound, the ice-cubes had been dropped into their glass.

'You were saying that it was last Friday that you'd discovered the Countess was missing.'

'Yes.' She took a thoughtful swig of her drink. 'I'd

been for a dress fitting. Natalia was supposed to come with me – I'd been offering to take her to my dressmaker for absolutely ages, poor darling – but at the last minute, she changed her mind. So I went off by myself.'

'How long were you away?'

'Not much more than an hour. Perhaps an hour and a half. When I got back, she was gone.'

'And why do you think,' Rowlands asked, 'that she changed her mind about going with you?' She thought about it, swirling the ice around in her glass. 'I think she was frightened,' she said at last. 'It was seeing the report in the paper that did it. About that other unfortunate girl.'

'Elsie Alsop,' he said.

'Oh, you know their names, do you?' She shivered slightly. 'That must make it all seem more *real*, I suppose.'

'Yes. But surely,' he said, 'she must have been reassured to know there'd been an arrest?'

She thought about it. 'That's the funny thing,' she said. 'It didn't seem to make the slightest bit of difference. She kept saying, "He knows where I live."' Both were silent a moment. Lady Celia finished her drink. 'I believe I'll have another one of these,' she said. 'Are you sure you won't join me? I do so hate drinking alone.'

'In that case, how can I refuse?' he said. 'Did she say anything before she left – the Countess?' he went on as she got up to make the drinks. 'Anything at all which might give a clue to where she was going?'

'Not a word. I've thought and thought. Except . . . Oh!'

'What is it?'

'She did ask if I could lend her some money. She was always terribly hard up, poor Natalia.' There came the rattle of the cocktail shaker. 'Ooh!' she cried. 'That's cold.'

'And did you? Lend her money, I mean.'

'Only what I had in my purse. About five pounds.' She handed him his drink. 'I put a splash of lime juice with it. It's called a gimlet.'

He took a sip. 'It's very nice. You know, you're going to have to tell the police,' he said. 'By leaving your house, the Countess has put herself in very grave danger.' A thought occurred to him. 'Wasn't there a constable watching the house?' he said. 'Surely he . . .'

'It seems he was recalled to his other duties,' Lady Celia said. 'After they made the arrest.'

'Ah.' He thought he detected the hand of Inspector Graves. *He* wouldn't think much of wasting a man for the sake of a few scrawled words and a playing card. 'So nobody saw her go?'

'No. She seems to have slipped out without any of the servants noticing. Although how she'd have managed, even with the little luggage that she had . . .'

'It's only a few steps from here to Sloane Street. She could have picked up a cab quite easily. And you're *sure*,' he persisted, 'that she didn't mention anyone to whom she might have gone? A family member, perhaps?'

'She had no family. Or not to speak of. No, she didn't say a word,' said Celia West. 'I see now,' she went on 'that I've been terribly remiss in not ringing the police straight away. But you must see how bad it will look for me. With my history . . .' She gave a little shudder. 'Who will ever believe that I wasn't involved in some way?' The words were out before he had time to think. 'If you like,' he said, 'I could tell the Chief Inspector what you've told me.'

'Oh, *would* you?' She must have leapt up from her seat, for a moment later, he felt her clasp his hand in both of hers. 'That's so good of you. I can't tell you how grateful I am.'

At that moment, the door opened. There was a startled silence, then: 'I seem to be interrupting,' said a voice.

'Hello, Johnny. I wasn't expecting you till later,' said Lady Celia. 'Oh, don't get up, Mr Rowlands,' – since he had risen to his feet. 'You needn't go on Lord Edgecombe's account.'

'Well, I must say,' said Edgecombe, sounding far from amused, 'I call that a *very* nice welcome!'

'Don't be a bore, Johnny,' said his fiancée lightly. 'Now that you're here, you might as well make yourself a drink.'

'I should be going,' said Rowlands.

'Yes, why don't you?' said Edgecombe coldly. 'Nobody's stopping you.'

'Johnny, you're being perfectly foul,' said Lady Celia. 'I shall ask you to leave in a minute if your manners don't improve.'

'It's quite all right,' Rowlands said to her. 'I think we've covered everything. I'll let you know when I've spoken to . . . to our friend, shall I?'

'I'd appreciate that,' she said.

'Goodbye, Lady Celia.' Rowlands started to move towards the door. He found his path blocked, however. A hand shoved him, none too gently, backwards. 'You stay where you are!' said Johnny Edgecombe. 'I'd like to know what this is all about.'

'Don't be ridiculous, Johnny.'

'Is it blackmail? Because I can tell you, I know how to deal with people like you.' Another shove.

'If you touch me again,' said Rowlands quietly, 'I'll break your nose.'

'What, *you*?' came the sneering reply; but Rowlands' tone of voice must have been sufficiently convincing for his adversary not to want to put it to the test. He reached the door.

'Johnny, if you knew what an absolute fool you've just made of yourself . . .' he heard Celia West start to say. He closed the door behind him. 'My coat, please,' he said to the hovering maid. As he descended the short flight of steps to the street, he found he was shaking: pent-up anger at the insult he'd received mingled with something else – he supposed it was fear. Not that he was afraid of that great oaf, Edgecombe; he'd met men like him before, in his army days. They were all swagger; when it came to a fight, they collapsed like pricked balloons. No, he wasn't afraid of Johnny Edgecombe.

What he felt was a different kind of fear. Because, throughout his conversation with Lady Celia, one possibility – not alluded to by either – had been very much in his mind. It was that, far from having run away to a place where her killer couldn't find her, Natalia Rostropovna might already be dead. What if, instead of leaving Cadogan Square of her own free will, she had left it at the point of a knife? Shivering a little in the icy wind, that seemed cold enough to have blown from the Russian Steppes, he raised a hand to call a cab, to take him to Scotland Yard.

Rowlands had prepared himself for the Chief Inspector's anger at the news of the Countess's disappearance; what surprised him was that most of that anger was directed, not at Lady Celia, but at his own colleagues. 'I knew I should never have listened to Charlie Graves when he said there was no need to keep a man at Cadogan Square. Now we've lost our best chance of finding the killer.'

'Do you mean that you thought something like this would happen? That she'd try to run away . . .'

'. . . and lead us to the murderer? Aye,' said Douglas. 'It had occurred to me. I'd have preferred it if she could have done so before she was murdered herself – although you can't have everything,' he added drily. 'Now, thanks to your lady friend . . .' Rowlands started to protest. 'All right, thanks to the *lady* who's your *friend*, we've lost almost three days. She could be anywhere. I suppose,' he went on sarcastically, '*she* wasn't able to say where she thought our missing Countess could have run to? Lady Celia, I mean.'

'No. She hadn't the least idea.'

'Convenient. I don't suppose she helped her to run away?'

'She said you'd think that. And no, I don't think she's involved.'

'Which leaves us precisely nowhere.' The Chief Inspector let out a gusty sigh. 'We've three dead females, and one missing. I've the Chief Constable breathing down my neck, and the Press asking awkward questions about public safety. It looks as if our Playing Card Killer is winning.'

'The game isn't over yet,' said Rowlands.

'No, but we're running out of time.' Douglas rolled a pencil that was lying on the desk in front of him, then rolled it back again. He did this several times. 'Hang it!' he exclaimed suddenly. 'A clue. That's all I need.'

'We've several clues. The playing cards, for one.'

'Those damned cards . . .'

'Then there's the advertisement wanting artists' models. Do we know if Elsie Alsop saw it?'

'Not to my knowledge. But then Graves wasn't very interested in that.' He wouldn't be, thought Rowlands. 'Speaking of which,' said Douglas, 'how are you getting on with Loveless? I don't suppose *he* could have spirited our Countess away?'

'I can't see him as a murderer,' said Rowlands.

'No? I'm rather afraid,' said Douglas, in his driest tone, 'that you're letting personal feelings get the better of you.'

'Perhaps. But what are your grounds for suspecting Loveless? Only that he's an artist . . .'

'He was at that party.'

'So were a lot of other people. Le Fevre, for one.'

'*Now* you're letting your dislike of Mr Le Fevre affect your judgement.'

'That's as maybe. But he does know the Countess, it would seem. He was talking to her for several minutes at the party, you know.'

'Was he?' said the policeman sharply. 'I don't suppose you overheard what they were saying?'

'Unfortunately not.'

'Then how . . .'

'It was Lady Celia who told me about their conversation, as a matter of fact.'

'Ah,' said Douglas. 'And, as you've told me yourself, she has reasons of her own for disliking Maurice Le Fevre.' He gave another sigh, this time of exasperation. 'I mean, these kinds of speculations are all very well, but . . .' At that moment the telephone rang. 'Confound it,' he said. 'I gave orders I wasn't to be disturbed.' He snatched up the receiver. 'Yes? I thought I said no calls.' The voice at the other end of the line said something too faint for Rowlands to hear. 'I see,' said Douglas, in a changed voice. 'When did this happen exactly?' The voice spoke again. 'All right,' said Douglas. 'I'll be there as soon as I can. Don't let anyone else into the room.' He replaced the receiver. 'It seems,' he said heavily, 'that there's been another death.'

Chapter Sixteen

The Major must have been listening out for the car, for he came out to greet them as the Crossley drew up in front of the Lodge, and they got out. 'Very good of you to get here so quickly, Chief Inspector,' he said. 'Your sergeant said you were rather tied up this afternoon, and so I was afraid . . .'

'It was nothing that couldn't wait,' replied Douglas. 'As Sergeant Withers should have known,' he added darkly. The latter accepted the rebuke manfully. 'Sir.'

'Mr Rowlands has kindly agreed to join us,' the Chief Inspector went on. 'Seeing as how he's an old hand here.'

'Ah,' said the Major, sounding less surprised than Rowlands might have expected. 'It's good of you to come, Rowlands. Dreadful business, this.'

'Yes.'

'The men are very shocked, of course.'

'We'll need to talk to them later,' said Douglas. 'But first things first.'

'Of course. It's this way, round past the house. There's a path that leads to some outbuildings. You remember the way, I expect, Rowlands?'

'Yes.' It was a path Rowlands had taken every day for six months when he was learning how to type. Of all the skills he'd been taught here, it had been the one which had proved the most useful to him. That, and telephony, which had taken him another six months to learn. Without those, he'd never have found himself such a good position at Saville & Willoughby's. He felt a brief pang of regret for the job, which he'd left two years before, under circumstances which had made it impossible to remain.

'I'm afraid it's rather icy underfoot,' the Major was saying. 'We've tried to keep it clear, but with all the snow we've had these past few weeks, it's been impossible.' His voice rattled nervously on, accompanied by the grim tramp of feet as the little party made its way towards the sheds. These were usually hives of industry, with the cheerful sounds of hammering and whistling to be heard at all hours. Now, the buildings were all but deserted, the cold having kept even the keenest of the carpenters and boot-makers away. 'Which one is it?' asked Douglas.

'Oh, I'm sorry – didn't I say? The carpentry shed. Second on your right.'

'And at what time did you discover the body?' said the Chief Inspector, pausing on the threshold of the wooden, purpose-built hut. 'About an hour ago,' was the reply. 'You see, he hadn't come in for breakfast – although they don't always if they've made a night of it – and then when he didn't appear at luncheon, we started to wonder if something was amiss.'

'We?' said Douglas.

'The men and I. We had a brief conference to discover if anyone had spoken to him that day. It appeared not. So I sent out a search party, and . . . and after about twenty minutes, someone thought to look in here.' The Major opened the door, and the four of them – Douglas, followed by his sergeant, then Rowlands, and lastly the Major himself – went in. A smell of death, mitigated somewhat by the extreme cold, greeted them. There was a moment's silence, then: 'Who cut him down?' said the Chief Inspector, in what anyone who didn't know him better might have thought was a friendly tone.

'I did.' The Major's tone was no less amicable. 'That is, I ordered two of the men – Bingham . . .'

'Here, sir.'

'And Pryce – to do so. But I take full responsibility,' added the Major. 'We couldn't have left him hanging there,' he went on, in the same tone of calm authority. 'It wouldn't have been decent. When a man chooses to take his own life, his reasons for doing so are a matter for conjecture. Despair, perhaps.' He paused. 'Or shame. We can only guess at what might have driven him to this. But what we *can* do is to treat his mortal remains with respect.'

'All right,' said Douglas, almost, but not quite, containing his exasperation. 'Well, now that you've done your bit, perhaps you'll allow me to do mine?'

'With the greatest pleasure.'

'Thank you. So you found the body an hour ago, you say?'

'Yes. That's right, isn't it, Bingham?'

'It was at fourteen hundred hours,' said Bingham. 'Pryce can confirm the time, if you like.'

'Where *is* Pryce, by the way?' asked the Major. 'He went back to the house,' was the reply. 'Felt a bit queasy, poor chap. It was he who found the body – or stumbled into it, rather! It's shaken him up. I said it would be all right for him to go as long as one of us stayed.'

'Quite all right,' said the Major. 'Time you got back in the warm, too. Rowlands here can take your place.'

'Oh, are you here, Rowlands? Bad business, this.'

'Yes.' The two men shook hands. 'Well, I'll be off, then,' said Bingham.

'I'll want to talk to you later, Mr Bingham,' said Douglas, resigned, it seemed, to this subtle undermining of his authority. 'Stay close at hand, won't you?'

'Will do.' Bingham opened the door of the hut, letting in a gust of cold air – although the temperature inside wasn't a great deal warmer, Rowlands thought – and closed it again behind him. His footsteps on the snowy path had a muffled sound.

'So, just to get things absolutely clear,' said Douglas, evidently having mustered his reserves of patience. 'You found him at two o'clock. You cut him down . . .'

'I checked his pulse first,' said the Major. 'But there was no sign of life, poor fellow. He was quite cold. He'd evidently been dead some hours.'

'Yes, Well, the MO will confirm the time of death when he gets here,' said Douglas, somewhat irritably. 'Where could he have got to, I wonder? You telephoned him as soon as you'd finished talking to me, didn't you, Sergeant?'

'Yes, sir. He said as he'd another job on. Young woman that gassed herself in Chelsea.'

Yes, yes,' said his superior officer impatiently. 'We don't need to know about that. You'd better go and wait out in front for him. We don't want him getting himself lost,' he added sourly. He must have knelt down by the body then, for there followed the effortful grunt of a heavy man lowering himself to that position. 'As you say, quite cold,' he said after a moment. He got up again. 'While we're waiting for the good doctor to appear,' he went on, 'you'd better tell me all you can about the late Reginald Vance.'

The Major was silent a moment. 'I'm afraid I didn't know him awfully well,' he said guardedly. 'He'd only been with us about three months. I can get my secretary to look up the exact date, in his file. You see, he was one of the gas cases,' he added.

'Meaning?'

'He hadn't lost his sight until fairly recently. We've a number of men in the same situation here – Rowlands has talked to a few of them, haven't you, Rowlands? They're a generation older than our initial intake were – the Men of 1914, as we call them. Most of *them* were still youngsters. Vance was nearly forty when he went blind, I believe. It was a lot harder for men like him to adapt.'

'I see,' said Douglas. 'And was there any other reason, apart from this supposed difficulty in adapting to his condition, why Mr Vance might have wanted to kill himself? Any money troubles that you know of?' he asked slyly.

'As to that . . .' Again, the Major seemed to hesitate. 'He was always rather flush, if anything. Sometimes I wondered . . .' He let the sentence tail away. 'To tell the truth, Chief Inspector, I'm afraid that Vance might have been involved in something rather unpleasant. Gambling, I mean. Rowlands here knows my thoughts on the matter. I've no definite proof, of course, but . . .'

'We'll look into it, sir, you may be sure,' said Douglas. 'Was there anything else you can think of which might cast some light on the matter?'

'No. Yes. The fact is,' said the Major, sounding increasingly agitated, 'I blame myself for what's happened. If I'd only *listened* to what he had to say.'

'And what was that?' asked Douglas softly. 'I wish I could tell you,' replied the Major unhappily. 'All I do know is that he was worried about something. Said he wanted to talk to me about it. Now I wish I'd paid more attention.'

'But you did,' said Rowlands. 'It was just that he didn't follow up his initial approach.'

'Oh, you knew about this conversation too, did you, Mr Rowlands?' said the Chief Inspector, in a faintly acid tone. 'A pity you didn't think to mention it.'

'But why on earth should he mention it?' said the Major. 'It was said in confidence.' The uncomfortable silence which followed this remark was broken by the arrival of the Medical Officer and his assistants, stamping snow off their boots as they entered the building.

'You took your time, Bill,' said Douglas affably as the two men shook hands. 'Major Fraser, this is Dr Hargreaves. He'll be examining the body. Major Fraser's the man in charge here, Bill. You can address any questions about the deceased to him. And this is Mr Rowlands, who also knew the deceased.'

'So I take it they can both identify the body?'

For a moment nobody spoke. Then Douglas said, with an embarrassed laugh, 'That might prove a little awkward, Bill. You see . . .'

'I believe I can describe Mr Vance,' said Rowlands. 'Five foot eight, or thereabouts. Average build. Wears a toothbrush moustache and uses – that is to say, *used* – a good deal of brilliantine on his hair. Will that do?' he added innocently. 'I'm afraid it's by no means a full description, but . . .'

'It'll do to be going along with,' said the Chief

Inspector, in an amused tone. 'Agreed, Bill?'

'It'll do for me. All right, Jock,' – this to one of his two assistants – 'you can turn him over onto his back.'

'You're full of surprises today, Mr Rowlands,' said Douglas. 'Next thing, you'll be telling me that you can see as well as I can.'

'Oh, blind men have their ways of seeing,' said the Major. 'It's just a matter of using one's intelligence, isn't it, Rowlands? If you've finished with your questions for the time being, Chief Inspector, I'd like to go back to the house. I don't want to leave the men too long without a word. This had been a great shock to all of us.'

A few minutes passed. 'Well, it certainly looks like suicide,' said Dr Hargreaves, pulling off his rubber gloves with a snapping sound. 'Quite efficiently done, too – which isn't always the case with a hanging. One end of the rope tied around that beam, the other made into a nice, neat noose. Then he hops up onto the chair, slips the noose around his neck and . . . Bob's your Uncle. Yes, a pretty clear-cut case of self-murder, I'd say. But I won't know for certain until I do the post-mortem. You can take him away,' he said to his assistants. 'That is,' he added, addressing Douglas, 'if your chaps have finished.' The Chief Inspector gave a laugh that was more like a groan. 'Oh, we've finished,' he said. 'For what it's worth. The fact is, by the time our friends had done their worst – what with cutting down the body and trampling all over the scene – there wasn't much for us to find.'

'I'm sure the Major meant no harm,' interjected

Rowlands. 'He was just doing what he felt had to be done.'

'That's as may be,' was the dry response. 'In any case, it hardly matters, as we're dealing with a suicide. What *does* interest me is what our Mr Vance has been up to, these past few weeks – apart from playing cards, that is. The first thing we'll do is search his room.'

'Do you think he might have been responsible for the murders?' asked Rowlands.' Hard to say, at present,' was the reply. 'But if he was the killer, then there's a good chance we'll find something. They tend to keep things, these series killers,' he added, with the air of a connoisseur explaining some arcane point of detail to a layman. 'Mementos,' he said.

'So how did it go today?' asked Edith as he walked in, a little after seven. He must have looked blank, for she said: 'The painting. Is it finished yet?'

'Nowhere near.' He took his usual seat as close to the fire as possible and rubbed his hands together to restore the life to them.

'You look exhausted,' said his wife. 'You shouldn't have let him keep you so long.'

'I was only at the studio for a couple of hours,' he said. 'I've been with the Chief Inspector the rest of the time.'

'Why? What's happened?' He told her. After he had finished speaking, she was silent a while. 'I don't like this,' she said at last. 'I wish you'd never got involved.'

'You were all for it, at the beginning.'

'I know. Oh, it's all so hateful!' she cried. 'First those murders, and now this awful thing with Mr Vance. What do you think made him do it?'

'I couldn't say. I hardly knew the man.'

'Do you think there's any connection – with the murders, I mean?'

'I imagine that's what the police are trying to find out at this moment. You know, I could do with a cup of tea,' he said, hoping this might prove a diversion. All through the drive to the station in the back of the Crossley, with Douglas sitting preoccupied and taciturn beside him, and then in the crowded train home, he'd been able to think of nothing but Vance's dreadful death. He'd as soon have given the topic a rest. But Edith, having been at home all day in the company of small children, was eager to talk. 'Suppose he – Vance – were the killer,' she said.

'What of it?' he said wearily.

'Then he might have felt a sudden attack of remorse. Decided to end it all, rather than face up to what he'd done.' The thought had also occurred to him. But he didn't feel like discussing it. 'We'll have to see what the police dig up,' he said. He realised he was dog-tired. 'You know, I think I'll turn in early . . .'

'And then there's the Countess,' said Edith. 'Where does she fit into all this, I wonder? If Vance was the murderer, then surely she's got nothing more to worry about?'

'Let's see if she decides to come out of hiding, shall we?' he said, amused in spite of himself by her persistence. 'Come here,' he said, stretching out a hand to her. 'I feel as if I've hardly seen my wife all week.' He drew her down beside him on the sofa. After three children, she still had a waist as slim as a girl's. He drew her to him, and buried his face in her hair, breathing in the spicy, animal smell of it. He kissed her neck. 'I think we should both turn in early,' he said.

'No, Fred – be sensible for a moment, will you? I know what we should do. We should put a notice in the Personal column of *The Times*, saying something like, "*The knave is dead. The queen of hearts is safe once more*", or words to that effect. Since we know that she – the Countess – keeps an eye on the papers.' He sighed. 'My wife the detective. All right, have it your own way. But it's just possible, you know, that your theory's wrong, and that poor Vance isn't the killer. Then where would that leave us?'

But instead of replying, she suddenly sat bolt upright. 'A fine detective I've turned out to be! All the while you were telling me your news about Mr Vance, I had something to tell you. There's a letter.' With the same energy with which she did everything, she jumped to her feet, and shot out into the hall where the day's post was to be found on top of the hallstand. In another moment, she was back. 'Here we are!' she cried. 'It's addressed to you. A Lewisham postmark. Looks like a woman's hand. Rather round and schoolgirlish, but perfectly legible.'

'Well, go on, then – let's have it,' he said. She needed no further telling.

'"*Dear Sir,*"' she began. '"*You said if I had something to tell you I was to write and so I am writing. It isn't Fair what they said*" – capital 'f' for 'fair', by the way – "*he couldn't of done it. Albert Mullins is a Good Man*" – capital 'g', capital 'm' – "*I know the Truth of it . . .*"'

'Capital 't' for 'truth', no doubt?'

'Yes. "*I know the Truth of it and am willing to say what I know. Don't come to the W. H.—*"'

'I suppose that's the White Hart.'

'"*I will meet you Tuesday 4 p.m. Bettys Tea Shop*" – no apostrophe – "*by the station. Yours Truly Ruby M. Tyler (Miss)*". She doesn't say which station, but I imagine it'll be easy enough for us to find,' said Edith, folding the letter up.

'Us?'

'Oh, didn't I mention it?' she said. 'I thought I'd come with you. Mother can look after the girls.'

'I can see you've thought it all out,' he said.

'I have. And there's another thing,' said his wife. 'I think we should pay a visit to the grandmother – Mrs O'Reilly. Ever since you told me about her being left with that poor little boy, it's been on my mind. I thought there might be something we could do for them,' she said.

The house was one of a terrace in Drysdale Street, off Hoxton Square. They rang the bell. It seemed that a long time passed before somebody came. The woman who opened the door had a soft Irish voice. 'If it's the Mission Society you're collecting for, you're wasting your time' she said. 'We have our own collection for the orphans at St Monica's.'

'We're not from the Mission Society,' said Rowlands. He hesitated a moment, trying to think how best to say what it was he wanted to say. But it was Edith who spoke first. 'We wanted to speak to you about your daughter, Mrs O'Reilly. It *is* Mrs O' Reilly, isn't it?'

'And what if it is?' All friendliness was gone from the woman's voice. 'Are you from the poliss – is that it?' she demanded. Rowlands shook his head. 'We – that is, my wife and I – are assisting the police in looking into your daughter's murder,' he said. 'If you could see your way to answering a few questions, it would be a great help.' For a moment she seemed to hesitate. Then she sighed. 'You'd better come in,' she said. The two of them followed her into a cramped hall, and from thence into a cheerless parlour. The smell here was of furniture polish and soot. There was no fire. A dim memory of a similar room in his late mother's house in Camberwell came to Rowlands' mind. The windows with their lace and chenille curtains, and the heavy chairs, with their antimacassars, on either side of the fireplace. The elaborate overmantel with its mirror and shelves of knick-knacks, and the Benares brass-topped table, on which the oil lamp stood, with its pink glass mantel, and the painted roses on its china base. This room, though doubtless as respectably furnished, seemed drearier, somehow. Perhaps it was the cold. 'I don't suppose,' he said, 'that we could sit in the kitchen?'

'It's not very tidy,' said Mrs O'Reilly, evidently reluctant to allow the company beyond the boundaries of her best room.

'Oh, don't worry about that,' said Edith quickly. 'I'm sure we'd all rather be cosy, wouldn't we?' The kitchen was certainly that. A smell of boiling linen, from the copper on the stove, mingled with a lingering odour of cabbage.

'I was after doing my washing,' the old woman said apologetically as she went to turn the gas down. But Rowlands had become aware of another presence on the far side of the room: a small scuffling, as of someone getting ready for flight. This must be the child, he guessed. 'What are you doing there, Daniel?' said Mrs O'Reilly, confirming this supposition. The boy said nothing. 'The teachers've sent them home today, because of the snow,' she added, for the Rowlands' benefit. 'Although how I'm to cope . . .' She let the sentence tail off. 'Will you have a cup of tea?' she went on, brightening a little.

'If it's not too much trouble.'

'Oh, it's never a trouble. Daniel, if you keep picking at that loose thread in your jumper, you'll make a hole.'

'Hello, Daniel,' said Edith. 'I've got a little girl at home just about your age. That's six, isn't it? Or are you seven?'

Still the child said nothing.

'You mustn't mind him,' said the boy's grandmother, busying herself with filling the kettle. 'He hasn't said a word since it happened. 'Cat got your tongue, has it?' she added, to the child.

'It's all right,' said Rowlands. 'I'm sure when Daniel has something to say, he'll say it, won't you, Daniel?' A clatter of feet in boots a size too big was followed by the slamming of the kitchen door, Daniel evidently having had enough of this interrogation.

'I'm sure I don't know what to do with him,' sighed Nora O'Reilly. 'He was never much of a talker, but now . . .'

'It'll come back,' said Edith gently. 'May we sit down?'

'You may. And here's me forgetting my manners.'

When they were seated, at a kitchen table whose worn pine surface spoke of many years of diligent scouring, and the tea – now brewed to a powerful strength – had been poured and set in front of them, Rowlands returned to the subject about which they had come. 'Tell me about your daughter.'

'Mary? Ah, she was a lovely girl,' said Nora O'Reilly. 'Never the least bit of trouble to me. An angel from Heaven.' She paused, and took a drink of tea. 'At least, she was until she met that man . . .'

'What man was that?' he said.

'Why,' she replied. 'The one she married. That Thomas Lintott. A waster,' she added, 'although God forgive me for saying so of my own grandchild's father. A waster, a liar and a rogue. He broke my Mary's heart,' said the old woman fiercely. 'And for that I can never forgive him.' What followed was an all too familiar tale of innocence corrupted. 'He took her heart, and then he took her money,' said Mrs O'Reilly. 'She'd a good job then, at the Brewery in Brick Lane. Brought home fifteen shillings a week. And didn't he take it all, for his dogs and his drink, the rascal? Then of course the child came.' So the sad litany went on. The young mother deserted by her faithless spouse. The struggle to make ends meet and the need to take whatever came her way. The inevitable drift into low company. 'No, I'll never forgive him for what he did to her,' said Nora O'Reilly. 'It's him – Thomas Lintott – I blame for what happened as much as the other one.'

Rowlands guessed it was her daughter's killer she meant. And she was right, of course: Mary O'Reilly's dreadful death had been the culmination of a series of unlucky events. A bad marriage, financial troubles, a loss of self-respect. 'I'm sorry,' he said, when she had finished speaking. It seemed that, after all, there was little more to be learnt here. 'We should be going,' he said to Edith. 'Oh!' cried his wife. 'I almost forgot.' She rummaged in her travelling bag and withdrew a parcel, wrapped in brown paper. 'I've a few things here I thought might fit Daniel,' she said to Mrs O'Reilly. 'A couple of jumpers that my eldest has outgrown. A few pairs of warm socks.'

'That's kind of you,' replied the other woman. 'But . . .'

'You'd be doing me a favour by taking them off my

hands,' Edith rushed on, to avert what seemed a certain refusal. 'Children *do* grow so fast, don't they? I'm sorry it's not more, but . . .'

'Thank you,' said the old woman. 'I'm sure they'll come in useful.'

They had by now reached the front door. 'It was good of you to talk to us,' said Rowlands. He opened the door, and he and Edith stepped out. 'Perhaps, if anything else occurs to you . . .'

'I saw him, you know,' said Nora O'Reilly suddenly. 'Standing just over there, he was, under the lamp. It was when she stopped by to leave the child, you know. She used to do that, when she was going to be late of an evening. They didn't like it, at her lodgings, if she left him—'

'Who was it you saw?' asked Rowlands, interrupting this rambling explanation.

'Why,' she replied. 'Who else but the man who killed my Mary?' It took a moment for the implication of what she'd said to sink in. 'Have you told this to the police?' he asked, stepping back inside the hall, and motioning to Edith to do the same. 'Sure, and didn't I try to tell him, that great lump of a feller that came to the house to tell me she was gone?' cried Mrs O'Reilly. 'He wrote it all down in his little book, right enough. Said he'd be back to tell me if there was any news. But that was the last I heard.'

'Could you describe this man – the one that you saw under the lamp, I mean?' said Rowlands.

'Well, he was wearing a hat and coat, you know, so I couldn't tell you much about him, other than that he was a tall feller. Well-built, I'd say.'

Tall. Well-built. It could have been said of any number of men. At least it confirmed his earlier supposition. But Rowlands couldn't help feeling disappointed that there was nothing more. It was Edith who asked the obvious question – which hadn't occurred to him, because it had been so long since he had formed his impressions of others in that way. 'Did you see his face?'

'I did,' was the reply. 'It was only for a moment, mind. But I'd know that face in a thousand, so I would.'

Chapter Seventeen

When they left Drysdale Street at last, it was still only half past two, with well over an hour to go before they were to meet Ruby Tyler. Rowlands' first thought was to find a public telephone box, from which to call the Chief Inspector – what Nora O'Reilly had told them being of too great a significance for any further delay. But Douglas wasn't in his office, it transpired; nor did his sergeant know when he would return. 'Perhaps you could take a message?' asked Rowlands. 'I can do that, sir,' was the reply.

'Good.' Conscious that his three minutes was fast running out, Rowlands kept it brief. 'Tell him that Mary O'Reilly's mother can identify our man. Apparently she saw him outside her house on the night of the murder.'

'Did she indeed?' Sergeant Withers let out a low whistle. 'Why didn't she come forward before now?' Rowlands hesitated. The last thing he wanted was to drop someone in it. But he had no choice. 'She says she did. Only it wasn't followed up.'

'Is that so?' said the sergeant as the pips began to go. 'Then I reckon *somebody's* guts is going to be made into garters.'

They caught the bus from Old Street since they'd plenty of time in hand, climbing the stairs to where there were some seats at the front so that Rowlands could have his smoke and Edith could get the best view. Although it was still bitterly cold, the sun had come out, and a hard bright glare was reflected from the windows of buildings along the City Road. They passed Bunhill Fields, and Wesley's house, and Royal London Ophthalmic Hospital – these and other landmarks remarked upon by Edith, as was her habit when they shared a journey – then arrived at London Wall, and the purlieus of the City. 'Your old stamping ground,' said Edith.

'Have we passed Threadneedle Street yet?'

'Not yet.' The bus lumbered on. 'If she really *can* identify this man . . .' his wife began. 'Don't let's talk about it now,' he said. Old habits of caution died hard. When you couldn't see who was sitting behind or beside you, it made sense to behave as if all the world was a spy. 'All right,' said Edith. 'Would you like me to go on describing things?'

'Yes, please.'

'We're passing the Bank of England now. Mansion House is up ahead. There aren't many people about, at this time of day. A few businessmen in bowler hats. Oh! *There's* a woman – wearing a rather chic costume, and a very pretty hat. Perhaps she's been lunching with her husband.'

'Or her broker.'

'There's a news stand at the corner of Lombard Street – "*Goddard case latest*" it says.' The trial of a police sergeant accused of taking bribes from an Italian nightclub owner had knocked everything else off the front page, in recent days. It was a shocking case, Rowlands thought: that even the *police* were not exempt from bribery and corruption. 'We're almost at the Monument,' she said.

'How's my old office looking?' He kept his tone light.

'Just the same. That big clock under what used to be your window is still five minutes slow.' She was silent a moment. 'You know, Fred,' she went on, 'I really think . . .'

'Let's talk about it later,' he said. This wasn't the time or place for a discussion of their future. 'I suppose we must be at the river?'

'We're crossing it now. Tower Bridge is to our left, you'll recall. Quite a queue of barges and ships waiting to go through. If I look the other way, I can just see the dome of St Paul's.'

'I'm glad it's still where it was,' he said. Just then, the

clock on Southwark Cathedral chimed the half-hour. 'If the traffic isn't too bad,' he added, 'we should be in good time for our rendezvous.' He liked to be early for any meeting. This wasn't mere punctiliousness on his part, but a way of regaining some of the advantage lost by not being able to see. On this occasion, however, he found himself pre-empted.

'There's a young woman in a black cloth coat and fur collar – not *real* fur, I don't think – sitting by herself at a table next to the window,' said Edith as they reached the tea shop next to New Cross Gate Railway Station. 'She's wearing a *very* smart hat . . .' This meant it was a little too smart, in his wife's estimation, 'and rather too much lip rouge.'

'It sounds as if it might be her.' And indeed as they came in, the woman spoke: 'You didn't say as there'd be two of you.'

'Miss Tyler? I'm Edith Rowlands. My husband thought you might be more comfortable talking to him, with another woman along.'

'Keeping an eye on yer property?' was the tart reply. 'Well, you needn't worry yourself on *my* account.'

'If you'd just say what it is you have to say,' Rowlands put in hastily, 'I'd be grateful. It was about Elsie Alsop, wasn't it?' But the girl didn't answer right away. 'Bring us another pot of tea,' she said to the waitress; then to the Rowlandses: 'I take it you'd like some tea?'

'That would be very nice,' said Edith stiffly.

'And bring us some cakes. Fancy ones,' said Ruby

Tyler to the hovering girl. 'And not them stale ones, neither,' she added sternly. From what Rowlands could tell, Betty's Tea Shop was far from full. A couple of elderly women comparing their respective medical conditions over a pot of tea at one table, and a man noisily drinking soup at another, comprised the rest of the clientele. Even so, he lowered his voice before repeating his question: 'What was it you wanted to tell me about Elsie Alsop?'

Miss Tyler allowed a pause to elapse, for dramatic effect. 'Elsie Alsop was a right little cow,' she said. 'Even if it *is* speaking ill of the dead to say so. Playing her little games, oh-so-sweet and butter-wouldn't-melt-in-her-mouth, when all the time she was stringing a good man along.'

'Bert Mullins, you mean?' said Rowlands.

'Yes, and what of it?' she said hotly. 'Seems to me I've got a right to say what's true. Because even though there wasn't a ring, it was understood that she and Bert were engaged. 'Least, it was understood by *him*,' she added gloomily.

'Are you saying there were other men?' asked Rowlands. 'I'm not *saying* anything,' was the reply. 'All I'm telling you is what she told me herself.'

'And what was that?'

'She was meeting someone, wasn't she?' said Ruby Tyler flatly. 'A man. She was all excited about it. "He's going to make me a *star*, Ruby," she says to me. "He says as with *my* looks I should be up there on the silver screen, 'stead of pulling pints." Silly little tart,' said Miss Tyler, her tone evenly poised between scorn and pity.

'Did you see this man?' put in Edith. ''Fraid not,' was the reply. 'All I know is he spun her a lot of yarns about his rich and famous friends – one of 'em a countess, would you believe?'

'He said that, did he?' Rowlands tried, without success, to keep the excitement out of his voice. 'I mean, about knowing a countess?'

'Oh yes.' The girl took a bite of cake, and washed it down with a sip of tea. 'Don't think as I'd forget something like *that*.'

This interesting remark aside, there was not a great deal more to be learnt from Ruby Tyler. 'Of course, she's in love with that young man,' said Edith mischievously as the cab that was taking them to Charing Cross sped along the Old Kent Road. (Rowlands had had enough of buses for one day – and if he couldn't treat his wife to a ride in a taxi occasionally, then what sort of a man was he?) 'Albert Mullins, I mean.'

'Yes, I'd rather gathered that,' he said. 'You will see to it that they let Bert out of prison, won't you?' Miss Tyler had begged as they took their leave of her outside Betty's. 'Only he never done it. He ain't capable. I'll vouch for him,' she'd added stoutly.

'A formidable young woman,' he remarked. Edith gave a snort.

'Formidable's the word. And what a figure! Junoesque about describes it.'

'Oh? A pity I'm oblivious to all such charms,' he said.

'Stuff and nonsense,' said his wife. 'Why, if I hadn't been there, you'd have been holding hands over the teacups.'

'I resent that! Besides, I thought we'd agreed that she's in love with young Mullins?'

'That – as you reminded me not so very long ago – doesn't stop some people,' said Edith darkly.

After dropping his wife off at the station, Rowlands took the cab on to Scotland Yard. What Ruby Tyler had said hadn't amounted to very much, it was true, but it had added a small but important detail to the picture of the murderer he and the Chief Inspector were trying to build. For this was a man, it had become clear, who relied on seduction in order to gain his ends. Flattery, and the promise of money and social advancement, seemed to have been his weapons. Then there was the remark about the Countess. If it were true – and there was no reason to suppose that Ruby Tyler had made it up – then it made the connection explicit between the murdered women and the woman Rowlands had come to believe was the *real* focus of the man's obsession. For that it *was* an obsession he was now in no doubt. He can't help himself, he thought as, having paid off the cab, he entered the great edifice of red-and-cream brick that was the nerve centre of the Metropolitan Police Force, and took the lift to the third floor. 'Ah, Rowlands, there you are,' said Douglas as he walked in. 'I was just going to telephone you about the latest development. The fact is, it changes everything.'

'Yes, I thought it was rather significant, myself,' said Rowlands, sitting himself down on one of the pair of rickety deal chairs that stood in front of Douglas's desk.

'What? Oh, you mean the new evidence that's been turned up on the O'Reilly murder? Yes, that was a good bit of sleuthing, on your part.' said the Chief Inspector. 'I've got a sergeant round there now, taking a statement. But it wasn't that I meant.'

'Then what?'

'I've just received the medical report on our late friend Reginald Vance,' said Douglas. 'Seems he didn't kill himself, after all. Somebody did it for him.'

'But . . . he hanged himself, surely?'

'He was garrotted, not hanged,' was the grim reply. 'There's a superficial resemblance – good enough to fool anyone who didn't know what they were looking for, but the signs are quite unmistakeable, the MO says. Something to do with the pattern of bruising around the throat. Then whoever did it fixed it up to *look* like a hanging. Had the rope all ready, you see. One end tied to the beam, the other already fastened into a nice, neat noose, to slip over the victim's head once he'd done the business. Then all he had to do was haul the unfortunate man into place, knock over the chair, and wait until the suicide was discovered. Clever,' said the Chief Inspector gloomily. 'Very clever.'

'I suppose we've no idea who?'

'Not as yet,' said Douglas irritably. 'Although I gather

from what your Major said that Mr Vance was not without his enemies. People he owed money to – or who owed *him* money. We're working through a few of the suspects now. But so far we've nothing conclusive.' Rowlands felt suddenly in desperate need of a smoke. He took his cigarettes from his jacket pocket and offered the pack to Douglas. 'Thanks, but I prefer my pipe,' said the other. 'What's so damned annoying,' he went on, 'is that it sounds as if he – Vance – was about to spill the beans about something. Or someone. If your friend the Major had only been a bit quicker off the mark.'

'It wasn't the Major's fault,' said Rowlands.

'I never said it was,' snapped the Chief Inspector. He let out a gusty sigh. 'This is proving a damnably complicated case,' he said. Rowlands lit his gasper and drew in a lungful of smoke. Ah, *that* was better. Things seemed clearer, all of a sudden.

'Do you think there's any connection between this and the other murders?' he asked. Douglas took his time considering the question.

'Well, I did think – when we first discovered the body – that Vance might be our man, you know,' he said at last. 'Remorse for his crimes being the motive for his suicide. But *this* rather washes that theory out.'

'I suppose so.'

'Yes, I'm afraid *this* murder may be no more than a particularly nasty way of settling a bad debt.'

'A debt incurred over a game of cards,' said Rowlands.

'There is that,' murmured the Chief Inspector, busying

himself with filling his pipe. A few moments passed while he completed this operation. 'What was it you wanted to see me about?' he asked, once the pipe was lit and drawing nicely. 'I take it there *was* something?'

'One small thing.' Rowlands repeated what Ruby Tyler had said about the man Elsie Alsop had been meeting, and his boasted connection with a countess.

'Interesting,' said Douglas. 'I don't suppose she got a look at him – your barmaid friend, I mean?'

'No such luck.'

'Pity,' said the Chief Inspector. 'But then we've not had a lot of luck with this case so far. We've one old woman as eyewitness, and one piece of hearsay linking our murderer to the Russian Countess . . . if it *is* the Countess our mystery man was referring to. It's not a lot to be going on with, is it?'

'It's more than we had yesterday,' said Rowlands.

'True. And we've one more murder victim than we had yesterday, too,' said Douglas. For a few moments, the two men smoked in silence. From outside in the corridor, came the sound of voices: 'I'm telling you, it was offside . . .' 'Rot! That was a perfectly good goal . . .' Then someone else said something and the voices were instantly hushed. 'Young devils,' said Douglas. His voice betrayed his exhaustion. 'Hearsay or no,' he went on, picking up the thread of the conversation, 'it's the best link we've got to what we might call the Countess's world. Your Lady Celia's world, too,' he added slyly. 'Speaking of which, how're you getting on with having your portrait painted? It must be nearly done by now, I'd have thought.'

Rowlands corrected this assumption. 'Good,' said the Chief Inspector. 'Then you've a reason to return. I'm still not convinced that we won't find our murderer amongst the Chelsea set. There's something about all this – artists' models, countesses, games of cards – that smacks of Bohemia,' he said.

Loveless didn't seem surprised to see him; in his world, Rowlands surmised, people came and went with a casualness not permitted to the working man. 'Oh, you're here, are you?' was all the greeting he received. 'I was just taking a look at the big piece. It's shaping up rather well,' he went on as Rowlands followed him across the cramped sitting room that doubled as his sleeping quarters, to the studio. 'I've got the composition more or less as I want it. Now it's just a matter of working up the individual figures. *Yours* has been giving me a bit of trouble,' he added. 'Can't decide whether to have you looking into the centre of the picture – towards the dead Christ, you know – or off to the side. Averting your gaze from the sight, as it were.'

'Yes, I can picture that.'

'In fact, now you're here, I'd like to try a few different poses. No, you needn't sit down. Just stay as you are.' There came the now familiar sound of paper being expertly torn to size, then the rapid scratching of charcoal as the artist got his impressions down on that paper. Surprised into immobility before he was quite ready, Rowlands now wished he'd taken up a more comfortable stance. There was an itch on the end of his nose he'd like to have scratched. It'd be hell after ten minutes. But, as it turned out, he didn't even have to hold it for two. 'All right, you can relax,' said Loveless. He considered his drawing. 'Not bad,' he said. 'But I think we can do better. Now, stand with your back to me. That's right. Turn your face to the side. Yes, that's it. A three-quarter view's what I'm after.' He drew rapidly. 'Good,' he said after a minute or so had elapsed. 'I think I've got it. You can rest now. Cigarette?'

Rowlands accepted gratefully. Knowing Loveless's appetite for work by this time, he supposed the break would be no more than momentary, but the artist, to his surprise, seemed disposed to chat. 'So tell me,' he said when both had their smokes and a pot of tea was brewing, 'has anything been seen of the lovely Natalia since we last met?'

'Not to my knowledge,' said Rowlands guardedly.

'How very mysterious!'

If the man knew anything about the Countess's whereabouts, he was playing his cards very close to his chest, thought Rowlands. 'Lady Celia thinks she left of her own free will,' he said. 'And what do *you* think?' Was there a note of sly teasing in Loveless's voice, Rowlands wondered. He thought, it's a game to him. It was the murderer of whom he was thinking. 'I don't know,' he replied. 'But I'm rather afraid that the

Countess's life may be at risk.'

Loveless yawned. 'I think Natalia's quite capable of looking after herself,' he said. 'That type always are.' He didn't elaborate. 'Shall we get on?' This time, it was the seated pose he wanted. 'I think we're almost done with this,' he said. 'Another session should do it.' He must have levered the lids off some of his tins of paint, for the smell of it filled the room. Years afterwards, that smell would conjure that moment for Rowlands: the studio, with the cold north light falling upon his face. The rapt attention being given to that face by the man behind the easel. The long periods of silence, broken by inconsequential remarks. 'You know,' said Loveless, 'it's not just your face that interests me, but your expression. You have what I'd call a rather inward look. Hardly surprising, under the circumstances, but quite difficult to catch. It's a good thing we artists like a challenge.'

Since no response was possible – or rather, permissible – Rowlands contented himself with listening. It was something which had become second nature over the years. It wasn't just what people said, but the manner in which they said it, that was revealing. He'd already worked out that Loveless's bluster was a blind, to conceal a more sensitive spirit. Now, as the artist worked away, occasionally murmuring instructions to himself, 'No, no, that won't do . . . a touch more rose madder on the cheekbone, I think,' he thought, could this man be a murderer? It hardly seemed possible, and yet . . . 'You still haven't told me,' said Loveless casually, 'how it is you know Celia West.'

'I did her a service, once.'

'Ah! "A verray parfit gentil knyght,"' said the artist. 'Yes, I'd imagine Celia would fit rather well into the role of the Cruel Fair.'

Rowlands made no reply.

'Yes, yes,' drawled Loveless. 'I know it's not the act of a gentleman to discuss a lady with another gentleman, but then, I've never paid much attention to such niceties. Can I ask you something?'

'Ask away.'

'Are you some kind of private detective?'

'You could say that,' said Rowlands warily.

'Only I can't otherwise account for your interest in our missing Russian.' Loveless went on painting for another few minutes; then he said: 'We'll stop now. The pub for lunch today, I think. And then I'm going to a private view in Cork Street. You can come with me, if you like.'

'That's kind of you,' said Rowlands. 'But I don't think . . .'

'You might find it of interest,' said Loveless. 'In your profession, I should have thought it made sense to cultivate as wide a circle of acquaintance as possible.'

The Tyro Gallery, it transpired, was one of the smaller ones, sandwiched between an establishment specialising in Old Dutch Masters – several of which were displayed in the window, to judge from Loveless's scornful comments – 'Old Masters, my eye! Most of 'em very poor copies of the real thing – painted in gravy, from the look of 'em' – and another, no less expensive place, whose stock-in-trade was the new Surrealism. About this, Loveless expressed a grudging approval. 'Some of the stuff's all right. I like that De Chirico. Quite a witty parody of Classical Formalism. But I don't think much of the Dali. All that half-baked dream symbolism and flabby eroticism. It sells, though,' he added gloomily. 'Like most mediocre work. Try to do anything first rate, and you can be sure that the *herd* will take fright at it.'

He was still talking loudly as they entered the gallery, which was already full to bursting, it appeared. The discreet clamour of educated English voices engulfed them. 'Interesting work, although not quite . . .' said a voice close to Rowlands' ear while another, a few feet away, opined that 'the Paris show was too, too divine.' A third asked plaintively, 'Any chance of another?' It was not yet four and already wine was being consumed in copious quantities. 'Oh God,' muttered Loveless, helping himself and Rowlands to a glass of the same. 'What possessed me to come? Half the bad artists in London seem to have turned up. There's Halliday, of course, with his coterie of eager young acolytes – Gatling amongst them. *He* wouldn't be a bad painter if he could only get out from under Gordon Halliday's wing. What a fraud that man is! He seems to think that wearing red trousers and sleeping with the maids makes him some kind of Communist. As for that cow-like wife of his, she couldn't paint to save her life. But of course, it wouldn't be polite to say so, of the divine Vanora's pretty little daubs . . . Ah, Goldberg, there you are! Quite a good turnout you've got.'

'Thanks,' said the artist drily. 'I knew you'd arrived even before you came in the door. Half of Mayfair must have known it, too.' His accents were those of Mittel Europa, filtered through the rougher tones of the East End.

'This is a friend of mine,' said Loveless, ignoring Goldberg's remark. 'Name of Frederick Rowlands. Goldberg and I are old Pals – from the Artists' Rifles,' he added, in parenthesis, to Rowlands. 'Rowlands is doing me the favour of sitting for me,' he went on. 'My big Crucifixion piece, you know.'

'Yes,' said Goldberg. 'That will be a fine piece – if you ever finish it. You have a good face,' he said to Rowlands. There was no suitable reply to this, except a smile. It struck Rowlands that his face had never been more complimented.

'I'm afraid I shall have to rely on Mr Loveless to tell me about your paintings,' he said. 'As you may have noticed, my appreciation of all such things is somewhat limited.'

'But that is wonderful!' cried Goldberg, rather disconcertingly. 'We will leave Loveless to look at the paintings, which, by the way, are of two kinds: the domestic – portraits of my dear wife, Hannah, and our children – and those with a martial theme. That is to say, they are reminiscences of the war. I cannot seem to forget what I have seen,' he added softly. 'Although it is no longer the fashion to paint this kind of subject . . . But come, I have something else to show you – something of which you will have a particular appreciation.' He drew Rowlands with him through the crowd, which seemed comprised of a fair cross section of the London art world – to judge, at least, from the fragments of talk Rowlands heard in passing:

'. . . not sure about his use of *impasto* . . .'

' . . . fetched eighty guineas for my last big piece . . .'

'. . . a good price, wholesale, from my dealer in Whitechapel . . .'

'. . . and don't even *mention* Max Ernst . . .'

'Here we are!' Goldberg had come to a halt in the middle of the room. It was, Rowlands felt, like being at the centre of a vortex of slowly circulating bodies. 'Give me your hand,' said the artist. Rowlands did so, and at once felt it being placed on top of a smooth, rounded surface. Some kind of metal – bronze, he supposed. He brought his other hand up to explore the object. A head, of course. Somewhat stylised, as was the fashion, he knew. Slowly, he ran his fingers over forehead and eyelids, across the cheeks and down the delicate curve of the nose, to the full, rosebud-lipped mouth and small, round chin.

'It's very beautiful,' he said.

'It is my son, David,' was the gratified reply. 'He was

ten years old when I made this. Do you have children, Mr Rowlands?'

'Three girls.'

'You are fortunate. But here is somebody who knows you, if I am not mistaken. A friend, perhaps?'

Rowlands shook his head. 'I hardly think so. Apart from yourself and Mr Loveless, I don't know anybody here.'

'But how extraordinary!' said Goldberg. 'I could have sworn that he . . . Did you see him, Loveless?' he asked as the latter joined them. 'The man who was here just now. Tall – and with *such* a face! He has seen terrible things, that man, I think.'

'I didn't see him,' was the reply. 'It's such a crush in here. Why? Does he owe you money?'

'I rather think it is Mr Rowlands to whom he owes money,' said the other gravely. 'He took one look at him, and then he turned and ran out, as if he had seen a ghost.'

'Good Lord! Any idea who that might be, Rowlands?'

'No.'

'Curiouser and curiouser,' said Loveless. 'Although it doesn't surprise me,' he added slyly. 'Rowlands here knows all sorts of interesting people. Some nice work, by the way, Isaac. Even though I still prefer your earlier stuff.'

'Loveless and I do not agree about Abstraction,' his fellow artist explained to Rowlands. 'The work he likes best of mine was made before the war when we thought we would change the world, he and I. He still believes this, whereas I . . .' His remarks were interrupted by a little commotion – no more than a just discernible increase in the volume of conversation – at the end of the gallery nearest the door. Someone, it appeared, had effected an entrance. Who it was became apparent to Rowlands a moment or two before the others had noticed. A voice that was all too familiar was saying, in tones that mingled amusement with the faintest irritation: 'I honestly don't see why you wanted to come. It's not really your sort of thing at all – is it, my sweet?'

Instinctively, he turned his face towards the sound. His companions must have followed suit, for Loveless said, 'Ah, here's La Belle Dame Sans Merci herself! A pity she's brought her tame Blackshirt with her.'

'Yes, I'm glad he and I meet in Mayfair, and not in Whitechapel,' murmured Goldberg. 'Good of you to come, Lady Celia,' he said in a louder tone. 'And Lord Edgecombe, too. I am honoured.'

But Celia West, as was her wont, paid scant attention to these conventional civilities. 'Hello, Isaac,' she said, 'This is a nice crowd you've got here.'

'The dregs of Western civilisation,' said Loveless.

'Oh, that's putting it a bit strong, don't you think? It's just a lot of men in art silk bow ties and shapeless tweed jackets going on about Significant Form – and women in hand-spun smocks and amusing silver jewellery letting them do it. A typical London art crowd, in fact. But what are *you* doing here, Mr Rowlands?'

'Didn't I tell you?' said Loveless to Goldberg. 'Rowlands knows all the most interesting people in

London. Speaking of which, I don't suppose *you* caught a glimpse of this chap that Goldberg has been going on about, did you, Celia? Tall, with a menacing expression.'

'Not menacing,' said Goldberg. 'Frightened, I would say.'

'Seems he took exception to Rowlands here. Dashed off before the rest of us could get a look at him.'

'How very odd!' said Lady Celia. 'When was this?'

'A moment ago – just around the time that you came in. He must have rushed straight past you.'

'Well, I didn't see anyone of that description – did you, Johnny?'

''Fraid not,' drawled Lord Edgecombe; then, to Rowlands: 'Friend of yours, was he?'

'Not as far as I know.'

'Johnny, I'm beginning to find you rather a bore. I suggest you go outside and have a smoke,' said Lady Celia. 'I can't think why he wanted to come,' she went on as, with a disgusted snort, her lover walked away. 'He hates this kind of thing. Some lovely work, by the way, Isaac,' she remarked offhandedly. 'That charming drawing of Hannah, and . . . Oh! I *do* like this.' It was the bronze to which she was referring, Rowlands surmised. 'What are you asking for it?'

'It's not for sale.'

'You artists,' she said. 'No wonder you're all as poor as church mice. Perhaps, Mr Rowlands, you'll walk round with me? There must be *something* else here that I'd like to buy – and that Mr Goldberg is willing to sell.'

Chapter Eighteen

Lady Celia took his arm, and drew him close to her as they began to work their way, by degrees, through the dense crowd of artists – who smelt, for the most part, of turpentine and the cheap, hand-rolled cigarettes they favoured – and of art dealers (cigars, and expensive cologne). The fur collar of her coat tickled his nose. Her delicious scent was in his nostrils. When they had reached what he judged must be the far wall of the room, she came to a halt. 'Now, this is a nice one,' she said. '*Reverie*. It's a woman – naked of course – standing in front of a mirror. I assume it's Hannah – even though he's painted her in rather odd colours. A green face, and lots of mauve and green mixed up with the flesh tones. But it's a nice picture. Most of the best ones seem to be of her. *I* call it rather wonderful, to be still so much in love when you've been married for over a decade – don't you think?' He murmured his agreement. 'But I suppose you know all about that?' she went on. 'Having been married for quite a while yourself.' Sensing that he was being teased, he merely smiled.

'Tell me about the next painting,' he said.

'Oh, I don't like this one nearly so much! It's rather a grim subject. A dead man – I suppose he must be a soldier – tied to a post. He's been shot. There's a lot of blood on the ground at his feet. The colours are quite *violent*. Reds, browns and purples. It's called *The Coward*. No, I can't say I care for that one at all.' Rowlands, for whom her description had conjured up an all too vivid memory of a scene he had once been forced to witness during those last dark days in Ypres, was silent. His companion must have noticed his change of mood, for she said softly, 'Of course, you were there, weren't you? I always forget how many of my male acquaintance went thorough the war.'

'Well, it's been over ten years since it ended,' he said – although that was nothing to him. It might have been yesterday.

'Yes,' she said. 'I don't suppose,' she went on, still in the same subdued tone, 'that you've heard any news about Natalia?'

'I'm afraid not.'

'Only since we last met, I've been thinking . . . There was something very *odd* about the whole thing . . . Ah, *that's* a much nicer picture!' she cried. 'Such a dear little family – mother, father, three children – all gathered around a table. With one of those candlesticks with all the candles arranged like a kind of tree. It's all in shades of blue and violet, except for the centre of the picture where the candlelight falls, which is all gold . . . *Sabbath*, it's called. I do like it. Perhaps I'll buy it.'

'You were saying that you thought there was something odd. Something to do with the Countess . . .' he persisted, trying to recall her to her former train of thought. But Lady Celia seemed, momentarily, to have forgotten him – her attention now caught by something – or someone – on the far side of the room. 'I don't believe it!' she said, as if to herself. Then: 'Mr Rowlands, would you mind awfully if we looked at the paintings another time?'

'Not at all.'

'Only my fiancé seems to have taken leave of his senses.' She left him then, without further explanation. He heard the sharp click of her heels as she crossed the floor. It seemed to him that a hush had fallen over the room, although it was perhaps no more than a momentary lull in the conversation. Whatever the reason, it meant that – without moving a step nearer – he could hear every word of the ensuing confrontation. It was she who spoke first: 'I wish you'd tell me what exactly you think you're playing at.'

'I don't know what you mean,' was the reply. Johnny

Edgecombe sounded both sulky and shifty – not an attractive combination, thought Rowlands, who already had ample reason to dislike him. Then came another voice – deep and sonorous, with the faintest trace of a foreign accent. French, perhaps; or Swiss – Rowlands couldn't be sure. 'I believe that I am myself the unwitting cause of the lady's displeasure.'

'Oh hello, Mr Le Fevre,' said Lady Celia, with casual insolence. 'I didn't see you there. Come to look at the paintings, have you?'

'Now we're in for some fun!' said Percy Loveless, in Rowlands' ear. 'If there's one man Celia can't stand, it's Maurice Le Fevre. I suppose Edgecombe must have invited him, the fool. Rather usefully, for my purposes, as it happens,' he added mysteriously. But just then Isaac Goldberg, sounding rather more like a denizen of the East End than he had during his conversation with Rowlands, joined the group that was standing near the door. ''Evening, Le Fevre. I didn't expect to see you here.'

'Then I hope,' replied Le Fevre, 'that my presence is not *de trop*?'

'It's a free country, isn't it? Or it was when I last looked,' said Goldberg amiably. 'Take a look around while you're here. You might see something you want to buy.'

'I very much doubt it,' said the other, no less courteously. 'Your work is . . . how shall I say? Too *modern* for my liking.'

'Modern's one way of putting it,' said the artist, every

vestige of warmth gone from his voice. 'Decadent's another thing I've heard it called, by people like you.' The room was suddenly quiet. The heated argument which had been going on in a far corner between a Dadaist and a Surrealist tailed off into subdued muttering. A woman who'd had rather too much to drink laughed shrilly, then lapsed into silence.

'I think,' said Maurice Le Fevre, 'that it is you who is being offensive. I have said nothing about your work, other than that I do not wish to buy it. That is surely my right. It is, as you say, a free country. But I see that I am not welcome here. Lord Edgecombe, if you are ready, perhaps we should go.'

'And where, might I ask, are you going?' Celia West's tone, addressing her lover, was one of dangerous politeness.

'Celia, if you're going to make a scene . . .'

Again, it was Le Fevre who intervened, with the unctuousness of one pouring oil on troubled waters. 'Lord Edgecombe has agreed to lend me his house for a private gathering this evening – my own being insufficiently large for the purpose.'

'I see,' said Lady Celia. She sounded infinitely bored. 'Well, don't let me keep you.'

'Celia . . .'

'Where's Isaac got to? Oh, *there* you are,' she went on as if Edgecombe had not spoken. 'There's a painting of yours to which I've taken rather a fancy. The blue one – with the children sitting around the table, and the candlestick in the middle. I take it *that's* for sale?'

'To you – of course,' said Isaac Goldberg. 'Goodnight, Mr Le Fevre. I'm sorry you couldn't have stayed longer. You might have learnt something.' But Le Fevre was not quite finished, it seemed. For he had spotted Loveless.

'Ah, Mr Loveless! Another artist of the modern kind. Although not, perhaps, so modern as Mr Goldberg. I trust you will be there on Saturday night?'

'Oh, I'll be there,' replied Loveless.

'Good. I look forward to seeing you – and your friend, too, if you like,' he added, noticing Rowlands. 'The more good, true men – Englishmen – we have taking a part in our movement, the better.' Then he was gone, taking Johnny Edgecombe with him, Rowlands surmised, for a moment later Lady Celia was again beside him.

'I must say, Loveless, I'm surprised at you,' she said. 'Fraternising with the likes of Maurice Le Fevre. The man's a snake.'

'Ah, but I have my reasons,' said Loveless. 'Besides which, he serves a very good dinner, I'm told.'

Le Fevre's house was a relatively modest establishment in Upper Grosvenor Street. 'Handy for his rallies in Hyde Park,' said Loveless as he rang the bell. 'This is just his pied à terre – he owns a much larger place in Kent, near Sevenoaks. Hideous great Gothic pile. I've been there once. Not really my cup of tea – the house or the company Le Fevre keeps. Still, needs must,' he added cryptically. They were admitted by a functionary whose manners left something to be desired. ''Ee's in there,' he grunted as he relieved them of their coats.

'If his last place wasn't Wormwood Scrubs, I'm a Dutchman,' muttered Loveless. 'Brute's built like a prizefighter . . . Probably *is* one, too, if half the tales one hears about Le Fevre's bully boys are true.'

The room to which they had so unceremoniously been directed was already more than half-full, to judge by the volume of sound which greeted them as they entered. It was, thought Rowlands, a very *masculine* sound, composed of all the varying tones – from lightest tenor to deepest bass – of men's voices; no females were in evidence, it seemed. The prevailing smells, too, were masculine: odours of cigar smoke, whisky, brandy, and other spiritous liquors, mingled with those of Bay Rum and Bayley's Imperial Russian Leather. 'Looks like the usual crowd you get at these affairs,' said Loveless. 'Disgruntled younger sons of earls, whose title has ceased to buy them the respect they feel they're owed, disaffected Conservative MPs, cashiered army officers, and cranks.'

'Gentlemen, welcome,' said their host, coming over to them at this moment. 'Mr Loveless – and Mr Rowlands, is it not?' Rowlands admitted that it was. 'You served your country during the war, I perceive,' said Le Fevre. 'We have many former soldiers joining our ranks. Men who have made sacrifices, as you have, but have not seen that sacrifice rewarded as it should have been . . . But you don't have drinks.' He clicked his fingers, and at once another functionary appeared. 'Bring our guests whatever they want,' he said. Loveless asked for a whisky and soda; Rowlands followed suit. 'So, Mr Loveless, you enjoy the hospitality of your Bohemian friends on one evening, and now you come to enjoy mine.' The amusement in Le Fevre's voice concealed something uglier, Rowlands thought. It wasn't quite menace, but still . . . 'You like to have a foot in both camps, I see.'

The drinks arrived. Rowlands took a swig of his. He thought he was going to need it. He'd been in some unpleasant spots in his time, but this Mayfair drawing room beat them all. 'Oh, I don't see myself as belonging to any camp, as you call it,' replied Loveless. 'Artists aren't obliged to be partisan.'

'Ah, now *there* I cannot agree. Surely Art must serve the greater good? It can only do this by promoting healthy values.'

'And what are those?'

'That you have to *ask* is itself somewhat troubling, Mr Loveless. But here is Mr Babbington to take up your challenge.' The individual alluded to was a man of whom even Rowlands had heard. A writer famous for his Anglo-Catholicism and for his trenchant views, all too frequently aired in the columns of the *Daily Express*, on the deplorable spread of effeminacy amongst all classes of British society and the rise of what he characterised as *decadent* elements. 'Mr Loveless wants to know,' said Le Fevre to the new arrival, 'what the purpose of Art should be.'

'Oh, oh, my good Le Fevre,' exclaimed Babbington

who, despite the virulence of the ideas he expressed in print, seemed in person to be the soul of geniality. 'You do ask the most extraordinary questions! I wouldn't *presume* to tell such a distinguished practitioner as Mr Loveless here the purpose, as you call it, of his chosen discipline. For myself . . .' Here he paused, wheezing a little. The author of such bestselling novels as *Yesterday Upon the Stair* and *The Four Horsemen* was also renowned for being immensely fat. 'I would say that the purpose of Art is to promote innocence.'

'Clean-living, you mean?' asked Loveless innocently.

Babbington chuckled. 'Oh, Mr Loveless, you won't catch me out so easily,' he said. 'I have known many sinners who have been converted to saints, not through clean-living, but through confessing their faults, and becoming as little children again. Salvation, as I need not remind you, is available to us all.'

'Even murderers?' said Loveless.

'Why not? Our Lord made no distinction.'

But Maurice Le Fevre had evidently had enough of such theological hair-splitting. 'Gentlemen,' he said. 'I see that the card tables are set up. Shall I lead the way?' In the annex off the drawing room to which their host now conducted them, a game of poker was already in progress; Rowlands could hear the clacking of chips as they were thrown down. 'Straight Flush,' called out a voice triumphantly as he passed by the table. 'Here, we leave politics – and religion – at the door,' said Le Fevre. 'The next two hours are dedicated solely to the pleasures of the table – the gaming table, that is. We will dine later.'

'I never play cards,' said Loveless. 'Playing the art market's risky enough for me. I shall just enjoy this very good cigar, and take a look at your admirable collection of prints, Le Fevre. I hadn't realised you were such a collector.'

'I have my own preferences in art, as you see,' replied the other. 'Mr Rowlands? Surely you will not disappoint us? We have Bridge as well as Poker on offer, you know.'

There was an awkward pause. 'I'd like to play,' said Rowlands. 'But . . .' He spread his hands in the gesture signifying amused resignation. 'You see how it is.'

'Please don't worry yourself, Mr Rowlands!' said Le Fevre. 'It isn't the first time we've had to accommodate someone like yourself. I'm sure we can find a pack of cards to suit you.' He gave an order to another manservant, and the latter returned within a moment or two. 'Here we are, sir. Two packs of braille cards, like you said.' Rowlands tried to keep the surprise from showing on his face. That Le Fevre was familiar with the special cards was surely suggestive? But whether of guilt or innocence, he could not be sure. Of the twenty or so people assembled in Le Fevre's drawing room, four tables' worth of card players now arranged themselves. Two of these were for Poker, and two for Bridge – the Poker tables filling up first so that a couple of those who wanted to play were left with the second option. One of these was Johnny Edgecombe, evidently disgruntled at this outcome. He was even more annoyed to discover that he was to play at the same table as Rowlands. The braille cards, too, met with his displeasure; 'But these are *marked* cards!' he said with some indignation. When it was explained to him what they were, he seemed no less suspicious. 'It doesn't seem quite *cricket* to me, somehow,' he said sullenly. 'Giving one chap an advantage like that.'

It didn't seem worth pointing out that the advantage in question was a poor compensation for the greater advantage of sight. 'Well,' he said ungraciously to Rowlands, 'It seems we can hardly avoid one another these days.' There were only two ways of responding to this piece of calculated rudeness: the first was to respond in kind; the second to ignore it. Rowlands chose the latter course. 'Shall we cut for partners?' he said. To Rowlands' relief, he was partnered with the banker, Carrington, who was dealing. The deftness with which he did this was a good sign, Rowlands thought. His own hand turned out not to be too bad: five spades and four hearts was the best of it. North – Carrington – opened the bidding: 'One spade.'

'No bid.' This was said in a surly tone. If Edgecombe's card-playing was as bad as his manners, he would prove a tiresome opponent, thought Rowlands. 'Three spades,' he said.

'No bid,' said the Colonel.

'Our bid wins the auction, I think,' said Carrington pleasantly.

Several more games followed, with Rowlands' pair

taking most of the tricks. They'd already won the first two rubbers and looked set to win the third, he thought, if their luck held. So far he'd had nothing but good cards. Now it was East's turn to deal. He did so in a grudging fashion, flipping the cards carelessly towards each of the other players instead of laying them down tidily. Once again, Rowlands found himself with a good hand. The bidding began. 'Two hearts,' said Edgecombe. 'No . . . Oh damn! I don't mean that.'

'You'll have to stick with it, old boy,' his partner reminded him. 'No bid.'

'Two spades.'

'Four spades,' said Carrington. 'Ours again, I think.'

'I call it bloody unfair, this business with marked cards,' said Edgecombe thickly. 'If you want my opinion, it's little more than . . .'

'Careful, old boy!' said the Colonel in a warning tone. He was rather a decent sort, Rowlands decided. 'I don't think the fact that they're braille cards gives my partner any advantage,' said Carrington.

'Well, you *would* say that,' retorted the younger man.

'You're tight, Edgecombe,' said the banker, who obviously felt confident enough in his own no doubt considerable wealth to dispense with the other's title. 'I'd take a walk around the room if I were you.'

'Damned if I will!' said the other. But he pushed back his chair and got up. A moment later, he could be heard in the next room, calling angrily for a whisky.

'Sorry about that,' said the Colonel to Rowlands. 'He always was an unstable boy. Knew his father, years ago. Good man. He and I served at Ladysmith together, y'know. Edward – the eldest boy – was killed at Gallipoli. Great pity,' said the old man ruefully. Dinner was announced at that moment, and so the game, by mutual agreement, remained unfinished, with Rowlands' pair winning by default. Their table joined the rest of the party as it moved towards the dining room.

'Lose much?' said Loveless, falling into step beside Rowlands. 'We weren't playing for money,' he replied, surprised.

'The poker tables were,' said Loveless, sotto voce. 'Some quite large sums were being staked as far as I could tell from where I was sitting. Don't tell your friend the Chief Inspector, will you?' he added slyly.

The dinner, as Loveless had promised, was excellent. Mock turtle soup was followed by Dover sole; then a wonderfully gamey plate of pheasant. Rowlands was glad to find himself seated by his former Bridge opponent, Colonel Forster. They soon fell into conversation about the war. As they talked, comparing their respective experiences on the field of battle, Rowlands wondered what it was that had brought the old man to such a gathering. But then, downing his third or fourth glass of Le Fevre's fine hock, Colonel Forster began talking in rambling clauses of the generation that had been lost, and of the one that had superseded it: 'It's jus' not the same. Calibre of men you get nowadays. Wretched types. Pansies, most of 'em. One might as well have bloody *women* in charge.' There was more of this, and so, as soon as he decently could, Rowlands turned to his left-hand neighbour. This proved to be one of Loveless's 'disgruntled younger sons' – angry that the family estate had been parcelled up and sold off to the Jews, as he put it. 'Disgraceful state of affairs. We've let them take over, and now they're squeezing us dry.'

Across the table, Loveless was giving one of his lectures on the decline of Western civilisation: '. . . of course, Europe's completely finished. "An old bitch gone in the teeth," as our friend Mr Pound would say . . .' It all fitted rather too well into the general tenor of the evening, thought Rowlands. Loveless, he had decided, was something of a wild card. He enjoyed sounding off about contentious subjects, and was just as likely to switch to the opposite point of view to the one he had been expressing if it suited him to do so. Which was all very well, Rowlands thought, as long as those to whom one was talking understood the game. In company such as this, one ran the risk of being taken at one's word.

They had reached the closing stages of the dinner. The savoury had been consumed and the port was circulating. At the head of the table, Le Fevre tapped his glass to call for silence. A hush fell upon the room. 'Gentlemen,' said their host, 'I think we all know why we are here tonight . . .' There was a low rumble of agreement. Le Fevre allowed this to die away, then went on: 'We are here because we all – in our several ways – care very deeply about our country. We dislike very much some of the *tendencies* to which it has become prone, in recent years . . .' Another rumble of approbation. 'Tendencies,' said Le Fevre – he had the demagogue's trick of repetition, Rowlands thought – 'Tendencies such as usury. Inversion. *Socialism* . . .' He pronounced the last word as if it had a foul taste. 'We have decided, gentlemen, that we are no longer willing to tolerate such tendencies.'

Rowlands felt a tap on his shoulder. It was the man Loveless had described as the prizefighter. 'Tellyphone for you,' he said, adding as an afterthought, 'sir.'

'Oh?' said Rowlands. There could be only one person who would telephone him here. Murmuring an apology, he followed the manservant out. He trusted that the other guests were too drunk or too preoccupied with what their host was saying to pay much attention. The telephone was on a marble table in the hall. The receiver had been left off the hook; he picked it up and waited until he was certain as he could be that the servant had returned to his duties in the dining room. 'Yes?' he said guardedly.

'How are you getting on?' said the Chief Inspector, in a genial tone. 'Made any interesting discoveries?'

'Some.' In a low voice, he told Douglas about the braille cards.

'That certainly *is* interesting,' said Douglas. 'Anything else?'

'The rest'll keep till tomorrow.'

'All right. I'll send a car to your hotel at nine.' He rang off.

As Rowlands replaced the receiver, he was overcome by a curious sensation. It was as if someone were standing nearby – and yet, surely, he was alone? His hands, exploring the space around him, found only air. Yet he had a definite impression of a woman's presence. For that it was a woman, he was in no doubt. His outstretched hand touched the end of a curving bannister. Of course. There would be a staircase leading up to the next floor – a landing, or mezzanine, overlooking the hall. It was from there that the scent emanated. Tuberose, he thought, and something else – something musky and exotic. He knew now where he'd smelt it before. 'Is that you, Countess?' he said softly. But if the Countess Rostropovna was there, she made no reply.

'So you think she's been with Le Fevre all this time?' said Douglas. They were in his office at Scotland Yard; a dense fug of pipe smoke filled the room where Sergeant Withers sat patiently typing up a report – the tapping of the typewriter keys providing a counterpoint to the main theme. 'She was talking to him at that party,' Rowlands replied.

'Yes, yes.' There was an edge of impatience in the Chief Inspector's voice. 'The police can't follow up on every private conversation, you know.'

'And then there's what he said to Edgecombe,' said Rowlands. 'You have to admit it did sound rather fishy.' It had been as he and Loveless were leaving, the latter having to be extricated from a rather drunken conversation with Horace Babbington about the purpose of Art. They'd been standing in the hall, but the door to the drawing room was open, so that it was impossible to miss what was being said just inside it. A voice Rowlands knew all too well was saying, in accents slurred by drink, 'All I can say is you'd better watch your step, Le Fevre. If I hear there's been any funny business, I'll know what to do . . .' To which had come Maurice Le Fevre's reply: 'My dear *boy*! Surely you know me better than that?'

If the 'funny business' was to do with Natalia Rostropovna, then it all fell into place, Rowlands thought. Her being offered sanctuary at Le Fevre's house – for he was convinced that was where she was – would have been done as a favour to Johnny Edgecombe who, in turn, might have orchestrated the Countess's escape in order to spite his fiancée. But when he'd put this hypothesis to Douglas, the latter had seemed unimpressed. 'Why not run away with her openly if that was his game?' he said. The answer – which was that the woman wanted to avoid being tracked down by the man who had threatened to kill her – seemed too obvious to point out.

'All the same, it's damned peculiar,' Douglas was

saying. 'I mean, from all I've heard about Maurice Le Fevre, I shouldn't have thought he was at all the womanising type.'

'Perhaps she needed a *protector*,' said Rowlands.

'Perhaps. Whatever the reason, we need to get hold of the woman. She's still our only lead when it comes to solving this damnable case. Well, there's the O'Reilly woman's evidence, o'course. But the description she's been able to give us is vague, to say the least.'

It was then that Rowlands thought to mention the man who'd appeared at the gallery, the night of Goldberg's Private View. The Chief Inspector seemed interested in this. 'He was tall, you say? Well, that matches Mrs O'Reilly's description so far. And with a distinctive face . . .' He was silent a moment. The typewriter bell gave a ping as Withers reached the end of a line. 'Do you think your artist friend might be able to draw us a picture of the man he saw?' said Douglas.

'I can certainly ask him.'

'Good.'

'What's happened about Albert Mullins?' asked Rowlands, conscious that his promise to Ruby Tyler to see to it they let Bert out of prison was as yet unfulfilled.

'Oh, we've had to let him go,' was the reply. 'Not enough evidence against him – even if he and his young woman *did* have a row the night she was killed. Turns out he's got an alibi for both the other murders. Half a dozen witnesses saw him in the pub – the White

Hart, not the Shoreditch place – the night of Mary O'Reilly's murder. And on New Year's Eve he was with friends. Playing cards,' said Douglas drily. 'So we'd really no cause to detain him any longer. Charlie Graves's nose is out of joint about it, but I canna help that.'

'What about the Vance murder?'

'What about it? It seems there were quite a number of people who had cause to wish him dead. Most of 'em owed him money, from losing at cards to him. The only one without a satisfactory explanation of his movements at the time of the murder is a Mr Bingham. Says he was visiting his wife, but there are two or three hours he can't account for.'

'Bingham's a decent sort,' said Rowlands.

'So was Dr Crippen,' came the reply. 'But no, I can't see young Bingham as our murderer. Which leaves us with precisely nothing,' he added glumly. 'Sometimes I find myself wishing that the MO'd got it wrong. If it had been a nice, tidy suicide, we could forget about it, and concentrate on the bigger story.' There was another silence, broken only by the clacking of the typewriter.

'So what are you going to do? About the Countess, I mean,' said Rowlands at last.

'Och, we'll put a watch on Le Fevre's house. Not much more we *can* do. Unless . . .' Douglas broke off, and fiddled with his pipe. 'Damn this thing,' he muttered. 'It never draws well in cold weather.'

'Unless what?' prompted Rowlands, although he guessed the answer.

'Why, unless our murderer decides to show his hand once more. With this kind of killer, the only chance you've got of catching him is to catch him in the act,' said Chief Inspector Douglas. 'You say there's to be another gathering at Le Fevre's place in Kent, in a few days' time?'

'A week from now, yes,' said Rowlands.

'Good. Well, if nothing else turns up before then, you ought to be there,' said the Chief Inspector.

Chapter Nineteen

It was snowing again. Rowlands, ascending the steps that led from the heat and bustle of the Baker Street Underground, felt his breath whipped away by an icy wind that blew great handfuls of flakes, like scraps of torn up paper, in his face. All around the air throbbed with the sound of labouring engines and grinding gears as motor vehicles made their way through the slush and mud. He crossed the Marylebone Road, and once more made his way throughout the side streets towards Regent's Park. How often had he made this journey during the past ten years or more? He'd lost count. But always he found himself coming back to the place, as if it were, somehow, the fulcrum around which his life revolved.

He entered the park gates. The snow lay more thickly here on the wide lawns and paths, undisturbed, except by passing dog walkers and children. He could hear the shouts of boys skating on the pond that lay within the Inner Circle; it had been frozen hard for weeks. If he were back in time this afternoon, he thought, he'd take the girls out for a ride on the sled. Thinking about his children gave him a guilty pang; with all the time he'd been spending in London these past few weeks, it felt as if he'd hardly seen them. He resolved that when this wretched business was over and the weather was better, he'd take them all away somewhere for a few days – the girls and Edith. The money Douglas was giving him – his retainer, the man called it – wasn't a lot, but it would pay for a little holiday. Cornwall would be nice. He could look up old Ashenhurst while he was about it.

First, however, there was this matter to see to. Because things had gone far enough, he'd decided. It was time to come clean with the Major. 'It just doesn't seem right,' he said, pausing on the threshold of the Chief Inspector's office as he took his leave. 'Spinning him a yarn about a summer fête when all this time . . .'

'You've been working as a police informer,' said Douglas. 'Yes, I can see that it might go against the grain, Mr Rowlands. Keeping him in the dark, as it were, about your activities. But it's been necessary.' That, Rowlands thought, wincing at the memory, was a word his sister had once used to justify something terrible that she had done, something for which she was now paying the price, it was true. But to Rowlands' mind, necessity remained a dubious concept. One that could be used as an excuse for any number of atrocious acts. He reached the house and rang the bell. It was answered after a brief interval by the housekeeper. 'Back again, Mr Rowlands?' she said pleasantly; then, when he had stated his reason for coming: 'You'll find the Major in his office.'

'Thank you, Mrs Britcher,' said Rowlands as he stamped the snow off his boots. He took his time hanging up his coat and straightening his tie. It was hard not to feel apprehensive. What if the man he admired and respected above all others found his transgression impossible to forgive? As he made his way slowly along the network of corridors that led to the Major's inner sanctum, he felt a little sick at the prospect. Reaching the familiar door, he drew a deep breath. Well, here goes, he thought. He was about to knock when he heard his name called: 'Rowlands, old man – is that you?' And then when Rowlands turned, a little startled to be so hailed, 'I'd know that military step of yours anywhere.'

'Hello, Mortimer,' he replied, forcing a smile. Now he was here, he wanted to get this over with. But Mortimer seemed disposed to chat. 'I'm awfully glad to see you,' he said. 'There's been a great deal going on here, as you might have heard.'

'Yes,' said Rowlands. 'I was sorry to hear about Vance.'

'The man had made enemies.'

'Indeed. Mortimer, old chap, I've got something I need to talk to the Major about.'

‘Oh, don’t let me keep you,’ said the librarian. ‘Tell you what,’ he added, ‘why don’t we meet for that drink we’ve been promising ourselves when you’re done?’

‘That’d be nice,’ said Rowlands.

‘Splendid. Come and find me when you’ve had your chat with the Major,’ said Mortimer.

‘I’ll do that.’ He knocked on the door, and heard the familiar voice sing out, ‘Enter!’

In the end, like most things put off through dread or inertia, it wasn’t as bad as he’d feared. The Major had listened in silence to what he had to say, only voicing a remark when Rowlands himself fell silent. When he’d got to the discovery of Vance’s body, and his own part in helping to identify the man, the Major said, ‘I did wonder what you were doing there that day, with the Chief Inspector. It just seemed rather a coincidence, your having arrived at just that moment, you know. I didn’t realise quite how *much* of a coincidence,’ he added wryly.

‘I’m sorry,’ said Rowlands. ‘I wanted to tell you before, but . . .’

‘You had orders not to, I imagine,’ said Major Fraser. ‘During the war,’ he went on, ‘there were quite a number of us working in Intelligence. It wasn’t something I was ever involved in – didn’t have the brains for it, you know – but I knew several chaps who went quite far in the Service. It always struck me that it was difficult as well as dangerous work. Not just because one risked one’s life – we all did that, every day – but because one couldn't talk about what one was up to. I take it,' he added, 'that you've been cleared to talk about it now?'

'Yes.' Although Douglas hadn't been very pleased when he'd been told of Rowlands' intention of taking the Major into his confidence. 'I just hope he'll keep the information to himself,' he'd said sternly. 'I'll vouch for Major Fraser's absolute trustworthiness,' Rowlands had said, no less forcefully. 'He wants this murderer caught as much as we do.'

Well, if he was taking a risk in telling the Major about their progress – or lack of it – in the Playing Card case, it'd be on his own head, thought Rowlands. At least he didn't any longer have to feel like a hypocrite. 'So tell me,' the Major was saying. 'Do the police have any further leads on who might have killed Reginald Vance?' Then, when Rowlands hesitated. 'Apart from young Bingham, that is.'

'I don't think Bingham had anything to do with it,' said Rowlands.

'No more do I. Silly fool got himself into a bit of a jam, that's all. He'd lost quite a lot of money to Vance at cards,' said the Major grimly. 'Far be it from me to speak ill of the dead, but the more I hear of his activities, the more I have to conclude that Vance was a bit of a twister.'

'I'm afraid he was.'

'Still, just because a man does something dishonest, doesn't mean he deserves to be strung up like a butchered carcass,' the Major said. 'I've as much interest as you and your police associates have in finding out who murdered Vance. Probably more. You can rest assured that if I hear of anything which might further that end, I'll let you know.'

'Thank you, sir.'

'And what of these poor young women who've been killed – you don't suppose there can be any connection?' asked the Major. 'We've had the police here on that account, too, as you know.'

'So far, there doesn't seem to be any connection,' said Rowlands. 'But we're working on it.'

'Have you any leads, or is that something you can't discuss?' The Major took out his cigarette case, helped himself, then offered the case to Rowlands. 'There's a lighter on the desk in front of you.'

'Thanks.' Rowlands lit his cigarette, then handed the lighter back. 'As it happens, we've several pieces of new evidence,' he said. 'One witness actually caught a glimpse of the murder suspect. Says she'd know him again if she saw him. Then, just the other day, there was another sighting.' He told the Major about the man who'd made such an impression on Isaac Goldberg at the Private View. 'We've reason to believe he was following someone connected with the case,' he said guardedly, reluctant to mention Celia West's name in this context, even to the Major. 'If it really was the same man, then Mr Goldberg's evidence might prove very useful.'

'I don't quite see . . .'

'He's an artist,' said Rowlands. 'It's more than likely that he'll be able to draw this man's face from memory.

If our witness – the first one – recognises it as the face that she saw, then we're home and dry.'

'You'll still have to catch him,' said the Major.

He found Mortimer in the library, busy re-shelving books, as he had been on that first visit, nearly a month before. It seemed a Sisyphean task – no sooner completed, than begun again; but when he said as much to Mortimer, the other laughed. 'Oh, I don't mind it so much,' he said. 'Keeps me out of mischief, you know.' He replaced the last of the books – a three-volume edition of *The Way We Live Now*, Rowlands discovered in passing – and pushed the empty trolley back against the wall. 'But let's not talk about my rather dull job,' he said. '*You're* the one with the interesting life.'

'I don't know about that,' said Rowlands, rather taken aback by this description.

'Oh, come! You've a wife and kiddies. You run a farm. It must take a fair bit of work to keep it all going.'

'Well,' said Rowlands. 'You could say that, I suppose.'

'Although it seems to me,' Mortimer went on as, having quitted the library, they walked along the corridor towards the front of the house, 'that you must have a jolly good manager. Someone you can trust with the running of the place, I mean.'

'Yes,' said Rowlands.

'Otherwise you'd hardly be able to take as much time off as you do. Farming's a demanding business – nobody knows that better than *I*. So you must have found yourself a very reliable man.' Perhaps sensing from Rowlands' silence that he'd gone too far, he changed the subject: 'So what do you think of our murder, then?'

They were crossing the park by this time – heading for the Albany, Rowlands assumed. There was no one else about as far as he was able to tell. And yet it seemed indecent, somehow, to be discussing Vance's horrible death as if it were the latest cricket score. 'I don't think much of it,' he replied. But if he had hoped by this unenthusiastic response to close the subject, he was disappointed, for Mortimer went on: 'It's turned the old Lodge upside down, I can tell you! Police crawling all over the place. But I was forgetting,' he added slyly. 'You were here that day, weren't you? The day they found him.'

'Yes.' It struck Rowlands in the same instant that he hadn't actually spoken to Mortimer that day. 'It was the Major who told me you'd come,' said Mortimer, as if in answer to this unspoken question. 'With that policeman. Douglas.'

'The Chief Inspector. That's right.'

'Friend of yours, is he? Oh, don't worry,' laughed Mortimer. 'I won't give the game away! What's it to me if you've friends in high places? So you were there when the body was cut down?' he said.

'No. As a matter of fact, I didn't get there until some time after.' To Rowlands' relief, they had by now arrived at the pub. As, pushing open the doors with their heavy etched glass panels, they were greeted by the welcoming buzz of lunchtime conversation, he resolved to have no more than one drink with Mortimer before making his excuses.

'My turn, I think,' said Mortimer, already ahead of him at the bar. 'What'll you have?'

'Pint of Mild, thanks.' In that genial atmosphere, Rowlands felt his irritation at Mortimer's inquisitiveness start to lessen. He'd been on edge about his interview with the Major, that was all. And Mortimer had only been making conversation; as he himself had said, the poor chap had little enough excitement in his life. There was no reason to snub him. 'How're the others taking it?' he accordingly asked, when they were seated with their pints at a corner table. 'What happened the other day, I mean,' he added, hoping that Mortimer would be equally discreet in his choice of words. And Mortimer certainly seemed to have taken the hint.

'It doesn't seem to have made an awful lot of difference,' he replied. 'After the initial *upset*, and then your *friend* descending with his cohorts, it's as if it never happened. Of course,' he added, taking a sip of his pint, 'the man in question hadn't made himself very popular.'

'So I gather.'

'In fact, between you and me,' said Mortimer, 'there are some of us who feel that whoever did it did the place a service, if you get my meaning.'

After this, the talk turned to other things. England's triumph the week before in the Ashes. Chelsea's victory against Everton at Stamford Bridge (Mortimer was a

Chelsea supporter). Rowlands offered to buy another round; Mortimer declined the offer. 'Thanks, old man, but I'd better be getting back. When the weather's bad like this, the library's always full. Nothing much for the chaps to do except read – and play cards, of course.'

'Maybe next time, then,' said Rowlands as both got to their feet.

'That'd be grand. Hullo!' said Mortimer. 'Somebody's left a paper. Well, finders keepers, *I* say. Might have the match report in it if it's today's edition.'

'I suppose you'll get Miss Clavering to read it to you, will you?'

'What? Oh, yes,' said Mortimer carelessly. 'I might at that. Girl's got to be good for *something*, hasn't she?'

From Regent's Park he took the Bakerloo Line, changing at Oxford Circus for the Central, which took him to Notting Hill Gate.. A telephone call would've been quicker, but Loveless, true to his somewhat rackety existence, wasn't on the telephone. Nor was he at home, it transpired: several minutes' determined hammering at the door of his basement flat brought only an irate request from an upper window to 'stow that bloody racket'. Rowlands did so, wondering if it was worth hanging about on the off-chance of Loveless's return. *Damn and blast*. Why hadn't he thought to provide himself with pencil and paper? He checked his watch. It was a quarter to. They'd still be open, he thought. It was worth a try.

Loveless was in his accustomed seat by the fire. He

didn't seem too surprised to see Rowlands. 'I'll have the same again,' was all he said. Rowlands complied with this request, and bought himself a half. He oughtn't to get too fuddled if he were to carry out the plan he had in mind. When, after a decent interval, he put his proposal to Loveless, the artist gave a sardonic laugh. 'I knew the moment you walked in that you'd something up your sleeve. So: you want Goldberg to draw you a picture of the man with the wild eyes, do you? This doesn't have anything to do with our missing Countess, by any chance?'

'There may be a connection,' admitted Rowlands.

'Always the man of mystery! All right. I'll ask him,' said Loveless. 'In fact, you can ask him yourself. If I'm to trudge all the way to Whitechapel, you might as well come with me. Although,' he added as 'Time' was called, and people around them started drinking up, 'you may find poor Goldberg a little more distracted than usual.'

'Why's that?'

'Of course, you won't have heard,' said the other, putting down his empty glass with rather more force than necessary. 'But someone put a brick through the window of the gallery last night. No prizes for guessing who was behind it.'

Goldberg lived in one of the side streets off Brick Lane; Rowlands never did learn the name of it. If he'd been on his own, there'd have been no question of not committing address and directions to memory; as it was, he let himself be swept along in Loveless's wake. They went by Underground, because it was quicker than the bus – 'and God knows, a lot cheaper,' Loveless said, than taking a taxi – and were at Whitechapel Station by five minutes to three. Then it was a ten-minute walk, in the teeth of the wind, along the Commercial Road until Loveless said abruptly: 'We turn in here.'

The flat was at the top of one of the tall, narrow houses – built during the eighteenth century, Rowlands remembered once having been told, for the French silk weavers who had once flocked to this part of London, escaping persecution. Now, these once elegant dwellings had a ramshackle feel. Loveless, who had evidently been here before, didn't waste time ringing the bell, but pushed open the unlocked street door. 'This way,' he said. 'And mind how you go on the stairs – there are rotten boards.'

The staircase in question formed a kind of spine around which the house, like its fellows, was constructed. Up this they began to climb, passing successive landings, off which led doors to what had once been fine apartments. Now, stale cooking smells – and worse smells – hung in the air, and the sound of crying babies could be heard. '*This* is what one must avoid if one is to do anything worth doing,' muttered Loveless as they reached the attic floor. 'The hell of domesticity.' And indeed, most of the noise appeared to be emanating from behind the door in front of which they stood, and on which Loveless now thumped with his fist. 'They won't hear unless you hammer away,' he said as the screaming within reached a crescendo. 'How he stands it, I'll never know.'

The door flew open. 'Hullo!' said Goldberg. 'This *is* a pleasant surprise. Come in. Hannah's just putting the baby to bed. He's got a touch of colic, poor little beggar.'

The room into which they now trooped had a complex smell: olfactory remnants of last night's supper mingled with clouds of steam from the boiling of babies' napkins in the kitchen next door and smoke from one of Goldberg's ever-present cigarettes. Overlaying these, were the now familiar smells of oil paint, linseed oil and turpentine – although Goldberg, Loveless had explained, had a studio elsewhere. 'Otherwise I don't see how he'd do any work at all.'

'Take a pew,' said the object of these reflections, although this proved more difficult than one might have thought given that all the chairs seemed to be piled high with a detritus of baby clothes, old newspapers, children's toys and dog-eared books. 'Here,' said the artist, sweeping the mess off one of these onto the floor. 'You can have the *best* chair, Mr Rowlands. Loveless can make do with what's left. I must say,' he added, addressing the latter, 'I consider this something of an honour. I thought you never ventured further east than Oxford Circus?'

'Yes, as far as I'm concerned, this might as well be Moscow,' said Loveless airily, seating himself on a chair that creaked alarmingly under his weight. 'It certainly *sounds* like it. I haven't heard an English voice since we stepped off the train at Whitechapel.'

'Careful!' laughed Goldberg. 'You're beginning to sound like one of Le Fevre's speeches.'

'I was sorry to hear about what happened at the gallery,' said Rowlands, for whom the mention of the demagogue's name had prompted this association. He couldn't see Goldberg's reaction, but he guessed it must have been a shrug.

'A lot of broken glass,' he said. 'But no broken heads, I am glad to say. And none of the paintings were hurt . . . Ah, Hannah, my dear,' he went on, in a changed voice as that lady came in, having put down the baby with some success, judging by the blissful quiet. 'You know Mr Loveless, of course? And this is Mr Rowlands.'

'Please don't get up,' said a pleasing contralto voice as Rowlands made a move to do so. 'Sammy, come here . . .' – this to another child, Rowlands guessed. He thought of Celia West's description of the little family in the painting she had liked so much. Evidently, there was another side to the 'domestic hell'. Something of this must have struck Loveless too, for he said: 'What I can't understand is how someone with *your* looks, Goldberg – or lack of 'em – has got himself married to one of the most beautiful women in London.'

'Oh, she married me for my money, didn't you, my dear?' said Isaac Goldberg. His wife gave a snort of incredulity. 'I'll make some tea,' she said.

'So,' went on Goldberg once she had gone out. 'What

can I do for you, gentlemen? You didn't come here just to admire my wife.'

Loveless took it upon himself to explain. When he had finished doing so, his friend gave a soft whistle. 'So you think this man I saw might be a murderer?'

'It's possible,' said Rowlands.

'I thought he looked quite ill,' said the artist, thoughtfully. 'Not sick in his body alone, but in his soul, if you understand me. But yes, I will draw him for you. I take it,' he added gently, 'that my drawing will be shown to someone in a better position than yourself to appreciate it?'

'Yes.' Without mentioning her name, Rowlands told them about Mrs O'Reilly. 'What we're hoping . . .'

'He means himself and the police,' put in Loveless.

'Is that she – this person to whom I'm referring – will recognise the face. As you pointed out just now, Mr Goldberg, it's not something I can do myself. But with an accurate picture . . .'

'I'll do it at once,' said Goldberg. Within a matter of moments, the sound of a stick of charcoal moving swiftly and confidently across a piece of paper could be heard. 'There!' said the artist after a minute or two. 'I think that will do. If I say so myself, I believe it gets that look of his to a T.'

The sensible thing, he realised afterwards, would have been to take the drawing at once to Scotland Yard. That was surely what had been agreed – tacitly, at least – when he and the Chief Inspector had last met? And it was the only useful course of action, the drawing being of no practical use to Rowlands himself. However good his other skills of recognition, a blind man had no way of 'seeing' a face without touching it. So what spirit of perversity was it that had made him decide to go to Drysdale Street alone? Even Loveless, as the two of them took their leave of one another in the great roaring thoroughfare that skirted Spitalfields Market, had seemed uneasy. 'Sure you don't want me to go with you?' he'd said. 'This isn't the most salubrious neighbourhood. And it'll be dark as pitch in half an hour . . .'

'Thanks,' Rowlands had replied. 'But I'd rather go by myself. It might alarm her – the witness, I mean – if two of us were to appear. And I'm quite used to darkness.' Now, with the privilege of hindsight, he wondered if it hadn't been just his cussed pride that had made him do it so that – instead of thinking it over coolly – he'd seen it merely as a chance to prove himself. To show, in the teeth of all the evidence, that his blindness needn't make him any less effective than other men. And of course, he'd argued with himself as he climbed the stairs to the top deck of the bus that would take him along Shoreditch High Street to the edge of Hoxton Square, it would be stupid to go all the way back to Whitehall when the witness lived a mere stone's throw from where he was now. Uppermost in his mind was the thought of how impressed the Chief Inspector would be when he turned up later that evening with confirmation that the man Nora O'Reilly had seen on the night of her daughter's murder and the man Isaac Goldberg had glimpsed at the Tyro Gallery were one and the same man. He could hear Douglas's words of congratulation ringing in his ears already.

He found Drysdale Street without difficulty; one of the things he'd become good at, over the years, was memorising the details – from the layout of streets to landmarks – of any place he'd ever been. He found the house all right, too. There was nobody else about. The inhabitants of Drysdale Street kept themselves to themselves, it seemed. He rang the bell and, once again, heard its forlorn echo within the house. But no one came. He pressed the bell again, feeling the elation which had sustained him throughout the journey start to drain away. Perhaps, after all, she was out? He raised his hand to try once more, already half-resigned to the failure of his mission, when suddenly the door swung inwards. Caught off balance, he staggered slightly. 'Mrs O'Reilly?' he said. But there was no reply. He took a step inside the door and stumbled over something that was lying there. Then a savage blow to the back of his head sent a jolt of pain throughout his body. For an instant he saw shooting stars: red, blue, green; then he saw nothing.

Chapter Twenty

How long he had been lying there he had no way of knowing – was it hours, or only minutes? His head felt heavy as lead; when he tried to lift it, an agonising pain shot through him, and a sour taste of vomit rose in his throat. He lay still then. Since moving was out of the question for the moment, he'd try to get his bearings. Well, that was easy enough. He was lying face down on the floor. It was a tiled floor. Cold against his face. Someone was breathing . . . was anybody there? No, it must be his own breath that he could hear. There was something he had to do, he thought. Something about a drawing . . . Yes, he remembered now. He'd been on his way to show Mrs O'Reilly the drawing. He had it on him, didn't he? Yes. Inside pocket. God, his head hurt.

Whoever had hit him, had made a good job of it, he thought. There was a smell he recognised – sharp and metallic. It was blood, surely? Gingerly, he lifted a hand to touch the back of his head where the pain was worst. The hand came away clean. This puzzled him. But he had other things to think about just then. Getting himself upright being the first.

Fighting the waves of pain and nausea which threatened to overwhelm him, he levered himself up from the floor until he was crouching on hands and knees. Take it slowly, that was the way. He remained in this position for a moment, testing himself, to see if he was fit to carry on. Then, slowly and painfully, he began to get to his feet, steadying himself with one hand pressed against the wall to his right while with the other he sought the piece of paper which had been his reason for coming here. But the drawing was gone. At first, he couldn't believe it. Shivering a little with the effort, *he would* not *be sick; he would not*, he tried his other pockets. No, there was nothing there. Whoever had attacked him – and he was as sure he could be that it was the man who had murdered Winnie Calder, Mary O'Reilly and Elsie Alsop – had made certain that no evidence that could tie him to the crimes remained. A terrible thought struck him: could the murderer still be within the house? He held his breath, straining his ears to catch the slightest sound. Perhaps he was watching Rowlands at this moment? Enjoying his power over him before moving in for the kill . . .

The thought was intolerable. He had to get out of here, and quickly. The door. He needed to get to the door. Still steadying himself against the wall, he took a step towards where he supposed the door to be, and felt his foot skid on something slippery. He tried to save himself, but his fingers clutched only air. His feet went from under him and he fell, striking his hip painfully on the tiled floor. As, with a groan, he went to push himself up again, he found that his hands were sticky. That smell again. He knew what it meant now. Giddy with horror, he felt around blindly until his hands encountered what he guessed was lying there. It was her hand he found first, its palm curled upwards. She was on her back, then – her head only inches from where he had been lying. He shuddered at the thought that, in his scrabbling about, he might so easily have kicked her. Pity overcame the horror almost at once. Poor woman! To have lost her only child, and then to die in such a brutal way . . . It occurred to him suddenly that she might not, after all, be dead.

Steeling himself, he reached again for the hand he had let fall. He felt for a pulse, but there was nothing . . . or was there? He ought to make sure. Stretching out his hand, he went to touch her throat to see if any sign of life still lingered there. What he found instead was her hair, which must have tumbled down in the struggle with her killer, and which lay, heavy and wet, in the pool of blood that oozed from Nora O'Reilly's shattered skull. At the same moment, he became aware of the sound he had heard on first coming round: the sound of someone breathing. It was not, after all, his own breath, but that of the child who must have witnessed the whole dreadful thing. It was an effort to speak, but Rowlands forced himself to do so, turning in the direction from which the sound had come. The hall cupboard, he thought; the poor little blighter must have been hiding there all along. 'It's all right, Daniel,' he said gently. 'Don't be afraid. I won't hurt you. It's all over, now.'

His recollection of what happened during the next few hours was patchy. He must have got himself and the boy out of the house, because he remembered staggering around in the snow, looking for a telephone box. The police. He'd wanted to phone the police. Then someone – a man whose name Rowlands never did find out – came up to him. 'You all right, mate?' Perhaps it was he who'd telephoned in the end, because a policeman had come. 'Now, what seems to be the trouble?' Then, more sharply: 'Is this your boy, then?' He couldn't recall exactly what it was he'd replied, but it must have made some sense – enough for the young constable to do something about it. A police van had arrived. Somewhat to his surprise, Rowlands had found himself bundled into the back of it. 'The boy . . . What have you done with the boy?' he remembered asking, only to be told: ''*Ee's* all right. More than can be said for '*er* . . .' From which he gathered that they'd found Nora O'Reilly's body.

He must have blacked out then, because the next

thing he was conscious of was waking up in a police cell. He guessed it was a cell, because of the hardness of the bed on which he was lying – more of a shelf, really. The wall next to the bed was of limewashed brick. There was nothing else in the cell except a bucket, over which he tripped on his way to the door. The door was made of metal. He banged upon it. After a time, somebody came. 'What do *you* want?' a voice said. 'I need to speak to Chief Inspector Douglas urgently,' said Rowlands. There came a startled pause; then: 'You don't want much, do you?'

'Is this Shoreditch Police Station?'

'It is. Where didjer think it was? The Ritz?

'In that case, let me speak to your Inspector. Inspector Dawes, isn't it?'

'What if it is?' replied the sergeant, but there was a different note in his voice. He went away. A few minutes later, the door of the cell opened.

'You wanted to speak to me, I gather?' said a new voice.

'Inspector Dawes? The name's Rowlands. We haven't met, but I've information that may cast some light on the murder of Mary O'Reilly.'

'Well, I must say you've done yourself proud,' said the Chief Inspector. 'Getting yourself arrested on suspicion of murder while the real murderer gets clean away.' I call that a *very* good day's work,' he observed sarcastically.

'I'm sorry,' said Rowlands. 'I see now that I should

have come straight to you with the drawing, but . . .'

'As it happens, it wouldn't have made a blind bit of difference,' said Douglas gloomily. 'The woman was already dead by then. So any chance we'd have had of getting her to identify the man she saw was a lost cause, anyway. What I *can't* forgive,' he went on, 'is your putting yourself in danger so needlessly. He meant to kill you, you know. Probably would've succeeded if he hadn't been in such a hurry to get away.'

'Two minutes,' said a voice from the door. 'Then you'll have to leave. Visiting Time was over hours ago.'

'Right you are, Sister,' said the Chief Inspector, with surprising meekness. They were at the London Hospital, whence Douglas had insisted on driving Rowlands after springing him from his Shoreditch police cell. Inspector Dawes had been apologetic about the mistake, 'but what choice had Constable Perkins had?' he'd said. 'You find a man covered in blood, wandering about the streets, and a body with its head bashed in, and what are you to do? You have to arrest him.' Which was exactly what he himself would have done under the circumstances, said the Chief Inspector.

Any hopes Rowlands might have had of getting home that night had been swiftly scotched by the stern young Sister. 'You've got a nasty contusion on the back of your head, and a suspected concussion,' she said. 'You'll stay put, Mr Rowlands, if you know what's good for you.'

'But what about my wife? She's no idea where I am.' The memory of how upset Edith had been on that occasion two years before when he'd arrived home with a black eye and broken ribs now came to mind.

'I've already telephoned your wife,' said Douglas. 'She'll be with you first thing tomorrow. Now I suggest you get some sleep,' he added hastily as a pointed clearing of the throat was heard: the Sister again, Rowlands guessed. But there was one more thing he had to know: 'What's happened to the boy?' he said.

'He's quite safe,' was thc reply. 'Don't worry. We're not going to let anything happen to him.'

Edith arrived at Visiting Time, to find her husband packed and ready to go home. 'I was discharged this morning,' he told her. 'I was just about to ring you.' He kissed her. 'You needn't have come, you know. I'm quite capable of—'

'Getting yourself into scrapes,' she said tartly. 'I suppose *next* time, you'll be coming home in a coffin.'

'Edith . . .'

'I wait an entire day,' she said, ignoring his pleading tone, 'for a telephone call from you, to say when you'll be home – and when a call does come, it's from the police.'

'I'm sorry.'

'Don't you care at *all* how I feel?'

'You know I do.'

They were by this time standing in the street, having come out through the hospital's main entrance, opposite the Underground station. Edith went to take his arm, to guide him across the road, but his sharp hearing had caught the distinctive *tick tick ticking* of a taxicab's idling engine as it stopped to let off a fare. He held up his hand. 'Waterloo Station,' he told the driver, ushering his wife into the back of the cab.

'You realise that this is the second taxi we've taken in a week?' she said when they were hurtling along Aldgate High Street towards the City. 'I suppose you think we're made of money?'

'Not exactly,' he said. 'Let's just say I'm feeling flush this week.' And in fact when they'd met yesterday – how long ago it seemed! – Loveless had insisted on paying him the balance of what he was owed. Edith gave a disbelieving sniff. But her silence had a friendlier character. For the rest of the short journey they talked of this and that, both, by common consent, staying clear of the subject of what had taken place the previous day. Only when they were seated in an otherwise empty compartment of the Staplehurst train, did she refer to this, and it wasn't her husband's well-being which most concerned her.

'Oh Fred,' she said. 'What's going to happen to him – the child, I mean?' To which Rowlands had shaken his head.

'I don't know,' he said.

'Can't we do something?' But to this question he had no reply.

When they got back to the house, there was a surprise waiting. To the chorus of female voices welcoming him home – those of his daughters and mother-in-law – had been added another, distinctively masculine in tone. Rowlands knew the voice. Disentangling himself from the enthusiastic embraces of three little girls, he went towards the speaker. 'Ashenhurst, old man. Is it really you?'

'The very same.' His hand was firmly grasped. 'Ciss is here with me, too.'

'Mrs Nicholls – how very nice,' he said.

'Cecily, please,' said Ashenhurst's sister.

'But I'd no idea you were coming,' said Rowlands as they all went into the house – the children running ahead, followed at a slower pace by their grandmother. 'Edith never said a thing.'

'You're not the only one who can keep a secret,' said Edith.

Ashenhurst and his sister had come up from Cornwall for a family funeral, it transpired. 'Great Aunt Cecily's,' said Ashenhurst when the party was comfortably settled in front of a very good fire, with cups of tea and some of Edith's home-made scones. 'Ciss is named for her, of course. She was rather an old dragon.'

'Now, Jack . . .'

'Well, she *was* – she'd have been the first to admit it. When Mums and Pop died, she rather took over our bringing up. Not that she made a very good job of it, in my own case,' he added cheerfully.

'Never was a truer word spoken in jest,' said Cecily Nicholls. 'Delicious sponge cake, Edith. You must give me the recipe.'

'Oh, it's ever so easy,' said Edith.

The conversation rambled pleasantly on. Rowlands, feeling the life flow back into his chilled and exhausted frame, found it hard to believe that the events of the past few hours had ever happened. Sitting there, in the warm circle of his family and friends, it seemed a world away from that cramped hallway in Hoxton, and the horror of Nora O'Reilly's death. He thought, Edith's right. We must do something about the boy.

'Penny for them,' said Jack Ashenhurst.

'What? Oh, sorry . . .' He realised that he'd heard not a word of what his friend had just been saying. 'Rather a lot on my mind.'

'Yes, I gathered you'd been in the wars again,' said Ashenhurst. 'It all sounds very mysterious. But then, you've always like living dangerously.' This was an old joke – a reference to their early days together at the Lodge when Rowlands, eager to prove he could manage as well as his more experienced fellows, had taken a tumble down a flight of stairs and given himself a split lip in the process.

Edith got up to begin clearing the tea things.

'No, stay where you are,' said Mrs Nicholls. 'You've done enough work for one day. Now, girls, who's going to help me with the washing-up?'

'Ciss loves children, you know,' Ashenhurst said in a low voice when Cecily Nicholls had gone out with her team of helpers. 'Such a shame she's never had any of her own. I tell her she should marry again – not waste her life looking after her great useless lump of a brother. But she won't hear of it. Still, perhaps things'll change now.'

'In what way?' asked Rowlands.

'With the money, I mean,' Ashenhurst sounded faintly embarrassed. 'The fact is, we're Great Aunt Cecily's sole beneficiaries. She never married, you see. I don't mind telling you,' he went on, 'that it's come at exactly the right time. With the hotel business as bad as it is, I don't think we could have survived another month without dear old Auntie's timely bequest.'

'That *is* good news,' said Rowlands. He was genuinely pleased at his friend's good fortune, even though it was hard not to feel a certain chagrin at the contrast with his own lack of the same. Something of this must have conveyed itself in his voice, for Ashenhurst said: 'But that's enough about my affairs. How are things going with you?'

Edith had just that minute decided to follow her guest into the kitchen, and Mrs Edwards was asleep in her chair, so Rowlands was at liberty to be frank. 'I'm afraid we're bust,' he said. 'Unless something turns up pretty soon, we're going to have to sell the farm. It's heavily mortgaged, so . . .' He let the sentence tail off.

'I'm sorry,' said Ashenhurst. 'If there's anything I can do . . .'

'That's kind of you. But we'll manage.'

'Well, keep me posted, won't you?' Both fell silent. The only sounds, apart from Mrs Edwards' gentle breathing, were the ticking of the longcase clock and the soft crackle of a burning log collapsing in on itself. 'So many businesses are doing badly these days,' said Ashenhurst. 'Running a farm must be especially difficult, I'd have thought. You're far from being the only one who's found it hard to make a go of it. A lot of it's down to luck, I'd say.'

'That's true enough,' said Rowlands.

The next couple of days passed very pleasantly. With heavy snowfalls causing delays and cancellations of the trains between London and the West Country, it took very little persuasion on Rowlands' part for Ashenhurst and his sister to agree to stay on at the farm until the weather cleared. He'd forgotten how much he liked having people around; it was almost like the old days with Dorothy and Viktor, he thought. He'd always found Ashenhurst good company, and during the past few days, Edith and Ashenhurst's sister seemed to have become fast friends, too. There was talk of their all meeting up again in Cornwall when summer came. 'Because we've heaps for the children to do,' said Cecily Nicholls one day as they were finishing lunch. 'Being so close to the sea, you know.'

'Oh Fred, wouldn't it be lovely?' said Edith. 'Do you think we might?'

'Oh, Daddy, *please* . . .'

'We'll see,' he said, but he said it in such a way that it was perfectly clear to anyone who was listening – his children, not least of all – that the answer was yes. As the women were clearing the table, he and Ashenhurst went outside for a smoke.

'And don't forget we need some more wood for the fire,' Edith reminded him as he was putting on his boots.

'Aye, aye, Captain.' Rowlands took the axe from the nail in the scullery, and he and Ashenhurst strolled towards the orchard where a pile of logs was waiting to be split into pieces of a size suitable for burning. As they did so, they talked of this and that.

'Is there much hunting around here?' asked Ashenhurst. 'I should have thought it was quite good country for it.'

'The West Kent comes through here sometimes,' said Rowlands. 'Although mostly they hunt further over, towards Sevenoaks.'

'I used to hunt a bit. Before the war, you know. Always wondered what it would be like to get back on a horse again.'

'Mm,' said Rowlands, concentrating on what he was doing, which was setting up one of the larger logs to serve as a chopping block.

'There was that chap at the Lodge who used to ride quite a bit,' said Ashenhurst suddenly. 'Said there was nothing to it, once you let the horse know who was in control. *He* took up farming, too, I seem to recall.'

'Quite a number of the men did,' said Rowlands, not really paying attention. He got his first log into position – *carefully does it* – took aim, and brought the axe down with just the right amount of force to cleave the log neatly in two. 'Some of them must have been farmers before the war, I suppose.'

'Yes, but this wasn't one of those; he was new to the game, like you. Wish I could remember his name. Nice chap. Very good rower – you *must* remember him; you were mad about all that, too.'

'I suppose I was,' said Rowlands. He set up the next log, ready for the axe. One, two, three, and *crack*. Down it came. The two halves fell either side of the chopping block.

'Anyway, he – the chap I'm talking about – went into business with a Pal of his,' Ashenhurst went on. 'I *do* remember *his* name, because it was the same as mine. Jack. Jack Harker.'

Crack went the axe.

'No, not Harker. *Harper*, that was it!' said Ashenhurst. 'Jack Harper. He'd been an artist before the war. Rather a good one, I believe, before he lost his sight.'

'When was this?' said Rowlands.

'What? Oh, about ten years ago. It must have been just before I left the Lodge myself, in the summer of '19. The two of 'em bought a smallholding together – in Sussex, I think – but it all went rather badly wrong. The business failed – I suppose like so many businesses these days. There was a woman involved, too, as I recall. Anyway, whatever the reason, Harper killed himself. You must remember. It was in all the papers. Terrible business.'

At some point during Ashenhurst's narrative,

Rowlands felt himself grow very still. It was the feeling he'd had, years ago in Flanders when he'd got his sights lined up on a target. It was as if everything fell into place: *click, click, click*. What had been obscure was now sharp and clear. The cards were on the table. He didn't need to press Ashenhurst to remember the name he'd forgotten, because he already knew what it must be.

It had stopped snowing, but the train still seemed to Rowlands to be crawling along. Would they ever get there? he wondered. These branch lines were always slow. Even so, by his calculation, he ought to be in Sevenoaks by half past seven. Then it would be a taxi ride, always supposing he could find a taxi, which might take fifteen minutes – more if the roads were bad. He'd be there by eight o'clock at the latest, he thought; of that much he could be sure; everything else was as yet unknown. He tried not to think about it. Since that moment, a few hours before when he'd come to know for certain what he'd half-known all along, he'd been in a kind of frenzy. Because if he didn't act *now*, he knew, then it would be too late. The man Douglas, with his sardonic humour, had dubbed 'The Playing Card Killer' would kill again. The murders – five now, in all – which had led up to this, were only the prelude to a final *movement*; the *tricks* leading up to a *grand slam*. All along, he saw, it had been this which had been the killer's real aim. It was Rowlands' task to thwart that aim – and it was to that end that he found himself now rattling along in a half-empty train across a snowbound landscape.

'Are you sure you know what you're doing, old man?' Ashenhurst had asked when Rowlands had told him where he was going, and why. It was a question to which he hadn't had a ready answer. Now, as the train began to slow, with a harsh grinding of wheels on the icy track, he readied himself for what would surely be the most difficult game of his life. Queuing for a taxi outside the station, he overheard someone else ask for Avalon Hall. 'I say,' he interrupted, as the man stood haggling over the fare with the driver. 'I'm going that way, too. Perhaps you'd like to share?'

'All right,' said the other, ungraciously. Rowlands introduced himself. His new acquaintance hesitated a moment before doing the same, as if he might have preferred to remain anonymous. 'Hinchcliffe's the name,' he grunted as both settled themselves into their seats. The car set off. Rowlands checked his watch; five-and-twenty past seven. They were in plenty of time. 'From what I can recall,' Loveless had said, 'nothing much will happen until after dinner. There'll be drinks first, of course, and then when everyone's nicely pickled, Le Fevre'll do his rabble-rousing.' That would be the moment, Rowlands thought, to slip away.

'Been to the house before?' he asked his silent companion.

'No. Can't say I have,' was the reply. 'Why? Have you?'

'No,' said Rowlands. 'This is the first time for me, too.' And the last, if I have anything to do with it, he added silently. 'I've heard him speak, though,' he said. At this, Hinchcliffe seemed to thaw.

'Have you? So have I. Marvellous speaker, isn't he? So right about our *Hebrew* friends, wouldn't you say?'

'Oh, rath*er*,' said Rowlands. Distasteful as it was to have to agree with such a man's opinions, he couldn't help thinking it had been an excellent idea to tag onto him like this. With Hinchcliffe beside him, he'd be less conspicuous, he thought.

Chapter Twenty-One

'By Jove, what a place!' said Hinchcliffe as, having traversed a drive of perhaps a quarter of a mile, the taxi drew up in front of Avalon Hall. Other cars were disgorging passengers as the two of them got out and paid the driver. Hinchcliffe, although he had not proved an engaging companion, had his uses, thought Rowlands.

'Describe it for me, will you?' he asked, having put the other man in the picture as to his own limitations.

'Describe it?' Hinchcliffe sounded bemused. 'Well, I'd say it was a pretty sizeable place. A wing on each side of the main building and a sort of tower, with turrets and all of that in the centre . . . Dash it all, I'm not much of a hand at this. What else do you want to know?'

'That'll do fine.' Two wings. He'd have his work cut out then, he thought. 'No, there's no need for you to take my arm, thanks,' he added as they climbed the short flight of steps that led to the front door. This stood open to admit the group whose arrival had immediately preceded theirs. He heard voices: 'Bloody night for it, what?' 'Yes, isn't it?' then he and his companion entered in their turn, surrendering their coats and hats to the waiting manservant. To judge from the buzz of conversation emanating from the room leading off the hall, to which a second servant now conducted them, a sizeable crowd had already assembled. But if he had hoped his own presence might remain unobserved because of this, he was disappointed: almost as soon as he entered the room, he found himself hailed.

'Ah, Mr Rowlands!' It was their host. 'How very good to see you. So you decided to come and see for yourself how our little operation works, did you?' Le Fevre's tone was affable, but Rowlands thought he detected an ironic note. 'And Mr Hinchcliffe, too, I see. Come, gentlemen. You are welcome to Avalon Hall. Perhaps one day you will be able to say to your grandchildren, "*This* is where it all began . . ."'

'This', from what Rowlands could make out, was a large chamber – perhaps the size of the Great Hall in a mediaeval castle – in which were assembled around a hundred men. Numerous as this gathering appeared to be, it hardly filled the enormous room, in whose vaulted spaces even the deepest of bass voices seemed puny. 'It seems like a good-sized party,' he observed to their host as a waiter brought drinks.

'It is indeed, Mr Rowlands,' replied Le Fevre in a self-satisfied tone. 'But perhaps it surprises you that so many are drawn to the cause?'

'Not at all.'

Le Fevre laughed. 'You are not a man who likes to admit to being surprised,' he said. 'But I imagine that even *you* may find your expectations confounded. We are a growing organisation, Mr Rowlands.' Rowlands inclined his head politely in acknowledgement of this fact. 'We number many eminent men amongst our number. Men of science. Men of progress. Men – dare I say it? – of vision. But I must leave you gentlemen to amuse yourselves,' said their host as another guest – a Mr Simpson – was announced. A moment later, Le Fevre was gone.

'By Jove, is that who I think it is?' said Hinchcliffe, giving Rowlands a nudge.

'I'm afraid you'll have to be more explicit,' said Rowlands. 'You see . . .' But just then there came another interruption.

'What the hell are you doing here?' said a voice.

'Good evening, Lord Edgecombe,' replied Rowlands calmly. 'This is Mr Hinchcliffe.'

'What?' said Edgecombe. Then, coldly: 'How d'ye do?' If he had intended to say anything further, it was not to be, for at that instant he was as if struck dumb. Perhaps it was the presence of the mysterious Mr Simpson which had had this effect, thought Rowlands. Whatever the reason, it brought their ill-tempered exchange to an abrupt end. Without another word, Johnny Edgecombe walked away.

'You didn't say you knew Lord Edgecombe,' said Hinchcliffe, with what seemed a new respect.

'Didn't I?' Rowlands' attention was only half-given to what his companion was saying, the rest being focused on what was going on around them. Just now, from somewhere on his right, there came a voice – gruff and somewhat overbearing; the voice of a man used to having his opinions deferred to – 'The fact is, Baldwin's lost control of the Party. If we don't look sharp, we'll have a Socialist government before you can say "knife"...' Another voice – wheedling, appeasing; the eternal apparatchik – protested: 'Oh, but *surely* it won't come to that?' To Rowlands' left, yet another conversation was in progress: 'When you see what they're doing in Italy, you just have to admire it.' 'Couldn't agree more, old boy. I was just saying as much to Rothermere the other day.'

From all around, came the rumble of laughter, the clinking of ice in whisky glasses and the smell of cigar smoke, as the richest and most powerful men in the land deplored the way that civilisation was going. Rowlands had had enough of it. Choosing his moment, he set down his empty glass on an occasional table and threaded his way back towards the door through which they had come in. Once more in the cavernous entrance hall, he made boldly for the stairs. If challenged, he'd say that he was looking for the lavatory. But no challenge came. At the top of the stairs, he hesitated. Left or right? With no idea where to start, he'd need to work quickly, he thought. He chose the left-hand corridor. If the house were as symmetrical as Hinchcliffe had said, then there'd be another just the same, leading the other way.

He tried the first door. The room into which it opened was empty, although a smell of hair pomade lingered. Evidently, some of Le Fevre's guests were staying the night; Rowlands trusted to fate that they'd all be in the Great Hall by now. If he *were* to find any of the rooms occupied, he'd pretend he'd got himself lost. Another door yielded the same result, only this time the smell was of gentlemen's cologne. He didn't bother to go into any of the rooms. What he was in search of was a different kind of scent. Four doors, five. The fifth one was locked. He rattled the handle, but no sound came from within. 'Hello,' he said softly. 'Anybody there?' He pressed his ear to the door, but could hear nothing. Voices were coming from the direction of the stairs. '. . . runs like a dream, even at sixty,' someone said. Hastily, Rowlands tried another door. This led to a bathroom; he ducked inside. The voices went past, still talking of the joys of motoring. He waited a moment or two until he guessed that the coast was clear. Then, trying to look as if he had every right to be there, he started back along the corridor, trying the facing doors. Seven, eight. Now he was back at the top of the stairs again. He stood for a moment, listening. Was that a floorboard creaking? No. His nerves were on edge, that was all. As he stood hesitating, he heard dinner being announced, and the sudden lull in the drone of conversation that followed as people made their way to the dining room. He hadn't much time.

With a growing sense of urgency, he plunged down the right-hand corridor, trying doors as he went. One door. Two. Perhaps, after all, he'd got it wrong, he thought, and had come all this way for nothing. But then the third door opened easily to his hand and, as it did so, the scent of tuberose told him he'd found what – or rather *who* – he was looking for. Had he been in any doubt, her sharp exclamation would have confirmed the suspicion – 'Oh!' – and then, in a more imperious tone: 'What do you think *you're* doing here?'

'I'm sorry if I startled you, Countess,' he said, closing the door behind him. 'But I had to speak to you.'

'You've certainly got a nerve,' she said. There wasn't a trace of a Russian accent now. 'If Maurice finds you here, he'll kill you.'

'I'll take that chance,' he said, thinking it was probably no more than the truth. 'The fact is, I wanted to warn you. It isn't safe here. Not now.'

'What are you talking about?' she said scornfully, but there was a note of uncertainty underlying the scorn. 'Nobody knows I'm here.'

'That's where you're wrong,' said Rowlands. 'He's

known for some time. He's just waiting for his chance . . .'

'I don't know what you mean,' she said. 'If you'll just think about it for a moment,' said Rowlands, ignoring this, 'you'll see that the best thing you can do is to come away with me tonight. There'll be a car arriving in two hours' time to take me to the station. You could be in it.'

'And why,' said the woman he knew only as the Countess Rostropovna, in a voice that trembled slightly, 'would I want to do that?'

'Because five people have died already,' said Rowlands. 'He's not going to give up now. It's you he wants – as you've known all along,' he added, not attempting to conceal his disgust. 'If you'd gone to the police in the beginning . . .'

'It wouldn't have stopped him,' she said.

'It might have saved three lives.'

'Perhaps,' she said indifferently. Then for a long moment, she was silent. He heard her get up and start to pace about the room. 'If I did come with you,' she said, 'where would I go?'

'To the police, first of all,' he said.

'I can't do that,' she said. 'You see . . .'

But she never got to give a reason, because just then the door opened, and whatever she had intended to say was lost in a choking cry, at the sight of whoever it was that had just come in. A moment later, Rowlands felt something cold and hard – it was the muzzle of a gun, he realised – being thrust against the back of his neck. A voice said: 'I should stand absolutely still if I were you, old man. You've caused me rather a lot of trouble, one way and another. I wouldn't have the slightest qualm about shooting you.'

'All right,' said Rowlands. The gun withdrew a fraction. 'Although,' the interloper went on, 'I suppose I ought to be grateful to you, in a way. If it hadn't been for you, it might have taken me a lot longer to find my way here. As it was, all I had to do was keep you in my sights, and here we are.'

'You fool,' said Natalia Rostropovna, addressing Rowlands.

'Hold your tongue, Nettie,' said the third member of their party. 'I'll do the talking. And sit down – yes, over there on the sofa will do very well. I want you where I can keep an eye on you. I must say,' he went on, with what seemed no more than polite interest, 'you've done very well for yourself. Very well indeed. Quite a grand place, this. But then you always were an ambitious girl.'

'Arthur, please . . .'

'*Shut up*,' said the other viciously. 'You'll speak when you're spoken to. Oh, and in case you're thinking of trying anything funny . . .' – this was to Rowlands – 'I should tell you that I've no compunction about shooting *her*, either.' At this, the Countess – because that was how Rowlands still thought of her – began to cry. 'Stop that noise,' said the man holding the gun. 'Or I'll stop it for you.'

'Somebody's bound to hear,' said Rowlands.

'What, with all the rumpus they're making downstairs? I think not. But even if anyone did hear something – a shot, shall we say? – it'd be too late,' said the hateful voice. 'For both of you.'

'You don't have to do this,' said Rowlands. 'You can stop now. Get away while there's still time.'

'What – and throw in my hand while I'm still winning? Why should I want to do that? The fun's only just beginning. Besides which,' the voice went on, 'they'll still hang me for the other ones, you know.'

'Be that as it may,' said Rowlands. 'You can let her go. You've won. There's no need for any more of this.' A silence ensued. From where he was standing, a few paces into the room, Rowlands tried to gauge the distance between himself and his gaoler. It couldn't be more than a foot or two. If he were just able to catch him off guard . . .

'So she's got you too, has she?' said the other man, suddenly. 'Twisted you around her little finger, the way she did to Jack and all the others.'

'Arthur . . .'

'Didn't I tell you to be quiet?' The voice was a snarl, barely recognisable as that of the man Rowlands had once thought of as his friend. 'Because it's not going to work with *me*,' the voice went on. 'I've always known you for what you are, Nettie Roberts – a liar and a whore. You broke Jack's heart. Now you're going to pay the price.' There was the sound of a gun being cocked. A low moan of fear from the girl.

'When was it,' said Rowlands, with a calmness he did not feel, 'that you found you could see again?'

Mortimer laughed. It was a chilling sound. 'Oh, I've been able to see for a very long time,' he said. 'Long enough to see what was going on in front of me, at any rate – worse luck for anyone who was trying to pull the wool over my eyes – eh, Nettie?' The latter gave a sob, but made no other reply. 'Yes, it started to come back that summer – the summer of 1919. You remember that time all right, don't you, Nettie? You and Jack were living in Cooksbridge. A smallholding,' he added, for Rowlands' benefit. 'Not a big concern – there was a cottage, with three or four acres; a few pigs, some goats and half a dozen chickens – but it was Jack's pride and joy.' He was silent a moment, then went on: 'I was at a loose end at the time, and Jack needed someone to help with the rough work and so I volunteered. There was a room for me, Jack said, and Nettie wouldn't mind . . . which she didn't, or at least not to my face,' Mortimer added. 'For a while it was all right. Jack and I got on with the work, and *she* kept herself busy with whatever women do. Gardening. Cooking. Although she was never much of a hand at *that* – Jack did most of it. He was a very good cook, was Jack,' he added, with a certain wistfulness in his voice which had not been there before. 'Still, it was pleasant enough while it lasted. Country life.' *I tried it for a while, but it didn't work out* . . . That seemingly inconsequential remark, which had meant nothing at the time, now came back to Rowlands. He thought, the clues have been there all along. I just haven't allowed myself to see them.

'I don't know whether it had anything to do with the life I was leading,' went on Mortimer, 'with all that fresh air and exercise, you know, but it was around that time – the spring of '19 – that my sight started to come back. It wasn't all at once, you understand, but bit by bit. So that at first things were pretty hazy. Later, they became clear . . .' He was silent for such a long time that it seemed to Rowlands that he'd forgotten their existence, caught up in his vision of the past. For those few moments, he became an absence for Rowlands – a blank, in the middle of the quiet room. Only the faint crackle of the fire and the measured ticking of a clock gave a feeling of substance to the place. From below, came muffled sounds of revelry: shouts, and laughter, and what might have been the thumping of fists upon a table. On the sofa next to the fire, the girl – Nettie Roberts – wept quietly. 'Crystal clear,' said Mortimer, as if suddenly recalled to the here and now. 'Oh yes. I could see what was in front of my eyes *then* – couldn't I, Nettie? Even though you and that fancy man of yours weren't aware of the fact that there was a witness to your carryings-on.'

'It wasn't like that,' the girl burst out.

'Wasn't it? It looked pretty much like it to me. Making eyes at each other across the table, in front of Jack and me. *Touching* each other at every opportunity.' Mortimer's voice was thick with disgust.

'I never meant it to happen,' she nevertheless

persisted. 'Gus was just a friend, in the beginning. Jack's friend, more than mine.'

'A fine friend,' said Mortimer. 'Accepting a man's hospitality, and then stealing his wife from under his nose. Not that you tried very hard to stop him . . . Oh, quit your snivelling, can't you? It won't wash with me. Yes, you led him on, I'd say. Letting him have his way with you – kissing and fondling and rubbing up against you like a dog in heat – and all the while your poor blind husband was sitting there oblivious to what was going on. Oh, you led him on, all right!' She wept harder, and this time, he didn't attempt to silence her.

From downstairs, the shouts and laughter grew in volume. No one would have heard anything, Rowlands thought. They were as cut off in this wing of the house as if they had been at the ends of the earth. 'I remember the first time I saw what you were up to, the two of you,' Mortimer went on after a moment. 'Perhaps you remember it, too? We were all sitting around the table after supper, and Jack suggested a game of Whist. He always loved his game of cards,' added Mortimer, in a softer tone than the one he'd used hitherto. 'Yes, there we all were, sitting under the lamp, and I suddenly found I could see as plain as day. The lamplight shining on your hair, Nettie – such pretty golden hair you've got. The kind that men are fools for. I could see the faces of the others, too. Dear, kind Jack, with his scarred face, and that funny, faraway smile he had – you remember his smile, don't you, Nettie? And handsome Gus

Kirkwood. Oh yes, I can see it all now. He was dealing, wasn't he, Gus, because he was North and you were on his left, which meant you were East and Jack's partner. And I remember,' said Mortimer, in the voice of someone telling a troubling dream, 'how as he was dealing the cards, old Gus, he put a card into your hand – it was the queen of hearts, I seem to recall. And then he ran his fingers up the inside of your bare arm – it was a hot night – until he reached your breast, and let his hand lie there for a moment. And you let him do it, didn't you, Nettie? You let him touch you like that, in front of Jack and in front of me—'

'It was because of the portrait,' she said, cutting across him. 'None of it would have happened if it hadn't been for that.'

'You think so, do you?' said the murderer in an interested tone. 'Well, you'd have reason to know, I suppose. Taking your clothes off so that Gus could paint you must have given him a good deal of encouragement.'

'It was Jack who asked him to paint me,' said Nettie Roberts, in a pleading tone. 'Because he couldn't, any more . . .'

'Being blind. No, I do see that,' was the sarcastic reply.

'It was only supposed to be the head and neck,' she went on, with what seemed to Rowlands an unfortunate persistence.

'But you gave him the rest of your body nonetheless,' said Mortimer. 'Generous to a fault, our Nettie.' Too late, she fell silent. But Mortimer still had things he wanted to say. 'Yes, I can see it all now,' he said. 'Playing cards around that table, night after night, and the two of you unable to keep your hands off each other. Poor Jack sitting there, smiling that faraway smile, unaware of what was going on . . . if indeed he was unaware, which looking back, I rather doubt.'

'No . . .' she started to protest, but he must have given her a look or made some gesture that silenced her, for she said not another word.

'Once,' went on Mortimer, 'I saw him slide a hand up under your skirt – had you left your drawers off on purpose, perhaps? Holding the cards in one hand and calling out his bids, as cool as you please, while the other hand was busy at its work between your legs.' Mortimer gave an odd little laugh. 'I could see what you were both up to, of course – although you were blissfully unaware of the fact – but I could also *smell* it . . . the smell that was on Kirkwood's fingers afterwards. I couldn't help wondering if Jack hadn't smelt it too. The smell of his wife, excited by another man.'

'That's enough,' said Rowlands sharply. Mortimer giggled. 'That's where you're wrong,' he said. 'It's only just begun. You'll die first, of course. A single shot through the head. Suicide,' he added, in a gloating tone. 'Atonement for your crimes, including this one. The murder by strangulation of the Countess Rostropovna, alias Nettie Harper, née Roberts. That'll be up to me to do since you'll be dead, but I think I can safely say it'll be laid at your door with all the others. It's funny to think that the police suspected a blind man, all along.'

'What about Vance and Mrs O'Reilly?' said Rowlands. 'The police are hardly going to accept that I was responsible for *those*.'

'Oh, Vance had a lot of enemies,' said Mortimer coolly. 'Young Bingham amongst them. I think you'll find *he'll* take the blame for that. As for the old woman – that was a burglary gone wrong. An unknown assailant. You got in the way, that's all. But you won't get in the way *this* time – I'll make sure of that.' Once more there was the sound of a gun being readied for firing. 'So long, old man. A pity it had to end like . . .'

In that split second, Rowlands flung himself sideways, towards where he knew his adversary was standing. He felt the crunch of muscle against flesh and bone as his shoulder made contact with Mortimer's ribs. The two of them crashed to the floor. In the same instant, the gun went off, and the woman screamed. Everything else was lost in a roar of deafening sound. The gun. He must get hold of the gun, he thought. But where it had got to, he had no way of telling. Perhaps it was still in Mortimer's hand. He was confronting this possibility when the door burst open and there was the thud of heavy footsteps. The room was suddenly full of people. One of these was the Chief Inspector; Rowlands heard him say to one of his men: 'Catch hold of him now – that's right.' It was Mortimer he meant.

'Is he hurt?' asked Rowlands, getting painfully to his feet.

'Winded,' said Douglas. 'You know, you took rather a chance, knocking him down like that. He might have blown your head off. As it is, he's just made a rather nasty hole in the ceiling.'

'Yes,' said Rowlands. 'I must say, you left it rather late.'

'Och, I'm sorry about that. I came as soon as I got your message,' replied Douglas. 'It was the devil's own job to find this place.' Then, as Mortimer was hauled to his feet: 'Arthur Mortimer, I am arresting you for the murders of Winifred Calder, Mary O'Reilly, Elsie Alsop, Reginald Vance and Nora O'Reilly, as well as the attempted murders of . . .'

'Oh, get on with it,' said Mortimer wearily.

'You do not have to say anything, but I should warn you that anything you do say will be taken down and may be used in evidence against you.'

'As a matter of fact, I *do* have something to say,' was the reply. 'She killed him – that bloody bitch – as surely as if she'd put the rope around his neck with her own hands. It was me that found him, you know. Cut him down, too, but I couldn't save him, poor Jack. Not that he'd have thanked me if I had. He left a note, you see,' he went on shrilly as the handcuffs were put on. 'It said: "I'm sorry old man, but I can't face living without her." Murderess!' he spat.

'That's quite enough of that,' said Douglas. 'Take him

out.' Then, to the woman, who had said nothing all this while: 'Are you all right, Countess?'

'I never knew there was a note,' was all she said.

As their party descended the stairs – Mortimer in front, escorted by two police officers, followed by Douglas and the Countess, with Rowlands bringing up the rear – a hubbub broke out. A number of Le Fevre's guests had come out to see what the fuss was all about, Rowlands surmised, their host being one of them. 'Natalia, what's all this about?' he heard Le Fevre say, and then her subdued reply: 'I don't want to talk about it, Maurice.'

'But Natalia . . .'

'The Countess has had a nasty shock,' said Douglas. 'She can't talk to you now. Countess, if you'll go with Constable Griffiths, he'll escort you to the car. Now then, gentlemen,' he went on, addressing the rest of those assembled, 'there's no cause for alarm. If you'd all return to the dining hall, I'll send Sergeant Withers in to take your statements in due course.' There was some muttering about this, but the crowd of onlookers duly complied with the Chief Inspector's request. Only Le Fevre stayed behind.

'I think I ought to point out that there are some very important people amongst my guests tonight,' he said. 'One in particular,' he added, in a lower tone. 'I'm sure I don't have to tell *you*, Chief Inspector, that this . . . regrettable *incident* has to be kept as dark as possible. It wouldn't do for the papers to get hold of it.'

'We'll certainly do what we can, sir,' came the reply.

'But I can't promise anything.' 'The idea!' Douglas remarked to Rowlands later when they were on their way back to London. 'That we'd forego the chance of a nice big headline in the early editions – "*Police Trump Playing Card Killer*" or some such – in order to spare the feelings of Le Fevre's guests. Even if one of 'em *is* a Very Important Person.' This exchange having been concluded, the Chief Inspector took charge of his prisoner. 'This way, Mr Mortimer, if you please.' He – Douglas – seemed in unusually high spirits. And of course, Rowlands thought, as far as he was concerned, it had been a successful evening. When he and his party had gone out, Rowlands found himself momentarily alone with Le Fevre. 'Well, well, Mr Rowlands,' said the latter. 'You are a man of many parts, I see! A friend of artists and, it would seem, of policemen.'

'A bloody spy, is what he is,' said another voice, thickened by drink and aggression. Once again, Rowlands found his way barred by Johnny Edgecombe. He could smell the whisky fumes as Edgecombe thrust his face close to his.

'Let me pass, please,' said Rowlands in a civil tone, but the other hadn't finished.

'Sniffing and spying and toadying around your betters,' he sneered. 'Dirty spy. It's time you were taught a lesson.'

'Oh, let him go,' said Maurice Le Fevre, in a bored tone. 'There's nothing he can do to us.'

'Anything the matter, Mr Rowlands?' came the voice

of the Chief Inspector from the open door.

'Nothing at all,' said Rowlands.

'Good,' said Douglas. 'Then let's go, shall we? I'd like to be back at Scotland Yard before midnight. Goodnight, gentlemen,' he added to the demagogue and his friend. 'I trust you'll be as co-operative with the police enquiry as possible.'

Chapter Twenty-Two

'I must say,' said Mortimer. 'It *has* been rather amusing, these past few weeks, watching you tie yourself up in knots. That first day you came to the Lodge, asking questions.' He gave a not very accurate imitation of Rowlands' voice: '"Now do tell me all about what you were doing on New Year's Eve, won't you, old chap?" I was laughing my head off.'

'You must have been.'

'Oh, I guessed you were up to something from the very beginning. Snooping around in the library, asking your daft questions. It didn't make sense. And then when you said the girl's name . . .'

'Winnie Calder's, you mean?'

'Yes, her. Silly tart thought she could twist me round

her little finger. They all think that, the women,' said Mortimer with contempt. He adopted a wheedling, feminine tone: '"Oh, Arthur, why don't you step inside for a nightcap? It'll be ever so cosy, just the two of us." Oh, it was *that* all right!' He gave a soft little laugh, that made the hairs on the back of Rowlands' neck stand up on end. 'Ever so cosy.' A silence elapsed. They were sitting on either side of a deal table in Mortimer's cell. A prison guard sat with them. He took no part in the conversation so that if it hadn't been for an occasional throat-clearing or the creak of a heavy body shifting its weight on a flimsy chair, it would have been easy to forget he was there. Not for Mortimer, of course, Rowlands reminded himself. For him, the man would be a silent, but ever-present reminder of where he was and what had brought him there. 'Yes, it was a good joke while it lasted,' went on Mortimer after a moment. 'Watching you stumbling around in search of *clues*. You've no idea how foolish you looked!'

'I can imagine.'

'You wouldn't leave it alone, would you, old man? Always poking about and prying. It got on my nerves, I can tell you!'

'I expect it did,' said Rowlands, fingering the tender spot on the back of his head with a rueful air. 'And all the while,' Mortimer said, with evident self-satisfaction, 'I was one step ahead of you. First you led me to Nettie . . .'

'It was seeing the photograph that put you onto her, I suppose?'

'Yes. That was a lucky break for me. Seeing her in the paper like that. The funny thing is, it was you I recognised first. I know that face, I thought, and it was only then that I saw who it was you were with. Yes, you did me a good turn, there, and no mistake! Although I'd have tracked her down in the end,' he added, with the supreme confidence in his own cleverness which had been the hallmark of his behaviour from the start. 'It was only a matter of time and of using my wits.'

'I suppose,' said Rowlands, 'you must have thought it was all over once you knew where she was staying. It must have been quite a blow to find yourself thwarted by the police.'

'When they put a man outside the house, you mean? *That* merely told me she was safely inside.'

'You were watching the place yourself, weren't you?' said Rowlands.

'Oh, you worked that out, did you? Yes, I was there the night of the party. Saw you go in, with that other fellow, that artist . . .'

'Percy Loveless.'

'Yes, him. Ridiculous he looked too, in that great swirling cloak and top hat. Fancies himself quite a one for the ladies, doesn't he?' Rowlands shrugged. 'Oh, I know you were quite thick with him for a while . . . You and your artist friends!' laughed Mortimer. His laugh ended in a coughing fit. 'Damn these wretched lungs of mine,' he gasped when he could speak. After a moment, he gathered enough breath to go on. 'Yes, I saw quite a lot that night. A lot of to-ings and fro-ings. Bloody cold it was, too. I had to keep stamping my feet to keep from freezing. Well, around midnight I saw you leave, and then I thought I'd seen enough. Decided to make myself scarce. It was a good thing I didn't, though, because it was then that I saw Nettie.'

'Did you?'

'Oh, yes, I saw her quite plain – her and that bounder, Edgecombe. He came out first, and then she came out after him. They were standing on the steps in front of the house. I saw them kissing.'

'Ah.'

'You might very well say "Ah!" Not very nice of her, was it, to steal her best friend's boy? But that was Nettie all over. So I thought I'd got her, then. All I had to do was to wait until she was alone.'

'But she ran away before you got your chance,' said Rowlands.

'Yes, that *did* make things more complicated. At first I thought I'd lost her. But then I realised that all I had to do was stick to you like glue, and you'd lead me to her . . . which you did, you know, old man,' said Mortimer happily. 'Yes, you've been a great help to me all along. If it hadn't been for you, I'd never have found out what Vance was up to.'

'You were listening at the door that day,' said Rowlands.

'Of course I was. The minute I saw you go into the Major's office, I knew something was up. And I was right, wasn't I? As soon as I heard Vance's name mentioned, I knew he must have been shooting his mouth off. He tried to blackmail me, of course,' he added. 'Said he'd tell the Major what he'd found out about me.'

'And what was that?' This was something which had puzzled Rowlands. Because surely Vance couldn't have twigged that Mortimer was the one responsible for the killings? Mortimer's reply made it all clear: the reason Vance had had to die. 'Why,' he said, 'it was that I used glasses for reading. Vance trained as an optician before the war. He knew a bit about lenses, as you'd imagine. One day, he took a telephone message from the local branch of Dollond and Aitchison, saying that my new prescription had come in. He knew what it meant, of course. Threatened to peach on me unless I made it worth his while not to. I had to put a stop to that,' he said flatly. A brief silence followed this bald statement, during which Rowlands could not help but think of what putting a stop to Vance had entailed.

'You must have been eavesdropping that other time,' he said at last. 'When I told the Major about the drawing.'

'That's right,' was the reply. 'I heard every word. So I knew I had to act fast. It wouldn't have done to have let the old woman clap eyes on my portrait. Quite a good portrait it is, by the by.'

'So it *was* you that Goldberg saw that night at the gallery, then?' It was hardly necessary to offer these prompts, Rowlands thought. Mortimer, enraptured by his own cleverness at having fooled them all, was only too eager to tell.

'Of course it was me! That's why I had to have the drawing, even after the old woman was dead. I couldn't risk having someone else recognise me. Yes, I took the thing. It wasn't a bad likeness, as I've said.' The drawing, Rowlands knew, had been found amongst Mortimer's things when his room was searched. Evidently, he hadn't been able to bring himself to part with it. What was it Douglas had said? 'They tend to keep mementos . . .'

'I wish I could have seen it,' said Rowlands. 'He's supposed to be very good – the artist, I mean.'

'Oh, I wouldn't know about that,' said Mortimer.

'You know, you almost gave yourself away that time,' said Rowlands. 'When you called my name, outside the Major's office. I hadn't said a word, so there was no way you could have known it was me – unless you could *see* me, of course. It was that which made me wonder if you were quite what you seemed. Then later in the pub when you found the newspaper, with the football results . . .'

'Yes, I was afraid you might have thought it was a bit odd,' said Mortimer. 'Was it that which put you onto me?'

'Not exactly. It was something Ashenhurst said. About your having once helped to manage a smallholding. He . . . he mentioned what had happened to Jack Harper. That there'd been a woman involved. Then it all sort of fell into place.'

'I kept you guessing for quite a while, though, didn't I?'

'You did. One thing I don't understand, though,' said Rowlands, 'is how you knew I'd be at Avalon Hall that night.'

'I didn't. It was a lucky break. It was Edgecombe I was following, as it was that time at the gallery. I thought where *he* was, *she* wouldn't be far away – and you see I was right. Then I saw *you* arrive, and I knew my instinct hadn't let me down. All I had to do was keep you in my sights, and let you lead me to her. When you went upstairs, I followed you.' That footstep he'd heard on the stairs, thought Rowlands. 'But what made you go there on that particular night?' he persisted.

'How you do love to tie up loose ends, you detective chaps!' laughed the other. 'Well, there's no great mystery about it. It was in the paper, the day before, in bold fourteen point type.' He adopted a pompous tone: '"Evening Lecture – 'The Decline of Western Man: Inevitable or Avoidable?' Dr Horace Babbington will talk on this important topic at Avalon Hall, near Sevenoaks – 8.30, Saturday 26th January 1929 – Entrance: 3*s*. 6*d*.; All Welcome." You see?' said Mortimer. 'Not such a mystery, after all.'

Another silence fell, during which there was no sound except the faint creaking of the prison officer's chair, and Mortimer's laboured breathing. When he spoke again, it was in a different tone of voice. Reflective. Almost wistful. 'I was at Langemarck in '15,' he said. 'You remember that beastly show?'

'Yes.'

'Of course, you artillery boys were well out of it! Decent respirators, for one thing – and then you were on higher ground.'

'Not always.'

'No? Well, it certainly seemed that way to us. Anyway, there we were, Jack and me, and the rest of our platoon, with that filthy HS coming over. It wasn't like the other stuff, with its sulphurous stink. This was a different kind of smell – like mustard, they said. I couldn't see it myself. To me it was always the smell of death. You're smiling. What's funny?'

'Nothing.'

'But you were smiling. Go on, tell me what you were thinking.'

'I was thinking that you must have got to know that smell quite well.'

'Death, you mean?' Mortimer's laugh ended in a cough. 'Oh yes. I know what death smells like, all right. What it *looks* like, too – which is more than *you* can say, eh, Rowlands old man?'

'I've seen my share of it,' said Rowlands drily.

'Yes – *then*. But you don't see very much of anything now, do you?'

'No.'

'Where was I? Ah. Langemarck. Yes. The gas shells coming over that day. Did you see what it did to men, the gas?'

'Yes.'

'Quite horrible,' said Mortimer, wheezing a little, as if

in sympathy. 'Why, there was one poor bloke I saw who'd turned blue as sailor's serge. Thick pus simply pouring out of him every time he coughed, poor devil. Drowning in it. He died at last, thank God. With some of them, it took days. You were well above it all, you gunners, but down in the trenches we saw it all.' Mortimer was silent for a moment, perhaps recalling the sights to which he had referred.

'Was that how it happened?' asked Rowlands.

'Was that how what happened?'

'Your losing your sight.'

'Yes. Bloody stupid, really. I'd taken off my respirator for a minute, because the goggles had steamed up, and I couldn't see a blessed thing. Got a face full of HS – it felt as if someone had thrown burning acid in my eyes. Gummed them up good and proper.'

'That was hard luck.'

'Oh, you got yours too, in the end, didn't you?' said Mortimer, with a bitter little laugh. 'We all did. Including Jack. Although his was a bullet through the head. Lucky to survive it, the doctor said. Quarter of an inch to the left and it would've been curtains. Turned him stark blind, though, from that moment on. I don't suppose you remember him, do you?'

'Before my time, I'm afraid.'

'Yes. He left the Lodge in the spring of '17, to get married to that girl of his. That bitch,' said Mortimer with barely suppressed violence. 'God knows what put the idea into his head. Seems to have thought she was doing him a favour. Instead of which, it was all the other way about.'

'Perhaps he was in love with her,' said Rowlands.

'*Love*!' was the withering reply. 'Then he chose the wrong person to fall in love *with*, that's all I can say. She didn't know the meaning of the word. It was all self, self, self with Nettie . . . I say – you haven't got a cigarette, have you, old man?' Rowlands lit one for him, and then one for himself. 'Thanks,' said Mortimer, taking a deep drag. 'I'm not supposed to, with the state my lungs are in, but what does it matter now? They'll hang me within the month – that is, if I don't peg out first.'

Rowlands said nothing to this.

'You know, it's funny, in a way,' the other man went on. 'The gas did for me in the end – only it wasn't my eyes, but my lungs. Oh, it's ruined me, all right! Not only my lungs, but – another part of me. Fucked. If you'll pardon the indecency.' Then he said nothing more for a while, but sat and smoked his cigarette as Rowlands was smoking his, down to the barest stub: a habit contracted in their soldiering days. 'It was for *him* I had to do – what I did,' he said, in a softer tone. 'For Jack. You do see that, don't you, old man? I couldn't let her get away with it. Letting him down the way she did.' His voice trembled a little. 'Her going off like that was what killed him, you know. Drove him to it.'

'But what about the others?' asked Rowlands. 'Those girls. What had *they* done?'

Mortimer made an impatient movement. 'They were

all the same,' he said, in an indifferent tone. 'Out for what they could get, just as she – Nettie – was out for what she could get. That girl Mary was the best of 'em, even though she was a tart. Forced into it, of course because of the kid. I didn't want to hurt her,' he said softly. 'But by then she'd seen my face, hadn't she? That other one – that Elsie – was a nasty piece of work. Hard as nails, for all she looked so soft and pretty. She was engaged to that young chap, Mullins, you know, but she ditched him as soon as she thought she'd got a better offer. That was what Nettie was like, too. First she took what Jack had to give her, and then she got what she could from that rotter, Gus Kirkwood. "Augustus Kirkwood, RA", as I suppose he calls himself now. Oh, she was well in with *that* crowd, for a while! The Chelsea set,' he added, in a jeering tone. 'But even *that* wasn't grand enough for our Nettie.'

'I still don't see . . .' Rowlands began; but then he realised that there was no point in pursuing the question he'd just asked. For Mortimer, caught in the toils of his obsession, the deaths of the young women who had, in his twisted fantasy, stood in for Nettie Roberts, were of little consequence. 'And Mrs O'Reilly?' he nonetheless persisted. 'What had *she* done?' But Mortimer wasn't interested in talking about Mrs O'Reilly.

'That, I must say, was rather *your* fault, old man. If you hadn't insisted on getting hold of that drawing, she'd still be alive and well today. To tell the truth,' he went on, 'I'm pretty tired of it all. I can't say I'll be sorry when it's all over, and I go to join the Great Majority. Who knows?' he added, with his wheezing laugh as, at a word from the prison officer, Rowlands got up to take his leave. 'Maybe Jack'll be there to meet me. We were always such Pals you know, Jack and me. I'd like to think we might see each other again some day.'

'So she knew all along who he was,' said Celia West when Rowlands had finished speaking. 'That day the police came – that you came – she already knew who had sent that letter.'

'Yes.'

'Yet she said nothing.'

'She was afraid,' said Rowlands. He hesitated a moment before saying what was in his mind. 'Perhaps as much afraid of being found out for what she was, as of being found by the murderer.'

'Yes, I see that,' she said thoughtfully. 'Either way, she was taking a frightful risk. More tea? Or would you rather have something stronger?'

'Tea will do fine.' They were in Lady Celia's drawing room; a day and a half had passed since the events in which the woman of whom they had been speaking had played such a central role.

'What I find extraordinary,' went on Lady Celia, 'is how she got away with it for so long. Oh, I don't mean lying to the police – although I suppose that was bad enough – but the deception.'

'She was – *is* – a good actress,' said Rowlands. Again,

he hesitated before saying what he had to say. 'Also . . . people see what they want to see. Or rather, what they *expect* to see.'

'You mean that if someone tells you she's a Russian Countess, you're rather inclined to believe it than not? I must say,' said Lady Celia with a wry little laugh, 'it does make one feel an awful fool for having done so.'

He shook his head. 'You trusted her, that's all.'

'Yes, and I wish I hadn't! I wonder,' she went on, what would have happened if she'd met a real Russian? There are lots of them about just now, you know.'

'I imagine she'd have thought of something,' said Rowlands.

'Yes. Natalia – I still think of her as Natalia – was nothing if not resourceful. And of course, she *looked* the part. You'll have to trust me for that.'

Rowlands smiled.

'But there's still all the rest of it.' He knew it was the subtle codes of behaviour and speech by which the upper classes distinguish themselves from the rest to which she was alluding. 'How *did* she get away with it?'

'As I said, she was a good actress.'

'Well, she took *me* in all right,' said Lady Celia. 'Most of the time, that is. I did start to have my doubts towards the end.'

'Did you?'

'Oh, yes. Although it wasn't until the night I told you about – when I heard her crying – that I really began to think something was up. It was when she said that strange thing.'

'"What have I done?"' said Rowlands softly.

'That's it. Except that there was something odd about the way she said it – I thought so, even then.'

'She didn't have a Russian accent when she said it.'

'That's what it must have been, of course. Then when I spoke to her she became "the Countess" again. Extraordinary, really, that she fooled so many of us for so long. So, you're telling me she was really an artist's model?'

'That was later,' said Rowlands. 'After she left her husband for Gus Kirkwood.'

'I met him once, you know. Kirkwood,' she said, which didn't surprise Rowlands in the slightest; Celia West knew everybody. 'Rather full of himself, as I recall. He's supposed to be rather good, although Loveless would be furious if he heard me say so. Natalia was his mistress, you say?'

'For a year or so. I rather think,' he said, with the faint embarrassment he was unable to suppress when such matters were discussed, 'that she expected him to marry her.'

Lady Celia let out a crow of laughter. 'He'd have run a mile, of course. I mean, Natalia's very good-looking, but she's no great shakes as a conversationalist. He'd have been bored to tears.'

'Well, whatever the reason, it didn't last. After that, she rather disappeared from view.' What Douglas had said, following the police interview, had been cruder: 'When Kirkwood threw her out, she was on her uppers for a while. I don't think she was too particular about how she made her living, if you get me.'

'Then she reappeared, in due course, as a member of the Russian aristocracy,' said Lady Celia. 'How did *that* come about, I wonder?'

'I gather she had a friend – someone she shared lodgings with during that time – who was Russian. A ballet dancer,' said Rowlands. 'It was from her that she picked up the accent – and no doubt a few salient points about the Russian way of doing things.'

'Black tea,' put in Lady Celia. 'Her old nurse used to make it in the samovar, she told me.'

'Indeed,' said Rowlands. 'It wasn't, perhaps, too difficult an illusion to sustain,' he went on. 'Given that she'd told everyone she met that her entire family had been wiped out during the Revolution. So if any awkward questions arose about her past, she could say the subject was too painful to talk about – or even that she didn't remember.'

'Well, I must say, she seems to have been very clever,' said Celia West, grudgingly. 'But what I don't understand is how she managed to *dress* the part. She never had any money, of course, but she had some very good clothes. Jewellery, too.'

'I imagine,' said Rowlands, feeling more and more awkward, 'that she must at some time have had a . . . a protector.'

'What a wonderfully Victorian word!' she laughed. Then she grew sombre. 'Yes, of course. Stupid of me. Poor Natalia. That's exactly what must have happened. She'd have found some rich old man to keep her. And all the time I thought she was merely an impoverished émigré, living off the remnants of past glories. I rather liked her, you know. Although she was really rather a bitch when all's said and done. Hardly surprising that Mr Mortimer wanted to murder her. I suppose,' she added, in what might have seemed a casual tone, but was not, 'they'll hang him?'

'Yes,' said Rowlands. 'There's no doubt of that.'

She gave a little shiver. 'I suppose one ought to be glad,' she said. 'And yet I can't help feeling that it's all rather pathetic.'

Taking his leave of her at last – and how long would it be, he wondered, before he held those cool slim fingers in his own once more? – he thought about what she'd said. Pathetic. Yes, it was certainly that. A sad, rather squalid affair. Walking back through Hans Place to catch the Underground, he thought of the conversation he'd had with his wife the night before. 'You know in a way I feel responsible,' she'd said, not for the first time since it had all come out. 'If only I'd told you in the first instance what I'd seen.' What she'd seen, glimpsed in passing from the police car on the way to Regent's Park Lodge, had been Arthur Mortimer, buying a newspaper from the stand outside Baker Street Underground. 'Only I thought I must have been mistaken. If only I'd *said* . . .'

'You weren't to know,' he said.

'No. But I *should* have known! If I'd said something, he might have been stopped. It just never occurred to me.'

'It doesn't matter now,' he said. 'And in any case, I'd already worked out that it must have been Mortimer you saw. It was after he found that newspaper in the pub, and I guessed he could see.'

'You're just saying that to make me feel better,' said Edith.

'Now, would I do that?' he said. 'Let's change the subject, shall we?'

But the subject of Arthur Mortimer had proved difficult to leave. 'Is he mad, do you think?' Edith had asked, some moments later. 'Almost certainly,' had been his reply. 'The way he planned the whole thing. The ritualistic aspects . . .'

'Those playing cards . . .'

'Exactly. It all suggests a mind deformed by obsession.'

'Then they'll lock him away in Broadmoor, won't they?' said Edith, who was all too aware of what her husband felt about the death penalty. His own part in bringing Mortimer to justice was, she knew, already weighing heavily on his mind.

'I doubt it,' Rowlands had said. 'Even if it might be argued that the killings of those three young women were acts of madness, the way he covered his tracks afterwards will be seen as the action of a sane man.'

'The murder of Mr Vance, you mean?'

'Yes – and that of Danny's grandmother.' It was thus they had taken to referring to Nora O'Reilly, the fate of whose motherless grandson had become a pressing concern.

'Well, in my opinion, he deserves to be hanged for that alone,' said Edith firmly. 'You agonise about these things too much, Fred.'

'You're right,' he said.

Still, it wouldn't stop him from rising at six one morning three weeks after that conversation when the trial was over and the sentence – never in doubt – had been passed, to sit, with his mug of tea and cigarettes, and share the last hour on earth of Arthur Mortimer. If what he had done was abominable, his reasons for doing what he had done were harder to condemn, thought Rowlands, cradling the battered enamel mug in his cupped hands. One might even say he had done it out of love – or at least a desire for justice – for the man who had been his Pal. Thinking of his own deep affection for Ashenhurst, Rowlands wondered if he, too, might have been capable of murder if Ashenhurst had suffered a similar fate . . . and indeed, it hadn't been so very different; it was just that Ashenhurst had chosen to go on living after *his* girl had left him. Some might say it was the more difficult choice.

He finished his cigarette and lit another. The hands on his braille watch read a quarter to seven. Overhead, he could hear the sounds of his baby daughter waking up: a contented cooing; Joan seldom cried. What was it

Mortimer had said, that last time? 'I can't say I'll be sorry when it's all over . . .' Well, he would have his wish before long. They'd have moved him a week ago to the cell next to the execution shed. Here, he'd have been having his meals and playing cards with the two men set to guard him, and laying his head down at night on a pillow not yards from the place he was to die. The hangman would have looked in on him a couple of days before to measure his weight and height. They said you didn't have time to know too much about it . . . He recalled that summer's day by the river at Putney when he and a crowd of other sports-mad men had cheered themselves hoarse as Mortimer and his eight had beaten the Goldie crew by a length. What a fine chap he had been – so full of life and vigour. The poison that was already eating away at him had not yet taken its dreadful toll.

Rowlands found that he was praying. *Let it be over*. A tear ran, suddenly, down his cheek. He touched his watch face. Seven o'clock. The door opened, and Edith stood there. She didn't say anything, but after a moment, she came and put her arms around him.

Chapter Twenty-Three

It was a beautiful day in June – the perfect day for a garden party. The lightest of breezes, smelling of new-mown grass, brushed their faces as they walked across the wide lawns of Regent's Park towards the gates of the Lodge. From somewhere within its grounds, came the sound of children's voices, rising above the deeper notes of adult conversation and laughter and the strains of a jazz band playing popular favourites – 'Happy Days Are Here Again' was one he recognised. Someone cried, 'Oh, I say! Good shot!' The games were under way, Rowlands surmised. They went in – his daughters running ahead, as usual. 'Slow down!' he called after them. 'The ices won't run away.' He and Edith, following at a more leisurely pace, were greeted a moment later by the Major.

'Is that you, Rowlands? Thought I recognised your voice. And Mrs Rowlands, too, I suppose?'

'Oh, yes,' said Edith. 'As far as I'm concerned, this is the event of the season.'

'It is now,' replied the Major gallantly. 'Won't you come this way? I believe there's tea, and cakes, and all that sort of thing. A good turnout,' he went on as the three of them strolled towards the tea tent. 'Which is largely thanks to your efforts – and your husband's, of course.'

'Oh, we enjoyed doing it, didn't we, Fred?'

'Rath*er*,' he said. Around them, other family groups met and mingled. Exclamations of pleased recognition were heard: 'Well, blow me down! Is that really you, Frank?' and the reply: 'It's me all right, old chap. Mabel, this is Bob. We were in Signals together. Bob, I don't think you've met the missus . . .'

Yes, a good turnout, thought Rowlands, and a satisfactory end to what had been a troubled era. From the Major's general air of calm good humour, he gathered that there had been no repetition of the painful events of last January when the *esprit de corps* he had tried so hard to preserve seemed to have broken down, and an atmosphere of suspicion and dread prevailed. With Vance dead . . . but he didn't want to think about Vance, or Mortimer, or any of what had happened – not today. Today was a day of celebration. Of restoration, he supposed. 'Daddy!' Anne came running up, excitedly. 'Daddy, when's the tug of war to be?'

'Soon, I expect.'

'Daddy's going to be in the tug of war, aren't you, Daddy?' she informed the Major. 'His team'll win, because he's very strong.'

'Now then, Anne,' said her mother, but she was laughing as she said it. 'That's quite enough boasting for one day.' Leaving Edith talking to Laura Bingham, with whom she was to judge the Iced Cake Competition, the two men wandered off, pacing slowly across the wide lawn towards the house. Their companionable silence, borne of a long acquaintance, was broken only by occasional greetings from other guests – 'Hello, Major! Jolly nice day for it . . .' and the Major's courteous replies. At one point the latter cleared his throat as if there were something he wanted to say, but he wasn't sure how to begin saying it. After another moment, he said, 'I feel I ought to thank you.'

'No need,' said Rowlands, and the subject was closed.

'Well, I suppose I ought to go and see about my speech,' said the Major when they had reached the house. 'Rather a bore, really, but people expect it.'

'Yes, sir. Good luck,' said Rowlands, knowing how little the Major enjoyed public speaking.

'Thanks.' Then he was gone. Rowlands lit a cigarette and strolled on for a few paces, enjoying the feeling of being, for once, at a loose end. Snatches of conversation floated towards him: 'Jolly good shot! A coconut for the young lady!' '. . . so looking forward to the concert, aren't you?' '. . . I say, we seem a bit short of mallets for the croquet . . .' 'More tea, anyone?' A moment later, he almost ran into somebody. 'Hi, Rowlands!' said a familiar voice. 'That you?' Edith said I'd find you somewhere about.'

'Hello, Ashenhurst,' he said. 'Enjoying the party?'

'I'll say.' His friend gave a comical groan. 'I'm supposed to be organising the egg-and-spoon races for the kiddies later. Don't know what I've done to deserve it, frankly. Listen, there's something I'd like to talk to you about.'

'Oh?' They began walking back towards the tea tent. There was a beer tent, too, but Rowlands thought he'd better wait until after his tug of war duties were over before indulging.

'The thing is, it's about Danny,' said Ashenhurst. This was a discussion they had been having, by letter and telephone, for some months – ever since Edith had collected the child from the Foundlings' Hospital where he was then lodged, and had brought him back to Staplehurst for the week. It had been when Ashenhurst and his sister were staying with them. The idea of adopting him had come from Cecily Nicholls, with strong support from her brother. 'A year ago, when business was so bad, I'd have said it was no go,' he'd said. 'But we've money now. We can give him a decent start.' Inevitably, there had been complications in the furtherance of this plan – not least those resulting from the interventions of Thomas Lintott, Danny's absentee father. It was about the latest of these that Ashenhurst wanted to consult his friend, and so the two of them went in search of a quiet corner where they could have a smoke and work out a plan of action. 'He's after money, of course, the rogue,' said Ashenhurst. 'Well, let him have it, I say.'

As Rowlands listened, throwing in a cautionary remark from time to time, he thought how strange it was, the way things fell out. That a child's future could depend on a throw of the dice – or in this case, the fall of the cards. Six months ago, the boy had had a mother and grandmother to look after him. Now he was a virtual orphan. How infinitesimal were the moments that could decide a life! An overheard telephone conversation. An intercepted glance. A bullet missing the brain by a quarter of an inch . . . It was all part of the great Game of Chance in which they were caught up – he, Ashenhurst, Danny, Arthur Mortimer, and the woman Rowlands still thought of as 'the Countess'. He became aware that Ashenhurst was saying something.

'Sorry,' he said. 'I missed that.'

'You haven't been listening to a word I've said, have you?' said his friend, with some amusement. 'Thinking about your next case, I suppose?'

'What? Oh no. Nothing like that,' said Rowlands.

'Look – if you're worried about the loan, forget it.'

Against his wishes, but under duress from his wife – exacerbated by their parlous financial state – Rowlands had accepted a modest loan from Ashenhurst in order to tide him over, as the latter put it, until he could sell the farm. It had been on the market for five months, but they'd yet to find a buyer.

'No, it wasn't about that, either,' he said. 'Although, now you mention it . . .'

'Shh,' said Ashenhurst. 'The Major's about to speak.' And indeed there came the prefatory howls and whistles from the microphone, which had been set up on the terrace behind the house that now served as a temporary stage.

'Ladies and gentlemen,' began the Major when the instrument had been got to behave. 'It gives me great pleasure to be standing here on this glorious afternoon, and to welcome you all – former and present St Dunstaners – to the dear old Lodge.'

There was a ripple of applause; then the crowd fell silent.

'I hope,' the Major continued, 'you will agree with me when I say that, delightful as it is to be here on such a day – to enjoy the pleasures of the gardens and the splendid range of activities on offer – what has united us here today is more than just the prospect of an afternoon's entertainment and the chance to meet up with old friends. It is an idea. A conviction, if you like,' the Major went on, his voice growing stronger as he spoke, 'that life is worth living, no matter what, and that even though some of us may feel we have been dealt a bad hand, we can go on to win the game, in spite of this . . .'

'I love this place,' whispered Ashenhurst. 'I wouldn't be anywhere else for the world.'

'No,' said Rowlands. 'Neither would I.'

Another afternoon, later the same month, and another social event – this one considerably grander than the St Dunstan's garden fete. The invitation – deckle-edged and printed in what Edith said was a 'very elegant' cursive script – had been sitting on the mantelpiece for a fortnight. Now, having passed through the great arched gateway of the famous Palladian mansion, and crossed the courtyard with its statue of Sir Joshua Reynolds, they entered the building which lay directly ahead, and climbed the marble staircase to the first of the galleries. Rowlands was in morning dress, 'as if it were a smart wedding,' he'd joked that morning as they were getting ready; Edith wore a floor-length gown of figured chiffon. It had been bought for the occasion; the pretty summer dress she'd worn to the garden party wouldn't have done for this. 'I hope I look all right,' she nonetheless muttered as they crossed the wide expanse of marble floor, already crowded with their fellow invitees. 'My pearls are good, that's one thing . . .' He squeezed her hand. 'I'm sure you look perfectly lovely.'

As was his habit, he took a moment to get his

bearings. Even if he hadn't been aware of its size already, he would have been able to form an idea of the enormous scale of the room in which they now found themselves, from the echo that resounded from its walls and lofty ceiling. The murmur of voices that came from all directions around him added variation to this continuous note, incorporating as it did the polite coughs, discreet trills of laughter and occasional remarks thrown out by the knowledgeable and the Philistine alike: 'What's *that* supposed to be, d'you think?' 'Heaven knows. He's frightfully *the thing*, though.'

'I wouldn't mind taking a closer look at some of these smaller paintings,' said Edith. 'There are some things I rather like.'

'You can tell me about them later,' he said. 'The one we've come to see will be a big piece. Quite unmistakeable, I imagine.'

'I think it must be that one on the far wall,' she said. 'A crucifixion, isn't it?'

'Yes.' They began to make their way, with some difficulty, through the slowly perambulating crowd. But before they could reach their goal, they were intercepted. 'Mr Rowlands!' said a voice he knew. 'How very good to see you.'

Mr Goldberg,' said Rowlands, holding out his hand, which was seized and vigorously shaken. 'Do let me introduce my wife.'

'Delighted,' said Isaac Goldberg, adding vaguely,

'Such a pity my Hannah couldn't be here. But the children, you know . . .'

'Do you have a painting in the exhibition?' asked Rowlands politely.

'Oh, yes. A couple of small things,' was the reply. 'My *Card Players* is the best of them – a homage, you know, to Cézanne.'

'I'm looking forward to seeing it,' said Edith. 'Oh!' Because they had now reached the far wall and the painting they had come to see.

'A fine piece, isn't it?' said Goldberg. 'One of his best, I think.'

'But . . . that's you,' said Edith to her husband. 'Or at least . . . your back view. But he's caught you exactly. The way you stand. The way you turn your head. Not that it's at all realistic. I'd call it rather stylised, in fact. And yet you can see precisely who it is.'

'I assume, given the subject, that there are other figures in the painting apart from my humble self,' said Rowlands drily.

'Well, yes . . .' she began.

'Mrs Rowlands has shown her impeccable artistic sensibility in going right to the heart of the composition,' said Goldberg. 'The figure of St Peter – that's you, Rowlands – stands in for the viewer, directing our gaze upward, as his is directed, towards the figure on the cross.'

'I'm glad you approve of my centripetal structure,'

said another voice. Loveless, of course. 'I worked rather hard to get it right.'

'I wonder if Maurice Le Fevre will admire it as much,' said Goldberg slyly.

'I don't know what you mean,' said Loveless.

'Only that the figure of Judas – the hanged man, to the right of the picture – bears a striking resemblance to our black-shirted friend.'

'Does it?' said Loveless innocently. 'I can't say I'd noticed. Glad you could make it, Rowlands. I take it this is your better half?'

'Yes.' It was with some trepidation that Rowlands performed the introductions, knowing, as he did, the dim view Loveless took of matrimony. But, as it turned out, the artist could not have been more charming.

'Have you ever been painted?' he said to Edith. 'Because you ought to be. My God! What a bone structure! I won't insult you by calling you a beauty,' he added judiciously. 'You're much too interesting for that.'

Afterwards, Edith reproached her husband for having given her a false impression. 'From all you'd told me, I was expecting someone rather uncouth and dishevelled,' she said. 'But he was a perfect gentleman. Immaculately dressed, too.' It seemed that Loveless had woven his spell over yet another woman's heart.

When Loveless's *pièce de résistance* had been duly admired in all its bravura glory – its reds and blacks and ochres; its swooping curves and plunging vortices –

there remained another work to see. This, an altogether *quieter* piece than the other, was to be found in one of the smaller rooms, adjacent to the main hall. Here, the crowds were less dense and the murmur of voices less obtrusive. For a moment, they stood at the centre of the room while Edith scanned the walls. 'Ah,' she said at last. '*There* you are.'

She took Rowlands' arm and drew him across the room to where the portrait was hanging. Both stood for a few moments in silence – Edith studying the painting, Rowlands recalling the hours during which it had been created. 'It's very like you,' his wife said. 'Much more obviously so than in the big picture. He's caught your expression very well. Your faraway look.' She must have leant forward at that moment, the better to scrutinise something, for she gave an exclamation. 'It would appear that it's already been sold,' she said. 'There's a red dot in the bottom right-hand corner.'

'Guilty, I'm afraid,' said a voice, from behind them. It was Lady Celia. 'I simply couldn't resist it,' she laughed. 'Marvellous painting, isn't it? I made Loveless promise he wouldn't sell it to anyone else. It'll have to go into store, of course.' Rowlands' surprise must have shown on his face, for she went on: 'Oh yes, we're off to New York next week. I've no idea when we'll be back in London again. That rather depends on Eliot, doesn't it, darling?'

'On what happens on Wall Street, certainly,' said a pleasantly deep voice, in the accents of New England.

'Oh, forgive me,' said Celia West. 'I haven't introduced you, have I? Mr and Mrs Rowlands, this is my fiancé, Mr Hamilton.'

'Pleased to meet you, M'am,' said Eliot Hamilton. 'Rowlands, I guess I oughta be jealous of you. It isn't often that a man has to buy another man's picture as an engagement present for his fiancée.'

'Well, I'm not asking you to live with it,' said Lady Celia cheerfully. 'I rather thought you might like to keep it for me,' she said to Edith. 'Although you've got the original, of course.'

'Thank you,' said Edith.

'He's awfully good, isn't he?' said Lady Celia, meaning the artist.

'Very good,' replied Rowlands' wife.

A pause ensued, during which a great deal that might have been said remained unspoken. All that had passed since their last meeting – his and Celia's – the day after Mortimer's arrest. The trial, which neither had attended; the sentence, and its execution. The announcement in *The Times* a few weeks after – read out to him by Edith over the breakfast table – of the forthcoming marriage of the Countess Rostropovna and Lord Edgecombe. Although she was well out of *that* affair, in Rowlands' private opinion.

'Well,' said Celia West. 'I mustn't keep you. So glad we had this chance to chat. I'll get the painting sent to you as soon as I'm able. Do send my love to the darling children, won't you?' Then she was gone, in a rustle of silk and a delicious waft of scent. For a moment neither Rowlands nor his wife said anything. Around them, the murmur of voices was like the sound of waves breaking on a distant shore. Then Edith, leaning for another look at the painting, began to laugh. 'I've just noticed the title your Mr Loveless has given it. It's *Portrait of a Spy*,' she said.

Christina Koning has worked as a journalist, reviewing fiction for *The Times*, and has taught Creative Writing at the University of Oxford and Birkbeck, University of London. From 2013 to 2015, she was Royal Literary Fund Fellow at Newnham College, Cambridge. She won the Encore Prize in 1999 and was long-listed for the Orange Prize in the same year.

christinakoning.com